The Great Engine _____ in Ondinium, but the _____ y's industrial zone and the _____ vas inescapable . . . Civilization had its price, _____ had its advantages . . .

"I feel sometimes there is nobody in Ondinium who cannot be replaced," Lt. Amcathra said. "We are like the gears in one of Exalted Forlore's clocks. That is a strength, because the clock will keep running even after every gear inside it has been replaced. But it is a weakness because it is impossible to respect a man when one thinks of him as nothing more than a replaceable part. 'We must have a dedicate here. Go, send a lictor there.' A man's name and spirit become unimportant."

"Maybe that's why terrorists throw bombs," Taya suggested. "So people will remember their names."

"Yes, that is why terrorists throw bombs," Amcathra agreed. "They have not been taught to respect life. How can a man learn to respect life in a city of clockwork castes?"

"You're a philosopher, lieutenant." Taya reached the bottom of the stairs and leaned against a wall, rubbing her shoulders. "But a grim one."

"Perhaps an icarus, whose eyes are fixed upon the horizon, cannot be other than optimistic. Those of us who do not fly so high are not as fortunate." He turned and began pacing down the hall, his blue eyes moving over the walls and floor like one of his hunter kin.

CLOCKWORK HEART

CLOCKWORK HEART

Dru Pagliasotti

JUNO

Clockwork Heart

Juno Books
Rockville, MD
www.juno-books.com
info@juno-books.com

To my family and friends, and in memory of my mother, Skydancer.

Chapter One

Taya cupped her wings and fanned them, slowing as the iron struts of a wireferry tower loomed before her. The massive construction blocked the gusting winds, and she sighed with relief as her thick boot soles hit the girder. Bending her knees to absorb the impact, she crouched and folded her arms, ducking into the safe harbor.

The wind in the wires sent vibrations thrumming through the metal under her feet, and the tower swayed. She took a moment to lock her armature into tight-rest, tailfeathers snapped up and wings tucked in. With a wriggle, she pulled her arms out of their leather straps and ran a safety line from her harness to one of the narrow girder struts. She made a short loop around the iron bar and locked the line back to her belt.

"Oh, that's better," she groaned, rubbing her shoulders. After a moment, she pulled off her flight goggles and wiped them against her sleeve. The glass was smeared with dead bugs and the inevitable greasy soot that collected whenever she flew past the city's refineries.

Usually, the trip up from Tertius was easy. Thermals from the smelting factories provided plenty of lift, but today the late autumn gusts of the *diispira*—the winds that blew over the Yeovil Range every year right before winter—made soaring risky. For a few minutes, when one of the winds had stolen her thermal away and sent her into a stall, Taya had been forced to flap like a foundering duck. Her shoulder muscles were still twitching, and the sweat from her efforts was drying beneath her flight leathers.

How much longer until she was off-duty, anyway?

She slipped her goggles back on to keep protect her eyes from the wind and surveyed the mountainside spread beneath her. Terrace upon terrace of closely placed buildings descended into the dark haze of factory soot that perpetually mantled the lowest sector of the mountain. That was Tertius, the sector where the famulate caste labored in the mines and manufactories, providing the metals and goods that maintained Ondinium, the capital of Yeovil. Tertius— where she'd been born and where her sister was about to get married.

Thick stone walls ringed the mountain, dividing the major sectors from each other: Primus, for the exalteds; Secundus, for the cardinals; and Tertius, for the plebeians. Gates pierced the walls at regular intervals, but each portal was guarded by stern-faced lictors whose job was to prevent the indiscriminate mixing of castes.

Only icarii like Taya and the occasional authorities who rode the suspended wireferries could pass freely from sector to sector. And even wireferry passengers were checked at waystations whenever they changed cars, especially at Primus.

Taya searched the soot-blackened towers that rose at regular intervals along the sector walls, looking for a clock.

Seeing one, she smiled. Another hour before she could go home and prepare for the wedding. With a little luck she could deliver the report from the College of Mathematics and linger long enough at Oporphyr Tower to avoid picking up another job. As long as the decatur didn't give her another message to carry, she'd get to the party in plenty of time.

The metal beneath her feet jolted and shuddered. Taya grabbed the strut next to her with one heavily gloved hand. Usually she loved flying, but today's winds were the worst she'd—

The girder jolted again, and the high-pitched shriek of straining metal cut across the whistling wind and humming cables. Chilled, Taya jerked her head up, looking for the source of the noise.

There. One of the wireferry girders, suspended in midair several yards away from her, was starting to bend under the weight of an approaching car. Gears ground and began to spin as the heavy wire cables slipped, loosening as the girder started to buckle.

Taya leaped to her feet, banging her head against a low strut. She winced, looking around. Didn't anyone else see the danger?

Yes—wireferry workers were racing up the tower ladders from a nearby station, alerted by the sound of straining metal. But they were far away; too far away to do the people in the car any good.

The people in the car!

"Oh, Lady," she groaned, unsnapping her safety hook and tucking the strap back into her harness. Even though the rational part of her mind was screaming warnings about the danger of flying next to a collapsing girder, of maneuvering around wires that could snap at any moment, she was already dredging up memories of old aerial rescue drills, calculating wind direction and target height, her best angle of attack and the loadbearing capacity of her ondium armature.

Heart pounding, Taya slid her arms back into her wingstraps and crouched.

It had to be done. Her armature tugged her upward, its buoyant ondium straining against the weight of her compact body. Shifting to put her head into the wind, Taya threw herself into the air, her boots smacking the girder for extra thrust.

Metal girders shot past as she plunged through their deadly network. As soon as she was clear of the support structure, she threw her arms wide, snapping her metal wings to full extension.

Broad ondium feathers closed as she swept her arms downward, propelling herself up toward the endangered ferry car. She kicked her tailset down and slid her ankles behind its bar. A gust of air tugged her and she rode it aloft, then swept her wings again as the gust veered off, broken by an obstruction current from the girders around her.

Metal shrieked again. Wires snapped and twanged.

Time was running out. Taya strained forward, flying up and over the ferry car to get a clearer grasp of the situation.

Two passengers clutched the car's leather-covered seats—
an adult and a child. The adult was wearing robes and a
mask. An exalted.

"Scrap!" Taya swore and wheeled around, searching for
assistance. Engineers were scrambling over the breaking
girder, but she could tell from their hand signals to each
other that they weren't in any position to help. A small
group was trying to string another support wire through the
struts to keep the straining girder from crashing hundreds
of feet to the streets below, but that wouldn't help the
passengers if the car cable snapped.

One person at a time, she counseled herself. The wind was
suddenly icy on her face as sweat trickled down from her
hairline. *Just concentrate on rescuing one person at a time.*

She circled back to the ferry and began to brake, her tailset
down and her wings cupped. She kicked her feet free.

Momentum and uneven winds sent her crashing into the
side of the car. Taya's knees buckled against her chest and
she gasped, twisting one hand out of its wingstraps to grab
a service handle on the side of the car.

An arm reached through the window and caught the
harness straps along her shoulder. Taya looked up and saw
a woman staring at her, her dark eyes wide but her ring-
covered hand gripping the leather harness like iron.

Taya breathlessly nodded her thanks, then took a tighter
grip on the door handles. The woman released her and
Taya yanked the ferry door open, grabbing the sides of the
door frame. Her ondium wings scraped against the sides of
the ferry car and she flinched.

"Take Ariq," the lady said, her voice shaking. She swept
up the little boy at her side. "Save him."

Ariq screamed, staring at Taya's goggle-masked face,
and tried to kick away. He couldn't have been any older
than four, his round face still free of castemarks.

"I've got him," Taya said. She braced the edges of her
feet against the door frame to steady herself as she took
the boy from his mother. Ignoring the child's shrieks, she
pressed him against her stomach and snapped safety cords

between his legs and under his arms, just like the practice drills had taught her. It wasn't as easy with a squirming child as it had been with a stuffed dummy. "I'll be back as soon as I can."

The mother nodded. Her castemarks, sweeping blue waves tattooed across each cheek, stood out sharply against her pallor. She'd let her ivory mask fall to the floor, and she'd stripped off her jeweled public robe to free her arms.

Taya finished securing the terrified boy to her harness and slid her arm back into its wing.

The car jolted again, dropping a few more feet as the girder bent and the cables slipped. The woman gasped and Taya threw herself backward, free of the doorway.

For one nauseating moment she was in free fall, and then she twisted around, spreading her wings. They checked her descent with a violent jolt, ondium and air currents fighting gravity. The boy screamed, one long howl of terror.

The engineers at Cardinal Station Six were the closest. Taya flapped without any regard for her dignity, concerned only with maximizing speed and lift as she compensated for the unfamiliar and frantically shifting weight against her midsection. The stubby metal work dock several yards beneath the breaking girder was her target.

Several of the workers saw her coming and stretched out their hands. She swooped down, braked, and let them grab her by her legs and harness to haul her in. Holding her wings over her head, she panted, staying as motionless as possible as the workers steadied her with brusque efficiency. Ariq howled again as they stripped away the straps and buckles that held him, roughly tucking them back into her harness.

"There's another one up there!" a man shouted, as the tower shuddered. Everyone looked up fearfully, but the gears and girder were still holding. Barely.

"I know." Taya waited just long enough to make sure Ariq was in safe hands, then turned and kicked off from the work dock as engineers and repairmen ducked her sweeping wings.

Another icarus had spotted the danger and was circling the threatened car, seeking a safe approach. Taya swept up, foundered a moment under an unexpected crosswind, then caught herself. The other flier saw her and rocked his wings left and right.

Relieved to have backup, Taya angled toward the ferry again.

The exalted was standing in the door frame, staring up at the bending girder with her hands clamped over her mouth. Taya swept her wings backward and slammed into the car.

"Grab me!" she shouted, as the car lurched. The woman reached out—and then, with a horrifying screech, the tower buckled and the ferry plummeted.

Taya's foot slipped from the car's door frame and she tumbled backward, feeling the exalted's arms tighten around her neck as they dropped. Both of them screamed. Taya instinctively spread her wings to catch as much air as possible, but the edge of the falling car clipped her flight primaries and sent her into a spin.

Wires! Taya thought with alarm, beating both wings in a desperate attempt to get lift. If a loose wire hit them, it would slice them in half. If a girder hit them, it would smash them to a pulp.

Her sister would never forgive her if she died just hours before the wedding.

But the plummet continued. Her armature hadn't been built to carry another adult. Taya had hoped to have enough time to go into a controlled glide, but—

Her wings caught an updraft and their descent slowed, almost imperceptibly. The woman clutching her shoulders moaned, the only sound she'd made since that first scream.

Taya wanted to tilt, but the woman's excess weight was dragging her down vertically, and all she could do was try to control their fall by flapping as hard as she could. The exalted's fingers dug between her shoulder straps and her flight suit. Her legs were wrapped around Taya's waist, and her face was pressed against Taya's neck.

Somewhere metal crashed against metal, and people shouted, but Taya couldn't look up to see what had happened. She felt a strange drag on her wing — clipping the side of the car must have damaged one of her feathers.

"Taya!" The shout was barely audible over the wind in her ears. The other icarus swept past, wings locked. A locked glide was a dangerous maneuver at the best of times, especially so close to the wireferry girders, but it was the only way he could free an arm to yank loose one of his safety lines. "Grab on!"

"Exalted! Listen!" Taya shouted into the woman's ear. "There's a safety line dropping toward us. You have to hook it to my harness!"

For a moment the woman's arms tightened around her, and Taya could feel the exalted's heart hammering. But then, with the same desperate courage she'd shown in the ferry car, the woman looked up.

"I can't!"

Taya swept her arms down again, straining to keep them from entering complete free fall.

"Grab the line or we're both dead!"

The line swung past. The woman took a halfhearted pass at it, but the line slipped through her fingers. Taya shuddered as she nearly missed a beat.

The icarus above them made a tight circle. The line swung past again. This time the exalted caught it, then clutched Taya's shoulders. Taya felt the safety line's clasp slide through the rings in her back harness.

"It's done," the woman gasped.

Their fall slowed as the icarus above them shared their weight. They were safe.

A CROWD HAD GATHERED on the street to watch the drama unfolding hundreds of feet above their heads. Arms reached up to grab her and her passenger, and Taya had to shout at them to back off so she'd have enough space to land. For a second she hovered, backbeating. The exalted slid off and collapsed to the ground, shaking.

Then Taya's boots hit the street and she staggered, taking a few steps forward. She barely remembered to yank her arms free and unfasten the safety line before she, too, sank into a crouch, wrapping her arms around her shoulders and trembling with relief. Strangers surrounded her, touching her floating wings for luck and saying things to her that sounded like an incoherent rumble.

Lictors appeared, barking orders, keeping people back. After a moment, Taya drew in a deep breath and pulled her goggles down around her neck. She turned and knelt next to the exalted.

"Are you all right, exalted?"

The woman rolled over, her gold hair ornaments clinking against the cobblestones, and opened her eyes.

"Is my son safe?"

"I left him at the tower station." Taya jerked her head upward. "He's all right. Just a little scared."

"Thank you." The woman closed her eyes again.

"Excuse me. Exalted." A lictor stepped forward, his eyes averted, and held out a rough scarf. Taya took it from him.

"Your face, exalted," she said, draping the scarf over the woman's head. "It's bare."

"Oh, Lady save us," the woman snapped with disgust, then sat up, holding the scarf in place. The exalted's hands were unsteady, but she wrapped the scarf around her face, leaving only her eyes visible. Taya gave her a crooked smile. Sometimes caste restrictions weren't very practical.

"Tell me your name, icarus."

"Taya, exalted." Taya pressed a leather-gloved palm against her forehead and ducked her head, sketching as much of a bow as she could while squatting in the cobblestone street. Her loose wings tugged at her armature as they swayed.

"I am Viera Octavus, Taya, and I am in your debt."

"Are either of you hurt?" The lictor sounded more confident now that the noblewoman's face was hidden again.

"No, by the Lady's grace, neither of us has been injured. Give me something to cover myself," Viera demanded. "And bring me my son."

"They're carrying him down now, exalted." The lictor obediently unbuttoned his greatcoat and shrugged it off. He handed it to the woman as she pulled herself to her feet.

"Taya! Taya, are you all right?" A familiar voice. Taya looked up.

The icarus who'd slowed their descent pulled off his goggles and cap, revealing a shock of curly black hair. His wings were locked high and his straps neatly bundled.

The crowd let him through, and even the lictors reluctantly stepped aside.

"Hi, Pyke." Taya let him grab her hand and haul her to her feet. For a moment she leaned her forehead on his broad chest, gathering her strength. "Thanks."

"Anytime." He patted her shoulder. "Wings up, babe."

Her metal wings were drifting horizontally, knocking into bystanders who tried to crowd too close. With a groan, Taya slid her arms back into them long enough to lock them in a vertical line up her back and over her head.

She winced as she pulled her arms back down. Her shoulders were going to be killing her tomorrow. She pulled off her flight cap and ran her hands through her short, sweat-dampened hair. The cool breeze felt good against her scalp.

"Taya Icarus." Exalted Viera Octavus turned. Barefoot, wearing a borrowed greatcoat and a makeshift mask, she looked more like a child playing exalted than a full-blooded member of the ruling caste. However, the steady, dark eyes over the veil revealed that she was already recovering her dignity. "Will you please introduce me to your friend?"

"This is Pyke, ma'am. He's the one who threw us the safety line."

"At your service." Pyke tapped his palm against his forehead and gave a perfunctory bow. Taya glared at him, and he lamely added, "exalted."

"I am grateful for your assistance, as well, Pyke Icarus." Viera looked up. Taya followed her gaze.

The girder had collapsed, and twisted metal struts were trapped in the wireferry lines that held them suspended overhead as if in a metal net. The ferry car had slammed into the side of one of the station towers and was nothing more than a tangle of wreckage. Several of its dislodged ondium keel plates had floated up and tangled in the cables.

"Scrap," Pyke breathed, shaking his head. "You owe the Lady a couple of candles next holyday, Taya."

"I sure do," Taya murmured, staring.

"Exalted, if you'll please follow me, I'll escort you inside," a lictor was saying, beside them. "We'll bring your son to you and semaphore up to the tower to notify your husband."

"Very well. We shall speak again, Taya Icarus. House Octavus shall not forget what you have done for it today." Viera touched one of Taya's wings before allowing herself to be led away. Taya looked after her a moment, admiring the exalted woman's elan. After a few thousand rebirths, maybe she'd be that self-possessed after a near-death experience.

"Excuse me," another lictor said, politely but less deferentially, to Taya and Pyke. "I must now hear your account of this occurrence." He was tall, pale, and fair-haired—Taya didn't even need to analyze his accent to guess he was of Demican descent. However, the black lictor's stripe tattooed down one side of his face proved that he was a full citizen of Ondinium.

"I don't have much to say." Taya stripped off her gloves and loosened the top buttons of her flight suit. "I didn't see anything until I heard the girder giving way."

"Interviewing witnesses is a mandatory procedure," the lictor insisted. "You must follow me, icarii."

"All right," Taya acquiesced. Arguing with a lictor, especially a Demican lictor, was worse than useless. One of the selection criteria for the caste was stubbornness.

"You don't have to interrogate us," Pyke protested, balking. "We didn't do anything wrong."

"Pyke, come on," Taya urged him. "The sooner we give our statements, the sooner we can get out of here."

"This is harrassment! We're innocent—why do *we* have to be questioned?"

She rolled her eyes.

"He's just doing his job. And I'm almost certain that people are never beaten and brainwashed for rescuing exalteds."

"You never know," Pyke said darkly. "Octavus is a decatur."

"I know." Octavus was among the many names she'd memorized while cramming for the diplomatic corps examination. "So?"

"So, you know what that means." Pyke gave her a meaningful look. "*Council.* Do you think it's coincidence that a wireferry broke while his wife was riding it?"

"Oh, Lady, not a new conspiracy theory." Taya grabbed his arm and started walking, pulling him along after her. "Come on. Let's go."

"But what if the stripes are in on it?" Pyke objected, digging in his heels. "It could be a military plot. They might decide to get rid of the witnesses."

"Pyke. I'm tired, and I have to attend a wedding tonight. Let's just answer the man's questions and go, all right?"

"You're too trusting," Pyke growled.

"Uh-huh." Several months ago she'd gone out a few times with Pyke. At first his gloomy mistrust of authority had been amusing, but after a few weeks, his conspiracy theories and complaints about the government had gotten on her nerves. "The thing is, I don't feel particularly threatened by the lictors, all right?"

"Well, they're probably not as much of a threat as collapsing wireferries," Pyke admitted, looking up again. Taya laughed, despite herself, and his eyes warmed.

She looked away.

It was too easy to like him. Pyke was a skilled flier and a thoughtful friend, and he had all the good intentions a girl could want. Not to mention broad shoulders, a strong chest, and hard muscles in his arms and legs from years of flying. Add to that his Ondinium-copper skin and dark hair and eyes, and he was a difficult man to resist.

Her best friend, Cassilta, said she was crazy to cut Pyke loose, but Taya hadn't been able to take any more lectures about corruption and cover-ups. She'd ended the relationship with the reliable "just friends" excuse. To his credit, Pyke had taken the rejection well. In some ways, Taya would have preferred a more contentious breakup; at least then their relationship would be clearer.

Fortunately, Cassi now considered Pyke fair game, which gave Taya some breathing room whenever the three of them were together.

"If you will please follow," the Demican lictor insisted.

"You were great up there, Taya," Pyke said as they trailed after the official. "Just wait until the eyrie hears about it."

"Not great enough. I think the car clipped one of my feathers." She craned her neck, but she couldn't see the tips of her wings without stumbling over her own feet.

"It's just a little bent. The smiths will fix it in no time."

The lictor led them up a short flight of steps into the nearest guard station, and Pyke waved a dramatic good-bye as they were parted.

"If you wish to remove your wings, you may," the Demican lictor said, leading her into a small office. Taya hesitated, but her body ached, and she wanted to sit down. Deciding she deserved a break, she unbuckled the harness straps and swung open the metal keel. Her back prickled as the leather flight suit pulled away from her sweat-covered skin. She turned and looked at the armature.

It swayed in the air, its metal wingtips touching the ceiling. Taya frowned as she inspected the feathers. Two primaries were bent out of shape, but Pyke was right. They wouldn't be hard to repair.

She'd been lucky.

"You were very brave," the lictor said, pulling two chairs away from desks and swinging them around. "I will not make you stay long. Sit down. Do you wish to have something to drink? I can bring you water."

"That's all right. I'm fine." She sank into a chair and rubbed her neck. Her muscles twinged like plucked strings. "What's your name?"

"I am Lieutenant Janos Amcathra." The soldier dropped into the other chair and pulled out a sheet of paper.

A Demican name. From his accent, he had to be a first-

or second-generation citizen. Taya switched to Demican and held out a hand.

"Well met in peacetime, Lieutenant Janos Amcathra."

"Well met in peacetime, Taya Icarus," he replied in the same language. He took her hand and clasped it, then switched back to Ondinan as he picked up a pen. "This will not take long. Please describe everything that happened."

Taya recounted the event. It took her longer to tell it than it had to live it. Amcathra took detailed notes, then nodded when she was finished.

"Then it was a coincidence that you were close to the accident scene," he summarized. "If you had not stopped to rest there—"

"We all got lucky."

"Yes." Amcathra handed her a printed form and a pencil. "The last thing I must have is your signature and eyrie number. We will send you a message if we need to talk to you again."

Taya blinked, surprised.

"That's it? I thought we came in here because it was going to take a long time."

"We came in here because you needed to be away from the crowd."

"Oh. Well, thank you."

"We do not often beat and brainwash Ondinium's citizens," he said, dryly.

Taya grinned. "Don't mind Pyke. He's harmless." She picked up the form and skimmed through it.

Amcathra watched as she signed it, and then he added his own signature.

"Your friend may be correct about one matter. The collapse may not have been an accident."

"What do you mean?" Taya remembered Pyke telling her about stacked contract bids and substandard building materials in one of his anti-government rants.

"Incidents of political violence have been on the rise."

"Is Octavus . . . political?" She knew from her studies that Octavus was a technological conservative. That made him popular among the laboring plebeians but alienated many of the cardinal castes who depended on technology for their living. His enemies labeled him an Organicist, a reactionary who wanted to get rid of all technology.

Amcathra shrugged.

"I am only speculating. An icarus flies high and sees much. If you spot anything suspicious among the wires, I hope you will report it to me."

Typical. It was just like a lictor to drop enough hints of criminal activity to make a person uneasy, and then try to use that uneasiness to his own ends. Suspicion was a way of life for the military. And icarii were always asked to help out their investigations.

Best just to agree and get out.

"Of course. Is that all?"

Amcathra glanced up at her floating armature. "Do you require any assistance with your equipment?"

"No." She rose to her feet, suppressing a flinch. Her back and arms hurt.

"Fly safely, icarus," he said, nodding and leaving.

"Thanks."

Taya set about strapping herself back in, moving more slowly than usual. The metal exoskeleton and leather straps had left bruises all over her body. A hot bath would be nice. With luck, she'd have enough time to take one before the wedding.

Once the armature was strapped on, its buoyant ondium helped support her aching muscles. Taya's legs had stiffened up after sitting, and now they twinged as she walked.

Back out on the street, lictors were keeping the crowd of rubberneckers out of the way as engineers scrambled over the wireferry towers, running more cables back and forth like a giant safety net to keep the wreckage from hitting the street.

Taya stood on the wide station steps a moment, wondering how long it would take to lower the broken girder safely to the ground. She was glad she didn't have to rely on the wireferry to move from sector to sector. The cars would have to be rerouted around the accident site, and a lot of important people were going to find themselves delayed on their way home.

A few members of the crowd began to cheer. She looked around and realized they were waving at her. She lifted a hand, embarrassed. Scattered applause greeted the gesture.

Uncomfortable at being the focus of attention, Taya limped across the street to the base of the wireferry tower. She considered waiting for Pyke, but she had no idea how long it would take him to give his statement. She smiled. With his attitude toward authority, they might decide to hold him for the night.

The lictors allowed her to climb up to the lowest launch dock on the tower, only fifty feet off the ground. It was high enough. She rolled her shoulders one last time and pulled on her cap, goggles, and gloves. Muscles protesting, she slid her arms into the wings, unlocked them with a backward shrug, and ran to the edge of the dock.

The citizens below clapped as if they'd never seen an icarus take off before. Taya made a face and swept her wings out, searching for a thermal to lift her away from the broken girders and the unwanted attention.

CHAPTER TWO

According to the clock she passed as she soared up the mountainside, she was officially off shift. She could land at the eyrie and ask someone else to carry her message from the College of Mathematics to the Oporphyr Council. No one would blame her, after the day's excitement. And she really had to wash and change before Katerin's wedding.

But flying was working the aches out of her muscles, so she decided to push onward and deliver the message. Until she heard back from the examination board about her scores, she didn't want to do anything that might reduce her chances of being accepted into the diplomatic corps. Not all of the examination was pen-and-paper. The board would be looking at her personnel records, and some icarii whispered it had even been known to set up secret tests for prospective envoys, to see how they behaved when they didn't know they were being watched.

Rescuing a decatur's family has got to help my chances, she thought with a sudden burst of good humor, swooping past the landing docks and heading up the cliffs. Other icarii tilted their wings as they flew past her, running their own messages across Primus and back and forth from Oporphyr Tower.

The "tower" was really a small but ornate palace built on the very peak of Oporphyr Mountain, overlooking the city of Ondinium. A number of slender stone towers pierced the sky, topped by slate roofs that shed the annual rain and snow and ringed by narrow balconies that provided safe docks for the icarii who were constantly coming and going at the Council's orders. The tower's grounds were covered with arched walkways and fountains to make up for their lack of greenery—few plants grew well this high above the mountain's long-since-vanished timberline.

Oporphyr Tower had once housed the king of Ondinium, centuries ago when the realm had still been a monarchy. At that time, the tower's location had been a matter of security. Foreigners often wondered why the Council still met in such an inaccessible location, now that Ondinium was no longer torn apart by war, but the tower was more than just a building. It was also the doorway into the hollow shell of the mountain, where Ondinium's clockwork heart floated—the colossal Great Engine, each giant gear, pin, and lever cast out of pure ondium and suspended in the center of the mountain, ticking away in constant motion as it calculated Ondinium's future.

Taya soared up on an air current, rising above the unruly gusts of the *diispira*, and circled the tower. She loved being this high, where her ondium wings swept her effortlessly through the clear air, their metal feathers gleaming in the late afternoon sunlight. The Yeovil Range stretched out around her. The three mountains immediately surrounding Ondinium were dotted with townships and mining camps, lumber yards and herders' crofts. None of them were as crowded as Ondinium Mountain, where every square inch was covered by buildings, streets, or walls, but they formed a secure barrier between the capital city and the wilderness that enveloped the rest of the range.

Then she wobbled and remembered the damage to her flight feathers. *I don't need any more excitement today*, she scolded herself. She tilted and landed on one of the docking balconies.

The balcony doors were closed against the late autumn chill. Taya let herself in and pulled off her goggles, cap, and gloves. The room was dim and not much warmer than outside. Ondinium's engineers had tried running gas lines to the tower, but the pipes had kept breaking during the winter storms. As a result, the Council still conducted its business by the archaic light of fireplaces and oil lamps.

One of those lamps lit the single lictor who sat at a desk, feet up, nose buried in a cheaply printed magazine.

"I've got a message to deliver," Taya announced.

"Destination?" The guard moved her boots and set aside the magazine. Taya read the upside-down title. *The Broken Lens*—political commentary and satire. Pyke's kind of publication.

"Do they really let you read stuff like that in here?" Taya pulled the package from her back pouch.

"Are you kidding? The decaturs buy it wet off the press. The Lens' reporters know more about what's going on in Council than they do."

"That's not very reassuring." Taya tilted the package toward the light, looking for the address. "Decatur Forlore. Delivered by Taya."

The lictor dipped her pen into an inkwell and wrote as Taya stole another glance at the magazine's cover. Maybe she should pick up a copy tonight and see if it said anything about Decatur Octavus. Of course, Pyke might already have one . . . but borrowing it would mean listening to his latest political rant. *No thanks*.

Maybe Cassi would have a copy. Her best friend didn't give a tin feather for politics, but she lived for gossip and scandal.

"Okay, you're all set." The guard told her how to find Forlore's office and waved her through.

Taya strode through the high halls, taking the opportunity to stretch the kinks out of her arms, legs, and back. Most of the strangers who passed traded respectful nods with her—dedicate clerks, librarians, and programmers, and the occasional lictor. Once a masked and robed decatur paced past, and Taya joined everyone else in the hall in stepping aside, bowing with her palm pressed against her forehead. The lower-castes who worked in the tower had developed a fast and perfunctory bow around their decatur employers—a necessary compromise between intercaste formality and day-to-day work life—but Taya carefully followed protocol. If she became a diplomatic envoy, precise decorum would become her life.

Decatur Forlore's office was in one of the highest towers, and by the time Taya had finished walking up several flights of curving stairs, she was grateful for her wings. Their lighter-than-air metal made the climb a lot easier. Even so, she was breathing heavily in the thin air by the time she reached the doorway.

She knocked.

"Decatur Forlore? Icarus. I have a package for you."

"Enter."

She swung the door open and ducked through. Most of the city's buildings had been constructed with wings in mind, but doorways could still pose a problem.

The decatur's office was crammed with shelves of books, stacks of paper, and odd knickknacks strewn here and there on top of chairs and small tables. Two men stood at a table in the center of the room, examining a clock.

Neither was covered, although Taya spotted a set of public robes thrown over a chair in one corner, its ivory mask laid on top. Despite the lack of ritual garments, and even though they had their backs toward her, it was easy to pick out which one was the decatur. His clothes were made of beautifully dyed silks, and his long black hair was bound back in an ornate style held together with glittering gold clasps, just like Viera Octavus's. Taya saw the flash of rings on his fingers as he set the clock down.

Then the decatur glanced over his shoulder and smiled. He was a handsome man, with a generous mouth and green eyes that twinkled amiably.

"Wait for me a moment, icarus. I'll be right with you."

He looked back to his guest, who wore the short hair and somber black suit of a famulate craftsman.

"Thank you, Cris. I'm impressed. But in truth, I'm always impressed by your work."

"*I'd* be impressed if I knew how your guests managed to knock it off the mantel," said the repairman, one hand resting possessively on the clock case for a moment before rising to adjust his wire-rimmed spectacles. "This clock isn't light. What in the Lady's name were they doing?"

"It was an accident," the exalted said, lifting a dismissive shoulder. "High spirits and too many of them, I'm afraid. I appreciate your bringing this all the way up to the Tower. You could have simply taken it around to the mansion."

"I didn't want to visit the mansion. And I wish you'd send a servant to pick up your packages, instead of expecting me to bring them to you. I have other work to do, you know."

Taya shifted uncomfortably at the repairman's sharp tone. He sounded better-educated than most famulates and used the formal speech patterns of the ruling caste, but that didn't excuse his taking such a familiar manner with an exalted. He and the decatur must know each other well. Maybe the decatur broke his clocks on a regular basis. From the looks of his office, Exalted Forlore wasn't very careful with his possessions.

"Yes, well, at least this way I have the opportunity to see you once in a while." The decatur held out a hand. The repairman shook his head, but they clasped.

"You could always come down to visit me, for a change." The man turned and Taya drew in a startled breath.

The repairman was exalted, too.

The contrast between the wave-shaped castemarks on his cheeks and his somber black famulate suit was so shocking that it took her a moment to collect her thoughts. She'd heard of exalts who'd rejected their caste, but she'd never actually seen one before. She'd always considered them as unreal as dragons and unicorns.

Instead of an exalted's traditional long, ornamented hairstyle, the repairman had cut his black hair carelessly short, as if he didn't care at all what impression he made. His face was narrow and sharp, with cold grey eyes behind silver-rimmed glasses and a thin mouth set in a skeptical twist.

Taya dragged her gaze away, afraid she was staring, but he seemed to be looking just as intently at her. His chilly examination made her wonder if she'd somehow offended him. Should she have bowed? Then he took another step forward and she realized it was her armature that had attracted his attention.

"Your straps are loose," he said critically, then lifted his gaze. For a moment the lenses of his glasses flashed white in the lamplight. "And two of your feathers are damaged."

Taya swallowed.

"Yes, exalted. I was in an accident. I'll get them repaired as soon as I return to the eyrie." She looked down at her harness and wished she'd taken the time to re-coil all her lines and re-fasten all her buckles. She'd been in too much of a hurry to finish up for the day. "I'm sorry."

"Don't be so unpleasant, Cristof. The young lady appears to have been working hard today."

Taya glanced up and saw Decatur Forlore smiling at her. He was young, for a member of the Council—he couldn't be much into his thirties, and most council members were in their sixties. She remembered seeing his name on her list of important people. Forlore. He was a programmer, but he hadn't voted often enough to be politically categorized yet.

"It's a matter of safety." Cristof's voice was stern. "An armature is a sensitive piece of machinery. It shouldn't be mistreated like this."

"I didn't mistreat it!" Taya protested. The exalted's eyebrows rose, and she bit her bottom lip.

"Then what happened to you?" Forlore asked, before Cristof could respond to her outburst. Taya bowed, eager to explain before she was criticized again.

"One of the wireferry girders broke, exalted, and—"

"Viera!" The decatur pushed away from the table. "You were the icarus who rescued Viera? We were told what had happened when Caster was called away from the Council. Is she well? How is Ariq?"

"They're both safe, exalted. Neither was injured."

"Thank the Lady."

"What caused the accident?" Cristof asked, his grey eyes narrowing behind his glasses.

"I don't know."

"Who cares? What's important is that no one was hurt," Forlore said impatiently. "That is—no one *was* hurt? None of the rescuers were injured, were they?"

"No, exalted. I don't think so."

"That's good. By the Forge, Cris," the exalted said with a touch of irritation, "you need to get your priorities straight."

"The icarus had already told us Viera was safe. I asked the next logical question." Cristof gave the decatur a sidelong look, pushing his glasses higher on his nose. "You should wonder why it happened, too, Alister. It could have been you in that car."

"Oh, would you stop worrying over hypotheticals? I've told you before—statistically speaking, you're less likely to get into an accident on a wireferry than you are walking through the city streets," Forlore said. "It was probably metal wear. I should adjust the weather variables on the Engine's repair program; the last few winters have been more severe than most."

"We would all be safer if you did," Cristof said, stiffly. "Good evening, Alister. Icarus."

Taya stepped aside as he brushed past her, wondering again whether she should bow. At last she did, but he was already through the doorway.

She turned back to Decatur Forlore, who shrugged.

"Cristof is brilliant with machines but terrible with people. Come in, icarus. Tell me everything that happened."

She took a cautious step deeper into the room, afraid her wings would knock something over.

"You had better take those off. There's no point trying to walk through this mess with twelve feet of metal strapped to your back. Here, let me find you a chair. Were you part of the rescue team? You must be exhausted."

"I can't stay long, exalted—"

"I insist you stay for a few minutes. I intend to hear the entire story before you leave." The decatur turned, working his way to a desk. "Would you care for a glass of wine?"

"No, thank you. I have to fly back," she said with regret. Wine was a luxury she could seldom afford, and it was unheard-of for an exalted to offer a glass to a mere icarus. But flying required precision work, especially with damaged feathers. She glanced at the clock on his table, thinking of Katerin's wedding. Time was slipping by. At this rate, she was going to have to choose between a bath and dinner, if she wanted to get to the ceremony on time.

Well, there'd be food at the reception.

"I hardly imagine half a glass will impair your judgment." Forlore pulled out an open bottle and rummaged until he found two glasses. "Consider it a command, if you wish."

"Well, exalted, if you put it that way . . . ." She set the package aside and unbuckled her harness. When she looked up, she saw him smiling at her. She instinctively smiled back, then blushed. *Exalted*, she reminded herself, pulling off her flight cap. *Mind your caste!*

"What's your name, icarus?"

"Taya, exalted." She left the armature bobbing behind her and gave him a proper bow, trying to restore a safe formality between them. He was still gazing at her, looking bemused. Her short hair was probably standing on end. It always did, after a long day of flying.

"I don't believe I have ever seen you here before. I'm sure I would have remembered you."

"I'm here every couple of days, exalted, flying one errand or another."

"Is that so?" He poured a half-glass and handed it to her, then filled a glass for himself. He tilted the glass in a brief toast. "I should get out of my office more often."

Was he flirting? Did she want him to be flirting? Flustered, Taya looked around the crowded room, seeking a noncommittal response.

"I can see where getting out of here might pose a problem."

He laughed.

"I know this must appear chaotic, but I assure you that I have a very scientific filing system."

"And the floor is part of it?"

"The system is deeply encrypted."

Taya smothered her smile. Lady, what was she doing? She had to get back to the eyrie.

"I brought you something to add to it, then." She handed him the package from the College of Mathematics, then sipped her wine as he opened it.

Definitely a new Council member, she thought, watching him as he read. No exalted had ever poured her a drink before, or engaged her in small talk. They seemed peculiarly thoughtful gestures for a member of the ruling caste. The exalteds, forged by the Lady with the superior insight and intellect they needed to protect Ondinium, seldom wasted much time on the lower castes.

Superior insight and intellect. Her lips quirked as she let her gaze roam across the clutter that surrounded them. *You'd think the product of a thousand fortunate rebirths would be a little more organized.*

"Well, I can't say I'm delighted by these statistics, but I appreciate your delivering them." Forlore set the papers down and looked up. "You're still standing. Sit down. You can remove that bust from the chair behind you. Set it on the floor."

"Are you sure I won't disrupt your filing system?" she asked, moving the head away and taking a seat.

"Not at all. It belongs there with the other P's." Forlore leaned against the table, watching her.

"I see." She returned his look, keeping her face impassive. "Would that be 'P' for Abatha Cardium or 'P' for astrologer?"

"'P' for plaster."

She laughed and he beamed, his green eyes warm with pleasure.

"May I ask you a question, exalted?"

"You may."

"How long have you been a decatur?"

"I've been a decatur for a little over a year. I was elected to the Council after Decatur Neuillan was . . . released from duty."

Of course. She should have guessed the newest member would be Neuillan's replacement. The older decatur had been caught selling programs to the Alzanan government.

Most of the city had demanded his execution, but Ondinium law reserved the death sentence for murder. Instead, the decatur had been stripped of his caste, blinded, and flogged out the city gates as a traitor.

"Is there a reason you ask?" Forlore gave her a curious look. "Do I seem different from the other decaturs, somehow?"

He did, but she wasn't about to tell him that.

"I was just wondering why I've never delivered a message to you before."

"Oh. I'm afraid that's because I spend a great deal of time down at the University with my programming team." He grimaced. "I've come to the conclusion that the Council keeps its new members in line by assigning them so much work that they're unable to find the time for any potentially disruptive pursuits, such as framing legislation. But my team has just finished a major project, so I'm free now to attend meetings."

"Is attending meetings better than programming?"

"It is different, at least. I'm afraid my job must seem quite dull, compared to yours. Now, tell me about the accident. What happened?"

Taya recounted the story a second time, gratified by his rapt attention. When she was through, Forlore gave a long, low, and very un-exalted-like whistle.

"Astounding. I'm relieved you were there. My cousin Viera is as close as a sister to me. I'd be devastated were I to lose her."

"She was very brave," Taya ventured.

"Viera has always been brave. She's also honorable; she won't forget she owes you her life, and neither will her husband. Caster Octavus is a very traditional man in matters of caste and honor."

"What are his politics?" she asked, eager to learn more about the man. Forlore blinked, looking surprised by the question.

"Well . . . that's rather difficult to say. Caster's enemies call him an Organicist, but it's a misnomer. He depends on the Great Engine as much as the rest of us, at least in matters of industry and agriculture. But he doesn't care for programs that simulate human behavior, so he's objected to a few of the trade and policy calculators that the Council has adopted."

Taya studied the decatur's face, trying to see if he were joking.

"You have programs that act like humans?"

"Not precisely." Forlore smiled. "I imagine you saw that play down in Secundus last year, didn't you? The one about the analytical engine that goes insane and orders the city's lictors to kill anyone that challenges its calculations?"

Embarrassed, she nodded.

"You needn't turn so red! I was among the exalteds who went to see it, myself. I found it very imaginative, but its playwright didn't have any idea how analytical engines really work. What we call a human-behavior simulation program doesn't give an engine any capacity for independent thought. What happens is that programmers like my team collect a great deal of data about how one person behaves, or about how many people behave, under certain circumstances. They boil the data down and develop a behavioral model, code it onto cards, create a program, run it, and the Great Engine uses the program's parameters to calculate the most statistically likely behaviors a hypothetical person sharing the same traits might adopt in a given situation or over a finite period of time."

Taya gave him a dubious look. He smiled.

"You've taken loyalty tests, of course."

She nodded. Icarii took a loyalty test each year, on the anniversary of their Great Examination.

"Your answers to each test are fed into the Engine, and it compares your new responses to your old responses, notes any changes that have occurred over the years, compares them to established risk factors, and predicts whether or not you're a threat to the city or the Council. If there's a reasonably high probability that you're becoming a security risk, you'll be summoned before a Board of Inquiry that determines the truth of the matter."

"Isn't the Engine always right?"

"Many people make that assumption, but it isn't true. If the Engine has a well-tested, reliable program and enough data, its predictions can be have a high level of validity. But it's impossible to collect enough data to cover all the potential variables. That's why humans make the final analyses." He smiled. "If the Great Engine were infallible, Ondinium wouldn't need a Council."

Taya thought of Pyke. "I know someone who always criticizes the Council, but he's never been called up to a Board of Inquiry."

"Criticizing the Council doesn't automatically make a person a security risk." Forlore paused, taking a sip of his wine. "In fact, Council members criticize each other all the time. A group that doesn't question itself usually makes bad decisions. Your friend may not be happy with Ondinium's government, but apparently he hasn't shown any inclination to sabotage it."

"He wouldn't do that," Taya hastened to assure the decatur. She didn't want to get Pyke into any trouble. Forlore looked amused, as if reading her mind. "Do decaturs take loyalty tests, too?"

"Yes, but . . . ." the exalted paused, glancing at her. "As I said, the Engine isn't infallible. If it were, it would have caught Decatur Neuillan."

His moment of hesitation was enough to remind Taya that she wasn't chatting with a friend; she was talking to an exalted. Why was she dawdling here, anyway, when her sister was getting married tonight? She stood.

"I'm sorry, exalted. I've been taking up too much of your time."

"Not at all." He reached out for her glass. She faltered, then handed it to him. Exalteds weren't supposed to take dirty dishes. "I've enjoyed talking to you, Taya."

"Thank you. And thank you for the wine."

"My pleasure. I look forward to seeing you again."

"I'm sure you will, exalted." She began strapping on her armature again.

"Yes. I'm sure I will, too."

She glanced up. He was watching her with a thoughtful look, the lamplight glittering off the gold clasps in his dark hair and burnishing the smooth copper of his skin. But even without the ornaments, it would be obvious that he had been born exalted—his Ondinium coloration and features were flawless.

Taya smoothed her short auburn hair, the all-too-apparent sign of her mixed heritage. To her chagrin, she took after her Mareaux-descended father more than she did her Ondinium mother. Then she blushed and looked down to check her harness once more.

Lady, there's a reason exalteds wear concealing masks and robes! She had no right to notice Decatur Forlore's face. The only features that mattered between them were her wings and his castemarks.

Think of this as a diplomatic test, she advised herself. *Act like you would if you were already in the corps.*

"Is that everything, exalted?" She took a deep breath and looked up, smoothing her expression into one of calm professional interest.

"For the moment." He held her gaze. "Fly safely, icarus."

"I will. Thank you." She bowed once more, her palm against her forehead, and made her way out as quickly as she could. She felt his eyes on her and had to struggle to resist the urge to glance back.

As soon as she reached the hall, she rubbed her hands against her cheeks, trying to convince herself they weren't burning and he hadn't seen her blush.

Lady and spirits. I'm going to have to rush to get to the wedding on time.

Chapter Three

Taya's father ran an iron smelting factory in Tertius, and her sister was marrying one of his chief engineers. Most of the factory workers had come for the festivities, along with the family's friends and neighbors.

Taya held a cup of weak punch and watched Katerin dance, a flash of white moving through the dark suits and dresses of the other guests.

"That'll be you down there, soon enough," her father said, at her elbow. Taya started, then smiled.

"I'm not in a hurry, Papa," she said.

"Too busy working, are you? Heard from the exam board yet?"

"No. It's still too soon. Even if I do well on the exam, they'll be running background checks and talking to my employers and friends."

"You've not a thing to worry about." He kissed her on the forehead. "I've faith you'll pass your test, and nobody will speak poorly of you, not under the wires nor up in the air. Now, doff those wings and join the dancing. You've done your duty today, haven't you, and then some."

"I wasn't planning on staying much longer." Taya glanced up at the wings that curved over her head. The two primaries were still bent. She'd returned to the eyrie too late to ask the smith to repair them, and she'd needed her armature for the wedding. Icarii were considered good luck, especially at weddings, so she'd promised her sister she'd wear her wings to the ceremony.

"Tired?"

"It's been a long day."

"I suppose it has, and the longer for spending time with us instead of your own caste."

Taya glanced at him, worried, but her father was smiling, one hand on her arm while his eyes followed his youngest daughter with contented pride.

Filled with affection, Taya leaned over and kissed him on the cheek. His red hair, which she'd inherited, was streaked with grey now, and dirt from his job had ingrained itself into his skin like another tattoo, revealing his caste as clearly as the black circle on his forehead. Taya knew some icarii who were embarrassed to come from the famulate caste, but she'd always been proud of her father.

"I wouldn't have missed this for the world," she said. "Tomas seems like a good man."

"He is that." Her father smiled. "We're glad you came down. Katie's told anyone who'll listen that her sister the icarus was going to be at her wedding, hasn't she?"

"She's not jealous of me leaving the caste, is she?"

"Of you, sweetness?" Her father's eyebrows rose. "Lady, no. She thinks you've a dismal enough life, full of long days and risky work and not a decent man in all those crowded eyries of yours."

"There are too decent icarii!" Taya protested, shooting her oblivious sister an annoyed look.

Her father chuckled and moved away to talk to his guests.

Taya stuck it out for another hour, exchanging polite inconsequentials with childhood acquaintances who came up to ask about the wireferry wreck and touch her wings for good luck. They were all famulates, and Taya felt the familiar discomfort of having left her birth-caste behind whenever the conversation faltered or turned to local affairs. A few children, clearly on the verge of their Great Examinations, asked her how to become an icarus, but she couldn't give them much advice. She knew that being small and not being afraid of heights were important, but she couldn't begin to guess what other variables the Great Engine calculated when it made its decisions. *Decatur Forlore would know*, she thought, then smiled at herself and dismissed the thought.

At last she kissed Katerin and Tomas good-bye and left the party with a distinct sense of relief.

TERTIUS SPRAWLED at the base of Ondinium Mountain, where it primarily housed members of the famulate caste — miners and metalworkers, engineers and smiths — and those foreigners who'd managed to purchase a labor or residency license, or who were visiting the city on business or out of curiosity. Even during the day, the streets of Tertius were shadowed by the network of wireferry towers and girders that surrounded the mountain with a metal web, and darkened by the ever-present blanket of smog from the factories that turned the sector's sky a sickly yellow and covered everything in a thin layer of soot.

Taya looked up but couldn't make out the stars, only the lights from Secundus and Primus. Returning to Tertius always gave her a twinge of nostalgia for the sights and smells she'd left at age seven, but her father was right — she didn't belong here anymore. Icarii moved between all the castes but fit in well with none of them, a social position that could be as awkward as it was liberating.

Breathing in the smoky, metallic air, she walked through dark, narrow stone streets toward the Great Market. When she'd been a child, she hadn't noticed how dirty everything was on Tertius, or how shabby.

The Great Engine ensured that nobody starved in Ondinium, but the difference between the heart of the city's industrial zone and the luxury of Oporphyr Tower was inescapable to someone who moved freely between them every day.

Still, she thought, *Ondinium is better than most countries*. It might be dirty and crowded, but she'd rather breathe a little soot than hunt and skin her own dinner, like the residents of neighboring Demicus.

Civilization had its price, but it also had its advantages.

Lost in thought, Taya was about to pass beneath the broad stone arch of a footbridge she had played on as a child when she heard footsteps scrape on the cobblestones behind her.

She turned.

Two men stood under a gas lamp, five yards away. One was tall and fair-haired: a Demican, wearing his people's rough native garments. The other was shorter and had the stocky build and bright vest of an Alzanan. Their faces were uninked. Foreigners.

"Can I help you?" she asked, trying to sound confident. Her gaze flickered to the sky. The way was clear enough, although she hadn't had to take flight from a flat run for years. But flying meant locking her arms into her wings, and she didn't want to make herself that vulnerable unless it became necessary.

"We am lost, Icarus," the Alzanan said, struggling with Ondinan. "How we go Blue Tree Hotel?"

The Blue Tree Hotel? That was a nice place . . . too nice for them. *Still, they might be meeting someone there*, she told herself, trying to keep an open mind.

Then the thought flickered past: *This could be one of those secret diplomacy tests*.

"It's on Jasper Street in Secundus," she said, speaking Alzanan. "This bridge goes up to Secundus, and you can ask the guard at the sector gate how to get to the hotel. You'd better hurry, before the midnight lockdown."

"This bridge?" The Alzanan began walking forward, his neck craned. His tall companion followed, wearing the flat, stoic expression Demicans cultivated. "How do we get up to it?"

"Go back a block and turn right on Damper, then right again on Alumina. There are access steps on Crate Street. Look for the signs directing you to Whitesmith Bridge."

"But we were on Crate Street, and we didn't see any way up," the Alzanan protested in his own language, still advancing. Taya touched the utility knife strapped to her chest harness.

"Please don't come any closer, gentlemen," she said, still speaking Alzanan.

The two men paused.

"You don't need to be afraid of me." The Alzanan looked hurt. "I'm just asking for directions."

"Go back a block. Make two rights." Taya's heart was pounding. This could be a test, but it could also be the prelude to mugging. She was on Tertius, for the Lady's sake—people were attacked down here all the time. "Please go."

"Can I touch your wings for good luck?" The Alzanan took another step forward. Taya stepped backward, her hand tightening around the knife grip.

"I'm sorry, but I—"

Then she heard the scrape of metal against stone above her. Instinct took over and she threw herself forward, but heavy coils of rope hit her, jarring her wings and dragging at the metal feathers. Taya staggered, off-balance, and looked up. A second Alzanan leaned over the side of the bridge, leering down at her.

A net. Taya swore, feeling it encumbering her wings, its awkward weight threatening to pull her on her back.

This isn't a test!

The first Alzanan and the Demican lunged forward. Taya yanked at her harness buckles with one hand, slashing out with her knife when the Alzanan drew near.

"Help!" she shouted, feeling a buckle give way beneath her fingers. She began pulling at the next. The Demican drew a dagger from the back of his belt, his face hard.

They were going to kill her.

"Help! Guards!"

The Alzanan darted in like a knife-fighter, a thin blade materializing between his fingers and snapping across her harness. Its razor-sharp edge cut the backs of her fingers. Taya stabbed at him. He danced backward. A small nick marked his bare forearm.

The second buckle opened and her wings slid to one side across her shoulders. Taya tugged at the buckle around her waist, her fingers slippery with blood. If she could get out of the armature, she'd be able to fight. But right now her wings were nothing but deadweight.

"Guards!" she shouted again, angry. "Dammit, somebody get help!"

The Demican shoved his partner aside, stalking forward with menacing intensity. Taya worked harder to pull the waist strap open. Demicans were hunters and warriors, hardened by their nomadic life outside civilized lands. And this one was about two feet taller and wider than she was.

"What's going on here?" a hard voice snapped with authority.

The two men looked around, and Taya abandoned the buckle, taking the moment's opening to even the odds. She lunged forward and thrust her utility knife through the Demican's wool shirt and into his chest.

He roared with anger, grabbing her wrist and yanking her aside. The net tangled her feet and she sprawled, losing her knife. She wrenched her waist buckle open with both hands and twisted aside as the warrior's knife slashed down. The point of the blade caught her shoulder as she rolled away, leaving the net behind her.

Scrambling on all fours, Taya snatched her utility knife off the cobblestones.

Something gave a sharp, machinelike hiss. Behind her, the Demican grunted, sounding surprised.

Taya spun, rising into a fighting crouch.

The Demican was staring down at his chest. Two long metal needles stuck out from his shirt, blood spreading around them to match the growing stain where she'd stabbed him.

"Forget her! We go!" the Alzanan shouted in Ondinan, and ran. The Demican staggered, looked at his fleeing companion, and then followed.

Taya craned her neck, but there was no sign of the second Alzanan who'd been on top of the bridge.

Her wings floated a foot off the ground, trapped by the heavy rope net. Taya hurried over to them, hoping she could untangle the armature from the ropes without damaging it any further.

The newcomer's footsteps sounded behind her. She glanced over her shoulder, expecting to see a lictor.

Her rescuer had crouched to study the drops of blood on the cobblestones. The hem of his greatcoat dragged on the street, and he held a bulky iron airgun in one hand. Taya had seen the air rifles carried by Council guards, but she'd never seen one that was pistol-sized before.

Then the man looked up, lamplight flashing from the wire rims of his glasses. For a moment he and Taya stared at each other with mutual recognition.

"Exalted." Taya ducked in a clumsy bow, remembering their disagreeable meeting in Decatur Forlore's office. "Thank you for rescuing me."

Cristof was silent a moment longer, then stood. He slipped the gun into his coat pocket, where it made an unsightly lump. The cold night breeze ruffled the uneven ends of his dark hair. Taya had to look up to meet his eyes—like most icarii, she was small and slight, whereas he had an exalted's height, six feet tall or more.

"Well, icarus," he said, frowning. "You're either very careless or very unlucky."

His words irritated her. She turned back to her armature before he could see the annoyance in her expression.

"Actually, I consider myself very lucky," she said, working hard to keep her tone even. "I'm still alive."

"You're bleeding."

She glanced over her shoulder at the dark stain on her flight suit. The wound stung, but it was less inconvenient than the cut across her fingers.

"It's just a scratch." She turned back and tried to find the bottom of the net.

"Don't. You'll break it if you try to untangle it here. Take it back to my shop and do it in the light."

She hesitated. She didn't like his manner, and if she weren't so worried about her wings, she'd take great satisfaction in turning him down.

But it wasn't worth damaging her wings for the sake of pride.

"Is your shop close?"

"A few blocks away." He stepped next to her and began gathering the net's loose ends. She scooped the whole

bundle off the ground. He turned his frown on her again.
"I'll get it."

"I can do it, exalted," she insisted. "It's not heavy, and
they're my wings."

He gave her a cool look, then handed her the rest of the
net. As soon as she'd gotten all the ends wrapped up, he
began walking, one hand jammed in his coat pocket.

Taya followed, silently, and wondered if this might be a
test, after all. Her classes in diplomatic protocol had never
covered how to deal with an outcaste exalted.

CRISTOF'S WORKSHOP was small, tucked into the basement
of a larger building that was filled with small businesses.
They descended three steps from the street to get to the
door, which he unlocked with two keys.

"Be careful," he said, leading her in. Taya followed,
tugging her floating bundle behind her.

The first thing that struck her was the sound—a loud ticking,
whirring, and clicking that came from every direction at once.

Cristof struck a lucifer match and lit a lamp. Taya looked
around with wonder as he turned it to its brightest level
and hung it on one of the low ceiling beams.

The exalted's shop was filled with clocks and watches,
pumps and wind-up toys, every kind of clockwork mechanism imaginable. Most were in motion, their hands turning,
pendulums swinging, and gears rotating.

"You have so many!" Taya breathed, her annoyance
forgotten. She clutched her bundle and stared. Enamelwork
and metal gleamed in the lamplight like moving jewels.
Cristof had a small fortune hanging on his walls and sitting
on his shelves. "Did you make them all?"

"No. Not all." He hesitated, then walked to a desk. The
lamplight reflected off his cheekbones, making his face
look even thinner. The exalted's waves tattooed on his face
seemed to move in the unsteady light. "Put the net on the
table. Make sure the armature doesn't float too high."

Reminded of her business, Taya tied two ends of the net
to the table legs, letting the rest of the bundle float. Cristof

returned with two knives and offered one. His hands
were covered with dark smears—dirt or machine oil, she
guessed. It was another indication of his outcaste status.
Exalteds were fastidious about their appearance.

"It'll be faster to cut the ropes," he said. "That way we
won't bend any feathers."

"If those bastards broke my wings, I'll kill them." Taya
grabbed the knife, sawing at the cords.

"You might have, already. The man you stabbed was
losing a lot of blood."

Taya cut through a rope and attacked the next. Then she
set down the knife a moment, looking at the blood welling
from the cuts on her fingers.

Had she really killed a man?

If he got to a hospital, he'd be all right.

Of course, he was a foreigner, and probably not even a
licensed resident. Physicians weren't obliged to treat anyone
who didn't pay Ondinium's taxes, and any respectable
doctor would ask questions about those wounds that the
Demican wouldn't want to answer.

Why did she care what happened to him, anyway? He'd
tried to kill her.

"Scrap," she muttered, angrily.

Cristof paused, on the other side of the table.

"What?"

"What about you? You shot him, didn't you? If he dies,
he'll probably die from that."

"Maybe." The exalted studied her. "Although needlers
seldom kill at range. They're intended as deterrents."

"Oh. So if he dies, it's my fault." The thought depressed
her. How would inflicting a fatal injury on a foreigner
affect her chance at the diplomatic corps?

"If he dies, it's his fault for going icarus-hunting, not
yours for defending yourself." Cristof went back to work,
his slender fingers tugging at the net strands. "And it's
his fault for letting himself be led around by Alzanans. A
Demican should know better."

Not feeling very comforted, Taya picked up her knife again.

"I guess you don't like Alzanans."

"Half the Alzanans in Ondinium are spies. Maybe more." He sawed through another rope. "It doesn't surprise me that they'd want an operational armature. They could demand a king's ransom for these wings."

Taya began working on another rope, considering his words. She knew her wings were valuable, of course, but she'd never thought they'd attract thieves.

"Do you think they were specifically looking for wings?" she asked.

"They came with a net. That isn't a standard mugger's weapon. Did anyone know you'd be on Tertius tonight?"

The rope unraveled beneath her blade, and she sighed.

"Just about everybody in the neighborhood. I was at my sister's wedding."

Cristof was silent. Taya kept working, ignoring the fresh trickles of blood that ran over her hands as she worked.

She didn't like the thought that those men had been hunting her. They must have heard she would be attending the wedding in armature and—what? Had they waited to see if she'd leave alone? Had they guessed that an icarus would find it easiest to launch from the Market Tower? Was she that predictable?

She could have foiled their plans if she'd done something unexpected, but why would she? No one harmed icarii. They were Ondinium's couriers and rescuers; its alarm system and its luck.

Of course, those three had been foreigners. They wouldn't have an Ondinium citizen's respect for icarii.

The armature jerked as the net slid apart. Taya grabbed the harness before it could hit the ceiling and hauled it back down. Without a word, Cristof tied one of the severed ropes to a harness strap and anchored it into place over the table.

"It doesn't look too bad," Taya said, inspecting the wings. The net had yanked them out of their locked position, which meant they might have sustained damage to the joints, but she wouldn't know until she tried them on again. She caressed the metal feathers closest to her, tugging them. They still seemed to be securely fastened to the wing struts.

On the other side of the table, Cristof was doing the same thing, frowning as he concentrated. His dirt-stained fingers moved confidently as he tested the feathers and their housing.

Taya surreptitiously studied him. His coat was as plain and well-worn as any other craftsman's. He didn't wear any rings or necklaces. He didn't have any pins in his lapels or any clasps or jewels in his short black hair. Even his spectacles were ordinary. There was nothing in his appearance to indicate he was anything other than a simple famulate mechanic, except the curling blue waves tattooed on his cheeks.

Once you get past the discrepancy between his castemarks and the way he dresses, he's not so bad-looking, she thought. He still had an exalted's features, after all. His copper skin was smooth and his badly cut hair was thick and glossy. His features were sharp, though, and there wasn't much extra weight on his tall, thin frame. Grey eyes were unusual for an exalted. He must have foreign blood in his ancestry; Demican, maybe. His pale eyes were what made his face so cold, their light color emphasized by the silver rims of his spectacles.

"This wing seems all right," he said at last. She collected her thoughts.

"Mine, too, unless some of the joint mechanisms have been damaged."

He glanced at her hands.

"You're getting blood all over everything. Sit down."

"They're just cuts." She looked down and made a face. He was right. She'd smeared blood on her flight suit, and blood had dripped on the table beneath the armature. The scratches weren't deep, but working with her hands had been keeping them open.

Cristof pulled off his greatcoat and threw it over a chair, then vanished through a doorway. Relieved to be free of his critical gaze for a moment, Taya curled her bloody hand in her lap and looked around with wonder.

All of the clocks and timepieces indicated the same time, but otherwise they varied widely, from the somber black long-case clock standing in one corner to the fanciful jeweled stag-shaped clock set on a high shelf to the open-geared clock under a glass case that took up two feet of the top of a tool cabinet. Three short shelves next to a worktable were covered with wind-up toys, the kind Taya had played with as a little girl. Two caught her eye: small birds that floated over the top of the shelf, tethered with pieces of string. She stood and walked over to them, holding her bleeding hand close to her chest to avoid making any more of a mess.

The birds were cunningly crafted with tiny, bright enameled feathers and little beaks of gold. The miniature keys between each set of wings looked gold, too. The birds' eyes sparkled in the lamplight, and Taya wondered if they were made of cut glass or gemstones. Gemstones, she guessed, if they were the expensive toys they seemed to be.

"They have ondium cores," Cristof said, returning with a basin and two hand towels. He put them on the table beneath the floating armature. "Wash your hand."

"They're beautiful." She pulled herself away and dipped her hand in the cold water. Blood stained the cold water as she rubbed the cuts clean. "Are you repairing them for someone?"

"They're mine." Cristof held out a handkerchief, and she pressed it against her cuts. He'd washed his hands, too, she noted, but dirt still smudged his shirt cuffs and the sharp bridge of his nose, where he must have touched his face to push up his glasses.

"Do they really fly?"

"Let me see your shoulder. The cut might not bother you now, but your harness will irritate it."

"I don't think it's too bad." She tried to crane her neck around to see it. "It stings, but it doesn't hurt much."

"Let me see," he repeated, impatiently.

She made a face, then unbuttoned the flight suit's high collar, down to the top of her breasts. A clock repairman wouldn't be her first choice of physician, but she supposed he was better than nothing.

"This may sting." Cristof lifted the suit away from her bare shoulder. The suit's cotton padding stuck to the coagulating blood as it peeled away, and Taya winced. Cristof pressed a wet towel between her suit and skin.

Taya shivered as cold water dripped down her back. The outcaste's fingers were cold, too, as he touched the edges of the cut.

"You're right. It's shallow. Have a physician look at it tomorrow. It shouldn't impair your flight tonight." Cristof's voice was as detached as it had been when he'd reported on the status of her wings. She remembered Decatur Forlore's quip about the repairman's way with machines and felt a flash of amusement. He *had* worried about her armature first and her wounds second, hadn't he? She imagined the exalted touched his broken clocks with exactly the same care and dispassion with which he'd touched her bare shoulder.

He laid the bloodstained towel on the table and picked up a clean one, pressing it over the cut. "That will be enough of a bandage for the flight to your eyrie."

"Thank you." She buttoned her suit back up and reached for the floating harness.

"Give the cuts on your hand a few more minutes to clot." He pushed up his spectacles, turning away. "Do you want to see them fly?"

Taya studied his back, confused by the sudden change of subject. Then she remembered the toy birds.

"Please. If you don't mind."

He untied one of the birds, holding it gently and turning toward her once more as he wound the key. For a moment the lamplight flashed on his glasses again.

"My mother gave these to my brother and me, when we were little." He held the bird up with both hands and spread his fingers, releasing the bird.

The clockwork wings beat and the little bird took off, darting across the room and hitting the opposite wall. It floated there, its beak pressed against the wall, its wings still flapping uselessly.

Cristof walked across the room and turned it with one finger. The bird flew away again, coming to an abrupt stop at the next wall.

"They're meant to be used outside," he said. "Or in a very long hallway, preferably with an unsuspecting adult at the other end."

Taya laughed, and for a brief moment Cristof's thin lips twisted upward in response. He retrieved the bird. Its wings were winding down, their beating slowing, but its ondium core kept it aloft. It floated between his hands.

"My brother broke this one and threw it away. I decided to fix it for him. It took me six years to learn how, but now it flies as well as ever." Pride shone in his pale eyes as he regarded the tiny mechanism. "They aren't made anymore. Using ondium in a children's toy is considered too much of an extravagance now that the main veins have been tapped out."

"I think they're wonderful." Taya smiled. "Did you ever give the bird back to your brother?"

"No. By the time I'd fixed it, he'd moved on to other toys and didn't want it anymore."

"Oh. That's too bad."

"It's typical." He turned and tied the bird back to the shelf. "Alister adores his toys until they disappoint him. Then he throws them away." For a moment his voice turned sour.

"Alister?" Taya felt a jolt of recognition. She'd already heard Cristof use that name today. "You don't mean—" But of course he did. It made perfect sense. "Decatur Forlore is your brother?"

Cristof's hands stopped.

"I thought you knew."

"No, I didn't." She faltered. "But, if he's your brother, why are you living down here?"

"What do you mean?"

"Well, he's a decatur, and he's still speaking with you. So why doesn't he bring you back to Primus?"

"I have no interest in going back to Primus." His voice had turned cold, but Taya forged on.

"But you don't *want* to be outcaste, do you?"

Face twisting in rage, Cristof turned and slammed a hand down on the table.

"My brother and my caste are none of your business, icarus!"

Taya flinched, then slid off the chair and dropped to one knee, pressing her palm against her forehead.

"I'm sorry, exalted," she said, furious at herself. How could she have forgotten her manners around an exalted, even an exalted in exile?

Some future diplomat!

"Stand up." Cristof's voice was tight.

She glanced at him. His face was pale with anger. She bowed again, feeling sick.

"I'm sorry, exalted," she repeated.

"Dammit, icarus, stand up!"

She scrambled to her feet, bracing herself for a slap.

"Look at me!"

She risked another glance and saw him glaring at her. She dropped her eyes again, not daring to anger him any further.

"You see?" he asked bitterly. "That's exactly what I hate about my caste. You're brave enough to stab a Demican who's twice as tall and as strong as you are, but all an exalted has to do is raise his voice and you're on your knees."

"I apologize," she said. "I was out of line."

"Look at me when you talk. You're not a slave."

She swallowed and looked up.

He started to say something, then closed his mouth and scowled. For a second the only sound in the shop was the ticking and whirring of the clockwork around them. They stared at each other.

"What's your name?"

"Taya Icarus, exalted."

"Icarii stand outside the caste hierarchy. The next time an exalted shouts at you, stay on your feet and answer him like an equal."

"I can't do that, Exalted Forlore."

"Why not?" His voice was sharp.

"It wouldn't be respectful. An exalted could take away my wings, if he wanted." She shivered at the thought. "I'm sorry I made you angry."

"I'm not going to take away your wings, icarus. I'm barely an exalted now, anyway."

"You still wear the castemarks."

He touched his copper-skinned cheek, his scowl deepening.

"Do you think wearing them makes me a coward? Do you think I should burn them away, or ink them over?"

"No," she protested, sensing she was on dangerous ground again. *This man is a test in diplomacy all by himself.* She reached for her armature, pulling it toward her and untying it from the table. The sooner she could get out of here, the better. "I think you'd be foolish to give up your caste. The Lady granted you an exalted rebirth for a reason, and it would be sinful to treat it lightly."

He fell silent, and she slipped on the armature and reached for her buckles.

"Do you like being an icarus?"

"Yes, exalted." She tightened the straps. The cut on her shoulder was going to hurt on the way back up, but she was eager to leave. "I wouldn't want to be anything else."

"Then it would be foolish of the Council to take away your wings at the whim of an angry exalted. The city barely has enough icarii as it is. If you understood how valuable you were to Ondinium, you wouldn't be so intimidated by authority."

She didn't answer, busy with her armature.

"I have to adjust this outside," she said after a moment, sliding her arms into the wings long enough to lock them into tight-rest, which pressed them close to her body. She lost no time in escaping the small, noisy shop but, to her dismay, Cristof followed.

Outside, the light from the gas streetlamps washed the narrow street in black and white. Taya unlocked her wings and spread them out, testing the joints and tilt, making sure the feathers closed and opened correctly. Everything seemed to function.

"Go straight back to your eyrie until you can get your shoulder tended," Cristof directed.

"I will." His peremptory tone was grating, especially after he'd made such a fuss over icarii being equal to exalteds. She had to bite back the urge to point out his hypocrisy. "I—"

The clocks in his shop began to chime, a hundred different bells ringing at the same moment.

A loud explosion ripped through the air and the ground trembled.

Taya whipped around and saw flames rising in the distance. She took a step forward.

"Don't!" Cristof snapped.

"They'll need—"

"Others will attend to it." Cristof grasped her arm. "Your armature is damaged and you've been hurt. You'll only be a danger to yourself and the rescue crew."

Taya laughed humorlessly and pulled away from him.

"Sorry, exalted. Equal to equal, I've got a job to do, and I don't have time to argue with you about it."

He cursed as she ran down the street and lifted her wings to catch the wind.

Chapter Four

The cook at Taya's eyrie brewed tea out of the bitterest black leaves ever exported from Cabiel. Normally the drink was enough to give the twenty or so icarii who lived at the boarding house the jolt they needed to face the day, but this morning Taya yawned over her cup and wondered if she could get away with going back to bed for a few more hours. Her muscles ached, her cuts throbbed, and her wings were in the smith's shop, being repaired.

"Hey, Taya!" Pyke burst in, waving a newspaper. "You're awake!"

"Barely." She grimaced as he sat next to her and spread out the pages of *The Watchman*. The ink smelled fresh, and Pyke's fingers were smeared with black as he stabbed at the headline that blazed across the front page.

TERRORISM!
Torn Cards Attack Wireferry, Refinery
Night of Horror!

Taya frowned and skipped down the stack of headers to the story.

"You're in there," Pyke said, pointing. "Both of us get a mention, but you're the hero, see?"

"I don't remember seeing any reporters there." She read further, then gasped. "Look! They quoted me! I never said that!"

Pyke laughed and read the paragraph aloud.

"'I was only doing my duty,' the modest icarus said. 'I'm grateful that Lady Octavus and her son are safe and that I was given this chance to serve my city.' Like you wouldn't have said that if they'd asked."

"I don't think Taya would have used that 'serve my city' line," Cassilta said, breezing in and dropping into a chair at their table. "It sounds so fake."

"It's all fake," Taya protested. "The only person I talked to was Lieutenant Amcathra, and that was just to give him my statement."

"Well, that's the glory of having a free press." Cassi grinned at her. "It's free to make up anything it wants."

"You should be flattered," Pyke grumbled. "Nobody faked an interview with me."

"You were just as important," Taya assured him. Without his help, both she and Viera Octavus would have died, or at least been crippled on impact. But only another icarus was likely to realize that.

"I'd love to hear what *you'd* tell the papers, Pyke." Cassilta pried the cup of tea from Taya's hand and took a sip. "Ick, it's cold. Stay there. I'll get us fresh cups."

"Believe me, I'm not going anywhere."

"Late night at the wedding?" Pyke leaned back in his chair.

"Not really. But—"

"Don't talk about the wedding until I'm back!" Cassilta shouted across the dining room, balancing three cups in her hands. She wove back through the tables and rejoined them. "Okay. How was it?"

Taya began to tell them about the ceremony. After a few minutes Pyke returned to his paper, leaving the discussion of food and dresses and babies to the two women. She didn't mention that she'd nearly been mugged. She didn't want to hear their lectures about walking alone through Tertius at night.

"Hey, Taya, did you see the fire last night?" Pyke interrupted, peering over the paper. "It wasn't far from your old neighborhood."

"I saw it." Taya took a sip of the stomach-dissolving tea to collect her thoughts. "I flew over in case I was needed, but they got everything under control pretty fast." She'd lingered long enough to report the icarus-hunters to the lictors. They'd promised to look for the three men as soon as they had a chance.

"*The Watchman* says the stripes think it was a bomb. Apparently they're suspicious because the refinery blew up right at the stroke of eleven."

"Yes, it did." Taya remembered the clocks ringing the hour in Cristof's shop. "Did they find any bomb parts?"

"Not by the time the paper went to press." Pyke turned a page. "I'll pick up a copy of the *Evening Dispatch* tonight. Maybe they'll know more by then."

Taya looked at the ink stains on his fingers and remembered Cristof's fingers. She'd thought the repairman's dirty hands had meant he didn't care about cleanliness, but his workshop had been neat, and he'd been annoyed by the mess her bloody hands had made.

And he'd washed his hands as soon as he'd left the room.

So, why had they been dirty in the first place?

Could he have been walking back from the refinery?

No. That was ridiculous. A thousand blessed rebirths did not produce a terrorist. An outcaste, just maybe, but not a terrorist.

"Hey, Taya!" An icarus with her wings folded down walked into the dining room, waving a letter. "Message for you!"

"I'm here." Taya stood, surprised. Mail was usually kept for icarii at the dispatch office. She took the heavy parchment envelope with curiosity. A large, painted wax seal and gold ribbon held it closed.

"I brought it straight from the Octavus estate." The icarus grinned at her. "I was told to put it in your hands. I'm glad you're not out flying messages already."

"You're Ranelle, aren't you?" Taya remembered the younger girl; she'd been a few classes after Taya's.

"Yes." The girl looked gratified at being recognized. "That was really amazing, what you did yesterday. Everyone's talking about it. All the fledglings are begging their teachers to run rescue drills today."

"Thanks." Embarrassed, Taya turned the envelope over in her hands.

"Well . . . I'd better get going." The girl sounded reluctant. "Bye, Taya."

"Fly safely."

Taya felt the whole eyrie's eyes on her as she sat back down. She put the letter on the table and stole a glance at her friends.

"You might as well open it here," Cassi said pragmatically. "Whatever it says, it's going to be all over the eyries in a matter of minutes."

"It'll be a thank-you," Taya guessed, picking up a butter knife and wiping it clean on a napkin. She eased the seal up, unwilling to break such a beautiful object.

The letter was on vellum, inked in three colors; black for the text, red for the proper names, and gold around each capital letter. Cassi gasped, leaning over her shoulder. Neither of them had ever seen such ornate writing before.

"Must be nice to have that much time to spend on a letter," Pyke remarked. Cassi elbowed him in the ribs. "Oh, sorry, the *exalted* didn't have to spend any time on it. Some poor sap of a dedicate clerk did all the work."

"'To Taya Icarus, Greetings,'" Taya read aloud for her friends. The rest of the dining hall fell silent as everyone listened. Even the cook stood in the doorway, drying a platter. "'To offer thanksgiving and gratitude for your timely rescue of Exalted Viera Octavus and Exalted Ariq Octavus, and to celebrate perils overcome, you are invited as the guest of honor to Estate Octavus for a formal evening of dinner and dancing.'"

The other icarii in the room broke into applause. Taya turned red, reading further. "Oh, scrap! What am I going to wear?"

Pyke groaned.

"I don't believe that was the first thing to come out of your mouth," he said with disgust. "How about an observation about the comparative value of dinner and dancing to the life of a wife and a child? Not to mention your own life, which was equally at risk."

"What would *you* want?" Cassilta asked, scornfully.

"A purse of gold masks," he replied at once. "Five hundred, a thousand, maybe. Something *useful*. I notice the exalted didn't send me an invitation."

"Pyke, you're cute but shallow," Cassi said. "Prestige is a lot more useful than money."

"Sure. That's what they want you to think. That's how they keep us in line. Prestige won't buy an army. Poor people can't fund a revolution."

"Cassi!" Taya turned to her friend, mentally running through her limited wardrobe. She was an icarus, for the Lady's sake! She didn't own any fancy clothes. "Can I wear my armature? Please tell me I can wear my wings."

"You can *not* wear your wings," Cassi said firmly. "Not as the guest of honor. When's the party?"

"Three days from now."

"No problem. Pyke, tell Dispatch that Taya and I are taking the day off."

"Why? To go dress shopping? The boss will love that."

"He will if he wants our caste well-represented in front of the exalteds," Cassi retorted.

"I'll tell him," volunteered an icarus from the next table. "Don't worry, nobody's going to make a fuss. Taya deserves a day off, anyway."

"Thanks," Taya said, chewing on her lip as she re-read the invitation. Clothes. She'd never thought about clothes. But a diplomatic envoy would need clothes, right? Why hadn't she thought about that earlier? Oh, Lady, she was going to have to learn how to wear fancy clothes.

Cassi led her out of the dining room and up the three flights of stairs to her bedroom, where Taya set the invitation on top of her bookshelf. She pulled on her groundling boots and a threadbare coat bearing a stylized feather on one lapel, then tucked the slim leather wallet that held her identification papers into the coat's inner pocket. Meanwhile, Cassi was rummaging through Taya's wardrobe, shaking her head.

"How can you only have two dresses and one pair of nice shoes? Don't you ever go out?"

"Yes. In flight leathers." Taya pulled out her bank book and looked at the balance. She saved as much of her slim salary as she could, but a fancy dress would set her back by months.

Maybe she could rent a dress. Or—did theaters lend out their costumes?

"Didn't Pyke ever take you anyplace nice?"

"Like where? One of his conspiracy meetings? We mostly stayed in and talked."

Her friend tsked, muttering about brains, biceps and waste—or was it waist?—before closing the wardrobe door.

"Well, this is hopeless. We'll have to start from scratch."

"Do you think I can find something at the Great Market?"

"A readymade for an exalted's party? Taya, you make me despair for all womankind." Cassi grabbed her hand and tugged her down the hall to her own room. There she pulled on a jacket and grabbed her purse. "Don't worry. I have a secret weapon. My nephew just finished his apprenticeship and is opening up his own couture business. You should see his designs. They're fantastic."

"I can't afford a custom-made dress."

"Don't be silly. He should pay *you* to wear one his dresses to the party." Cassi hurried down the stairs, and Taya followed, feeling out of her depth. "This could be just the break he needs. Now come on. Jayce is a miracle-worker, but three days isn't much time, and we've got a lot to do."

CASSI'S NEPHEW had rented a hole-in-the-wall shop in a respectable part of Secundus. As soon as Cassi explained Taya's predicament, he canceled all of his appointments and summoned a small army of friends and associates to help. At first Taya questioned the wisdom of putting herself into the hands of a baby-faced twenty-year-old dedicate, but after an hour of gazing at his designs and listening to his rapid-fire orders, she surrendered to his artistic vision and meekly let him do whatever he wanted.

After an hour, Cassi abandoned her to find shoes and jewelry.

"I can't afford jewelry!" Taya yelped as her best friend vanished out the door.

"Don't worry. She'll get it on loan." Jayce ran a strip of measuring tape around her breasts and Taya flinched. "Straighten up. You do *not* want your dress to sag here."

Taya stiffened her back.

"I can't believe you icarii," he grumbled. "You're thin enough, but none of you have any breasts. And your legs are too short. And your arms! We'll have to hide your shoulders."

"What's wrong with my shoulders?" Taya protested. "I mean, aside from the cut?"

"You're cut? How badly?" Before she could argue, he'd pulled up her shirt and was groaning to himself. "Not even bandaged. I don't believe this—do you *want* a scar? Fine, fine, no problem. I can work around it. It's too cold for bare shoulders, anyway. Especially shoulders like yours."

"What's wrong with my shoulders?" she insisted.

"Muscles aren't ladylike." He scowled, his pencil flying over a sheet of paper. "I feel like I'm dressing a boy. Fortunately, I've made dresses for Cassi before, so I know a few tricks."

"I'm not a boy. And my breasts are just fine, thank you very much."

"They're fine for a flier. They don't give a designer much to work with. Too big in front and you need too much internal support. Too little and the front won't stay up on its own." He chewed on the end of his pencil a moment, then started scribbling again. "I'd sell my soul for perfect breasts."

"You and me both." Taya grimaced and sat, sneaking a glance down at her chest. Nobody had ever told her that her breasts were too small before. Great. Now she had something else to worry about.

By the time Cassi returned and dropped several bags in front of Jayce, Taya was ready to go. She wasn't allowed to leave for another hour, though, only escaping a little before noon.

"Don't worry," Jayce assured her. "I won't let you down. Cassi, I need her three hours before the party. Minimum. Four would be better."

"She'll be here," Cassi said, grinning. "Make the family proud, Jayce."

Released from the shop, they hurried to a tearoom not far from the University and took refuge from the cold autumn wind.

"Thanks," Taya said, after half a cup of the house's strongest black brew had steadied her nerves again. "I really appreciate your help."

"Oh, it's no problem." Cassi smiled. "My uncle's a tailor and my aunt makes jewelry. Couture's in Jayce's blood. This is a big opportunity for him, getting his work in front of the exalteds so quickly after graduation."

"He said I wasn't ladylike and I have small breasts," Taya admitted. Cassi laughed.

"Jayce likes to whine. You know, if you get into the diplomatic corps, you're going to need a new wardrobe. You won't be able to wear your flight suit all the time."

"I know. Today made me realize that."

"Well, if the kid comes through for the party, keep him in mind. It'd be a real break for him."

"I'll remember," Taya promised. She wrapped her fingers around the teacup. "If he can make my chest look bigger, I'll owe him one, anyway."

They spent half an hour nursing their drinks, then stood and pulled on their gloves, stepping back out in the street.

"Since we've got the rest of the day off, I think I'll go visit my mother," Cassi said, glancing up at the University clock tower. "She had a cold last week. You don't mind, do you?"

"No . . . no, that's fine," Taya said, jamming her hands into her coat pockets. "I've got a couple of errands to run, myself."

"See you for dinner?"

"Sure." She smiled and waved, then turned and began walking toward Booksellers Row.

Taya liked to stroll through Ondinium's markets, not because of the goods they sold but because she loved looking at foreigners: cheerful, red-haired Mareauxans drinking shoulder-to-shoulder with canny, brown-skinned Alzanans; fur-clad, snow-skinned Demicans comparing weapons with black-skinned Cabisi wrapped in brightly woven long jackets; and swarthy, bearded Tiziri gesturing earnestly to golden-skinned, hairless Si'sierate. She wandered through the streets, listening for new words to add to her range of languages, until she finally reached the booksellers' and printers' line of stalls.

The customers in the Row were mostly Ondiniums, so she dragged her attention away from the crowd and browsed through the newspapers and broadsheets, searching for the latest news on the wireferry disaster and refinery bomb. The most recent printing was a three-hour-old broadsheet reporting the timeline for the wireferry repairs and the new passenger schedule. She looked for news about the disaster's cause, but nothing had been reported.

"You going to buy that, then?" grumbled the old woman inside the news stall.

"Oh . . . no, thank you. I don't take the wireferry." Taya handed the sheet back over the wooden counter. The woman took it with a gnarled, ink-stained hand, and Taya thought again of Cristof's hands.

Which direction had he been coming from?

Would a terrorist stop to help a woman in distress immediately after he'd planted a bomb?

Annoyed at herself, Taya turned, weaving her way through the narrow streets of book stalls and publishing houses until she reached Gryngoth Plaza. The plaza was dominated by a bronze statue of Lictor Gryngoth on horseback and was built on an outcrop that provided a clear view of the sweeping mountainside below and the majestic range of peaks around them.

She leaned on the low stone wall and gazed down at the smoggy haze that blanketed Tertius.

It was easy to envision Cristof planting a bomb, his long fingers setting the hands of a timer with painstaking precision and getting dirty as he slipped explosives inside grease-covered machinery. He was outcaste. That meant he was unreliable and quite possibly dangerous. Honest citizens didn't reject their caste and carry around air pistols. And he hadn't hesitated to shoot the Demican mugger, had he? He had a violent streak.

Wind disheveled Taya's short, auburn curls and numbed her ears.

On the other hand, Cristof was exalted by birth and by caste, and the brother of a decatur. Could the Lady have let a flawed tool slip through her Forge and get born into a sacred body? Taya wasn't a religious idealist. She knew that accidents happened; that sometimes a good tool was damaged by careless use. Still, exalteds were usually above question.

Usually.

Icarii stand outside the caste hierarchy.

"Fine!" Taya slapped a hand on the top of the wall and straightened. "Let's see if he believes it."

"I beg your pardon?" asked a woman next to her. Taya gave her an apologetic wave and strode back across the plaza, toward Whitesmith Bridge.

Ondinium's bells began tolling noon as she walked down the broad, switchback levels of the bridge, jostled by citizens of all castes and inkless foreigners visiting the city on business or to gape at its mechanical marvels. The sector gate between Secundus and Tertius was wide open, but the number of lictors guarding it had been increased, and the lines were long. Taya wished she had her wings as she stood in one of the citizens' queues, pulling out her identification papers. A number of the other Ondiniums in line gave her inkless face a curious glance, then saw the icarus pin on her lapel and turned back to their own conversations.

Taya had been mistaken for a foreigner before; it was one of the hazards icarii faced when they weren't in harness, especially if they didn't have the copper skin and dark hair of a full-blooded native. Taya had inherited her father's auburn hair and pale skin. Only her mother's dark eyes suggested that she wasn't pure Mareauxan. Once, when Taya had been younger, she'd dyed her hair black to try to fit in. The color had been flat and lifeless against her pale skin, and the dye hadn't set well. Every time she'd washed her hair, the water had turned dark. She had never repeated the experiment.

The lictor at the gate gave her a close look as she stepped up and scrutinized her papers. After a moment he snapped the wallet shut and handed it back with a polite nod.

"Travel safely, icarus."

"Thank you." She tucked the wallet back into place and stepped into Tertius.

Nothing differentiated the top of Tertius and the bottom of Secundus; smog and soot darkened both equally. But even though no part of Ondinium was completely free of heavy industry, the lowest sector of the mountain grew flatter as it spread out toward the foothills and rivers below, and thus it bristled with more chimneys and smokestacks per square mile than anywhere else in the city. The streets were narrower and dirtier, especially as one traveled further down into the sector's depths, and the residents, on the whole, were poorer.

Taya had studied other countries to prepare for her diplomat corps examination, and she knew that many foreigners, whose first encounter with Ondinium was through Tertius, considered her city to be a sulfurous hellhole. They objected to its smog and dirt, to its cable- and tower-filled skyline, to its tightly built streets and buildings, and to its caste system and strict, sometimes ruthless laws. But at the same time they envied Ondinium's

material wealth and rich culture; its high rates of education
and employment and low rates of poverty. They wanted
her city's technological resources and, most of all, they
lusted after its priceless mines of ondium.

Ondinium hadn't sent an army to war in two hundred
years, but it had weathered numerous attacks, and its lictors
were among the best-trained security forces in the world. Not
even Alzana, Ondinium's most aggressive rival, bothered to
attack the city directly anymore. Now warfare was carried
out with spies and thieves instead of soldiers and cannon;
with bombs and terrorism instead of armies and sieges.

Taya glanced around, but the site of last night's
refinery bombing was obscured by the walls and rooftops
surrounding her.

The streets in the lower sector were darkened by a gritty
haze of coal smoke and wood ash and by the crisscrossing
cables and iron girders that formed the lowest level of the
wireferry transit system. Buildings were constructed with
jutting upper levels that formed wooden arches over the
narrow streets, leaving only narrow slices of sky open to
view like skylights.

When she'd been a child, Taya had spent much of her
time climbing to the roofs of those buildings, playing on
the broken, sooty tiles and watching the bright-winged
icarii swoop overhead. None of her family or friends had
been surprised when she'd been chosen to join the icarii
after her Great Examination. She'd considered it a dream
come true.

But despite being gone so long, she remembered this part
of Tertius well. It didn't take her long to locate the street
where Cristof Forlore's shop was hidden among a row of
small workshops, most of them geared toward mechanical
repairs of one kind or another. The outcaste's basement
shop had nothing that set it off from the others; nothing to
indicate that its proprietor had a wave on his cheek instead
of a circle on his forehead.

Taya stopped at the stairs that led down from the street
to its basement door. Three grubby children, two boys and

a girl, were sitting on the steps, trading small chunks of metal.

One of them looked up at her. He was the oldest of the three, but his bare face indicated that he hadn't taken his Great Examination yet. Still under seven, then.

"Shop's closed," he said. "But the clockwright's coming back soon, should you wanna wait, then."

She glanced at the shop door. Just as the boy had said, a sign hung on the knob. *Closed.*

"He's not hiding inside?"

"Nope."

"Oh." Taya debated with herself a moment, then shrugged. If she had been wearing her wings, she wouldn't have thought twice about leaving and coming back later, but she didn't care to climb Whitesmith Stairs more than twice in one day. The clocks in the shop window showed that it was half past noon. "I guess I'll wait. Are you his friends?"

"Neighbors." The boy jerked a thumb at the shop next door, a wigmaker's.

"You wanna play pick-up?" The younger boy held up a small, vulcanized rubber ball. "We're playing for disks."

Taya crouched. "I don't have any disks." She remembered having them, once. Just like these three children, she and her friends had collected chunks of slag from the forges and used them as a makeshift currency between themselves.

"How about that feather, then?" the older boy asked, pointing to her lapel pin.

"Sorry—it belongs to the government." Taya dug into her pockets and found a few coins. "I'll play you for pence, though. Six disks to a penny."

"Four."

"Five."

"Done."

The youngest child, a girl who couldn't be older than four, drew an unsteady circle on the cobblestones with a nub of chalk. Taya and the three children knelt around it, concentrating on the bouncing ball and the bits of colored stone used as markers.

Taya lost the first five games and then won back three of her pennies as her old skills returned. She laughed, snatching the ball in midair as it bounced off the edge of a cobblestone and angled toward the steps. The oldest boy grinned.

"You did that on purpose," she accused, bouncing the ball into the circle for the next player.

"Just testing you, weren't I?" he replied, cheerfully.

The little girl's head snapped up from the circle and she looked down the street. "Clockite's back!"

Moving fast, the two boys swept up the remaining markers. Taya grabbed her three pennies before the oldest snatched them up — he gave her an unrepentant smirk — and turned. The three children flung themselves on top of the steps again.

Cristof's steps slowed as he drew nearer.

Even after meeting him twice, Taya couldn't help but feel an odd jolt as she compared his castemark to his naked face and simple garments. The outcaste was dressed much as he'd been last night, in a dark suit and greatcoat. He held a paper-wrapped bundle in the crook of one arm. The autumn wind played through his defiantly short hair, making it stand up in dark, uneven chunks that emphasized how poorly it had been cut.

He glanced at her, then fixed his gaze on the three children who stood in a line between him and his shop door. His expression was disapproving as he peered at them from over the top of his wire-rimmed spectacles.

"What are you three loathsome brats doing on my stairs?" he demanded.

Taya drew in an indignant breath, but her protest died as she saw that none of the children were upset by the outcaste's words.

"We cleaned 'em for you, din't we?" the girl piped up.

"Did you?" Cristof took a step forward and looked past the children. His expression as he gazed at the steps down to his shop door was one of profound disgust. "Am I to consider that clean?"

"Uh-huh." The girl squatted, her ragged smock pooling around her feet, and wiped her hand over the step. She held it up. "See, no dirt!"

Taya bit her bottom lip. The girl's palm was filthy, just as hers were, from playing pick-up on the street. But the shop steps, although stained, were free from the loose layer of ash that covered so much of the rest of the street.

"I see." Cristof gave the boys a skeptical look. "I suppose you two made your sister do all the work."

"Nope. We got three brooms." The youngest boy pointed to the twig brooms stacked at the bottom of the steps. "We all took a turn, din't we?"

"And you all expect to be rewarded for it, no doubt."

"Fair's fair," the boy declared.

Cristof turned his relentless gaze on the oldest boy.

"Nothing to say for yourself?"

"Sixpence for sweeping, then, and one for keeping your customer here while you was gone," the boy replied smartly, jerking a thumb at Taya.

"I doubt she's a customer," Cristof muttered. He dug into his coat pocket and pulled out a handful of coins, counting two pennies into each boy's hand and three into the girl's.

"Thank you, sir." "Thank you, Mister Clockite." "See you tomorrow, sir!"

The three grabbed their brooms and hustled off, waving to Taya. She waved back and turned to Cristof.

"Mister Clockite?"

His gaze narrowed, then he turned and headed down the steps.

"Jessica has trouble pronouncing her r's," he muttered.

"I think it's cute, exalted. They don't call you by your title?"

"I get enough titling from the adults around here." He fumbled with his keys. Taya lifted the bundle from his arm, smelling sausage and pickles. He grunted and unlocked the door, pushing it open and flipping the Closed sign to Open. The jangle of ticking and whirring greeted them as they stepped inside the shop's dim interior.

"What do you want?" he demanded, turning and retrieving his lunch. "Where are your wings?"

"I'm off duty today." Taya was suddenly reluctant to ask him about the night before. Cristof's little charade on the steps had made her doubt her suspicions. Loathsome brats, indeed. She went on the offensive, instead. "Why are you so rude to those children?"

"Because I'm a rude person." He pushed aside a large schematic, clearing a spot on the table. Then he unwrapped his bundle, pulling back layers of increasingly greasy paper until he revealed the sausage and pickles she'd smelled, and a hunk of pale cheese. Taya's stomach growled. All she'd had for breakfast had been tea. She made a mental note to buy lunch before heading back to the eyrie.

Cristof walked out of the room through the curtains in back.

Taya unbuttoned her coat and looked around. The jeweled birds were back in place, floating on the little pieces of string that tied them to a shelf. The shop shutters were open, but very little light came through the sooty window panes.

She cocked her head to read the schematic Cristof had shoved aside. It looked like a map of the city sectors.

She reached out and tugged it right-side-up.

It was a wireferry map, showing all the lines that ran from sector to sector and up to Oporphyr Tower. Symbols had been jotted all over it in pencil.

She leaned closer, worried. Was one of those marks over the vandalized spot?

Cristof returned with two tin cups and a short, dark bottle. Taya straightened and pulled her hand back. Ignoring her, the exalted broke off the bottle's wax top and set the cups on the table.

"It's a stout," he said, pouring.

Taya gave him another look, not certain what to make of the implicit offer.

"Thank you," she said at last. Even an ill-tempered outcaste couldn't object to good manners.

He handed her the drink without a word and poured for himself. She cradled the tin cup between her hands, watching. He had a deft hand with the bottle and knew how to keep the frothy head thin as he poured. She wouldn't have expected any bartending skills from an exalted who'd been raised with servants to bring him the very best wines and liqueurs. But maybe lower-caste tastes came with a lower-caste residence.

He finished pouring and looked up.

"I'm still waiting for you to tell me what you want." His voice was edgy. "Unless you have a watch to be repaired, I can't imagine what business we have together."

"I don't own a watch." She paused, considering her options. Honesty won out. "I came to ask you a question about last night."

"I've already reported the attack to the lictors." He took a sip of the beer, absently wiping his mouth with his thumb and setting the cup back down. He picked up a small knife, cleaned it on a smudged rag, and began slicing the sausage. "They said they'd inquire at the hospitals. I'm sure you'll be notified if they find the Demican we injured."

We. She was glad he hadn't put all the blame on her.

"Thank you. I talked to them, myself, last night after the fire. But that wasn't the question I was going to ask."

He cut the pickles in half and began carving off heavy slices of cheese.

"Then ask."

She set the cup down on the table. "Why were your hands dirty when you met me?"

The knife paused. He cocked his head and gave her a blank look, his grey eyes puzzled behind his spectacles.

"What?"

"Your hands were dirty when you met me last night. Saved me," she amended, to give credit where it was due. "I was wondering why."

He frowned, setting down his knife and straightening up. She paid attention as he reached for the rag he'd used to clean off the knife and wiped his greasy fingers on it.

"That's a strange question," he said, watching her. "Why would you—" He stopped, letting the rag fall to the tabletop. Then he smiled, without humor. "Oh. I see. You think I may have been setting a bomb."

Taya took a deep breath, then let it out and lifted her chin.

"It's a fair question. I wouldn't dare ask it of any other exalted, but *you* shouldn't mind being interrogated by an icarus."

A twitch of his jaw acknowledged the reference to their argument.

"You know, icarus, if I were a bomber, you'd be in a great deal of danger right now." Without looking down, he touched the knife with one slender finger.

Taya didn't look down at it, either. If Cristof were going to attack her, he'd do it without any warning. He was just being unpleasant again.

"Are you?"

He sighed and shook his head, lifting his hand away. "No. But you should be careful how you accuse a man. If you're suspicious of someone, tell the lictors."

"What about that?" Taya jerked her head toward the wireferry map. "I find that a little suspicious, too."

He picked up the map and folded it, his lips tight.

"I was plotting alternate routes to Primus and the tower. I dislike traveling by wireferry at the best of times, and I find the thought especially unpleasant after yesterday."

Taya frowned. He could be telling the truth, but she thought there was something a little strange in his haste to fold the map.

Cristof set the schematic on a shelf and turned, pushing up his spectacles.

"Now, if the interrogation is over, I have work to do."

Taya shook her head. "I'm sorry, exalted, but you still haven't answered my question. Why were your hands dirty last night?"

"Oh, for the Lady's sake!" Now his voice sharpened, giving her a glimpse of the same bad temper he'd showed last night. Oddly, his irritation reassured her. It was an honest emotion, unlike his strained good manners. "I was realigning the gears on a sector clock. It's been losing time all month, and I finally became impatient with it."

"You became impatient with something?" Taya struggled not to smile. "But you're such a self-possessed man, exalted."

He seemed taken aback for a moment, then glowered at her.

"Why didn't you wash your hands there?" she pressed.

"Clock towers don't come equipped with water pumps. I would have used the Market fountain, but I heard you shouting."

"Oh." Not guilty, then. She was surprised by the distinct feeling of relief the thought gave her.

Noticing that his expression was still dark, she flashed him a smile.

"Thank you, exalted. The question's been nagging me all morning, and I'm glad I have an answer. *Now* the interrogation's over."

He let out an annoyed hiss and took another swallow of his beer. His eyes fell on her cup, sitting untouched on the table. He picked it up and offered it.

"Then you won't be afraid to drink with me." His voice was still edged with irritation.

Surprised, Taya took the dented cup. She'd expected him to be eager to get rid of her.

"Your brother offered me a drink yesterday," she said. "And now you're offering me one today. No exalted has ever treated me so politely before. Is it a Forlore family custom?"

"Alister probably offered you a drink because he considered you a good-looking woman," Cristof said, sounding annoyed again. "I'm offering you a drink because it would be churlish to drink in front of you, and I'm thirsty."

Taya drank, not sure how to answer that. Had Alister Forlore considered her good-looking? The thought warmed her. She'd certainly found him handsome.

Still looking nettled, Cristof shoved half the sliced sausage, cheese, and pickles toward her. "Have you had lunch yet?" Without waiting for a reply, he dropped into a chair, picking up his food with his fingers.

"It would be churlish to eat in front of me?"

"Yes."

For a split second she considered refusing, but then her hunger got the better of her. After all, she rationalized, the invitation might have been ungracious, but it had been an invitation. And like all icarii, she had a healthy appetite.

She pulled up a chair and sat down.

"Thank you, exalted."

For several minutes they sat in the ticking, whirring room, working on the food. It was a crude but filling meal, reminding Taya of the workman's lunches she'd brought to her father in the smelting factory, back when she'd been a little girl. He'd shared them with her on a wooden bench outside the factory, covered with dirt and sweat but full of smiles for his oldest daughter.

Not at all like the dour-faced outcaste across from her.

Once the edge was off her hunger, Taya wiped her hands on Cristof's cleaning rag, picked up the bottle of stout, and refilled their cups. Cristof took his without comment.

"Do you get much business here?" she asked, searching for a subject that wouldn't annoy him as they drank.

"Yes." Cristof stared into his cup. For a moment she thought he'd stop with that curt reply, but then he elaborated, almost defensively. "It looks quiet right now, but most of my customers come by in the morning, on their way to work. I have three clocks and two watches to repair this week. I do well enough."

"Do many people on Tertius own timepieces?" Her family hadn't.

"The factories have clocks, and the overseers and managers bring their clocks and watches down from Secundus. My shop's easy to reach from Whitesmith Stair."

"Do you do most of your work for the Cardinal castes, then?"

"I get some work from Primus, too." He sounded sour. "Alister doesn't hesitate to recommend me, and he's so charming that the other exalteds are willing to overlook my eccentricities to please him."

"You must be good at what you do, or they wouldn't come back," Taya said, encouraging him. She felt a certain sense of satisfaction that Cristof was talking to her like a regular person.

"Anyone can do basic repairs, if he's willing to learn." The exalted looked up. "The difficult jobs are restoring heirlooms and one-of-a-kind pieces. That's my specialty, finding or making unusual parts and fixing old clockwork that's been allowed to degrade. I repair imports, too. I correspond with all of the major clockwrights on the continent. And sometimes I make my own timepieces."

"Then you're a more important clockwright than I thought," she said, pleased to have drawn him out. "May I see some of your work?"

His sharp cheekbones turned a darker shade of copper, and he looked away, straightening his glasses.

"I don't have anything here that would impress you," he said.

Taya's eyes were drawn to the wave tattoo on his cheek again. Seeing it here inside of his shop wasn't quite as jarring as seeing it out in the street. Except for his lack of robes and jewels, he could be any exalted who'd doffed his mask in private to speak to an icarus.

"Most of these clocks are common," he continued, the defensive note in his voice returning. "The ones I make on commission are more ornate, but I deliver them as soon as they're finished."

"Don't you have a clock of your own?"

"Nothing unusual." He hesitated, then slid a gold pocket watch from his plain black vest, unhooking its chain from a buttonhole. "I made this a long time ago. It doesn't look like much, but it's extremely accurate."

Taya carefully took the watch from his thin fingers, feeling the chain slip over her wrist. The warm, heavy case was made of pure gold and was the most expensive thing she'd ever held.

The watch seemed very simple, for an exalted's timepiece. No jewels or inlay adorned the case; just a simple engraved design of a gear. The case vibrated like a small heart in her hand, and she held it up to her ear, hearing it tick.

"Here." Cristof stood and leaned across the table, showing her how to open it. His fingers were just as cold as they'd been the night before.

The watch's face was a pearlescent grey, its quartile numbers and hands gleaming gold. Taya laughed, delighted.

"What?"

"Nothing. I mean, the outside was so plain that I was expecting the inside to be plain, too." She tilted the watch toward the dim light from the window, admiring it. "It's beautiful. This shade of grey matches your eyes."

Across the table, Cristof made a strangled noise and sat back down.

"It's mother-of-pearl, isn't it? I've seen jewelry made out of it, in the Markets. Did it come from the North Sea?"

"No. It's imported from the south." He was giving her a strange look. Taya blushed. Had her question been stupid?

"I'd love to see the sea someday," she said, to cover her embarrassment, and then felt even more ridiculous. "I mean, I'd like to see what seashells look like in the wild." She closed the case and handed it back, certain he was laughing at her. "Is the gear your personal insignia? Or is it a clockwright's symbol?"

Cristof dragged his eyes away from her face and slipped the watch back into his vest pocket, a line furrowing his brow again.

"It doesn't mean anything."

"It must mean something," she insisted. "Or you wouldn't have put it on your watch."

"I made the watch years ago." He picked up the stout bottle, realized it was empty, and set it back down again.

"I suppose I had some sort of asinine notion about taking the gear as my personal insignia, but I outgrew it. Besides, it's not what a watch looks like that's important, but how accurately it measures time."

Taya nodded. He was withdrawing again. She changed the subject. "That's true. We've got a really nice clock in my eyrie, but it's off by about ten minutes. My landlady keeps resetting it, but in a day or two it's right back where it started. We've all gotten to the point where we look at it and automatically add ten minutes. Then, whenever she resets it, we're ten minutes early to everything."

"Does she wind it at the same time every day?"

"I think so. It's a little hard to tell, with that clock."

"Tsk." Cristof's lips tightened. "What good is a clock that doesn't do its job? I can fix it, if you want."

"I don't think we could afford your services, exalted."

He gave her a sidelong look and lifted one thin shoulder in a casual shrug. "It doesn't cost anything for me to look at it."

Taya lowered her head so he wouldn't see her smile. His offer of help was as awkward and graceless as his offer of food and drink, but she had a feeling he meant it. He really did love clocks.

"That's very kind of you. I live in Three Alcides. I'm sure the landlady would let you in as soon as you explained why you were there."

"Maybe if . . ." He paused. "You said you're off-duty today? Is it a reward for saving Viera yesterday?"

"Who? Oh, no; well, not exactly." She remembered the morning's rush and blushed. "Exalted Octavus sent me an invitation to a party, so my friend Cassi and I took the day off to find an appropriate dress."

He slowly nodded. "Of course. Viera wouldn't have remembered that some people don't have a wardrobe full of formal clothes. Do you . . . do you want me to say something to her?"

"No!" Taya recoiled. "Don't do that! What would she think of me?"

"She could send you something to save you the expense—"

"No, please, I'm fine," Taya protested, turning red. "I have an excellent dressmaker." *I hope*.

"Well, if you're certain. I was only trying to help."

"I'm certain." Taya stood to prevent any further objection. "And I'm also certain that I've taken up enough of your time. Thank you for lunch, exalted."

"You don't—are you going back to your eyrie?" Cristof got to his feet, facing her across the cluttered table.

"Yes, I think I should." She checked one of the many clocks ticking around them. "It's a long walk back, and I want to check on my armature before the smithy closes."

"Will it be all right?"

"I think so. It didn't give me any problems on my flight back from the explosion, but I'll be happier when all the feathers are straight again."

"Of course." He blinked, as if suddenly remembering. "And your shoulder?"

"It's not bleeding anymore."

"Did it need stitches?"

"I haven't had time to see a physician," she admitted. "It wasn't bleeding this morning." She looked at the scabbing cuts on her hands. "I assume it'll be fine."

Cristof closed his eyes and pinched the bridge of his nose, looking pained.

"Careless."

"Huh?"

"I said last night that you are either careless or unlucky. I've decided that you're careless. You do realize that untreated wounds can become infected?"

"I'll have someone look at it when I get back to the eyrie," she said, nettled. "I've had a busy day."

"Yes, I'm certain that accusing me of being a bomber was far more urgent than seeing to your own health."

"Well, it would have been if you *had* been a bomber," she retorted.

He drew a deep breath, then slowly let it out and turned, picking up his greatcoat.

"Yes. I suppose you're right."

"Where are you going?"

"To look at the clock in Three Alcides."

"I—you don't have to do that today!" Taya protested. "You told me you had work to do."

"Nothing that can't wait." He picked up a small black bag. "I will examine the clock while you're at the physician's having your shoulder examined."

"Exalted!"

"Icarus." His voice was cool. "Why are you arguing with me?"

She flushed, not certain, herself. If he'd been wearing proper exalted's clothing, she would never have dared to raise her voice to him. It was easy to forget that he wasn't just another famulate, as long as she didn't pay attention to his castemark.

"Why do you want to come with me?"

"I intend to make certain you don't endanger the city by endangering yourself. If you had been injured yesterday, you wouldn't have been able to save Viera and Ariq."

"I promise, I'll see a physician before tonight. I don't need an escort through the city."

"That hasn't been my observation." He paused. "And I have no doubt that Viera would want me to see you kept in good repair."

Taya gave him an exasperated look, then turned and began buttoning up her coat. Fine. He was as stubborn as a lictor.

Still, if nothing else, I'll have someone to talk to on the long walk back up, she thought. *Or argue with, more likely.*

They didn't argue, however, and although she found herself trotting to keep up with his long-legged pace, she discovered one unexpected advantage of traveling with an exalted—the lictors took one glance at his castemark and waved them both through the gate ahead of the lines.

"Maybe I should draw a wave on my cheek, too," Taya mused aloud as they stepped off Whitesmith Stair and into Secundus.

"They know me." Cristof's voice was flat. "I'm the only exalted who lives on Tertius."

"I'm just joking. I don't even look Ondinium." Not to mention that fact that forging a castemark was a serious crime.

He nodded, studying her. "You're native though, aren't you? I've never heard of a naturalized icarus."

"Second generation. My father's grandparents moved here and became citizens when they were in their twenties. My mother was pure Ondinium. How long has your family lived here?"

"House Forlore's birth records go back seventy generations. The books before that were lost in the Last War."

"Is your brother the oldest in the family?"

"No. I am."

"Oh." For some reason that surprised her. "Are you two close?"

"I suppose so." He shrugged. "I'm a dissident and he's a decatur. We're as close as we can be, under the circumstances. I'm pleased with his success, and he does his best not to condemn me for my shortcomings."

"You said he recommends you to other exalteds. That doesn't sound like condemnation."

"Alister's too considerate. He shouldn't have anything to do with me. I'm a threat to his chances of ever becoming the head of Oporphyr Council. If he weren't such a brilliant programmer, they never would have made him a decatur; not with me in the family."

"I thought political positions were awarded on the basis of merit, not family."

"That's the theory. In practice, family is an important variable in the equation." Cristof stared straight ahead. "I try not to embarrass my brother too much."

Taya fell silent. They walked through the Markets, past the University and up until they reached the topmost point of Secundus and Cliff Road, which led into the icarus neighborhoods and then to the practice fields and flight docks. It wasn't an easy climb, and Taya longed for her wings.

"I've never had any reason to be in this part of the city before," Cristof said at last, during one of their rest pauses. He looked up at the tall houses built along the narrow, steep streets. "Who repairs the clocks here?"

"I don't know." Taya shrugged. "The city, I guess. I've never met an icarus who owns a watch, so I wouldn't know who to ask."

"I'll leave my card at the eyrie, then," he said. Taya looked at him, trying to decide if he were joking. She couldn't tell. She'd like to think that he was; that he might be making an effort to get along with her. But . . . she just couldn't tell.

They started up again. Cristof unbuttoned his coat, letting it flap around his long legs as they walked. The air was cold, but the afternoon sun beat down on Cliff Road and its steep rise was making both of them sweat.

The neighborhood was primarily inhabited by icarii, their families, and the businesses that catered to them. The air was clean; there were no factories in the neighborhood to pump soot into the air, and the coal smoke and wood ash were swept away by the strong winds that blew past the steep cliff. Hawks roosted in some of the highest rooftops, welcomed as good luck by icarii despite their tendency to prey on the neighborhood cats and dogs. Occasionally an icarus flew high overhead toward the docks, metal wings flashing.

Three Alcides was one of a number of barracks-like eyries that catered to unmarried icarii. Taya waved and greeted her friends as they drew near.

"Hey, Taya!" One of the icarii called to her from the eyrie porch, then paused to stare at Cristof, his jaw falling open. Then he collected himself and dragged his eyes away from the exalted's bare face. "Uh, you got another message. It's on Gwen's desk."

"Thanks." She opened the door and stepped aside for Cristof. The exalted's cold glower was back in place, and he kept his face down as he stepped inside.

"You didn't have to come," Taya whispered, giving him a concerned look. He ignored her, his grey eyes falling at once on the long-case clock that stood against the foyer wall, ticking loudly.

"You said you'd see a physician," he reminded her. He set the bag down next to the clock.

"Just a moment." She stepped through the doorway into the salon, where Gwen Icarus, the eyrie's landlady, kept her business desk.

"Oh, good. I have a letter for you, Taya," the woman said. She dug out a heavy parchment square and handed it over. Taya turned it. This one was sealed in wax, too, but it wasn't as ornate as the Octavus invitation.

"I asked a clockwright to look at our clock and find out why it's losing time," she said, raising her eyes. "He said he wouldn't charge anything just to see what's wrong."

Gwen scowled. "Can he be trusted?" She hoisted herself out of her chair. After she'd retired from flying, she'd put on a few pounds, although she had as much muscle as she had mass.

"Yes." Taya leaned forward, touching the woman's arm and dropping her voice to a whisper. "He's an outcaste exalted, so don't be surprised."

"An outcaste!" The landlady's eyes widened. "For the Lady's sake, Taya, what are you thinking, bringing an outcaste into my house? I run a—"

Taya tightened her grip. "An outcaste *exalted*! Exalted Cristof Forlore, and he's doing us a favor. His brother's a decatur."

Gwen snorted. "You're flying awful high, icarus."

"Not in his case," Taya said wryly, thinking of Cristof's basement workshop. "But he's touchy, so be diplomatic."

"Diplomacy's your job, not mine," Gwen said. "Now let go. I won't throw him out on his ear, but you know the rules—no strangers in the eyrie without an escort. Lady knows what this place would be like if I let you lot have free run of the place."

Taya sighed, trailing after the larger woman.

"What are you doing?" Gwen shrieked, when she walked into the foyer.

Cristof had taken off his coat and rolled up his sleeves, and he was kneeling in front of the clock as he unhooked its pendulum. He glanced over his shoulder, then turned back to his work.

"I can't figure out what's wrong unless I check the mechanism."

"I'm not going to pay you to put together what you've taken apart!"

"I'm not going to ask you to." Cristof laid the pendulum on the wooden floor and turned. He gave Taya a sharp look. "Don't you have someplace to go?"

"All right! Can I leave you alone here?" Taya was worried about Gwen. The landlady was staring at Cristof's castemark, her eyes wide despite Taya's warning. Gwen was a kind, motherly woman, but she wasn't very subtle.

"I expect so." Cristof glanced at the letter in her hand. "You'll see a physician before you deliver that, I trust."

"This letter is for me." Taya lifted it, studying the seal, and then turned it over. Her name was written across the front: *Taya Icarus*, in a firm, flowing script.

Cristof climbed to his feet and reached out. Taya let him take it, without protest, and he tilted the envelope up. His scowl darkened.

"What is it?" she asked.

"That's the Forlore seal."

"Oh!" Taya took another look at it, then broke open the letter.

> *Brave and beautiful Taya Icarus:*
> *Although I know Viera has already arranged to thank you for your rescue, I'd enjoy a chance to demonstrate my own gratitude for the assistance you've provided to my family. I'll send a driver by your eyrie tonight to see if you're available at eight; if so, he'll bring you to Rhodanthe's on Primus, where we can meet for dinner. If you have other business*

tonight, then I'll dine alone and hope that your duties
will bring you to Oporphyr Tower on the morrow.
Respectfully yours,
Alister Forlore

Taya glanced at the clock, now stopped at 2:10, and
swallowed, her cheeks burning.

"It's from Alister, of course," Cristof said, his voice flat.

"Yes." She bit her lip. "He wants to have dinner with
me tonight." She held out the letter, feeling like she had
to prove it.

"Of course he does." The exalted's hand hovered over
the note a moment, and then he took it, pushing up his
glasses as he read.

"But why?" She looked up.

"You've piqued his interest." Cristof handed the letter
back. "You still have time to see a doctor before you go."

Taya flushed. She knew what he was thinking. Icarii had
a reputation for moving as easily from lover to lover as
they did from sector to sector. But before she could say
anything, Gwen broke in.

"What's this about a doctor?"

"I got cut last night." Taya folded the letter back up.
"Exalted Forlore thinks I should have it looked at by a
professional."

"Exalted Forlore is my brother," Cristof corrected her.
He knelt in front of the clock again. "Master Clockwright
will do, if you insist on being formal."

"Whatever you wish, Master Clockwright." Taya
jammed the letter into her pocket. "I'm going. Please don't
wait for my return."

"I didn't plan to."

Taya shook her head and left the eyrie. Of course Cristof
wouldn't approve of his brother seeing an icarus—icarii were
hardly better than whores, in some people's eyes. But an
outcaste should know better than to believe in stereotypes.

Dinner with Alister Forlore. The thought of the decatur's
handsome face and bright green eyes was tempting, but

Taya knew she'd be a fool to accept. Alister probably assumed the same thing about her as his brother. Even if he were a gentleman over dinner, it wouldn't mean that he didn't have expectations, and . . . and, well, what on earth would she wear to a restaurant on Primus, anyway?

Besides, what if he made a pass and she couldn't resist it? She prided herself on being choosy about her lovers, but it had been a long time since the last one, and Alister was undeniably attractive.

No, all things considered, it would be best if she turned Alister's servant away tonight. She would meet the decatur at the Octavus party under safely reputable conditions, and then she'd see what happened.

Chapter Five

The physician cleaned and bandaged her cut, warned her not to rescue anyone from a wireferry accident for a week or two, and sent her on her way. Taya hurried back to the eyrie and felt a twinge of disappointment to find the clock back in one piece and Cristof gone.

"Taya!" Gwen shouted for her as she turned to head up the stairs, and Taya spun, changing direction to enter the parlor.

"What?"

"Your outcaste left. He gave me an estimate and took off looking like he'd been drinking vinegar." The landlady sniffed. "So, you got an invitation to dinner from an exalted?"

"Yes." Taya dropped into an overstuffed chair and made a face. "The cousin of the woman I rescued yesterday. He wants to thank me."

"And the outcaste disapproves?"

"His name is Cristof Forlore, and he's the exalted's brother."

"Oh." Gwen's eyebrows rose. "It's a family affair, is it?"

"It's not any kind of affair at all," Taya objected, nettled. "Cristof doesn't approve of me, and I don't want to cause any trouble between him and his brother."

"Who is a decatur."

"Decatur Alister Forlore."

Gwen looked impressed. "Well, if a decatur is asking you to dinner to thank you for saving his cousin's life, you can hardly say no. Is he well-mannered? Do you like him?"

"I only talked to him once, but he was very charming." Taya sighed. And dangerously good-looking. "I have to say no, Gwen. He's probably got the wrong impression about me—you know how it is. And besides, I don't have anything to wear."

"Go in your flight suit. That's perfectly acceptable attire for an icarus on business," Gwen said firmly. Taya wrinkled her nose.

"I don't think he expects this dinner to be business."

"He said it was to thank you."

"Yes." Taya didn't mention the letter's greeting, which was less than businesslike.

"Well, then he can't complain if you wear your flight suit. And if you don't want to give him the wrong impression, a flight suit is more than chaste."

Taya smiled. That was true. Alister might be disappointed if she showed up in a flight suit instead of a dress, but the few smocks she owned were more suitable for picnics over summer on Secundus than dinner during autumn on Primus. And a flight suit really was very difficult to get out of.

She chewed on her bottom lip, thinking about it.

"But his brother doesn't approve . . . ."

"His brother's a freak."

"He is not!"

"He's an exalted who walks around barefaced and dresses like a famulate. Taya, dear, he's a freak. And an ill-tempered freak, at that."

"He's not so grouchy when you get to know him." Taya wasn't sure why she was defending the clockwright. Gwen was right. Still . . . she felt a little sorry for him. It couldn't be easy, living the life of an outcaste.

"Well, he's not so important, either. If I were you, I'd worry more about offending a decatur than an outcaste. If you're going to fly with the eagles, dearest, you can't waste your time on the crows."

Crows. Taya's lips curved up. Cristof did look like a crow, and he certainly squawked like one.

"Then you think I should go?"

"You want to join the diplomat corps, don't you?"

"What—oh." Taya's voice dropped to a whisper as it suddenly dawned on her. "Oh!"

Exam scores were only part of the decision-making process. Diplomatic envoys had to work very closely with exalteds, so political acumen and personality were also important. The corps selection board would be inclined to favor a candidate who had friends on the Oporphyr Council.

"Oh. Oh, Lady," she groaned, suddenly seeing everything in a new light. "Why did you have to say that?"

"Hmph, some diplomat you'll make! You'd better start thinking like a politician, love. You have a golden opportunity to advance yourself, and there's no shame in making the most of it. You didn't rescue that woman for selfish reasons, and you didn't ask the decatur to invite you out to dinner. But as long he did, it's your duty to accept the Lady's gift and use it!"

Taya made a face. She hadn't applied to the diplomatic corps to dabble in politics. If politics had interested her, she wouldn't have been so bored by Pyke. She'd applied to the corps so she could interact with foreigners, get a taste of their cultures, and maybe even travel outside of Ondinium someday. It was the unusual and exotic that had attracted her to diplomatic work, not the politics and power plays.

"It just seems so . . . manipulative."

"Whether or not it's manipulative is up to you. I'm not telling you to accept the dinner, sleep with the man, and then start asking him for favors. Just go and do your best to impress him with your good sense and good manners."

"Yes . . . ." Taya drew in a deep breath. Yes, that was sound advice. "Thank you, Gwen."

The landlady smiled, pleased with herself.

"A decatur—you're a lucky girl, Taya. Who knows? This could be a turning point in your life."

CASSI DIDN'T AGREE that a flight suit was appropriate dinner attire, but after making a frenzied survey of the wardrobe of every icarus in the eyrie who was roughly Taya's height and build, she had been forced to agree that it was Taya's best option on such short notice.

"But," she warned Taya, "if this what your new life is going to be like, we're going to have to get you a better wardrobe."

"I'd be perfectly happy spending the rest of my life in this suit," Taya confessed, looking at herself in Cassi's mirror. They'd gone up to the docks to retrieve it and had spent two hours replacing worn straps and buckles and buffing the well-worn leather to a soft glow. "It's comfortable, practical, and warm."

"You're not going to catch yourself a man wearing comfortable, practical, and warm," Cassi said tartly. "About the only thing a flight suit has going for it is that it's tight."

"Big deal." Taya scowled at her chest, pressed even flatter than usual by the suit's snug fit. "I look like a boy, just like your nephew said."

"Well, we could pad you out, but your decatur might be surprised if you suddenly grew breasts."

Taya smiled. "This is just business. I'm not trying to seduce him."

"Good thing, if you're wearing *that*."

Taya sat on the porch stairs at eight, her hands in warm gloves and her collar pulled high. Their hunt through the eyrie for a suitable dress had spread the news of her dinner appointment, and the other icarii had started offering her scandalous advice about "what exalteds want." Explaining that her date was a cousin of the exalted she'd saved hadn't stopped the chaffing. Finally, she'd fled outside, preferring to sit in the cold than listen to more jokes.

At last she heard one of the city's small, one-horse hacks rattling down the street. She stood and waved to the famulate driver, who saluted and pulled over to the porch.

"Taya Icarus?" he asked.

"That's me." She watched as the coachman wrapped the reins around a rail and hopped down to open the door. "Where are we going?"

"Rhodanthe's, on Primus. Fare and tip are already paid." He smiled pleasantly at her. "Never carried an icarus as a passenger before. Always seems a little strange to see one of you without your wings, don't it? My map says I can get to Regent if I keep following Cliff Road, but I thought Cliff dead-ends at the flight docks. Is the map right, then, or am I?"

"Both, actually. Cliff Road forks, and you can get to Regent if you take the left turn, but it's not Cliff Road anymore. I think it turns into Catamount."

"Wide enough for us, you think?"

"It's used by delivery wagons making their rounds, so it must be," she assured him. "It's dark, though."

"I have lanterns. Well, in you go, then, and my thanks for the directions."

"Sure." Taya slid inside, then leaned forward as the coachman was about to close the door. "What's your name?"

"I'm Gregor, and my mare here is Bolt. We make the city circuit during the day, the two of us, but we can be hired special if you leave a message at any of the hack stations."

"I'll remember," she promised. He touched his cap and closed the door. In another moment, the hack lurched forward.

Riding in a hack, Taya decided after about ten minutes, was considerably more uncomfortable than walking, and a lot less efficient than flight.

Most Ondiniums walked. Because the city was so crowded and steep, only a few horse-drawn vehicles were licensed to operate in the sectors. Most of them were wagons for deliveries and hacks for the elderly and crippled. Exalteds used the wireferry or their own light carriages for travel, and icarii, of course, flew, delivering the post and acting as couriers and messengers to spare others the long walks from sector to sector.

Foreigners were the economic mainstay of the hack system. Few of them had the lungpower to manage the steep hikes through the city that native Ondiniums took for granted.

By the time the hack had reached the smoother streets of Primus and stopped, Taya was thoroughly shaken and disgruntled. She stepped out of the coach with a grimace and stretched.

"You all right, then?" Gregor asked.

"No offense, but next time I'll fly."

"Inside the sectors proper, you get a smoother ride." he apologized. "That Catamount needs to be cobbled, it does."

"It probably doesn't get used often enough." She looked at the restaurant door. The sign and facade were lit with gas. They were in the commercial part of Primus, but she'd never been to this street before. "Do you know this place? What's it like?"

"Mixed-caste. I ain't never been inside, but it's popular enough. I drive up plenty of fare from Secundus for business dinners, don't I? Now, I'm supposed to pick you up again in two and a half hours, and I'll wait here if you ain't out. If you leave before that, any hack will serve, but tell the man at the door about me, won't you? Otherwise I'll be sitting here all night waiting for you, I will."

"Don't worry." She smiled. Two and a half hours. Business for real. That relieved some of her concern. "I think I might rather walk back, though."

"Now, that wouldn't be safe, would it? 'Sides, you'd be chilled to the bone even under all that leather. You wait for me, and I'll pay particular attention you don't get too rattled up on the journey back."

"Fair enough. I'll see you in a few hours, Gregor."

He touched his cap and lifted the reins. Taya turned to the door.

The maitre d' looked surprised when she walked in. He recognized her flight suit, but he looked puzzled as his eyes rose over her shoulders and registered her missing wings.

"I'm Taya," she said. Through one of the doorways she could see a large dining room filled with well-dressed Cardinal castes, eating and laughing together. She was going to look very out of place among them, she thought, her stomach churning. "I'm a guest?"

"Taya Icarus, yes, you're expected," the man said, at once. "Please follow me."

To Taya's relief, he opened another doorway, leading her into a wide, empty hall lined with doors. He opened one of them and bowed her through, closing the door behind her.

The room was small and almost empty, with only three chairs and one low table. Another door stood on the opposite side of the chamber. A liveried servant bearing the circular caste-mark of a famulate stood and bowed.

"Taya Icarus?" The uniformed woman waited for her to nod. "Decatur Forlore awaits you." She opened the second door.

This door revealed a much more lavishly appointed room, and Taya suddenly understood. Of course, an exalted couldn't eat in the main room; not in a mixed-caste restaurant. These chambers must have been set aside for private dining, with the antechambers keeping the exalteds out of the sight of lower-caste guests and restaurant staff who might be passing by.

She stepped inside. Gas lamps on the wall brightened the room, their light reflecting off gilt-edged mirrors and well-polished tables and chairs.

Decatur Forlore was already on his feet, smiling.

"Taya! I feared you wouldn't be able to come. I apologize for the short notice, but I found myself at liberty this evening and hoped to make the best of my unexpected night off."

"I—I appreciate the invitation, exalted," Taya stammered, bowing and pressing her palm to her forehead.

He wasn't masked, of course, but he glittered with gold and jewels, and he wore the traditional three layers of flowing silk robes. Each robe was embroidered in silver and gold thread, and small gemstones glittered on their stiff cuffs and lapels. The exalted's long, shining black hair was swept around his head and held in place by golden combs and emerald-studded chains that reflected his green eyes.

"Sit." Alister stepped forward to take her arm, leading her to a chair. Taya stiffened at the touch of his fingers, her gaze flying to his face. He paused. "What's wrong?"

"I'm sorry, I just—" she stopped, confused.

He laughed and drew her forward, pulling out her chair.

"I was hoping we could avoid standing on caste tonight," he said. "Frankly, I find it tiresome, and I would like to talk."

"Of course." Taya was chagrined. "I'm just used to standing at arm's length from . . . exalteds."

"I never keep anyone I admire at arm's length." Alister gestured to the chair and Taya sat. He picked up a bottle. "May I?"

Taya nodded, remembering what Cristof had said about Alister pouring drinks for her. Color rose in her cheeks.

The exalted was acting like a man who expected an icarus to be available for his evening's pleasure. *No—no, he's not, he's just being polite,* she scolded herself. Wasn't he? How did exalteds act in private, anyway? She didn't have any basis for comparison. Except Cristof. And he didn't count.

Alister finished pouring and handed her a glass. "My servant will order for us and bring in the food. I told her to order a little of everything, so you should find something you like."

"Do you always have to be this circumspect when you dine out?" Taya asked, as he filled his own glass and sat down. Unlike Cristof, he didn't place himself on the opposite side of the table from her, but sat at the end, his chair angled toward her. Gas flames played off the golden ornaments in his clothing and hair.

"No, not always. We could have gone to an exalted-only restaurant, but people would have stared at you, and I was afraid you would find it embarrassing."

She nodded. "I would have. In fact, I'm—I'm a little nervous about attending Exalted Octavus's party. Am I going to be very out of place? Are any of the exalteds going to mind that I'll be seeing them without their masks?"

"Of course not. You will be our guest of honor, and we're all accustomed to dealing with icarii. I think you're very fortunate to be an icarus. It must be very liberating to move freely from Tertius to Primus and never worry about masks and propriety."

Taya glanced down at her glass. "I worry about propriety all the time, exalted. When you have to work with all the castes and foreigners, it's hard to remember which rules apply, even after taking the diplomacy exam. Like just now—one of the rules I was taught was never to touch an exalted."

"Certainly you wouldn't in public, but you can't believe that exalteds never touch lower castes in private."

"Well . . ." She blushed. Of course she knew that exalteds had personal lower-caste servants who saw them unmasked and helped them dress and do their hair, and she was sure that occasional cross-caste friendships and romances occurred. But those were special, necessary exceptions. "I've never touched an exalted before."

"Liar." His smile made the accusation playful. "My cousin told me she clung to you like a baby while you were falling."

"That's not the same thing." For that matter, she realized, Cristof had touched her to tend her wound. "I wasn't thinking about caste then," she protested, and it was true of both occasions.

"But you are now. That's understandable, but won't you try to set your qualms aside for a few hours? I could have waited to talk to you at Viera's party, but I wanted to get to know you before then. It will be more comfortable to have a friend at the ball, don't you agree?"

Taya gave him a shy smile. "I think you could make anyone feel like a friend, exalted."

"Alister. Call me Alister, but feel free to flatter me all you want, because I adore flattery." His green eyes twinkled. "Were you also taught that diplomats should flatter exalteds?"

"No! And I'm not a diplomat yet. I just took my exams a few weeks ago. I might not be accepted."

"So, you're still waiting for the board to make up its mind. I detested waiting for my examination scores at the University. I detest ambiguity of any sort. That was another reason I wanted to get to know you. Let the rest of Primus wonder what kind of person you are—I'll know first." He sounded like a mischievous child, and Taya couldn't help but grin.

"Will that matter, exa— Alister?"

"Only to me, but I'll take great satisfaction in it." He cocked his head. "Why do you want to become a diplomat? It can be dangerous work, and you might be sent away from the city to work in a foreign embassy, if you're especially unfortunate."

"No, that would be perfect! I'd love to see another country. Wouldn't it be wonderful to see Mareaux's famous vineyards, or a Demican bear hunt, or the Cabiel jungles?"

"I see. You're a true-born icarus, full of soaring dreams and aspirations."

"Haven't you ever been out of Ondinium?"

"I'm not permitted. Everyone who studies programming at the University signs a contract swearing to remain in the city. I've heard rumors of an elite group of lictors that is sent after escaped programmers to bring them back—dead or alive."

"No!" She stared at him. The story sounded like something Pyke would tell her. "Really?"

"I'm not making it up. Well, I am embroidering, a little. I expect the lictors are quite ordinary, and I imagine they would prefer to bring the wayward programmer back alive. Still, programmers are required by law to spend their life in Ondinium, in order to keep the city's technological secrets intact."

"Then you'll never leave?"

"I don't want to leave. I can enjoy the same wines and bearskins and jungle fruit here that I would in any other country. 'All roads lead to Ondinium,' after all." Humor lines crinkled around his eyes. "Now you'll think I'm boring and lose all interest in me."

"No. I love Ondinium, too. But I'd like to see more than wires and smog. I'd like to fly over an ice field or an ocean before I die."

"You must have been a merchant or a soldier in your last life."

"Or a bird. A lot of icarii think they used to be birds." She took a sip of the wine, then set it back down again. It tasted all right, but she'd feel more comfortable with a plain ale—something she was used to drinking.

"If you were a bird in a past life, you would have been one of those little hunting hawks I see carried by Mareauxan ambassadors," Alister speculated. "Red-headed and neatly trimmed, agile and fierce."

"Now who's being flattering?" she scolded him.

"Not at all, Taya Hawk."

"I'm a hawk without my wings right now."

"Just for tonight. I look forward to seeing you in your wings again the next time you come to Oporphyr Tower."

Taya looked down, reminded of her flight suit. "I'm sorry about the suit . . . I don't have anything formal to wear to dinner."

"Don't apologize. You look charming. Remember, I belong to a caste in which everyone hides their bodies under layers of heavy robes." Alister gestured to the glittering lapels stacked three-deep on his chest. "I'm enjoying the privilege of being able to sit here and ogle your legs without giving offense."

Taya laughed again. Cassi would enjoy hearing that. "Traveling to the lower sectors must be a real thrill for you, then."

"It would be if all the castes decided to adopt form-hugging fashions. Perhaps the Council should make it a law."

"Do you . . . do exalteds always dress so formally, even in their own homes?" Taya looked with open curiosity at his clothes, deciding that after his jokes he could hardly protest if she stared. Not that he seemed like the kind of man who'd object to being admired. "Isn't it hard to get any work done?"

"We wear lighter robes at home. Just one or two, made out of softer fabrics with less decoration." He tapped a flower spray embroidered across his top robe; small garnets picked out the shape of a bouquet of roses. "These are just for wearing in public. We have to be very careful when we choose them. One only purchases a robe that has gemstones sewn across the rear once."

"Sitting down in wings isn't much easier."

"I see we both suffer for our caste."

"What about your hair? Do you dress it when you're at home, too?"

He seemed amused. "Not as elaborately. If I intend to spend all day inside, I simply pull it back."

Taya nodded, imagining him in a light, open robe that would show off his well-built frame and dark copper skin, a curtain of black hair hanging loose over his shoulders. She felt a pleasant tingle. He was handsome in his exalted's jewels, but . . . .

A smile played on his lips as he watched her, and she dragged her thoughts away, afraid he might see them in her eyes. *Besides*, she sternly reminded herself, *I'm not that kind of icarus*. She'd never been able to shake off all her famulate ideas about respectability.

"And what do *you* wear in private, Taya?" he asked, with a teasing smile on his lips.

"Nothing very exciting. Trousers and a tunic, most of the time," she admitted, thinking for the first time that maybe Cassi was right and she dressed too plainly. "I was born on Tertius, so I'm used to wearing clothes for efficiency, not looks. But I'm having a dress made for the party," she added, hastily.

"Good. You look charming in that suit, but I'll see more of you in a dress."

"What will you wear?" she asked. "Your robes hide just as much as this suit."

His green eyes gleamed.

"As much as I would enjoy showing off for you, I'd scandalize Caster if I arrived in anything other than formal attire. I'm afraid that if you want to see me in casual clothes, you'll have to accept a dinner invitation to my house."

"I don't think I'd dare." She felt a thrill, knowing that she was on dangerous ground.

"I could invite a friend to chaperone us, if you insisted," he said at once, pretending disappointment.

Taya was saved from answering by a knock on the door. At Alister's summons, the servant came in, bearing a platter of food. The famulate had to make three trips from the antechamber before all the food was in. Taya wanted to leap up to help, but she forced herself to sit still, like someone accustomed to being served.

"Would you want anything else, exalted?" the servant asked, bowing. The woman didn't take any special pains to avoid looking at Alister's bare face, although for the most part she kept her eyes downcast. Another concession to everyday practicality, Taya thought, like the abbreviated bows and salutes in Oporphyr Tower.

"No, that's all, thank you."

The servant withdrew, closing the door again. Taya and Alister began to investigate the dishes, Alister recommending his favorites. Taya took a little of each. Most of the food was fancier than anything she'd ever eaten on her own.

"Do you know who's going to be at the party?" she asked, between helpings.

"The decaturs will all be present, and their families. Some of Viera's and Caster's friends, of course, and the usual political allies who are invited to every Octavus party as a matter of form." Alister named a few people whose names she recognized from her diplomatic studies and the city papers.

"You said that Viera's your cousin . . . will any of the rest of your family be there?"

"Viera and my brother are all the family I have, and Cristof never comes to parties."

"Because he's outcaste?"

"He's not, you know. Outcaste. He's chosen to live outside of his caste, but he's never been legally turned away." Alister's expression darkened.

"Then he could come to the party."

"He could, if he wanted. But he hated parties even before he left Primus. Cris never mastered the social graces, and now he's something of a scandal. Viera and I invite him up regularly—he's family, after all—but he almost always declines."

"Maybe he's trying not to embarrass you," Taya said, remembering what Cristof had said earlier that day.

"He doesn't embarrass me. I love him. I wish he would realize that."

"Does he get along with Exalted Octavus?"

"With Viera, yes. Our parents . . . our parents died when we were young, and Viera's family took us in. We're more like brothers and sister than cousins. But Caster's a traditionalist. He doesn't approve of Cristof breaking the rules of his caste, and even Vee's a little worried that he'll give Ariq strange ideas. It won't be too long before Ariq's seven, and then he'll have to start wearing a mask, himself. It wouldn't do for him to think that Cristof's behavior is normal and try to take off his mask in public."

"You don't think your brother's normal?"

"My brother is anything but normal." Alister laughed. "Don't get me wrong, little hawk. He's not insane. But it isn't normal for an exalted to cut his hair and take off his mask and move down to Tertius to live with the plebs." He sobered. "Cris has a bad temper. It's better for all of us that he went to live someplace where he can surround himself with machines instead of people.

"Why— why did he leave?"

Alister shook his head.

"I wish I knew. I think every exalted has daydreamed about throwing away the mask at one time or another. Caste restrictions can become tiresome. I'd love to go flying on a pair of metal wings without worrying that my bare skin might be seen by a stranger. Maybe you'll take me, someday? But Cristof's the only exalted I know who has ever acted upon the dream. Lady, the uproar he caused! I couldn't believe it, the day he cut off his hair—

he hacked it short with a pair of scissors, all by himself. It was horrible."

Taya tried to put herself in Alister's place, to feel his shock, but there wasn't anything comparable in icarus life. Icarii were free to wear whatever they wanted, to style their hair any way they wanted, to do whatever they wanted—as long as they carried out their duties. The central caste restriction on an icarus was to serve the city and its residents with loyalty and responsibility. Even if an icarus couldn't fly, for some reason, there was almost always a groundling job available in the eyries or docks, sorting mail or repairing armatures.

"My brother set up a small shop down in Tertius, buried in a basement where nobody can find it. I don't know why he hides himself down there—maybe he's ashamed of himself, after all. He could have made himself a celebrity. I would have, if had been in his place. I would have traded on my castemark and the scandal and made myself the darling of the gossip columns and fashionable salons. But Cristof keeps to himself, and most of the city doesn't even know that one of our caste has defected."

"I think I feel sorry for him," Taya said, at last. "It's awful, never fitting in."

"You have a kind heart." Alister's voice gentled. "Especially considering how he scolded you. He wasn't very polite to a weary icarus who had just saved his cousin's life."

"He wasn't so bad, later. I mean, he's not nice," Taya elaborated, "but I think he's well-mannered, behind that sharp tongue of his."

"I should hope he is. When did you meet him again?"

Taya related the story of the attack the night before, but she didn't tell him that she'd returned to the clockwright's shop that afternoon to accuse Cristof of being a bomber. Alister's brother had enough problems without her casting any undue suspicion on him.

"I'm surprised he helped you," Alister said, when she was through. He sounded puzzled. "Cris is such a gearhead . . . it's hard to imagine that he'd have the stomach to shoot a mugger. And where did he ever get an air pistol? But I suppose he's had to grow bolder, living on Tertius."

"It can be a dangerous place," Taya agreed.

"And you should be more careful when you go down there, too." Alister leaned forward to touch the back of her hand, looking at the scabs across her knuckles. "I'll add my voice to his in insisting the lictate investigate the mugging. Lately, they've been more concerned with hunting down terrorists like the Torn Cards, but attacking an icarus is a serious crime, too. And who knows; the two crimes could be linked. The king of Alzana has a number of spies funneling money to Ondinium's radical elements, hoping to unbalance the Council. He'd love to possess one of our armatures."

"Your brother doesn't trust Alzana, either." Taya realized Alister's fingers were still resting on the back of her hand. *Lady, he really is flirting with me*, she thought, torn between pleasure and panic.

"We both lost a dear friend to Alzana's conflict with Ondinium." Alister sighed. "But let's not talk about unpleasant matters. Tell me about your family."

Taya allowed him to change the subject, and their conversation wove back and forth as they ate, touching on families and friends, favorite foods and books. A loud knock on the door startled them both.

"The coach is here, exalted," the servant announced, without opening the door.

Alister slipped a watch from a hidden pocket inside his sleeve and opened it.

"Forgefire, I should have told him to come back in three hours," he muttered. He raised his voice. "Buy him a drink and tell him Taya will be out in a few minutes."

"Yes, exalted."

"I'm sorry," Alister apologized. "We haven't even had an after-dinner drink yet."

"That's all right. I have to fly early tomorrow." Taya eyed his watch. "Did your brother make that?"

Alister unhooked the chain and handed it to her. "He did."

The decatur's watch was gold, too, but the case had been engraved with a fancy sun-and-moon pattern, with an inlay of white and red metal. Taya opened it the way Cristof had shown her. The watch face was a shiny black surface filigreed in silver and gold, showing a repetition of the celestial pattern. Tiny diamonds marked the hours and looked like twinkling stars.

The vibration felt the same as Cristof's watch; like the steady beat of a tiny heart.

"Did you choose the design?" Taya asked, looking up.

"More or less. Cris said he'd make me a watch as a graduation present and asked what I wanted. I told him I'd like a sun on it, but he's the one who designed the pattern for the jeweler. That's platinum and red gold, and the face is an ondium and iron alloy. I didn't ask how he got his hands on ondium. Through the black market, I expect. He said it's perfectly counterweighted—if I ever took out the face and let it go, it would float without moving."

"It's beautiful."

"I'm sure it cost him a fortune, but since he barely touches his inheritance, I imagine our accountants didn't complain too much."

"He must love you a lot, to make you a present like this." Taya handed it back.

"Well, we're brothers." Alister tucked it into his sleeve, looking thoughtful. "Will you forgive me if I don't escort you to the door? I'd have to put on my overrobe and mask, and I wouldn't even be able to say good-bye."

"Of course. I understand." She bowed, pressing her palm against her forehead. "Thank you for dinner and the pleasant conversation, exalted. You've been very kind."

He grabbed her hand as she straightened and brought it to his lips, smiling as he kissed her fingers. Taya squirmed a little, meeting his eyes and melting at the humor and warmth she saw in their green depths.

"Nor could I do that in a mask and robes," he said, squeezing her hand.

"You're going to make it very awkward for us to meet again in Oporphyr Tower," she said, her heart pounding.

"I know how to admire from afar. I just don't enjoy it." He released her with a show of reluctance. "I intend to see you again. Before my cousin's party, if I can possibly clear my calendar."

"I'd like that." She stepped back. "Good night, exalted."

"Alister."

"Alister."

He called in his servant, who escorted Taya through the antechamber and out to the front door. Gregor was waiting outside, finishing an ale. He handed it back to the servant when he saw Taya.

"Eat well, then?" he asked, opening the coach door. Taya looked inside and sighed.

"Too well. I don't think I can stand being jolted around inside that stuffy box again, Gregor. Can I ride on top with you?"

"The exalted would have my head if he found out, he would."

"Don't be silly." Taya examined the side of the coach, gauging how to climb up. "Please? I ride on top or I walk."

The coachman sighed, closed the door, and helped her up.

THE NEXT DAY Taya went back to work, pleased to find her wings repaired. None of her deliveries took her to Oporphyr Tower, but Alister sent a note to the dispatch office, thanking her for a lovely evening and apologizing for not being able to get out of his obligations that evening. Taya felt a moment's regret, then tucked the note into one of her flight-suit pockets and finished her day's work.

On the day after that, she was amused to find a message asking for her by name, ordering her to fly to Exalted Forlore's office to pick up a package for the University. Alister did have a package for her, but he kept her chatting

with him for half an hour, shamelessly flirting and begging
her to take him flying with her someday. Taya promised to
make some inquiries. The dock kept a special set of wings
for visitors, but they were usually reserved to entertain
foreign ambassadors who didn't have to worry about caste
propriety. She didn't know what it would involve to borrow
them for an exalted. They'd have to go somewhere remote,
where he could fly without a mask and not be seen.

"I don't trust him," Pyke declared, after she told Cassi
about the day's meeting. They were sitting at their usual
table in the eyrie dining room, their voices pitched low to
keep the rest of the icarii from overhearing. "He's moving
too fast."

"Too fast?" Cassi rolled her eyes. "Dinner and a chat in
his office is hardly 'too fast.' It's a perfectly respectable
pace."

"But all this flirting . . . ."

"Is fine, as long as Taya doesn't mind. You should try
flirting, Pyke. Girls like to be flattered, you know."

"Alister flirts well," Taya said, smiling at the memory of
his lingering touches and long gazes. "It's harmless."

"And if he goes beyond flirting?"

"Then she's a lucky girl," Cassi said, with finality.

"I don't know," Taya admitted. "I don't know if he's just
having fun or if he's sincere."

"How can you possibly like a man you don't trust?"
Pyke exclaimed.

"It's not that I don't trust him! I just don't know him well
yet. But I'm having fun. If he wants to keep flirting and
flattering until we're both old and grey, that's fine. But it
would be kind of nice to know what he's thinking."

"And if he *is* serious? Do you really think a cross-caste
relationship between an exalted and an icarus can work
out?"

"I guess it depends on what you mean by 'work out,'"
Taya murmured. She'd been wondering the same thing.

"Well, that's the point, isn't it?" Pyke retorted. "We all
know what people think about icarii. What if he uses you

as a bed partner for a few months and then gets bored and moves on?"

"That might not be so bad," Cassi pointed out. "The exalted is handsome, rich, powerful, and charming. What makes you think Taya doesn't want a little no-strings-attached fun?"

Pyke scowled. "Taya's not that kind of girl!"

"Quiet," Taya said, reaching across the table to touch his wrist. Other icarii were glancing at them.

"If you're going to act like a jealous ex, go away," Cassi said, piqued. "Taya needs friendly advice, not offended masculinity."

"My friendly advice is to leave him alone," Pyke growled.

"And my friendly advice is to enjoy yourself and see what happens." Cassilta gave her an envious look. "Why doesn't some handsome exalted chase after me? I can't even attract an annoying conspiracy theorist." She kicked Pyke, who muttered under his breath.

"Taya Icarus?"

The three of them looked up at the icarus in the doorway. All the other icarii in the room raised their arms and pointed in their direction.

Taya stood and led the messenger out to the parlor. He wore a military corps insignia on his flight leathers. That made sense—courier icarii didn't fly at night, unless they were caught out past sunset or there was an emergency. Which meant—

"Is it my father?" she asked, fearfully. "Did something happen to my family?"

"Not that I know of." He handed her the note. "You're the Taya who rescued Exalted Octavus?"

"Yes." She unfolded the message, then breathed a sigh of relief. It was from Lt. Amcathra, telling her that a wounded Demican had been reported by one of the Tertius physicians and arrested on suspicion of being her mugger. The lieutenant wanted her to identify him.

"That was good work," the other icarus said with approval. "Have you ever thought about joining the military corps? You've got the guts for it."

"Actually, I just took the diplomacy exams. When you walked in, I thought you were bringing my results."

"They'll be delivered to your dispatch office. Diplomacy, huh? Too bad. If it doesn't work out, keep us in mind. You wouldn't need to memorize all that cultural scrap, and we could use a talented flier like you."

"Thanks." She nodded, although she didn't think she could take a job where she might have to kill someone. Just looking at Lt. Amcathra's note made her feel guilty all over again. "Does the lictor want me right now?"

"Of course he does. He's at Tallyfield Station. You want to walk, or should I get your wings from the docks?"

"I can walk down there in the time it would take you to sign out my wings," she said, with a touch of regret. "Tell him I'm on my way. Do they have the man in custody?"

"I don't know anything about it," he said, shrugging. "None of my business."

"Oh. Well, thank you. Fly safely."

"You too." He waved and ducked through the doorway. Taya told her friends where she was going, then ran upstairs to grab her coat and gloves.

The walk down Cliff Road was cold and long, but Secundus was still lively in the early evening, with people dining and drinking, attending plays and hurrying to friends' houses. In half an hour she was at Tallyfield Plaza, where the lictor station was lit by bright gas lamps and filled with guards hurrying in and out.

She stood a moment in the main foyer, blinking and pulling off her gloves.

"Icarus." Lt. Amcathra stepped out of an office and beckoned to her. "Very good. I require you to look at the face of the prisoner and tell me if he is the man who attacked you."

"Is he here?"

"He is in a hospital within the vicinity. His health is not good, or else I do not think we should have found him." The lictor grabbed a coat from one of the chairs along the hallway and pulled it on, striding outside.

"How bad is it?"

"Not good."

"Oh. You're handling the case, then? I thought you'd be investigating the wireferry accident."

"That investigation is also in progress."

"You must be the lictor who gets all the tough jobs," she joked, hurrying to keep up with him as he walked. He didn't answer, and although she studied his face, his black lictor's stripe and Demican stolidity made his expression impossible to read.

Deciding she'd get nowhere trying to engage him in small talk, Taya concentrated on following him through the crowds.

The hospital was a small private building tucked away in a back street. As soon as they entered it, Taya realized that it was under military control, with barred windows and lictors stationed at the doors. One of the lictors unlocked the door that led into the Demican's hospital room.

"That's him," Taya said at once, recognizing her attacker's face in the lamplight. Then she stepped forward, alarmed. He was breathing irregularly, and he looked pale. "What's wrong?"

"Infection."

"Oh, Lady." She felt a chill. "Was it—"

"The knife wound was deep, and he did not have it tended at once."

"Is he going to die?"

"I do not know. I am certain the physicians will do what they can." Amcathra sounded uninterested.

The Demican prisoner opened his eyes and looked straight at her. Taya recoiled, and Amcathra's hand fell on her arm, moving her aside. He stepped up to the bedside and looked down at his ancestral countryman.

"This icarus has positively identified you as the man who attacked her," he snapped, in Demican. "Do you understand me?"

The wounded man took a labored breath.

"I understand."

"You were working with two Alzanans."

"They left me to die."

"Of course," Amcathra agreed. "What else would you expect from a Southerner? A warrior should choose honorable companions, not thieves."

"I am shamed." The man fought for breath again, lips pale. "Please do not tell my family."

"Who were your partners?"

"Delfo," the man husked. "And Miceli. Delfo had the net. Leader."

"Where did you meet them?"

"A bar in Slagside. Red door."

"Name?"

"I do not know."

Amcathra nodded.

"Very well. I will return with an artist for a better description later. Rest and heal, warrior. You may live to regain your honor, if you are lucky."

The man nodded once and closed his eyes. Taya slipped next to Amcathra and touched the man's hand.

"You fought well," she said, also in Demican.

The man pried his eyes open once more, looking at her.

"And you," he replied, formally. "But the gun. That is not a warrior's weapon."

"It will be," Amcathra predicted, and then drew her away. "Come," he said, switching back to Ondinium. "Let him rest. I do not believe he will trouble you again."

Taya waited until they were outside. "Will he go free, if you catch the Alzanans?"

"That will depend upon the judge. Maybe he will die of his wounds."

Taya made a face at the Demican's cold pragmatism. "I hope not."

"You will not be found at fault, if he does. Your testimony and that of Exalted Forlore makes it clear that you acted in self defense."

"Forlore—you mean, Alister? The decatur?"

"No."

"Cristof?"

"Yes. I will ask him to identify the man tomorrow, also, but it is only to be thorough."

She made a face. "Icarii get called away from their dinners, but exalteds get to wait until morning?"

"Victims are called without delay, and secondary witnesses are allowed to wait until the next day," Amcathra corrected her. "Exalted Forlore's testimony is of less importance than yours."

"I'm sorry," Taya said at once. "That makes sense."

"You will tell your friend that we did not beat or brainwash you or your attacker."

Taya laughed. "I said I was sorry! But yes, I'll tell him."

"You were kind to compliment the prisoner's fighting, though he does not deserve such honor."

"Well, he probably would have killed me, if . . . if Exalted Forlore hadn't come along and shot him."

"Someday guns will come to Demicus," Amcathra said, with a touch of regret in his voice. "Every Demican will kill with the twitch of a finger, and a warrior's bravery will mean nothing."

"Ondinium doesn't sell arms."

"Not all countries are so cautious. If our elders are wise, they will seek guidance from the Council of Ondinium before Demicus embraces foreign weapons."

"They wouldn't do that, would they? I thought Demicans believed Ondinium is hell." Demican legends of hell included stories of black skies and flying spirits.

"Ondinium may be hell, but it is an orderly hell. Demicus will not be so orderly, once guns arrive."

Chapter Six

The day before the party passed quickly, with a note from Alister apologizing for not being able to see her but assuring her that he was looking forward to a dance. On the day of the ball, Taya and Cassi took a half-day off so Taya could return to Jayce's shop for last-minute tailoring and grooming.

"Good, good," Jayce murmured, seeing them come in shortly after noon, accompanied by a famulate hairdresser. "We're still finishing the sewing, but I'm glad you're here early."

"Do you have plans for Taya's hair?" Cassi demanded, pushing Taya down into a chair.

"Nothing that requires a particular style."

"Good."

"Bad," the hairdresser objected. "Look at how short this is! What am I supposed to do with it, then?"

"Make it gorgeous." Cassi turned to her nephew and began grilling him about the dress. The hairdresser rolled her eyes and combed her fingers through Taya's loose curls.

"Well," she said, "at least the color is interesting. I don't work with auburn very often. Mareaux, are you?"

"On my father's side. He was born a citizen," she added. To some Ondiniums, that mattered.

"Good you inherited his fair skin, then, ain't it?" the hairdresser commented, holding her coppery hand against Taya's hair. "Could be worse."

"I'm glad I'm not a complete disaster," Taya said.

"But it could be better," Jayce shot over his shoulder. "You could have green eyes. Or blue. I could work with blue. But red hair and jet-black eyes? Lady save us from mixed blood. And your figure!"

Taya slumped in her chair. All right. So she was a complete disaster.

By the time evening arrived, Taya understood why vigilante heroes in plays wore masks. She'd been poked, pinched, pinned, primped and put down to within an inch of her life. The next time she rescued someone, she was going to sneak off without telling anyone her name. That way she wouldn't have to dress up for a thank-you party.

"I can't do this," she said with despair, setting down the bowl of soup that Cassi had handed her. "I'm going to say something stupid and embarrass myself."

"Oh, don't be silly. You're the guest of honor." Cassi leaned over and patted her knee. "Exalted Octavus owes you her life, so short of throwing up all over the banquet table, there's nothing you can do that's going to offend her."

"Great." Taya looked at her bowl. "Is that why you're making me eat now? So I won't throw up?"

"No. I'm doing it because you're not going to be able to eat a thing once we strap you into that corset. Besides, it's more ladylike if all you do is nibble."

"Ladylike." Taya groaned. "I don't think I can do ladylike."

"You *will* do ladylike," Cassi's nephew commanded, in a voice like steel. He walked up, the dress draped over one arm. "You don't have a choice. Cassi, I'm going to sew her into this. You'll have to cut her out of it tonight. Use the back seam."

"So much for seducing that handsome decatur," Cassi said with mock sorrow.

Taya's cheeks burned.

"Once you're out of this dress, you're not getting back into it." Jayce pondered a moment. "However . . . it *would* be good for business if you seduced a decatur while you were wearing it. Very well. I give you my permission. But you'll have to wear something of his to get back home. And for the Lady's sake, bring me back whatever scraps you can salvage."

"I'm not going to seduce anyone!" Taya protested, her blush deepening.

"Well, I'm sleeping on your bed tonight," Cassi warned her, "so if you don't come home, I expect to hear *all* the details."

"What kind of person do you think I am, anyway?"

"A sexually deprived one," Cassi said, archly. "You and Pyke never got anywhere."

Taya drew in a sharp breath. "Did he tell you that? I'll kill him!"

"Ah-hah! It's true!"

"Cassi!"

"I was just checking," her friend said, sounding complacent. "I don't want to sleep with someone you've already slept with. It'd be tacky."

"Ladies," Jayce snarled, "we have two hours until the party. Divvy up your men while I sew."

One hour before the party, Taya stood in front of a mirror feeling more frightened than she had at any point during the aerial rescue.

"I don't dare move," she said, staring at herself.

Jayce and his assistants had decided to dress her in white and gold because "exalts always wear jewel tones. I want you to stand out." The top half of the dress was a slender, low-necked sheath that hugged her chest and waist like a second skin, growing looser on her hips to become a slit skirt that gave her room to walk. A tight corset beneath the dress kept her back straight and pulled her waist in another inch. Taya blinked at the unaccustomed sight of her cleavage being pushed up and out. Maybe she wasn't as flat-chested as Jayce had led her to believe. Of course, she couldn't breathe, but she thought the trade-off might be worth it.

Jayce had sewn a tight but delicate line of gold-edged white feathers up the dress, coiling along the bottom hem, over one hip, between her breasts, and up the low neckline to her shoulder. The dress straps were as slender as he could make them and still cover the healing wound on her shoulder, and her arms were bare.

She turned and looked over her shoulder. The line of feathers wound down to her waist to complete the circle around her body. Every time she moved, feathers rustled against each other and the feathers over her shoulders brushed her bare arm. The sensation was strange but pleasant.

Jayce had insisted she wear long white gloves to cover the healing cuts on her knuckles and to make her bare upper arms more striking. He'd found long, soft crosslaced white boots for her legs that hinted at an icarus's much more utilitarian footwear, and he'd run a line of white feathers down their sides. "Unusual. A little defiant," Jayce had said with approval, looking at her. "They'll be easy to dance in, and the fabric hides your calves."

"What's wrong—"

"'Muscles aren't ladylike.'" Cassi rolled her eyes at Taya. "Don't pay any attention to him. Jay-jay likes his women plump and cuddly."

"A man who prefers women with hard bodies might as well sleep with another man," Jayce retorted. Cassilta swatted her nephew across the head.

"Watch it, brat. Chicks might be cuter than eagles, but it's the eagles who bring home the dinner and defend the nest."

"Barbarian." Jayce placed a delicate gold net over Taya's hair and began weaving white and gold feathers into it, pulling them behind her ears. Taya stood motionless, watching as he created narrow, swooping wings from brow to nape. Cassi had already done her face for her, pulling a surprising number of tiny jars from her purse.

"You carry all this with you?" Taya had asked, amazed, holding up a small jar of lip paint.

"You don't?" Cassi had countered.

Now they both looked at her reflection as Jayce stepped back.

"That is a completely outrageous dress," Cassi said with delight. "I've never seen anything like it. Jaws are going to drop."

"I don't know about this," Taya fretted. She hardly recognized herself. She looked like she'd just stepped off the stage of some fairy-tale opera. Alister's joke about exalteds and their layers of embroidered robes returned to her, and she wondered how much of a scandal she'd cause, showing off her figure so brazenly at an exalted party. "Maybe I should wear something that . . . covers more."

"Covers more? You're an icarus!" Jayce reached forward to tease curls of her hair down around her face. "Freedom defines the icarus caste. You don't want to wear the same dowdy fashions the cardinal or plebeian castes would wear. And if there's one thing exalteds aren't, it's free. Besides, you're too small to carry off their heavy robes." He regarded her with satisfaction. "This sets a new standard for icarus fashion. I'm a genius."

"You're a genius, kid," Cassi agreed, hugging her nephew and ruffling his hair. "Now come on; let's see if Taya's coach is here."

ESTATE OCTAVUS STOOD on the highest street in Primus sector, surrounded by other exalteds' mansions. The street's cobbles were flat and smooth, laid together like pieces of a puzzle, and the gas lamps were small masterpieces of ironwork that stood every twenty feet to keep the neighborhood bright. Taya had visited the street before, but only to deliver messages. The mansions' peaked, slate-tiled roofs and forbidding iron gates looked more much imposing when she approached them at ground level.

Carriages blocked the road, and everywhere she looked, masked and robed exalts were flowing into the estate, followed by liveried servants.

Peering out the window of Gregor's coach, Taya touched her lips, worried. Was she going to be mistaken for a servant, showing up at the party without a mask? Then she pulled her fingers away before she could disturb all the work Cassi had done. To give her hands something to do, she stroked the soft velvet cloak Jayce had let her borrow for the night.

Lady, what am I doing here? She twitched the window curtain back even farther, impressed by the sight of ivory and gold masks glittering in the lamplight, of silk and silver hems sliding over spotless streets. Long embroidered sleeves hung well over the exalteds' fingertips, and only their long glossy hair, caught up around their heads in complicated braids and loops, revealed that the creatures beneath the masks might be human.

"Ostentatious incapacitation," Pyke had called exalteds' garments. Baroque, mouthless masks to prove they didn't need to give orders. Heavy, movement-inhibiting garments to prove they didn't need to run or carry. Everything an exalted might need to say or do in public was anticipated by their perfectly trained lower-caste servants. And if it wasn't, there was nothing the exalted could do about it without outraging tradition.

The way Viera Octavus had briefly outraged it, when she'd abandoned her mask and robe to lift her child to safety.

Despite Pyke's scorn for the exalteds, Taya thought the sight of so many masked and robed aristocrats was eerie and majestic. Very few people were privileged to see behind the masks, which gave exalteds an air of mystique that the nobility of other countries lacked. Maybe that's why other countries had so many revolutions. People there took their rulers for granted. Exalteds, by contrast, stood apart from the rest of humanity by virtue of their birth and their rules of conduct.

A footman approached her coach and spoke to Gregor, then tapped on the door.

"Taya Icarus?"

She drew in a deep breath.

"I'm here," she replied, as he opened the door. The cold autumn air made her pull her cloak close around her.

The footman blinked once, startled by her uninked face, and then bowed.

"May I escort you to the door? Lady Octavus told us to bring you in as soon as you arrived."

"Thank you." She took his hand and let him help her out of the coach, grateful for his assistance. Sitting and standing in a tight dress wasn't a maneuver she'd ever needed to practice before.

"Good luck, icarus," Gregor called out. "The man there says your transportation home's been taken care of already."

She turned and waved.

"Thank you, Gregor."

He gave her a cheery salute.

Heads turned as they walked through the street and entered the estate gates. Taya shivered under her cloak, feeling naked compared to all the covered guests around her. *Well, there's no turning back now*, she thought, squaring her shoulders. *If nothing else, this dress will confirm the fast-and-loose reputation of icarii everywhere.*

The doors were wide open and the foyer was lit by a thousand wax candles placed on high shelves and chandeliers, well above the long sleeves and dragging hems of the exalteds' heavy robes. Gold-framed mirrors reflected the light and the guests in an endless regression that made Taya dizzy. She swallowed as jeweled, featureless masks turned to watch her.

The footman led her through the foyer to the inner doors.

"May I take your cloak?" he asked. She glanced around and saw that here, safely away from the street, exalteds were shedding their public robes and pulling off their ivory masks, laughing and greeting each other like normal people.

"Of course." She pulled off the velvet cloak that had seemed so luxurious in Jayce's shop but now struck her as thin and tawdry compared to the exalteds' garments.

It doesn't matter, she reminded herself. *Nobody expects me to dress like an exalted.*

I hope.

Heads turned as the footman took it and revealed her bare upper arms and daring décolletage.

Bracing herself, Taya stepped inside the reception room, composing herself just as she would if she were on duty. Strangers turned to stare at her. For a moment she froze, wondering what to do.

A woman broke away from the crowd, and Taya recognized her hostess, Viera Octavus.

"Taya Icarus," she said, her strong voice carrying through the chamber. "We are honored that you have come."

Light applause greeted her words. Taya kept her gaze fixed on the woman as she walked across the ballroom floor. They met in the center of the ballroom and Viera grasped her hands, leaning forward to rest one blue-tattooed cheek against hers.

"Thank you," the exalted said, and then dropped her voice to a whisper. "Don't look so nervous."

Taya gave the exalted a crooked smile as they separated. Was it that obvious? Viera slid an arm through hers, leading her back to her husband, a tall, patrician man with silver hair and a lined face. Taya compared him to his wife. The decatur had married a much younger woman.

"Caster," Viera said, "this is Taya Icarus."

The elderly decatur smiled at her. Taya bowed, touching her gloved palm to her forehead.

"I am pleased to meet you, Taya." When she straightened, Caster took her hand and held it a moment. "I cannot thank you enough for saving the two most important people in my life."

This time Taya didn't start, and she was glad Alister had accustomed her to being touched by the upper-caste.

"I was just—" she remembered the fictional interview in *The Watchmen* and deliberately chose different words. "It was my pleasure, exalted."

"I doubt it was a pleasure, icarus, but I am grateful nonetheless. Come. I'll introduce you to the rest of the Council."

He took her arm and led her away, Viera on his other side. Taya was glad that her gloves kept her palms from sweating on Caster Octavus's embroidered silk sleeve.

Lady, please don't let me embarrass myself or my hosts.

Some of the decaturs Caster introduced her to were familiar—men and women whose messages she'd carried over the years. None of them had ever asked her for her name when she'd worn her icarus wings, and none of them recognized her now as they shook her hand.

Only Decatur Forlore smiled at her like a friend.

"I've had the honor of meeting Taya several times," Alister said, bowing over her hand. His fingers seemed to burn through the fabric of her glove. "She's always impressed me in the past, but tonight she's rendered me speechless."

"You've never been speechless in your entire life, Al," Viera teased. Her cousin ignored her, still holding Taya's hand and smiling.

Taya felt a blush creeping up her face. The decatur's eyes were intense, their emerald depths set off by his dark green outer robe, which was patterned with coiling vines. His under robes were lighter shades of green and lavender. Gold glittered on his fingers and in his hair, making him gleam like one of the Lady's immortal spirits themselves.

"On the contrary, Viera, tonight I have no words to express myself, for my steel-winged hawk has transformed herself into a silken swan." Alister lifted her hand and brushed the back of her glove with his lips.

"Enough, Alister. Taya has other guests to meet tonight," Caster said. Taya glanced at him, wondering she'd heard a trace of censure in the older man's voice. Alister released her, but she felt his eyes on her back as the Octavuses led her to the next decatur.

She hardly heard any of the other introductions, bemused by Alister's touch. Lady, he was handsome!

After Taya had been introduced to the entire Council, Viera reclaimed her and led her away.

"I promised Ariq I would take you to visit him tonight."

"I'd love to see him again." Taya followed the exalted through a small side door. "But does he really want to meet me? Our flight scared him."

"He was terrified," Viera agreed. "But then, so was I." Her eyes twinkled. "It took him a few hours to begin enjoying all the fuss being made over him. That's when he started bragging about how he went flying with you. Now I think he's completely forgotten his tears."

"I'm glad he's all right."

"Yes. By the way, you look lovely. Is that an icarus dress? I've never seen anything like it before."

Taya looked down, embarrassed. "Yes. It's an icarus dress."

"It's very flattering. I wish I had the freedom to wear something other than these layers of fabric every day."

Taya glanced at her. Viera, like the other women in the ballroom, wore several light silk robes in contrasting colors. The hems brushed her ankles, much higher than the dragging hems exalteds wore out in public—tailored for dancing, Taya assumed. Viera's outer robe was a deep blue, and her interior robes were rich saffron and crimson.

"If I could have come in my flight suit and wings, I would have," Taya admitted.

"You would have disappointed every man in the room."

They passed through a small hallway and up the stairs to the house's living quarters. Ariq was in his nursery, being read to by a famulate-caste nanny.

"Mommy!" The boy leaped up and ran to his mother. "You look pretty tonight, Mommy."

Viera leaned over and hugged him, then turned him around to face Taya.

"This is Taya Icarus, the woman who saved us," she said, her hands on the boy's shoulders. "I promised I would bring her up to see you before you went to sleep."

Ariq looked at her with open curiosity.

"Where are your wings?"

"I took them off for the party." Taya knelt, mentally cursing the corset for making bending over impossible. "I'm happy to see you again, Ariq."

Viera nudged the boy, who held out his hand.

"Thank you for saving me," he said solemnly.

"You're very welcome," Taya replied, shaking his hand. "Perhaps we can go flying again someday, if your parents agree."

"Maybe . . . ." he said with hesitation. Taya smiled up at Viera, who laughed, kissed her son, and stood.

"Good night, sweetheart. Mind your nanny."

"Good night, Mommy."

Viera led them back, pausing in an antechamber to pour two glasses of golden wine.

"Could you really take him flying?" she asked.

"We have a few pairs of trainer wings and guide harnesses that we use to teach the new children." Taya was careful as she held her crystal goblet, aware of what Cassi's nephew would say if she spilled anything on her dress. "There's even an adult set for the occasional visitor who wants to try flying. Foreign diplomats, mostly. Not many Ondiniums want to go aloft." Except Alister, she thought, amused.

"I suppose those who do are chosen to be icarii during their Great Examination."

"Do you plan to have Ariq take the Exam?"

"Oh, no, of course not." Viera sounded distracted, and after a moment of silence she sat down. "Taya, you have heard that the wireferry accident has been blamed on the Torn Cards, haven't you?"

"Yes."

"I can't help but wonder if the accident had been meant for my husband. He would have been on that car yesterday, if his Council discussion hadn't been extended."

"Do the Torn Cards have any reason to hurt him?"

"I don't know why they would." Viera looked distressed. "Caster is one of the most conservative anti-programming voices on the Council; you would think the Torn Cards would approve of that. But it doesn't make any sense for them to try to kill me, either. I have no voice in the Council at all."

"It could have been a random act of terrorism. Or maybe the lictors were wrong, and it wasn't the Torn Cards."

Taya remembered the question Cristof had asked her. "Did anyone else know that the three of you were supposed to be on that car?"

"Not all three of us *were*. The trip has been planned for several weeks, and our original plan was that Caster would come down to meet us at the gallery—one of our friends is holding an exhibit, and we had arranged to meet her for a private viewing." Viera looked troubled. "That morning, Caster had told me his meeting could run late, so I went up to the Tower with Ariq to see whether he was free. When it became clear he wouldn't be able to excuse himself, we headed back down by ourselves. But if everything had gone as planned . . . it could have been him on the wireferry."

"Has your husband considered hiring a bodyguard?"

"He's too proud for that. He has assigned extra lictors to us, but he doesn't want any protection for himself."

"I don't know what to say," Taya apologized, feeling awkward. "The fire at the refinery was blamed on the Torn Cards, too. Maybe it was just a day for random attacks."

"You didn't see anything suspicious around the ferry, did you?"

"No. But I wasn't looking for anything, either. It was just coincidence that I happened to be there."

Viera sighed. "I apologize. I don't mean to burden you with my concerns. I simply thought . . ."

"If I hear anything that might help, I'll tell you," Taya promised, just as she'd promised Lt. Amcathra. For a moment she thought again of Cristof's wireferry map, all marked in pencil—but no. Cristof wouldn't have hurt his cousin.

Alister's words returned to her: *"But Caster's a traditionalist. He doesn't approve of Cristof breaking the rules of his caste, and even Vee's a little worried that he'll give Ariq strange ideas."*

No—that's unfair, Taya chided herself. She'd already accused Cristof of a crime once, and he'd given her a perfectly good explanation for his whereabouts. Just because he was eccentric didn't mean he was a killer.

"Thank you." Viera stood. "I had better return you to your admirers. I have no doubt that Alister is hoping for a dance after dinner."

"What's Alister like?" Taya asked, trying to keep her voice innocent as they entered the main room again.

"Oh, he's impossible." Viera shook her head with affectionate dismay. "He's an incorrigible flirt. He ought to be married by now, but ever since he became a decatur, he's been locked up with programmers and the Council all day. The girls used to flock around him when all he did was throw parties, but they consider a hard-working man to be a bore."

"Then he's not . . ."

"Engaged?" Viera flicked a quick glance at her. "No. I have never known Alister to be serious about any of his paramours. I don't think he's ready to go wife-hunting yet, although Caster and I would like him to settle down. He needs to, if he wishes to pursue a political career. A good marriage would help balance the fact that he's the Council's youngest decatur."

Taya sighed. Well, there was her answer, very delicately put. If she wanted a temporary romance, she could have it, but she shouldn't expect anything else. Alister would marry for political advantage, and that meant marrying another exalted.

Disappointing, but . . . she was an icarus. She could enjoy herself with a handsome decatur, if she wanted. Pyke would be upset, but it would only be offended pride, and he'd get over it. Alister would be fun, she had no doubt, and she also expected he'd accept an to the affair quietly and kindly.

She closed her eyes, shaking her head. Is that all she wanted?

The announcement of dinner saved her from having to make any difficult decisions.

She was seated at the long table between Caster Octavus and another senior decatur, across from Viera, and she hardly had time to think as the dinner conversation buzzed around her. Cassi had been right—she couldn't imagine doing anything more than nibbling at the meal while she was locked into her corset, even if she hadn't been terrified of spilling something on her dress. But nobody seemed to notice that she wasn't touching the dishes that were served in a dizzying array. The conversation whirled around her at an alarming pace, and although Taya did her best to keep up, more often than not it dealt with subjects like paintings and novels and operas that she'd never had the time or the money to enjoy. She fell silent, listening and marveling over how little she knew about the world.

Flight, languages, armature repair, geography, cartography—she knew about those subjects. She knew which gesture would offend a Cabiel merchant but amuse a Demican child, and how to tell when a storm was approaching, and where the most popular assignation house in the city was located. But none of those topics would serve her here.

"Taya, what is it like, soaring over Ondinium Mountain?" Viera asked, catching her eye. "Is it true that icarii have flown through clouds?"

"Have you ever seen any of the Lady's spirits up there flying with you?" asked another guest, laughing.

Taya smiled gratefully at Viera as she replied. When the talk veered to the next subject, she relaxed, glad that she'd been able to say something interesting, at least.

Alister caught up with her after dinner as the guests left the table.

"I'm here to claim the first dance," he said, sliding his arm under hers.

"Is that proper?" she asked, suddenly breathless.

"Who cares?" He pulled her closer, tucking her arm under his as they walked. His silk robe was soft and cool against her bare flesh. Taya forced herself to exhale. "You look beautiful, little bird. I've changed my mind about the flight suit. It doesn't do your figure justice at all."

"You look very nice, too," Taya said, taking the opportunity to gaze at him again. "That green suits you."

"I'm afraid that next to you I'm going to make people think of a tree, but I'll have to live with it. I should have chosen to wear sky blue, instead."

"Are exalted dances the same as other caste dances?" she asked as they entered the ballroom. The musicians were playing. The rest of the evening's guests were trickling into the room, their faces flushed from the chill night air.

"Much worse," Alister confided. "They're very stately and slow. It's difficult to develop a graceful carriage when one is accustomed to being weighed down by ten pounds of gold and silk."

"Shouldn't you be that much lighter on your feet once you're free of your public robes, then?"

He smiled down at her.

"I'm afraid you're too optimistic. Do icarii dance in the air, Taya? Do you carry out secret winged ballets over the mountains when no other castes are watching?"

"Uh-oh. Somebody's been telling you our secrets."

His green eyes widened in playful surprise. "May I watch, someday? Will you take me dancing in the air with you?"

"Maybe." She turned away, amused by his persistence. Sometimes groups of icarii would fly out with extra ondium counterweights on their harnesses and engage in aerial acrobatics that were impossible in a normal rig. It was a dangerous sport, since their lighter weights made them more vulnerable to sudden gusts of wind, but every young icarus did it at least once. Taya was considered one of the better skydancers.

Too bad she didn't have a set of dancing wings here.

"The music's starting." Alister released her and bowed. "May I?"

She took another deep breath and held out her hand. He took it and pulled her out onto the dance floor.

He had exaggerated, of course. As far as Taya could tell, exalteds danced just as well as anyone else, and the steps weren't very different from those in the dances at icarus parties or her sister's famulate wedding. After the first few minutes, Taya relaxed and stopped thinking about what she was doing, letting Alister sweep her across the floor. The hand holding hers was very proper, but the thumb of his other hand stroked the feathers on her waist as he deftly guided her through the dance.

Lady, it would be easy to fall for him, Taya thought, as he pulled her closer a moment to sweep past another couple. *It would be just like a story, an exalted and an icarus loving across caste.*

Just don't forget how those stories always end up, she reminded herself. *It never works out well for the icarus. Alister Forlore is a charming flirt. Don't lose your heart to him, and you'll be fine.*

"What's wrong?" Alister asked. His grip tightened. "You looked very stern all of the sudden."

"Nothing," she said, becoming aware of the scent he was wearing. It reminded her of the spice markets of the foreigners' quarter, exotic but appealing. "Just . . . a thought."

"Are you worried about my brother?"

"Huh?"

"He's staring at you." Alister swung her around. For a moment Taya caught a glimpse of a dark figure in the middle of all the extravagantly dressed exalts, and then they turned again and he was gone.

"You said he never came to parties!"

Alister chuckled. "I believe you've made another conquest, Taya Swan."

"I doubt that! Although I'd like to talk to him."

"After this dance," he promised, pulling her closer again. "Right now you're mine."

She couldn't help glancing over his shoulder, seeking out Cristof's slim, severe figure every time they turned. Why was he here? To celebrate Viera's survival?

She hoped so, for the family's sake.

After the dance Alister waved off the other men who tried to break in.

"Back, back. The lady will dance with you as soon as she's had some refreshment," he scolded them. "Give the guest of honor a chance to rest."

He steered her toward Cristof, who was holding a glass of wine and regarding them gravely. *He really does look like a crow in a flock of fancy songbirds,* Taya thought, remembering Gwen's characterization. His somber clothes and sharp-featured face made the comparison even more apt. Anywhere else in Ondinium, she might have thought that he looked striking. Up here he just looked out of place.

Maybe as out of place as me, she admitted to herself as they approached.

"Why, Cris, what a delight to see you at a party at last," Alister said with mock surprise as they drew up to each other. "I noticed that you were staring at Taya while we were dancing. Could it be that my big brother's mind is finally turning to something other than clockwork?"

Cristof scowled, looking away. "I was studying the architecture of her dress."

"Architecture? Is that what they call them down on Tertius?" Alister teased.

Color rose in Cristof's cheeks.

"I was trying to figure out how the dress was fastened," he elaborated, with stilted dignity. "Dressmaking is as much a feat of engineering as bridge-building. More so. A bridge doesn't need to be comfortable."

"My dress isn't exactly fastened," Taya admitted. "It was sewn on."

Cristof choked in mid-swallow and set his glass down. Alister roared with laughter, making heads turn.

"Oh, Lady save us! That leads to all sorts of interesting lines of speculation, doesn't it?" He grinned at his older brother. "Are you all right, Cris?"

"I'm fine," Cristof said in a strangled voice. "Excuse me."

Alister watched him go, then turned and swooped Taya up and kissed her on the cheek.

"What was that for?" she gasped, holding on to his arms as he swung her around and set her back down again. His eyes danced.

"That was for flustering my brother. I don't get the opportunity to see his gears slip nearly often enough."

Taya shook her head with mild disapproval, but she didn't try to break away from his grip as he held her. Instead, she leaned on his arm and searched the crowd for Cristof.

She spotted him at once, because he was so tall and dark. He was still coughing into his handkerchief, and light gleamed off his wire-rimmed spectacles. She remembered how carefully he'd held Alister's toy bird and how he'd given her half of his poor lunch. Suddenly she felt sorry for him.

"Don't make fun of him, Alister. It's not nice."

"Nonsense. I'm only teasing. Cris takes everything so seriously. Sometimes I think his heart is nothing but springs and gears. I'd be the first to approve if he ever got his mind off his machines and started thinking about something as healthy as a pretty woman."

Taya sighed. As she was about to turn away, a footman approached and murmured something to the clockwright. Cristof's shoulders tightened, and he strode toward the ballroom door.

"I don't know," she said, troubled. "I have a feeling he thinks about a lot that doesn't have to do with machines."

"You believe the best of everyone, don't you? Now, tell me, was *that* what you wanted to say to him? That your dress was sewn on? I presume it will have to be dismantled before it's removed." Alister stroked the feathers over her shoulder and down her back. "What lucky soul will have that privilege tonight, Taya Swan? I hope your dressmaker was female."

She moved away before his finger could descend too far. "He's not, but he thinks I'm too boyish to be attractive."

"Only a madman would call you boyish."

Taya smiled, glad to hear it, even if it was blatant flattery. "Will you excuse me? I need to . . . check my hair."

"Of course. Over there." He pointed the way and she slipped away.

The foyer was empty of guests, although the candles and endless rows of reflecting mirrors made the room seem crowded as soon as she walked into it. The front door was open. Taya glanced at the door to the ladies' parlor, then turned and stepped outside. She didn't really need to relieve herself. She just needed a moment of solitude, before Alister's flirting could get any more suggestive.

The stone walls and iron gate blocked the light from the street, but the mansion's broad front porch was lined with small lanterns that provided a festive air. Taya shivered in the cold air and took a deep breath, leaning against the low porch rail. Tension uncoiled from her back and shoulders, and she realized how uneasy she'd been inside, despite Alister's charming company.

Or maybe because of it.

She looked up, hoping to see an icarus silhouetted against the stars or moon, but the night sky was empty.

This isn't me, she thought, looking up at the stars with a touch of regret. *I'm not meant to wear elegant dresses and flirt with handsome exalteds. The Lady forged me to wear leather and ondium and ride the wind.*

There was nothing to stop her from enjoying herself with Alister Forlore. Nothing but her own vague sense of unease. *Maybe it's because he outranks me*, she thought, testing the idea. Despite what Cristof had said, icarii didn't really stand outside of the caste hierarchy. Not as long as exalteds ran the city and owned their wings.

Perhaps she *should* borrow a pair of wings and take Alister into the air. Caste differences wouldn't matter once she was in her own element.

Or maybe I'm just getting too old for casual affairs. She'd never been as carefree as Cassi and so many of the rest of her peers. That's why she hadn't been able to sleep with Pyke. He'd been kind enough, but it hadn't seemed worth the effort of starting something that was doomed from the start.

". . . got them from Pins," someone murmured. Taya looked toward the voice and saw three men standing in the garden shadows, next to a small marble bench. Faint lamplight reflected from a small metal packet that changed hands. The man who took it shoved it into his jacket, and Taya bit her lip as she saw the silver circles around his eyes.

"You shouldn't have come. You could comp—" Cristof halted as one of the men looked up at Taya and made a warning noise.

"Excuse me," she apologized, stepping back from the rail. "I—I was just getting some fresh air. I didn't know anyone was out here."

"You see?" Cristof asked his companions, in a low, annoyed voice. He shook his head, waving the other two men aside. Taya caught a glimpse of their faces as they backed off. No masks. They weren't exalteds, then, but somebody lower-caste. It was too dark to discern their castemarks.

Cristof looked up at her. "Wait a moment, if you please, Taya Icarus."

"I'm sorry. It's cold," Taya said, feeling nervous. "I'd better get back inside." She caught a glimpse of his frown and turned, hurrying back to the safety of the house.

What was that? she thought in a panic, torn between fleeing to the sanctuary of the ladies' parlor and seeking the safety of Alister's company. *What did I just see?* The packet—it had looked like a stack of metal punch cards, the kind used to program analytical engines.

Like the engines that ran the wireferries. Or that switched refinery furnaces on and off at specific hours.

Chapter Seven

Taya smiled graciously, if somewhat absently, at the young exalted who escorted her off the ballroom floor. Her eyes searched the crowds, hunting for Cristof's angular face. She'd flung herself back into the dancing as soon as she'd re-entered the ballroom, using her partners to protect herself. During the first two dances she'd spotted Cristof watching her from the sidelines. Then he'd vanished, and now she felt safe enough to plead exhaustion.

Alister appeared at her side as she sank into a chair, her feathers rustling. The decatur held a glass of wine in one bejeweled hand.

"Allow me," he said to her partner, handing her the glass. The younger man bowed to him, then to Taya, and took his leave.

"You didn't need to shoo him off."

"If he surrenders you that easily, he doesn't deserve your company," Alister said, dismissing her concern. "I've been waiting for a chance to reclaim you."

"I'm glad you're here." She looked up. "Would you mind if I asked you a strange question?"

"Of course not." He looked intrigued. "What is it?"

"Have you ever heard of someone called Pins?"

Alister's pleasant expression vanished, and his gaze became intent.

"Yes. Why?"

"Just a conversation I overheard . . . in passing." She craned her neck, studying him. He didn't look happy. "Who is he?"

"She. She's a fence and a suspected smuggler. The Council keeps its eyes on her, but she's also a very clever woman, and so far she's avoided arrest." Alister touched one of the feathers in her hair. "You don't know her, do you? Have you ever carried any messages for her?"

"No, it's nothing like that." Taya gazed into her wine. This wasn't the reassuring answer she'd been hoping for. "You don't suppose she'd be involved in terrorism, do you? Like . . . the wireferry accident? Or the refinery explosion?"

He was silent. She glanced up. His face had grown even more still.

"Do you have any reason to suspect her of terrorism, Taya?"

"No! No, I don't. I was just wondering. I saw something strange, and I heard her name, and . . . well, a lictor asked me to keep my eyes open for anything suspicious, and Viera is worried about her husband, so of course now I'm reading sinister undertones into everything I hear." She forced a laugh.

"Maybe." He leaned over, putting a hand on her shoulder. His fingers combed through the feathers, caressing her bare skin and sending tingles down her back. "But if you know anything that could help the Council keep Ondinium safe, you should tell me. I'm in better position to order an investigation than a lictor or Viera."

"I don't know anything yet." She looked away, then took a sip of her wine as an excuse to avoid his eyes.

Viera joined them, gold gleaming in her hair and on her fingers. Alister's hand slid away from Taya's shoulder.

"Taya! How are you? You look tired."

"I am, a little," Taya admitted. "I don't usually stay up this late."

Alister slipped his ornate watch from his sleeve and glanced at it. "Why, it's only after midnight."

"After midnight!" Taya felt the urge to yawn. "No wonder I'm tired! I'm usually in bed by ten."

"I refuse to believe you're serious. The evening has only begun."

"Not when you have the morning flight shift," Taya countered. "In fact, Exalted Octavus, if you'll forgive me, I should be heading home now."

"Of course," Viera said. "I shall tell the servants to bring around a carriage for you."

"I would be happy to take her back in mine," Alister offered. "I should be heading home, myself. I'm supposed to inspect a new engine prototype tomorrow, and they want me down at the University by nine." He pretended to shudder, smiling at Taya. "A Ladyforsaken hour, indeed."

Ride home with Alister? Taya felt a surge of temptation. "I wouldn't want to inconvenience you," she said shakily. "The eyries would be out of your way . . . ."

"I know Cliff Road. It's not that far out of my way," Alister said, the smile still hovering around his lips. "And this will be my last chance to see my swan queen. After tonight, you will transform yourself back into a metal-winged hawk."

"Al, hush," Viera scolded him. "Taya must consider propriety. What sort of impression would it make if she returned home in your carriage?"

"Oh." Alister paused, and Taya thought he seemed taken aback. "But, Viera, surely an icarus . . . ."

"Should be treated with as much respect as any other guest I might invite to dinner," Viera said, her voice stern.

"Of course. I didn't mean any offense," he said, turning to Taya. "I simply hoped to enjoy your company a little longer."

Taya looked from him to Viera. The chance to spend more time with Alister, alone in a carriage, both tempted and frightened her. She was afraid it would be all too easy to forget her good intentions if she were alone with him in the dark.

"I'll do whatever you think is best," she said to her hostess. "I don't know anything about propriety. I'm used to flying myself home."

Both of the exalteds laughed, and Viera took her hand, pulling her up from the chair.

"It would be best if you went home alone," she said, kindly. "My cousin is a gentleman, but he isn't as careful of reputations as he should be."

"I'm very careful of reputations," Alister protested. "I'm a decatur. I have to be!"

"You're careful with your own reputation, perhaps." Viera raised an eyebrow. "Now say your goodbyes while I send for a carriage." She squeezed Taya's hand and strode off.

Alister watched her leave.

"Dear Vee. She's so protective. I suspect I owe my position on the Council to her," he murmured. "I'm certain she made Caster vote for me."

"Wouldn't he have voted for you anyway?"

"Perhaps." He turned and hooked his arm through hers. "May I escort you to the door this time, my swan?"

"I'd like that," she said, smiling up at him. She was glad Viera had told her to take another carriage. She could flirt now without worrying about where it would lead later.

"One thing, Taya Swan," Alister said, as they reached the foyer. She paused. He looked serious. "Please leave the investigating to the lictors. I would be devastated if you were hurt."

She gazed up at his face, touched by his concern. But what if he were the one hurt? If Cristof was involved in something illegal, Alister's position on the Council could be in danger.

"Taya Icarus." Caster Octavus stepped into the foyer. "Viera has informed me that you are taking your leave of us."

Taya shifted mental gears with an effort, turning and bowing, her palm on her forehead.

"I apologize for leaving so soon, exalted, but we icarii need to get off to an early start in the morning."

"I understand. Thank you very much for joining us, and thank you again for your brave rescue." He clasped her hand. "The Octavus family owes you a debt, and it will not be forgotten."

"I consider the debt repaid," she protested. "Tonight has been . . . well, I never imagined being invited to something like this."

"Don't be ridiculous. Tonight simply makes public our gratitude to you."

Taya studied him, her hand still in his. The white-haired decatur looked serious. This wasn't casual good manners, she realized. Exalted Octavus was making her a promise.

She slipped her hand from his and pressed her palm against her forehead again, bowing more deeply this time.

"Thank you, exalted."

To her surprise, when she straightened, he returned the bow.

"Fly safely, icarus."

"Yes, but not tonight," Viera added, as she entered the foyer. "Our carriage is waiting outside." A servant followed, holding Taya's borrowed velvet cloak and a heavy fur. "A cloak of feathers might be more appropriate, but it wouldn't be nearly as practical. Here, I'm giving this to you. I hope it will keep you warm this winter and for many winters to come." She handed Taya the fur cloak.

Taya's fingers sank into the thick beaver pelts, each one worth a month of her salary. She opened her mouth to protest, then closed it again when she saw Viera's expression.

"Allow me." Alister took it and wrapped it around her shoulders. The inside was lined with soft doeskin, warm against her flesh. He regarded her with mock criticism. "I approve of the brown against her hair, cousin, but fur doesn't flatter her dress. Now she looks more like a Demican chieftain than a swan queen."

Taya ignored him, running her hands over the fur. It probably *had* come from Demicus, she thought, overwhelmed.

"It's gorgeous. I don't know where I'll be able to wear it."

"You should wear it to the market and anywhere else you may need to go this winter," Viera said, practically. She reached forward and fastened the neck. Taya looked down and saw that the gold clasp had the Octavus sigil worked into it. "Good night, Taya Icarus. Fly safely."

"Good night, exalteds," Taya said again, draping her velvet cloak over her arms. The fur was heavy on her shoulders, but it was a solid, comforting weight.

They walked her out to the carriage and waved as she was driven away. Taya watched until the lights of Estate Octavus vanished around a corner, then let the window curtain fall and pulled her new cloak around her.

Pins, she mused, staring into the darkness. *Tomorrow I'm going to find Pins and see if I can track down the Torn Cards. For the Octavuses . . . and for Alister.*

"PINS?" Pyke set down *The Watchman* and narrowed his eyes. "Why?"

"Someone at the party bought something from her, and I want to find out what," Taya explained, warming her fingers on her second cup of tea. Cassi had made her stay awake to talk about the party for another hour after she'd gotten home, so she was working on only five hours of sleep and relying on the bitter drink to keep her eyes open. "Come on. You know her, don't you? I can tell."

"Yeah. She attends the same Inquiry and Liberation meetings I go to." Pyke still sounded suspicious.

"Spirits, Pyke. I can't believe the Council hasn't thrown you out of the eyrie yet," Cassi exclaimed, spreading jam over her breakfast roll. "Isn't I&L some kind of reactionary group?"

"You don't know anything about politics, do you?" Pyke looked disgusted. "It's a free-trade group. Did you know Ondinium levies a ten-percent import tax on spices from Si'sier, but when we send—"

"Pyke. Please. Don't." Cassi waved a hand at him. "I don't care. You know, you'd be a lot more fun if you took up a real hobby, like darts."

"You like men who play darts?" Pyke asked, dubiously.

"It was just an example. Although I'm pretty good at darts."

"Hello? Pins?" Taya waved a hand between them. "Please, Pyke, just give me an address. I'm not going to cause her any trouble."

"How can I be sure? You're hobnobbing with exalteds and decaturs now. Maybe they're turning you into their spy."

Taya rubbed her forehead.

"More like the opposite. They said she was dangerous and I should stay away from her. Look, I just want to ask a couple of questions, that's all. Then I'm gone. I won't tell anyone I saw her, and I won't tell her how I got her address."

"Dangerous?" Pyke rubbed his chin. "I didn't know she was dangerous."

"Pyke!"

"Taya, just go to Dispatch and look her up," Cassi advised. "It'll be faster than trying to get an answer out of tall, dark, and paranoid here."

"I'm not paranoid, I'm just cautious." Pyke frowned. "It's not a secret, I guess. She owns a copperwares shop on Operand and Cascade. There's a big beaten-copper basin in the front window. You can't miss it."

"Thanks." Taya finished her tea and stood. "Well, off to work. You two coming?"

At the dock, she and Cassi pulled on their flight leathers and strapped themselves into their rigs. When they were ready, they joined the line at the dispatch office to punch in. Taya dropped off a thank-you note to be delivered to Estate Octavus.

"Nice of you two to join us today," the dispatcher said dryly as they hung their time cards back on the rack. "All finished playing dress-up?"

"Better be polite," Cassi warned him. "Taya has friends in high places."

"Yeah, I get a nosebleed just looking at her." The dispatcher handed them their morning's delivery satchels. "Fly safely, ladies. It's cold and clear, but the *diispira* will be kicking up again this morning, so mind your tailsets."

"We will." Taya picked up the bag and began looking through it as she and Cassi left the warm office and joined the line at the icarus flight docks. The docks were long wood and iron strips that extended far out beyond the cliffs and provided clean drops down into the wind.

Morning breezes tugged at their wings, and sunlight turned the jagged mountain peaks around them a warm

gold. To the left, a group of seven- and eight-year-old
children were doing warm-up exercises, their training
wings giving their jumping jacks a little extra lift. Taya
thought of Ariq and grinned.

"I've got deliveries all over Secundus," Cassi said,
buttoning her bag closed again and hooking it to her belt.
"How about you?"

Taya glanced back down at the addresses once more.

"Some back-and-forth on Tertius. Shouldn't take too
long."

"Lunch?"

"Maybe. But if I'm not here by half-past, I probably got
caught up in other business."

"Business like a handsome decatur?" Cassi teased. Taya
laughed.

"I'm not planning on it, but who knows?"

Their names were called. Cassi waved. "Fly safely!"

"You, too!"

Flying in autumn and winter was a chilly endeavor, but
the blanket of smoke and soot that hung over Ondinium
always thinned out in the cooler weather. The air over
Tertius was never entirely clear, but today Taya could see
the rest of the city as she wove between towers and factory
smokestacks, delivering messages. Once she flew over the
street where Cristof's shop was located. She circled, but its
door was closed. She flew on.

By nine she'd finished her deliveries. In theory she was
supposed to head back up to the dispatch office to pick
up another bag, but instead she flew to the metal wares
markets in Secundus and landed on Cascade Street, locking
her wings upright.

Pins' shop was easy to find, but its door had been sealed
shut with black wax and a lictor's printed 'no trespassing'
order.

She stared, feeling a chill that had nothing to do with the
autumn morning. Then she turned.

A heavyset man across the street was wiping the soot
off his window and watching her in its reflection. He

nodded when he saw her looking at him. He had the same black circle castemark as her father, marking him as a craftsman.

"If you've a message to deliver, you'll have to take it to the lictors," he called out.

"Is that Pins' shop?" She crossed the street.

"Yup. Her daughter found her dead this morning, didn't she? Came in to open up and started screaming." The man leaned against his doorframe. "I sent my boy off to the lictors as soon as I figured out what was going on. Murdered, that's what they say."

Taya folded her arms over her chest, the chill returning.

"When?"

"Last night. Guess I would've been the last one to have seen her, then." He sounded proud of the fact. "She waved good night when I locked up around six. Must've been working late. I waved back and went inside. She was killed sometime after that."

She hated to ask, but she had to know.

"How did she die?"

"Strangled. With something thin, that's what the lictors said. I overheard 'em when I was giving my statement, didn't I?"

Taya thought of the men who'd mentioned Pins' name the night before. They'd been strong, rough-looking types. She didn't have any trouble imagining one of them strangling a woman.

But that would mean that Cristof was involved in murder. Maybe not directly, but . . .

Had he come to his cousin's party to give himself an alibi?

"So, if you've any message for her, you've got to take it to the lictor's station on Teague," the craftsman pointed out again.

"All right. Thank you." Taya turned and began walking toward Teague Street, her shoulders hunched.

Now she didn't just have a suspicion. Now she had a chain of coincidence. Cristof had gotten something from

Pins, Taya had overheard Pins' name, and Pins had been murdered. To stop her from talking to Taya?

She rubbed her gloved hands over her cheeks, reviewing her options. By rights she should go straight to the lictors to tell them what she'd heard. Lt. Amcathra would listen to her.

But if she talked to Amcathra, he'd go to Cristof for answers, and the ripples from that inquiry would inevitably reach Alister. Taya grimaced. If his brother were a murderer, Alister was going to be involved one way or the other. But if she told him first, he'd have a chance to control the damage to his family name.

Besides, she rationalized, *he's a decatur. He outranks the lictors.*

She found an open side street, spread her wings, and began to run.

"COME IN!"

Taya opened the door. Alister sat at the table in the center of the room, his repaired clock and a stack of books shoved to one side as he pored over a stack of papers. His exalted's mask was propped against a leg of the table.

He smiled when he saw her and pushed his chair back.

"As I predicted, my swan has become a hawk again. Good morning, Taya. Have you come to me with a pair of wings, so we can go skydancing together?"

"I have news," she said, ignoring his teasing. "Pins was murdered last night."

He stopped, his smile fading. Taya took another step inside, then remembered herself and bowed, palm on forehead. They weren't at a party anymore. This was business.

"You went to visit her? After I told you she was dangerous?"

"I had to. I know you didn't want me to, but I had to know how she was involved." Taya looked up at him. "She's dead. Somebody killed her last night."

Alister sat back down.

"Tell me everything you know."

Taya filled him in on the neighboring shopkeeper's gossip. Alister shook his head, his green eyes dark with concern. When he looked like that, serious instead of dazzling, she could see a closer resemblance between him and his brother. Both of them were intense, focused people. The difference was that Alister used his intensity to charm, while his brother used it to repel.

"So," she finished, "I decided to tell you. You said the Council had been keeping its eyes on her."

"Yes. We suspected her of being in alliance with the Torn Cards. You know what the Cards believe in, don't you?"

"They're anti-Engine terrorists. They think programs are infringing on our freedoms."

"Yes." He looked down at the papers in front of him. "I have read the report on the wireferry accident. A torn copper punch card was found jammed in a weld. That's their sign."

"Do you think they were after the decatur, or your cousin?"

"Caster, almost certainly. It was just an accident that Viera and Ariq were in the car instead of him."

"But why would the Torn Cards hate him?"

Alister sighed.

"There is an important vote coming up soon. Caster was initially against it, but he changed his mind. And he has a great deal of influence over other decaturs. Perhaps the Torn Cards learned about it."

"What kind of vote?"

"I don't know if I can tell you."

Taya bit her lip, reminded again of the difference between their castes. Alister looked up at her, and his expression softened.

"I apologize. It's just that this has been a controversial topic. It's an experimental program, and we don't want the newspapers getting wind of it until we have had a chance to give it a trial run. That is, assuming it gets approved by Council."

"Is it one of those thinking programs you were talking about?"

"Well . . . it does analyze behavioral patterns. I suppose I can tell you, Taya. You *are* an icarus and accustomed to dealing with secrets . . . but this is confidential. The Council doesn't want any information getting out until we are certain the program will work. Although if the Torn Cards already know about it . . . ."

"You can trust me," she asserted. "I'm an icarus."

"I asked you not to get involved with Pins, but you went down to meet her, anyway."

"That wasn't a secret. And besides, you didn't ask me," she objected. "You warned me."

His lips quirked up in a shadow of his usual smile.

"I should have known a hunting hawk would pay no attention to my warnings."

"So," Taya said, "what's this vote about?"

The smile faded again as Alister leaned back in his chair. "I've written a program called Clockwork Heart. It's meant to help people determine whether or not someone's going to be a good match for them. Romantically, at first, although I think it has applications in business and politics, as well."

"Romantically?" Taya wrinkled her nose. "You mean, it's going to tell us who we can marry?"

"No! No, I have no intention of taking away anybody's freedom of choice," Alister said hastily. "But let's assume you've fallen in love with someone. You'll both take a survey and we'll run your response cards through Clockwork Heart. The program compares your responses to one hundred key variables I've isolated from a multivariate analysis of a thousand successful marriages and a thousand unsuccessful ones. It then builds a series of statistical models according to the predictive parameters we've developed and calculates the likelihood of a stable marriage between the two of you under various hypothetical socioeconomic conditions. The greater the number of conditions under which your marriage is predicted to remain intact, the higher the confidence level that you're making the right choice."

Taya blinked, a little overwhelmed by his explanation.

"Well, I can see why the Torn Cards might object, since they hate machines, but why does the Council care about marriages?"

"Because stable marriages are integral to a stable society." Alister stood and began to pace. "The Great Engine has made Ondinium the most civilized nation in the world. Every citizen is matched to a job well-suited to his personality and skills, and our factories are fast, safe, and efficient. We can calculate resource supply and demand and make reasonable predictions to avoid shortages and avoid excesses. Now, why shouldn't we apply the same successful formulae to personal relationships? I don't want to take the excitement out of romance, but I do want to prevent truly disastrous marriages, the marriages in which wives and babies are abandoned, or beaten . . . or killed. If Clockwork Heart can prevent even one abusive marriage, then all the time I've put into it will be worthwhile."

Taya stared. She'd never seen Alister so worked up before. Maybe he wasn't all good looks and flirtation, after all.

"How will you know if it works?"

He took a deep breath.

"It won't be easy. So far we've only run simulations based on past cases. What we intend to do next, if the Council approves the experiment, is start a volunteer program. We'll run the couples' cards and monitor their relationships for a year or two. Then we will compare the experiment's successes or failures to those of a control group; couples that don't get any advice from the Engine. If we find a statistically significant difference between the two groups that proves the program's advice is having a positive effect on marriage outcomes, then we can begin to fine-tune the models. Clockwork Heart runs very slowly right now, but eventually, especially if the new prototype engine works out, we may be able to process a couple's data in just a few hours."

Taya shook her head.

"What if the Engine tells you a marriage won't work out, but that's really the person the Lady meant you to be with?"

Alister laughed, relaxing.

"Mere mortals can't defy the Lady of the Forge. If a marriage is meant to be, it'll come about, regardless of Clockwork Heart's computational robustness. People can always choose to ignore the program's findings, if they prefer."

"Do you really think it'll work?"

"Yes." He met her eyes, his chin jutting forward with determination. "I do. I've written the best program I can, I've tested it every way I can think of, and I believe it will make a difference. It still needs development, but if the Council gives me a chance, in our own lifetime we could see broken hearts and bad marriages become all but nonexistent."

Taya nodded, although she couldn't help harboring reservations. How could a machine possibly predict the vagaries of the human heart?

"Anyway," Alister said, leaning against the table, "you understand why it's causing so much debate. Clockwork Heart is a complicated, time-consuming program to run, and it's going to take a long time before the city sees any benefits from it. A number of decaturs aren't convinced it's important enough to pursue. Caster felt that way at first, but I showed him the data I've collected on the long-term economic impact of broken marriages and abandoned children, and he finally changed his mind. The simple fact is, strong marriages lead to strong societies. Caster agreed to approve the experiment and review our data after a year."

"So you think the Torn Cards found out he'd changed his mind?"

"It's possible. They wouldn't like this program. They don't like anything the Great Engine does." Alister sounded scornful. "If they thought Caster was slipping away from their agenda, they might have tried to kill him to keep the other decaturs from following his lead."

"But how would they know that Exalted Octavus decided to change his vote?"

"That's a good question." Alister shook his head. "I don't know how many people he has talked to about this."

"He'd only tell another decatur, right?"

"Any of his clerks might know, or a guard may have over-heard him talking about the vote. If he has discussed it with Viera, his house servants might know. I'm not trying to blame terrorism on the lower castes, but it doesn't make any sense for an exalted to work with the Torn Cards. We were born into this caste to protect Ondinium, not destroy it. And destroying the Great Engine is tantamount to destroying the city."

"But what if . . ." Taya faltered.

"What if?" he urged, after a moment.

"Last night, at the party, I heard some men talking, and they mentioned Pins. They were talking to an exalted."

Alister fixed his gaze on her.

"Who?"

"I didn't want to say anything, because I didn't know if something bad was going on." She felt miserable. "But now that Pins is dead . . . maybe one of the men I saw killed her. I don't know. I could be wrong. But I have to report my suspicions, don't I?"

"Yes. I think you do. Tell me, Taya, and I promise I will conduct a quiet investigation and keep your name out of it. Nothing will come back to haunt you if you've made a mistake."

"I hope I'm wrong. Really, I do." She took a deep breath and steeled herself. "Because they were talking to your brother."

"Cris?"

"He sounded like he was in charge." She didn't want to mention the night the refinery had blown up or the wireferry map she'd found in Cristof's shop. She'd had her suspicions then, but Cristof had explained everything. But this . . . Pins was dead. She'd witnessed Cristof receiving the package and heard him mention Pins' name. This was something she *couldn't* keep to herself.

She described exactly what she'd seen and heard at the dance.

"I'm sorry," she finished, feeling terrible. "Maybe it's just coincidence."

Alister stood still, his handsome face as blank as the mask on the floor.

"I didn't think it would be my brother."

"I don't know if it was! It might be a coincidence. He's probably got a good explanation for everything."

Another moment of silence stretched between them. Alister's blank expression transformed to amazement.

"I knew he was angry when he left, but I didn't think he would do anything this rash. Clock repair made sense. But to spend years pretending to be something he isn't . . . ."

"You think he's involved, then?"

Alister seemed to shake himself. "No. No. I don't think he is. I'm going to talk to him. He's family, Taya. Our parents are dead, and we're all we have left. It must be a misunderstanding. Or perhaps he doesn't realize what's he's gotten himself into. Cris can become so focused on his work that he doesn't notice what other people are doing around him. He could be an innocent dupe. And if he's not innocent . . ." Alister looked away, gazing at the clock on his table. "Then I'll tell the lictors. And, Taya—"

"What?"

"Stay away from him." Alister met her eyes. "He knows you overheard him last night. If he's involved with the Torn Cards, then you could be in danger. I don't want you to get hurt. That's one thing I'd never forgive him for."

Taya felt guilty for the warm feeling that filled her.

"I'll avoid him," she promised.

"Good." He pushed himself away from the table and took her hand. For a change, his fingers were cold, and she thought she felt them trembling. "Thank you for telling me, and thank you for letting me deal with this myself. Cris and I have our differences, but he means a great deal to me." He paused. "As do you."

The warm feeling intensified. Taya started to take a step back, to try to defuse the moment, but Alister wouldn't release her.

"Why do you keep backing away from me?" he asked, holding her hand captive.

She swallowed.

"You're an exalted," she said, unsteadily. "We're . . ." She gestured around them with her free hand, trying to indicate the office, the whole situation.

"I know things are confusing right now. But they won't always be like this." He moved closer, pulling her in. All at once her flight leathers felt too constricting, the harness straps too tight. Her heart hammered and she laid her free hand flat on his chest, meaning to hold him away. For a moment she faltered, feeling the hardness beneath his robes. Then she mustered her thoughts and pushed, stepping backward again.

"Not now," she said, struggling to maintain her dignity. "You're upset."

"Yes, I am," Alister agreed, releasing her. "So?"

Taya squared her shoulders. "It just—it doesn't feel right. I might be getting your brother into trouble. You should be angry at me!"

"I'm not. I'm grateful for your warning." The decatur studied her. Taya flattered herself that he looked disappointed that she'd pushed him away. She certainly was.

But she also knew she was right. To share a first kiss, now, after that kind of news—she didn't want the moment to be tainted by anything bad that might happen afterward.

"Talk to Cristof first," she pleaded.

Alister sighed, turning and looking out the window again. "Perhaps that's wisest, under the circumstances."

"Thank you." She felt a pang of regret as she gazed at his strong profile and watched the morning light gleam in the jewels and gold that caught back his long hair and brightened his neck and hands. The wave tattoo was dark against his cheek. A muscle there tightened as he stood, lost in his own thoughts.

"I wish you had brought me a pair of wings, instead of this news."

"I'm sorry." Taya took another step backward. "Will you send me a message when you know more?"

"Yes." He paused. "Fly safely, Taya Swan."

"I will. You be careful, too, exalted." She bowed and took her leave.

Chapter Eight

She hadn't lied, and she wasn't breaking her promise. She *was* going to avoid Cristof.

Just not his shop.

She picked up another set of messages from Dispatch, on her way down, and spent an hour and a half delivering them. Once they were gone, she flew to Gryngoth Plaza and landed by the statue, then hurried to Jayce's dressmaking shop.

Cassi's nephew allowed her to store her wings in his shop, but it took her half an hour to get away from his interrogation about the party. At last she promised to tell him everything over lunch later that week and grabbed another cloak to cover her flight leathers.

"That's two you've borrowed," Jayce pointed out as she left.

"I'll bring them both back tomorrow," she promised. "Really. And the dress, too."

"It's intact?" he asked, disappointed.

"Well, it was close," she admitted. "Or it might have been. But Viera Octavus was looking out for my virtue."

"Damn," Jayce muttered, waving her off as he turned back to his dressmaker's model. "Try harder next time."

She made a face at him and left, thinking ruefully about her almost-kiss. *Next time, I won't pull away*, she promised herself, heading down to Tertius.

When she reached the marketplace, she pulled the cloak's hood up to cover her face and hair. An "Open" sign hung on the front of Cristof's shop, but the door was closed against the autumn chill and the sooty air. Taya settled in to wait, crouching in an alley across the street.

I'll stay for an hour, she promised herself. *Then I'll report back to the dispatch office. And I'll work an extra hour this evening, to make up for all this lost time.*

Half an hour later, a man descended into Cristof's shop. Taya couldn't get a glimpse of his face, but shortly after his arrival Cristof left with him, pulling on his coat and, characteristically, frowning.

Taya waited until they were around the corner before she scurried down to the shop door.

The quality of locks in Tertius hadn't improved since she'd been a little girl. The loose frame wiggled under her hand, and with some ruthless jabbing with her utility knife, she managed to jimmy the locks and yank the door open. Cristof would notice, but this was Tertius. Break-ins happened all the time.

The dimly lit shop was still filled with whirring and clicking. Taya went straight to Cristof's desk, searching his papers.

Diagrams for clockwork mechanisms abounded, but none of them looked like a bomb to her untrained eye. She searched through the drawers, not sure what she was looking for. A torn punch card, maybe, or a half-constructed bomb. Instead, she found tools and broken clockwork.

Nothing. She turned to his filing cabinet. Bills, receipts, work orders. Cristof's filing system was as orderly as his brother's was chaotic. Even his handwriting was neat, each letter tiny and precise. He'd been telling the truth about getting most of his commissions from Secundus and Primus, she noticed.

She stepped through the curtains into his living quarters. Shelves of books; a wardrobe; a small, neatly made bed; an icon of Our Lady of the Forge on whitewashed walls. The room was monastic in its simplicity.

She opened the wardrobe and grimaced. Black, black, and black. And Cassi thought Taya's wardrobe was limited. Cristof had no imagination whatsoever. Wait—a spot of brilliance squashed in the back caught her eye. Taya pushed aside his suits and coats to see what secret vice Cristof was concealing in the back of his armoire.

"Oh." She stared.

It was an exalted's robe, wrinkled and musty-smelling. Its gems seemed dull in the dim light, and its gold-and-silver embroidery was dark with age. An ivory mask hung by silk cords from the robe's hangar. Taya touched the mask's smooth surface, feeling gritty dust covering it.

The robe reeked of old secrets and strong emotion. Of something hidden and tainted that Cristof couldn't quite bring himself to discard.

Of guilt, maybe.

Taya let the rest of the suits fall back to cover the robe and closed the wardrobe door. So far she hadn't found anything to warrant her trespass. On the one hand, she was relieved. Alister would be happy if his brother turned out to be innocent. But on the other hand, Taya couldn't help but hope she'd find something that would excuse her ugly suspicions. If Cristof didn't have anything to hide, she was going to owe him a very humble apology.

She looked at the books and felt a twinge of optimism. Most of them were about clockwork and clocks, but a number of other titles sat on the shelves, as well. She examined the spines. Books on programming and foreign customs, explosives and religion, exalted genealogies and icarus armatures. Weapons, poisons, anatomy. She shivered. The bottom shelf was full of dog-eared directories. The official directories weren't surprising, but her eyebrows rose as she pulled out badly printed, back-alley directories to gambling houses and brothels, "gentlemen's shows" and animal fights. Was this a side to the outcaste that she hadn't seen yet?

She found the wireferry map and opened it. Cristof's neat notes indicated time and distance from station to station. Other numbers were marked, too, and it took her a few minutes of reading to realize they were notations about repairs.

She refolded it, not certain what to think.

At the very end of the shelf she pulled out a small bundle of letters and official documents. Crouching, she paged through them, handling the old paper with care.

Coroner's Report: Emeline Forlore, Exalted. The notes were taken in Cristof's small, neat handwriting. She skimmed the medical jargon, noting the words that stood out. Lacerations. Perforation. Fracture. Hemorrhage.

She looked at the date and the age of the victim. Emeline Forlore had been thirty-seven when she'd died. Violently.

She grimaced, set the report down, and moved on to letters signed by Viera, dated twenty-five years ago, written in wide, childish script. *Don't worry, Father says everything will be all right. Give Alister kisses for me. Three more weeks!!! I can hardly wait to see you again. We are painting two rooms for you. You will love them.*

A small clipped obituary: *Emeline and Tadeus Forlore. No cause of death given. Survived by sons Cristof, 12, and Alister, 10.*

A tabloid-sized page from *The Keyhole Peeper*. Taya had never heard of it before. It was typeset on yellowing paper and dated around the time of Viera's letters.

Exalted Murder/Suicide Cover-Up?

She started to read the article when the shop burst into clamorous noise. Taya shrieked, then clapped a hand over her mouth. The clocks were chiming the hour.

Lady! She folded the article and jammed the bundle back where she'd found it. She'd lost track of time, and she had nothing to show for her search except a list of suspicious books, an inconclusive map, and some sad family secrets.

She wrapped her borrowed cloak around her and hurried back through the shop, cracking the door open to slip through.

The edge of the door hit Cristof in the face. He swore and recoiled, one hand over his nose.

"Oh." Taya stared at him, shocked.

"You!" He drew his hand away from his nose and looked at it. Blood ran over his fingertips. "Did you do this?" He pointed a crimson-stained finger at the jimmy marks in his door frame.

"No. I found the door that way, so I walked in," Taya lied, her heart pounding. "I didn't see you inside, so I was just leaving—"

"Give me your knife."

"What?"

He wiped a fresh trickle of blood from under his nose and held out his stained hand.

"Give me your knife. The one on your harness."

"Why?" She stepped back, alarmed.

"Because I'm going to match the blade to these marks," he said, glaring at her. "And if they look alike, I'm going to call the lictors and have you arrested for breaking and entering."

"Don't be ridiculous." She drew herself up. "I walked in to see if you were all right! Someone might have left you hurt, or tied up."

"Did you leave me any presents?"

"Presents?" Taya was taken aback. "What do you mean?"

"You know what I mean. The kinds of presents that start fires," he growled. "Or maybe just a mutilated punch card."

"Punch card? If there are any mutilated punch cards in here, they're yours!" she snapped, flushing. "Maybe the lictors will find them tucked inside all your books about explosives and poison!"

"You did break in!" Cristof crowed, triumphantly.

"I—"

A low, distant boom made both of them stop and look up.

An orange glow burned briefly on the side of the mountain far above them, just visible through the sooty haze in the air.

"Lady help us." Cristof sounded shaken, his face still turned upward. "What have you done?"

"My wings." Taya turned and ran, swearing at herself for leaving her wings behind while she was on duty.

Two minutes later, wailing sirens began to sound across the city, calling an emergency. Taya ran faster, pushing and shoving past the gawkers who stood in the streets and lined the bridges, staring up the mountain.

Jayce was standing in front of his shop when she reached Secundus. Taya dashed past him and grabbed her wings, dragging them outside. She stripped off the cloak and left it on the sooty cobblestones.

"What happened?" she asked, thrusting her arms through the armature and grabbing straps and buckles. Icarii were already circling overhead, summoned by the sirens to offer emergency assistance.

"I don't know. I heard an explosion. People are saying it's another wireferry."

"On Primus?"

"Higher, I think." Jayce squinted. "I think it's the ferry to Oporphyr Tower."

"Oh, no." Taya closed the keel over her chest and yanked its buckles tight. "Oh, Lady, no. Not another one. Where are the stairs to the roof?"

"Around back." Jayce kept staring up the mountain.

Taya folded her wings and pounded up the stairs, throwing herself off the roof and into the wind with furious abandon.

The *diispira* nearly swept her into a neighboring building, but a few strong beats of her wings raised her above the roofs and chimneys of Secundus. She kicked down her tailset and swept herself aloft as soon as she could, shooting up between towers and wires with reckless speed, heading toward the wreckage that grew more horrific as she drew closer.

Signalers were already standing on the towers on Primus, wind whipping their hair and clothes around them as their semaphores instructed the icarii about their approach pattern and civic duties.

Wireferry down. Search and rescue. Damage report. Maintenance escort.

Taya tilted and flew toward the other silver-winged searchers who circled the cliffs and rocks that jutted between Yeovil's peak and the top level of Primus. Up on the tower, response flags flapped in the strong winds, confirming the message below.

Wireferry down. Passengers aboard.

She swooped and turned, following the broken line.

Wires hung limp against the cliff, swaying in the wind. Two wireferry towers were bent. The cliff face had been

blackened by the explosion. Wreckage was strewn across
the rocks.

Taya felt sick, dropping closer to the ground. One of
other icarii wing-signaled to her. Cassi.

They teamed up and fell into a criss-cross search pattern.
Around them other icarii were doing the same, while
another team soared around the damaged ferry tower, then
swooped back to report its findings to the workers below.
Down on the icarus docks, training wings were being
prepared to lift signalers and engineers to the damaged
parts of the wireferry. Other icarii would start evacuating
the Tower. With the wireferry broken, the only way up or
down the peak was going to be by wing.

A shrill whistle announced a find.

The air above the mountainside was a silver, swirling
mass of icarii. Taya joined the circle, swooping low enough
to confirm the find, then flying back out, sickened.

There wasn't much left of the wireferry car.

She let herself soar upward on a thermal, closing her
eyes as soon as she cleared the active airspace.

That could have been Viera and Ariq.

It might still be. She gasped and opened her eyes,
searching for the tower's signal flags. They were moving,
being reeled around for update.

Two passengers.

She circled, joined by three, then six, other icarii,
waiting. The flags kept jerking as more were added. Her
heart skipped a beat as she recognized the house sigils
being strung along the line.

Octavus. Forlore.

Taya screamed, tilting her wings down and then folding
them close to her body for the long dive to Primus.

Lictors shouted and scrambled out of the way as Taya
threw out her wings at the last minute, back-beating
dangerously close to estate walls as she dropped onto the
wide cobbled street and skidded to a stop. The plaza had
been turned into a makeshift operations headquarters,

filled with rescue and repair equipment being hauled up
by wagons and wireferries. Engineers were poring over
a large schematic of the Tower wireferry line, trying to
keep the map from flying away in the gusting winds, and
signalers were decoding the messages from above, relaying
the news to lictors and laborers. Gawkers were held to the
side by a line of soldiers running cords across the street.

"What is it?" a lictor demanded, approaching as she
locked her wings high. "Another body?"

"I know who set the bomb," she said, shaking with fury.
"I know who killed them. Cristof Forlore, Alister's brother.
He did it!"

"The exalted?" The lictor stopped, his face registering
confusion. "That's impossible."

"It's not impossible! He killed Pins and Alister found out
so he killed his brother to keep from being caught!"

"Exalted Forlore is right there," the lictor said, staring at
her as if she'd gone mad. He pointed.

Taya spun, her heart leaping for one brief moment as she
thought he meant the other Forlore, but it was Cristof who
stared at her across the crowd of lictors and workers. For a
moment shock emptied his narrow face of expression, and
then it twisted with rage. He shouldered past the lictor who
was talking to him, striding toward her.

Taya clenched her fists and marched to meet him, shaking
with anger.

"You!" Cristof grabbed for her. Taya knocked his hand
away and slugged him in the stomach.

"You bastard!" she shouted, as he staggered back a step.
"You killed him!"

"I killed him?" Cristof straightened, lunging forward.
His fingers wrapped around her harness straps and he
shook her until her teeth rattled. "You scheming little—"

Taya rammed her palm up against his jaw, snapping his
head back and knocking his glasses askew. His grip loosened
and she tore herself away. He grabbed for her again and she
ducked under his arm, elbowing him in the ribs. He jerked
backward to keep from being slapped by her metal wings.

"Arrest him!" she shouted at the lictors, who were staring at them with slack jaws. "He killed his brother!"

"Arrest her," Cristof demanded, holding his side with one hand and straightening his spectacles with the other. "She's a Torn Card."

To Taya's amazement, the lictors jumped into action, grabbing her arms and flight harness. She twisted.

"Are you crazy? Don't believe him just because he's exalted! He killed his brother! He has books about explosives on his shelves! He murdered Pins!"

"Don't even try to blame your crimes on me," Cristof snarled. "Pins was alive when my men left her. She only died after you heard us talking about her!"

"You're lying!" Taya gasped as the lictors twisted her arms behind her back, beneath the jutting tertiaries of her metal wings. "You think you can get away with this because you're an exalted, but I know the truth, and so did Alister!"

"Strip off her wings and take her to the nearest holding cell," Cristof said, coldly. He rubbed his ribs, glaring at her.

"Any charges?" the nearest lictor asked, locking manacles around her wrists.

"Breaking and entering, and at least one count of murder. I'm sure we'll be able to add more later."

"Ask him about his books! Ask him how he knows Pins, ask him about the wireferry map in his bookshelf!" Taya twisted, but two lictors held her tight. The metal manacles pinched her wrists. "Alister was going to confront him and make him confess, and Cristof killed him for it!"

The lictors yanked her around, marching her off.

"Cristof!" she wailed. "You can't do this!"

The soldiers gave her a sharp shake and dragged her onward.

THEY MARCHED HER to a stationhouse on Primus, unlocked her manacles long enough to remove her armature, and then fastened them back around her wrists and locked her into a cell. Chains ran from her left manacle to a ring in the wall. Taya slumped on the floor, her hands suspended in front of her face, and closed her eyes.

Octavus. Forlore. The signal flags snapped and waved in her memory, superimposed over the dark wreckage that was all that had been left of the wireferry car.

Her eyes burned and she wiped her face on her sleeve. She was *not* going to cry. She wasn't going to give them the satisfaction of making her cry.

Hours passed. She heard voices through the cell door but couldn't make out any words. She stood and stretched a few times, rubbing her aching wrists, then sat against the wall again. The manacles chafed her flesh. For a while she lined up the evidence against Cristof, then thought about Pyke's suspicions about exalteds, then wondered if she'd be given a chance to defend herself at all, then thought about what she should have said to Alister before they'd parted. That just depressed her, so she fumed about Cristof again. Cristof, with all his angry speeches about exalteds and rights, who hadn't paused for a moment to use his caste privilege to force her into silence.

The light in the cell was fading when the door finally opened again. Cristof stood silhouetted in the light from the hall. He gazed at her for a moment, then stepped inside. He looked haggard, his ragged hair raked on end and his mouth bracketed with deep lines of stress.

"Don't even think about hitting or kicking me," he snapped, pulling a ring of keys from his coat pocket.

"Why are you here?" Taya asked, glaring at him. "Who let you in? Where are the guards? Guards!"

A passing lictor glanced in the doorway, then walked on.

"You don't need to shout for the guards." Cristof sounded impatient. "I'm one of them."

Taya jutted out her chin, staring at him with distrust.

"What would the lictors want with an outcaste like you?"

He scowled.

"I'm going to unlock you. But I swear, if you try to attack me, I'll have you thrown in the mines for the rest of your life."

"Is that the way the system works? Is that the equality between icarus and exalted you were telling me about the other night?"

He twitched.

"Murderers have no rights. Did you kill my brother?"

"No." She looked directly into his eyes. "Did you?"

"No."

For a moment they glared at each other with mutual suspicion. Then Cristof stepped forward and unlocked the chain around her left hand. She pulled it in close to her chest and stood.

He never took his eyes off her, watching as if he expected her to kick him without warning. His wariness made her feel more confident. *I'll bet his jaw still hurts*, she thought with satisfaction.

"Are you going to take these off?" she asked at last, holding out her wrists. He grabbed the manacles and unlocked them. Taya winced as she rubbed the chafed flesh on her wrists. Cristof let the metal bonds clatter to the stone floor.

"My men searched your rooms and questioned your acquaintances and family." His voice was cold. "We don't have enough evidence to hold you."

"Your men?"

"My men." He slid the keys back into his coat pocket. "I've been working with the lictors for fifteen years."

"Did your men search your rooms, too? Or doesn't an icarus's accusation mean anything?"

His eyes narrowed behind his wire-rimmed glasses.

"As a matter of fact, your accusation triggered a routine check that became rather more than routine once my superiors talked to the clerks in the Tower. I've spent all day in an interrogation room, thanks to you."

"Well, I've spent all day in a cell." Taya was unrepentant. They stood in silence again a moment. Then she took a breath, bracing herself. "Did they . . . have they . . . found him yet?"

"Probably." Cristof jammed his hands into his pockets, shoulders high. The muscles around his mouth were tense.

"It's going to take some time for the coroners to confirm who was in that car."

She rubbed her face, feeling the threat of tears again. She knew what that meant. The bodies were too mangled to be identified. *I'm not going to cry in front of Cristof*, she told herself furiously. "What—"

"They know it was a bomb." Cristof's voice was under tight control. "And Alister left the Tower today holding the clock I'd repaired."

Taya's head jerked up.

"Then why aren't you under arrest?"

"I was."

She waited. He was silent.

"Well? What happened?"

"Putting a bomb into one of my repair jobs in order to kill my brother makes about as much sense as you rescuing Viera and Ariq after sabotaging the wireferry they were riding on." He gave her a cool look. "It's not impossible, but it's improbable. And until more evidence is found, neither us can be held on an improbability."

She stared at him.

"Alister didn't know you worked for the lictors, did he? Or he would have realized you hadn't killed Pins."

"No. He didn't know. And thanks to you, he probably died thinking I was a terrorist."

"Why didn't you tell him?"

"Who cares? It doesn't matter now, does it?" Cristof's tone was bitter. "It wouldn't have made any difference if he had known. He'd still be dead." He turned his back on her, shoulders still hunched around his ears. "Get out of here, icarus. I don't want to see you again."

Taya drew in a hurt breath, then slowly let it out. She rubbed her wrist again and started out the door, then stopped. Her eyes burned.

Alister was dead. Caster Octavus was dead. Last night's party could have been a dream, for all it mattered today. And what was she supposed to do? Just walk away from it all?

She rested her head against the door frame a moment, getting a grip on herself, and turned toward him.

"I didn't kill your brother," she said, fighting to keep her voice from shaking. "I liked him. A lot. And I liked Caster Octavus, too. So I'm going to find out who did this. For both of them."

"No, you're not." He looked up, his expression bleak. "You're going to stay out of the way and mind your caste."

"Like you?"

"The lictors aren't going to let me investigate this case, either, thanks to your accusations."

"Fine. You can do what you want with your spare time. I owe it to Alister and Exalted Octavus to find out who killed them."

She started to turn, but the exalted reached out and grabbed her arm, his thin fingers digging in until it hurt. His face was twisted in anger and something else. Desperation? Despair?

"Don't be ridiculous. You wouldn't even know where to start."

Taya shot him a furious look. His eyes were red behind the lenses of his spectacles. Her anger diminished as she studied his face and saw the deep grief he was hiding beneath his sharp words.

Our parents are dead, and we're all we have left, Alister had said. And now Alister was gone, and Cristof was all alone in the world.

"Then help me," she said, simply. "He was your brother. You owe it to him, too."

Cristof's jaw tightened, and then he released her, scanning the hallway a moment before focusing on her face again.

"You have to sign for your wings. I'll meet you at the Wren and Cup, eight blocks east of the greenmarket in Secundus, in half an hour. They'll be watching us."

"I don't care."

He stared at her a long moment.

"You know what?" he asked, his voice flat. "Neither do I."

Chapter Nine

Heads turned as Taya walked into the public house, folding her wings close to get through the door. She'd only snapped the keel shut when she'd retrieved it from the lictors; her harness straps were tied together and tucked out of the way.

Cristof was sitting at a table in the back. She took a moment to lock her wings upright, out of the way of other patrons, and walked over to him. The tips of her metal flight feathers brushed the cobwebs on the ceiling beams.

The exalted slouched in his chair, staring at a tall pint of ale. His pocket watch was open next to his drink, gently ticking. Taya glanced at its mother-of-pearl face. She was just on time. Filling out the paperwork to reclaim her wings had taken her longer than expected.

"Can we talk here?" she asked, turning a chair around and sitting down. She folded her arms over its back.

"In generalities." He reached forward and picked up the watch, closing it with care and slipping it into his vest pocket.

"All right." She gave him a level look. "What are the lictors doing now?"

"The sun will set in twenty minutes. They're already calling in the search and repair teams and covering the supply wagons." Cristof stopped as a serving woman walked up with a fresh pint of ale.

"First one's on the house for rescue workers," the woman said in a brisk voice.

"I didn't do much," Taya confessed, looking up.

"Every little bit counts." The woman nodded and walked off. Taya stared at the ale, feeling guilty.

If she hadn't gotten herself arrested, maybe she could have done something useful.

"They'll wait out the night, then start working again as soon as there's light," Cristof continued. "Almost everyone was evacuated out of the Tower by wing. I understand a few lictors have volunteered to stay up there as a skeleton crew."

Taya thought of the cold, dark mountain and of mangled body parts, and closed her eyes. Ceaseless construction had driven the wolves off Ondinium Mountain, but smaller scavengers would be out as soon as the sun set, picking at any flesh they found among the rocks.

At any pieces of Alister and Octavus that hadn't been retrieved.

Her stomach twisted and she opened her eyes, grabbing the ale. Liquid spilled out of her mouth as she drank, seeking to drive away the gruesome mental image.

She set the glass down and wiped her mouth, shuddering.

"Do you know any Torn Cards?" she demanded.

"None that haven't already been arrested." Cristof shifted in his seat. "Tell me what you know. What Alister knew."

Taya recounted the morning's conversation, pausing every few sentences to swallow hard. She wrestled with her conscience over mentioning the Clockwork Heart program. She'd all but promised not to say anything about it, but if she kept it a secret now, Alister's murderers might go free. At last she sketched it out in as few words as possible, whispering to keep the other patrons from overhearing.

She didn't mention the end of that conversation at all, her voice trailing off as she grabbed the pint of ale again.

I should have kissed him, she thought with anguish. *I should have taken the chance.*

While she was drinking, Cristof pulled off his spectacles and pinched the bridge of his nose.

"All right. I know Alister was up early to look at a new engine. He was back in his office by the time you arrived.

He left nearly three hours after you spoke to him. What was he doing in that interval, and where was he going when he left? Did he tell anyone about your suspicions? If he said something indiscreet in front of a Torn Card spy, he might have triggered a reaction that got him killed."

"But there wouldn't have been enough time for a spy to plant a bomb in his clock," Taya protested.

"It wouldn't take that long, if the spy knew what he was doing and Alister were out of his office." Cristof shook his head. "But we don't know for certain if there *was* a bomb in the clock. It's just supposition." Cristof put his glasses back on. "And we don't know for certain the explosion was meant for him, either. The lictors believe the first attack was aimed at Caster, and this one may have been, too. That's the angle they'll investigate first. If the searchers have found any parts of the bomb, it would help explain what happened, but thanks to my arrest, I don't know what they may have discovered."

"Lady." Taya rubbed her face, wondering how he could talk about the attack so calmly. Every time she paused to think about what had happened, about who she'd lost . . .

"Why were Alister and Caster together?" Cristof continued, watching her. "Was it coincidence, or did it have something to do with what you said about me? Or was it something else? Were they talking about Council business of some kind?"

"I don't know." Taya felt daunted by all his questions. "How do we find out?"

"Talking to the clerks who were evacuated would help, but I don't have any access to them anymore. I'd like to search Alister's and Caster's offices in Oporphyr, but there's no way up." He shook his head. "We can't talk to Viera, yet."

"Poor Viera." Taya's heart ached. She'd only lost a hope. Viera had lost a husband. "I should go visit her."

"Not tonight. I haven't had a chance to see her, but the lictors told me she was in hysterics."

"Will she be all right?" Taya asked.

Cristof leaned forward in his chair and wrapped a hand around the base of his glass.

"She loved Caster," he said, voice low. "He was twenty-five years older than she was and Alister and I tried to discourage her, but she married him anyway, and he made her happy. We were arrogant idiots who thought we knew what would be right for her. I'm glad she didn't listen to us." He paused, tilting the glass back and forth. "I don't know what she'll do without him," he finished, and took a drink. Taya glanced down at the rings of condensation on the table, pretending she didn't see him wipe his eyes with his free hand.

Lady, she thought, alarmed, *if he loses control, I will, too, and we'll both be sitting here crying like babies*.

But Cristof took a deep breath, slamming his glass down on the table with a bang.

"My brother thought Caster was attacked because of the program he'd written?" he demanded.

"He suggested it, but I don't see why the Torn Cards would care about a program to predict happy marriages. The whole thing's silly, don't you think?"

"It's exactly the kind of program my brother would write. Alister wants everything to be just right, and he'll do whatever—" Cristof stopped and looked away. After a moment he continued, his voice rough. "Alister was an idealist. For him, things either worked perfectly or they didn't work at all."

"I thought you were the idealist."

"No." He looked back at her. "I know the world isn't perfect, and I don't think it can be. I just try to locate the worst problems and fix them. Alister would rather scrap the whole program and write a new one from scratch."

"Did someone break his heart once? Is that why he wrote the program?"

Cristof studied her a moment, then dropped his gaze to his ale. "Alister would never risk a broken heart. He preferred perfect flirtations to imperfect love. He wrote that program for our parents."

"But they—" she stopped. Cristof shrugged, his narrow shoulders slicing the air.

"We could talk to his programming team," he said, changing the subject. "Maybe one of them leaked information to the Torn Cards. I agree with you that it seems like a stretch. But they're probably the only suspects who are still available. Alister always stays up late at the University when he's working on a program."

A beat of silence followed his words. Taya looked down at her hands, and Cristof pushed his ale away.

"It's better than sitting here," he said abruptly, standing. "You don't have to come, if you don't want to."

"I'll come." She stood. People cleared a path for her as she led the way out, her wings scraping the ceiling again.

Night had fallen. Taya fastened the neck of her flight suit, grateful for its padded lining. Cristof buttoned up his coat and pulled up its collar. The winds had died down, but the night air had a bite. *We'll get snow in a few more weeks*, Taya guessed, looking up at the stars.

"You shouldn't walk around with your armature undone," Cristof said, breaking the moment of silence. "It isn't safe."

"I thought we might go someplace where I'd want to take it off." She looked down at the unfastened straps. "I guess not." She tugged them free and began running them through the buckles on her suit.

For another minute they stood in silence as she worked. Then Cristof shifted, his shoe scraping on the cobbled street.

"I apologize for shaking you," he said, his manner stiff.

"It's all right. You were mad. So was I."

"Even so." He turned, his sharp profile gleaming in the gaslight. "I never thought I'd raise a hand to a woman. I lost control."

"You were under a lot of stress." She tugged a shoulder buckle tight, feeling a twinge of guilt. "I'm sorry I hit you, too. I mean, I wouldn't have been sorry if you'd been the one who'd set the bomb, but since you're not . . . ."

He nodded once, falling silent again. Taya had the distinct feeling that he wasn't satisfied, but she didn't know what else to say. Instead, she finished fastening the armature. Cristof began walking, and she fell into step beside him.

People bustled through the streets of Secundus on their way home from work, their coats wrapped around them and their bundles under their arms. Gaslights and lit storefronts kept the streets bright. The lights of Primus rose overhead until they melded with the stars, and the lights of Tertius swept out below, vanishing in the furnace-red glow of the smelting factory chimneys.

Taya glanced at Cristof. He looked unhappy, huddled in his greatcoat as they walked.

"What will the lictors do if they find out you're investigating your brother's death?" she asked, to distract him.

Cristof shrugged again.

"Threaten me. Throw me in prison for a few days. Fire me, if they get really upset."

"You don't sound too worried about it."

"I don't need the job. I have plenty of money from my inheritance, and the repair business is good."

"Why didn't you give up your inheritance when you turned your back on your caste?"

"It's my money," Cristof snapped. "My parents died long before I decided I'd had enough of Primus."

His constant defensiveness irritated her.

"So all you really did was take off your mask and change your clothes," she observed. "You still have your money and your title, and you're still part of the government."

"So?"

"So, it wasn't exactly a heroic rebellion."

Cristof's laugh was short and bitter.

"You've got me confused with somebody else, Taya. I'm not a hero or a rebel."

"Then why are you doing this to yourself?" She gestured to his short hair and mercantile clothing.

"Alister never understood, either."

Taya took a deep breath, reminding herself that Cristof was under pressure, too. Diplomacy. She moderated her tone.

"Then maybe you need to explain it better."

They walked another block before he started to speak, pausing often, as if to choose his words with care.

"There are lower-castes who think exalteds aren't human. They think we're hiding some kind of grotesque deformity behind our masks and our robes, or that we're really spirits or demons. But the only thing exalteds are hiding is that they are human."

They turned down the broad, tree-lined street that led to the University's towering iron gates. Dry red and gold leaves rustled and blew around them, casting ghostly shadows in the light of the street lamps.

"The Lady permits us an eternity of rebirth to refine our base souls, and being born as exalteds is supposed to prove that we're close to the final forging. But the reality is that exalteds are as imperfect as anyone else and just as liable to shatter under pressure.

"My father beat my mother to death and killed himself. The caste covered it up. It wouldn't be in our best interest to admit that exalteds can go mad, you see. The lower castes might lose faith in our ability to rule the city." Cristof's voice dripped venom. "So we lie to them."

"Nobody would want to talk about something that terrible," Taya murmured. "It wouldn't matter what caste it had happened in."

"If you never talk about a problem, how can you prevent it?" Cristof stopped at the University gates and pointed to the motto inscribed in iron over the arch. *Knowledge is Power*. "Exalteds worship knowledge. We feed every scrap of data we can collect into the Great Engine—unless it's about ourselves. We don't want to know the truth about ourselves. My father's friends should have realized something was wrong. They should have stopped him long before he killed my mother. But everybody turned a blind eye to what was happening. They didn't want to see his wife's bruises or listen to his sons, who were asking them to do something, because if they did, they'd have to admit their caste wasn't perfect."

"So you left Primus because you were angry," Taya summarized, feeling sad. "Why don't you just say so?"

Cristof tightened his lips, drawing away.

"You think it's trivial."

"I didn't say that. You lost your parents. I was heartbroken when my mother died. She got the coughing sickness and the doctors couldn't do anything about it. I know a parent's death isn't trivial."

"It isn't about my parents." Cristof jerked around and began walking again, leading the way through the university commons. "I minded my caste for eight years after they died, finishing school and taking care of Alister. But I saw it happening, over and over again. Lies and cover-ups and pretense. Exalteds will do anything to keep from admitting they're as flawed as the lower castes. Finally I decided I'd be more useful repairing clocks than pretending to be perfect. Alister was already here at the University with a shining future ahead of him, so I left."

"Was your brother angry when you went?"

"Of course he was." Cristof's expression was blank. "I wasn't his ideal older brother anymore. But he got over it. Maybe he managed to reclassify me as the ideal exile. I don't know. But he started talking to me again, and he listened when I told him what was wrong with Ondinium. When he was named decatur last year, he told me he was going to make a difference. Lady." He raked his hand through his short black hair. "A marriage program. Some difference."

"He meant well," Taya said, hurrying to catch up with Cristof's long strides. "You dealt with your parents' deaths by running away. Alister dealt with them by writing a program to keep it from happening again. I think a lot of people would say his solution was more useful than yours."

"I wouldn't." Cristof turned to walk up the broad marble steps of one of the buildings. "A clockwork heart can't replace the real thing." He pushed open the giant carved wooden doors and walked inside.

Taya had to duck through the doorway to enter, but the vaulted ceilings inside the building were high enough to accommodate her wings and two span more. She'd visited the Science and Technology building before, receiving and delivering messages, but never at night. Now the halls were dark, the industrially themed frescos on the ceiling hidden in shadow. A low, steady chuffing and rattling from the bank of steam engines in the subbasement level echoed through the corridors.

Her courier duties usually took her upstairs to the offices, but Cristof headed down a short flight of steps to the basement labs. The sound of the engines grew louder, but not loud enough to drown out the argument going on in the analytical engine lab.

"—undefined terms in Cabisi would make it absolutely impossible—"

"We know their programs work!"

"But they're not trying to replicate their natural—"

"It doesn't matter anyway; nobody's going to learn—"

"Now, wait: that's exactly the kind of narrow—"

Taya and Cristof turned the corner.

Three men and two women were sitting around a cluttered room, ale flagons and beer jugs scattered around them. A board of bread and sausage shared table space with a variety of mechanical devices and tools, and a huge analytical engine spanned the wall behind them, clicking and chattering. One of the women was feeding it a set of cards with one hand and holding a tankard in the other. All of the programmers bore the spiral castemark of a dedicate over their right cheekbones.

"—we won't know until we get a Cabisi programmer in here to try it out," one of the young men was saying with finality. The others burst into argument.

"If you break that engine while you're . . . celebrating . . . you'll be blinded and sent into exile," Cristof said, in a cold tone.

"They wouldn't dare," the woman at the table said, turning. "We're too—" She stopped, staring at the two of them. "Oh, scrap."

The others turned, then scrambled to their feet, making awkward bows. Taya expected Cristof to shout at them the way he'd shouted at her, but instead he stalked forward, his lip curled with disgust as he inspected the mess around him.

"I assume you have some excuse for this?"

"I-It's a wake, exalted," one of the men stammered. Cristof froze.

"It's for Exalted Forlore," another added.

"You must be his brother," said the third man, looking up. "He told us about you. There can't be more than one exalted who goes bare-faced in public."

"This is Exalted Cristof Forlore," Taya hurried to say, before Cristof could respond with something unpleasant. "And I'm Taya Icarus. We're investigating Alister Forlore's death, and we need your help. There are things about his programming work that we don't understand, and we hoped you might be able to explain it to us."

The five programmers relaxed.

"You think his work has something to do with the accident?" one asked.

"Maybe." Taya left the answer hanging.

"Well, we can try," another man said, with an air of condescension. "What do you want to know?"

"How about your names?" Taya asked, forcing herself to give him a friendly smile despite the emotional turmoil she was feeling. "You were . . . you were Alister's friends, weren't you?"

"Yes, ma'am. We're his programming team." The man who'd recognized Cristof held out a hand to her. He was handsome in a conventional way, with brown hair and blue eyes. "I'm Kyle. The big guy over there is Lars, the one with the scary beard is Victor, the skinny one is Emelie, and the tall one is Isobel."

Taya greeted them all, shaking hands. Standing to one side, his hands in his pockets, Cristof seemed disinclined to speak. She was glad of it. She needed to do something useful to keep her mind off everything that had happened.

"I'm glad to meet you. I understand you've just finished an important program for the Council?"

"Yeah, although now that Alister's gone, who knows if it'll ever get run through the mill?" Victor grumbled, dropping back into his chair. He was pale and thin, with a bushy black beard and moustache that did, indeed, make him look a bit scary. "That's why we're running it here tonight."

Taya thought about Victor's use of Alister's first name. It would have been impossible for the exalted to work with a team while he was wearing a mask and robes. He must have trusted them with his first name and bare face.

Good. That would make this easier.

"It's sort of a commemorative voyage. We wanted to run it through once, in case the Council rejects it," Isobel added, turning back to the machine. She was still holding a box of punch cards. Her height and blond hair suggested Demican blood, although her dedicate castemark meant she had been born in the city.

"Is it his romance program?" Taya asked. "Are you running any names through it?"

"All of ours." Isobel flashed her a quick smile. "We wanted to see if any of us are romantically compatible."

"What happens if the program says you are?"

"The couple goes on a date, and we test the program's validity," Lars said. He turned to the table. "Can I get you anything, icarus? Exalted?"

"I'll have some of that beer, to toast Alister," Taya said, swallowing a sudden lump in her throat. "Since this is a wake."

"Refills all around," Kyle commanded. Cups were thrust forward. Taya was surprised when Cristof stepped up, his eyes hooded, and took a tankard.

"Will you make the toast, exalted?" Isobel asked, turning to him.

Cristof hesitated, then nodded. For a moment he stood silently, then lifted the tankard.

"To my brother, whose work I'll do my best to see preserved."

With a murmur of thanks, the group touched cups and flagons and drank.

"Can you do that?" Kyle asked, looking at Cristof with new interest. "Your brother told us you'd rejected your caste."

"I can try."

"Well, it'd be great not to lose a whole year of programming." Kyle tipped his cup toward the clicking analytical engine. "Clockwork Heart was Alister's obsession. Even when the rest of us went home, he'd be here, working away, running tests, trying new approaches. He pretty much lived in this room for several months."

"He was the best of us," Victor said heavily, pouring himself more wine. Before Taya could protest, he'd refilled her mug, sloshing some over her hand. "No one'll ever punch code the way he did."

"On the Clockwork Heart program?" Taya asked.

"On any of 'em. Lady knows what'll happen if something he wrote ever needs to be modified. It'll probably take the whole team to figure out what he did."

"What other programs did he work on?" Cristof inquired, finishing a long swallow. Taya expected him to wince at the flavor, but he didn't seem to notice. *I guess he really has lived a long time on Tertius.*

"Lots of things."

"Top-secret things."

"I heard he was fourth programmer on Labyrinth," Emelie said.

"Labyrinth Code was before his time," Lars objected.

"No, they brought him in for it," Victor asserted.

"Not a chance."

"I'm telling you, he worked on it."

"You don't know what you're talking about."

Cristof picked up one of the jugs and refilled everyone's drink as the argument continued. Taya was surprised by the amiable gesture until she observed that he didn't refill his own flagon. He wanted them drunk.

"Didn't he work on Project Refinery, too?" Isobel asked, giving Cristof a distracted nod as the exalted topped off her tankard.

"Oh, yeah," Kyle said. "He was second programmer on that one."

"And he got the job because of his work on Labyrinth Code," Victor insisted.

"What's—" Taya started, then caught Cristof's warning look and let the question die on her lips. The programmers didn't notice her, anyway, caught up in their argument. Then the analytical engine began to click, and Isobel flinched and began feeding it cards again.

"How much longer is that going to take?" Lars complained. "We've been running it all day."

"Not much longer. We're almost down to the bottom," Isobel said, hoisting the box as evidence.

"Good. Here's to us, beautiful." Lars lifted his glass and winked. She snorted, unimpressed, and went back to work, sliding cards into the machine.

"Why did the Council permit Alister to work on something as ridiculous as Clockwork Heart after he'd spent so much time on important programs?" Cristof asked.

"It's not ridiculous," Isobel objected.

"Oh, they kept him working on their projects, too, but Heart was always part of the deal," Kyle explained. "Alister agreed to work on the Council's programs as long as he was given equal time to work on his own. Tells you something about how much they needed him that they let him cut the deal."

"He charmed them, just like he charmed everyone," Emelie said with irritation. "Alister always got what he wanted."

"Hey, don't complain," Lars protested. "We're lucky he wanted us, or we'd still be punching accounting programs for the slagging Bank of Ondinium."

A chorus of groans greeted that comment.

"Besides," Isobel commented, "if he got everything he wanted, it wasn't entirely his fault." She gave Emelie an sly look. "Just because he asked didn't mean you had to say 'yes.'"

Taya felt her heart skip a beat. Emelie turned red and leaped to her feet, beer spilling on the ground.

"I thought he was—"

"Oh, please, you can't tell me—"

"What other programs was he working on?" Cristof repeated, raising his voice and cutting through the imminent argument. He turned, and Taya felt him study her red face a moment before addressing Victor. "What program would be worth killing him over?"

A silence fell over the room. Taya caught her breath and glowered at Emelie. The programmer was dressed in casual clothes, with her long black hair caught back but slipping from its pins. She wasn't as petite as Taya, but she was thinner, without an icarus's wiry muscles. She was good-looking enough, in kind of a careless, bookwormy way. Taya had a hard time imagining Alister being interested in her.

Of course, Taya couldn't figure out why Alister had been interested in her, either. Pressure started to build in her throat and she shook her head, denying it. Not now.

"Do you think that's what happened?" Lars asked, at last. "He was murdered?"

"Forgefire, Lars! He was killed by a bomb." Victor scowled. "What did you think 'bomb' meant? Natural causes?"

"Well, it might have been random . . . ." Lars looked at the others for support.

"It was murder," Cristof said, tersely. "It might have been aimed at him."

"Oh." The big programmer took another drink, subdued.

"He wasn't working on anything unusual," Victor said, slumping in his chair. "Encryption, decryption. Some modifications to Refinery."

"What's wrong with Refinery?" Cristof asked.

"Well, Decatur Neuillan slipped past it, so the Council asked Alister to look it over, figure out what it missed, and patch the holes in the algorithm."

The loyalty test, Taya realized. That's what Refinery was. It was the name of Ondinium's loyalty program.

"What holes?" Emelie sounded bitter. "That program was flawless. Neuillan just knew how to beat it. Alister told him."

"What?"

"Not a chance!"

"Alister would never do that!"

"Well, not in so many words," Emelie hedged. "But they were friends, or at least Alister thought they were. He told me he was afraid he might have let too much slip, that Neuillan might have been able to figure out from what Alister had said to him what kinds of answers would trigger the program to flag a profile."

"I don't believe that," Cristof objected, the lines around his mouth deepening as he frowned. "Neuillan was one of our guardians when we were orphaned. He was a good friend, but Alister wouldn't have compromised Ondinium's safety for him."

"He didn't do it on purpose," Emelie protested, looking around the room. "You know how much Alister liked to brag. Even if he wasn't supposed to talk about something, he'd still drop hints or tell you some little secret to make you feel special. That's how he made friends so easily. Everyone felt like he was trusting them with his confidences, and that made them trust him back."

"You're saying he was manipulative." Taya felt cold. Was that why Alister had so easily entrusted her with the "secret" of his Clockwork Heart program?

"No, no," Lars protested. "It wasn't like that. Sure, he tried to make friends with everyone he met, but there's nothing wrong with that. He wasn't manipulative. He was proud of his work, but we all are. Emelie's just got bent edges because he dumped her."

"He didn't dump me! I dumped him."

"Either way, it's coloring your perceptions. I liked Alister."

"We all did," Kyle agreed.

"He told me he thought Neuillan was his fault," Emelie repeated. Her tone was sullen. "He said he felt bad about it."

"Maybe someone else slipped through the program and was afraid that if Alister fixed it, he'd get caught," Victor suggested. "So he killed him."

"Doesn't have to be a 'he,'" Isobel pointed out.

"Women don't use bombs." Victor scratched his beard. "Women use knives. Or poison."

"I'd use a bomb!" Isobel sounded indignant. "Or don't you think I could figure out how to build one?"

"Oh, bombs are easy to build," Victor said. Isobel scowled. "But they're not clean enough for a woman. Men are slobs. We don't care if we get the walls dirty."

"Please—" Taya felt sick.

"Oh. Lady. Sorry." Victor slumped in his chair again. "Poor Alister. Have we helped you catch his killers yet?"

"It helps to know that he was working on something more important than a marriage program." Cristof's voice was strained. He reached into his coat pocket and pulled out the stack of cards Taya had seen the night before. "What do you know about these? Somebody smuggled them out of the Engine Room."

"Why do you still have those?" Taya asked. Emelie's comments about Alister had depressed her, and she was feeling contrary. "I thought you were suspended."

"These cards aren't officially linked to the investigation of Alister's death." Cristof narrowed his eyes. "And if it turns out they are . . . well, that wouldn't be my fault."

"Wait—what do you mean by 'suspended'? Are you working with the lictors or not?" Lars rumbled, looking suspicious.

"I'm working with the lictors and I'm investigating my brother's murder." Cristof turned, his angular frame diminished by Lars' girth. "But not at the same time."

"Are we going to get into trouble if we help you?"

"I'll try to avoid it. I can't guarantee anything."

The five looked at each other.

"Slag it," Victor said at last. "Alister's his brother. A man has to avenge his brother."

"Yeah."

"You're right."

"I would."

"Works for me."

"He spoke highly of you, you know," Kyle said, turning and taking the cards. The other four crowded around, and they passed the bundle back and forth. "He said you were logical and precise, and if the Council had brains instead of beads, it would have made you decatur, instead of him."

"That's not the impression he gave when he spoke to me," Cristof muttered.

"Really?" Kyle gave the exalted a long look over the bowed heads of his friends. "He told us he was modeling one of his most important programs after you."

Cristof made an angry sound and Taya looked at him, surprised. Kyle blinked, then looked back down at the cards.

"Anyway, if you'll give us some time, we need to skim through the perfs . . . the perforations, the punches. I have a pretty good idea of what this is, but we'll need to study it a little longer to be sure."

The exalted nodded and turned, stalking off to stand alone at the other end of the room.

Taya waited a moment, then joined him. She wanted to apologize for letting his status on the investigation slip, but the words died on her lips.

Cristof stood with his fists jammed into his coat pockets, his shoulders high and his eyes fixed on the metal dance of the analytical engine's pistons and gears.

He looked so miserable that she reached out and touched his shoulder.

"It would help if you just let yourself cry," she murmured.

He jerked his shoulder away.

"It wouldn't help anything."

"It would help you." She swallowed, her own grief too close for comfort. "You shouldn't hide your feelings. I thought the whole idea was that you didn't want to wear a mask anymore."

His breath hissed as he turned his back more firmly on her.

"I think it's nice that Alister talked about you to his friends," she said, trying one last time to reach him. "He told me about you, too. He said he loved you and that he wished you realized that. And he insisted he was going to talk to you before he talked to the lictors because he couldn't believe you were a terrorist. He said it had to be a mistake."

"Stop defending him," Cristof said, his voice harsh. "You heard what that skinny girl said. Alister was just worming his way into your confidence, the way he always did."

Taya drew back, stung. She'd been making herself sick thinking the same thing, but it was different to hear the words from somebody else.

"You don't know that," she argued, trying to convince herself as much as Cristof. She wiped her face, feeling a tear trickle down cheek. "That's a terrible thing to say. Alistser was charming and kind and sincere."

Cristof turned. She dried her face on her flight-suit sleeve.

"Don't." His voice was severe. "Don't start crying, icarus."

"I can't help it." She sniffed, tears streaming. "I can't believe he's gone. And Octavus, too. I lost two new friends in one day."

"Hey . . . do you need any help over there?" Lars asked, looking across the room at them. He sounded concerned.

"Just find out what's on the damn cards," Cristof snapped.

Taya swallowed, angry at herself for breaking down in front of strangers. She'd hoped to make it back home before the tears started.

Cristof dug into a pocket and thrust a handkerchief into her hands, then pulled off his glasses. "Spirits! Would you please stop?"

She looked up. Her tears had set him off. Just what she'd been afraid of, back in the bar. She wiped her eyes and handed back his handkerchief. He grabbed it.

"It's wet," he complained.

She gave a half-laugh, half-sob.

"Then you should have started first," she said.

"I have no intention of starting at all!" He sounded angry as he scrubbed at his face.

She tugged the handkerchief out of his hands again and blew her nose in it.

"Grieving's part of being human, you know." She looked up at him and took a shuddering breath, trying to get herself under control. "I bet even exalteds cry when they lose a brother."

He ran his hands over his face, his spectacles dangling from his fingertips, and walked away. Taya pressed her knuckles against her mouth. She'd upset him even more. Hot tears streamed down her cheeks—tears for Alister, for Cristof, and for herself. Ridiculously, she wished Alister were with her so that she could lean on him while she cried. Instead she crouched, her metal feathers scraping the floor as she buried her head in her hands and let her grief wrack her.

A few minutes later Cristof dropped to one knee in front of her. He pushed her hair away from her face. His fingers were cold on her hot forehead.

"Stop crying. Alister wouldn't want you to cry for him."

She looked up, sniffing, and wiped her nose on his handkerchief. He'd put his spectacles back on, although his eyes were red.

"His team knows that. Alister would have appreciated their wake." Cristof wiped a tear off her cheek. He looked weary. "He never had any time for grief."

"Not ever?" Taya asked, ducking her face from his hand and rubbing her eyes.

"I never saw him cry, after our parents' funeral." Cristof studied her. "That's better."

"No, it's not." She took a deep breath, steadying herself, and looked over his shoulder at the programmers. The five of them were studiously ignoring them. "Do you think he was manipulative?"

"Spirits." Cristof pressed his lips together a moment, then sighed. "What do you mean by manipulative? He liked smart, talented women. It wouldn't surprise me if he said things to impress you. I expect most men do. Is that manipulative or just natural?"

"Thank you." Taya forced a smile. "I didn't . . . I didn't like the way Emelie talked about him."

"Neither did I." He stood, reached down, paused, and then opened his hand. "Stand up."

She took it, grateful for the contact. His hand was cold but steady, his fingers thinner and harder than his brother's. She let him pull her to her feet.

"Okay." She squeezed his hand, then wiped her face one last time. "I think I'm all right now."

"Good."

She took a moment to adjust her flight suit, shoving his handkerchief into her pocket. Then she straightened her shoulders and walked back to the programmers. He followed.

"Is everything okay?" Kyle asked, giving her a quick glance.

"Yes. Just—just delayed reaction." She bit her lip and looked down at the punch cards lined up on the table. "So, what are they?"

"Well, they're obviously Great Engine cards." Kyle made room for her and Cristof. "You can tell because they're wider and longer than normal cards and made out of tin instead of heavy paper. The numbers on the edge identify the card's order in the program. You've got twenty-five cards out of a deck of a hundred here."

"Is that a lot? A hundred?"

"No. In fact, it's a very small program, for the Engine."

"What good would part of a program do anybody?" Cristof asked, pushing up his glasses as he leaned over the table to study the numbers. "What's the code in front of the number?"

"It tells the operator which program the card belongs to," Victor said. "After you've dropped a box of cards the first time, you realize how important it is to label them correctly."

"OCAE stands for Oporphyr Council Analytical Engine, the official name of the Great Engine," Isobel explained.

"SA stands for Security Access," Victor added. "Also known as Labyrinth Code."

Kyle tapped the numbers that followed. "Version three, copy two, card twelve of one hundred. We're not sure what these numbers are, but we think it's part of a randomizing formula."

"The Labyrinth Code is the Engine's security program, right?" Taya picked up one of the cards, examining its block of punches with wonder. She'd never seen the Great Engine or one of its cards before. "So if somebody got this, they could use the Engine?"

"Well, they'd need seventy-five more cards, first," Lars said. "My guess is that whoever stole these couldn't get the rest. A deck of tin cards gets heavy fast, so they're probably stored in four boxes of twenty-five each, and your thief only had a chance to grab one."

"It'd be easier to smuggle the program out one box at a time," Victor added. "He might have been planning to go back for the rest later."

"Since these cards are labeled as copy two, our guess is that they're part of the backup copy, which would be stored someplace on site in case one of the original cards got damaged," Emelie said. "A backup would be easier to steal than a working program. It could take months before anybody noticed a backup was missing."

Cristof straightened.

"How hard would it be to reconstruct the whole program if all you had were these twenty-five cards?"

The programmers looked at each other.

"Impossible," Kyle said at last. "It's called Labyrinth Code for a reason. Five different teams worked on it, each team under orders to create a code with no recognizable pattern. Then one high-security team assembled a metaprogram to govern each of the other five codes."

"People say it's impossible to write a program that's entirely random," Victor said, stroking his beard. "Humans aren't random creatures. But five teams trying to be random will create a program that's random enough for most purposes."

"But this set must include more than one team's work," Taya said. "I mean, if each team created equal programs, then each team would have twenty cards each, right?"

"If each part were exactly equal; but that may not be the case. Even if it is, it still leaves three teams' subroutines unknown, and the metaprogram would have required some rewriting of the original code. In addition, if we're right about the last numbers on the cards, this code can be fed into the Engine in different orders, which would make it even harder to replicate." Lars saw that he was losing her. "Okay, let me explain. Labyrinth Code is fed into the Great Engine once a day and once a night to make sure nobody can just dance into the Engine Room and run a new program while nobody's looking. The first time unlocks the Engine, the second time locks it again. Each of the five subroutines in the Code needs to be run, but they can be run in different orders. So let's say you're trying to guess a code with five variables. One's a number, one's a letter, one's a color, one's the name of animal, and one's, uh—"

"A musical note," Isobel suggested.

"Right. Pretty tough to crack, right? Lots of possible answers for each variable. But the code is going to be even harder to crack if the order of the five variables is shuffled each day—one day the musical note is the first key, and the next day the animal is the first key, and so on."

Taya nodded.

"So even if your thief manages to get all hundred cards, meaning he knows the note and animal and color and whatever else I said, he's still got to know which order to run the cards in on any given day. There are five variables— the subroutines—which means twenty-five possible order permutations." Lars shook his head. "Your thief sneaks in some night when the guards aren't looking and runs the program to unlock the Engine. Let's say it takes half an hour to run the cards through, and that's a modest projection. He doesn't get the order right the first time, so he's got to run the cards through in the next configuration. If his luck is really rotten, it could take him seven and a half hours to hit the right order. Figure about four hours on average."

"That's a long time to be feeding cards into the Engine." Emelie folded her arms over her chest. "Someone's sure to notice the thief working—a technician, or a lictor, or somebody."

"And then, don't forget that the thief still has to run whatever program he broke into the Engine to use in the first place," Lars finished. "Which could take several more hours. And then another half hour to reset Labyrinth Code so nobody knows he was there."

"Assuming he cares," Victor added.

"He'd save time if he knew what order he needed to run the program in. Who would know?" Taya asked. The programmers shrugged, looking at each other.

"That's not our area," Kyle said.

"The chief technician, maybe," Lars ventured.

"I'd randomize the order," Isobel said. "Toss some dice each evening to decide. That would make it even harder to guess."

"Dice have six sides. The program only has five subroutines," Kyle pointed out.

"Okay, draw lots. You know what I mean."

"Would anyone on the Council know what order the cards should be run in?" Cristof asked.

"I don't see why," Lars replied. "Decaturs don't work on the mighty machine. Even Alister handed his programs over to the engineers when he was done. None of us have ever fed a program into the Great Engine ourselves."

"You said Alister helped write the Labyrinth Code," Taya said, looking at Emelie. The programmer nodded and Victor looked vindicated.

"That's what he told me. He was just starting University. He said one of his professors was so impressed by his portfolio that she brought him onto the project to do code clean-up, and in no time at all he was on one of the teams."

"Is this his piece of code?" Cristof asked.

"Hard to say." Kyle sat down and poured himself a fresh mug of beer. As if it were a signal, the rest of the programmers sorted themselves out and began refreshing their drinks. "Do you know anything about programming, exalted?"

"I don't need another lecture," Cristof said, with a touch of his usual acerbity. "A simple yes or no will suffice."

Kyle grinned.

"Just like a punch card, huh? But it's not that easy. See, this program was assembled in a relatively simple language, and you've only got twenty-five cards here. That doesn't provide much room for a programmer's personal style to show up."

"But it *is* possible to figure out who wrote a program?" Cristof asked.

"Theoretically. After a while, you get used to seeing other people's programming shortcuts, and we reuse parts of our old programs whenever we can," Lars explained. "So, given a long enough program, we could probably parse out the author, especially if it was someone we'd worked with before, like Alister. We've been dealing with his programming quirks for nearly a year now."

"The problem is," Kyle picked up the thread, "Labyrinth Code was designed to avoid anything predictable, which includes any single programmer's preferences. And not only that, but if Emelie and Victor are right, this would be one of Alister's early jobs, before he developed most of the routines he uses now."

"In other words, you don't know," Cristof summarized. "You could have just said that."

The programmers looked at each other with a long-suffering air.

Taya reached out and touched one of the cards. For all she knew, there was a little bit of Alister in them. That made her feel better, thinking that his work would live on until his next rebirth.

"If you ran these twenty-five cards through an analytical engine, would they do anything?" Cristof pursued.

"No." Kyle chuckled. "That's your short answer. Your long answer is that feeding in a partial program would probably crash the engine. And that leads to another question, which is, which analytical engine would you try it on? People use 'analytical engine' pretty casually to refer to a lot of different calculating machines, but there are only five true analytical engines in Ondinium: the Great Engine, this University engine, the engine in the Bank of Ondinium, the engine in the Council building—and that one's old, hardly more than a difference engine—and the prototype down the hall. So it's not as though someone could walk up and start feeding cards into any one of them. Access is very restricted. And these cards, of course, can only be run on the Great Engine. They're too big for the others."

"What about reading the cards themselves?" Cristof picked one up, looking blankly at its perforations. "How many people in the city can do that?"

"Maybe twenty of us."

"Are any of you twenty inclined to sell the Labyrinth Code to another nation?"

"And lose our job security? Not to mention our citizenship and eyesight? We remember what happened to Decatur Neuillan." Lars shook his head. "We're not idiots."

"Besides, Cabiel's the only other country with advanced analytical engines, and they use a completely different assembly language," Kyle added. "There aren't any foreign nations that could run Labyrinth Code on their own engines."

"But if a country like Alzana could use this code to sneak in and misprogram our Great Engine, it could do a lot of damage to us," Cristof speculated.

The programmers looked at each other.

"You know, exalted, people call the Great Engine the 'Heart of Ondinium,' but it's really not that important to our day-to-day survival," Lars said, politely. "Slagging up some of the programs would be inconvenient, and it might cause us problems over the long run, but if Alzana really wants to cripple Ondinium, it just has to blow up our refineries or poison our water reservoirs. This little bit of code doesn't make a big difference in the grand scheme of themes."

Cristof was undeterred. "What about the Torn Cards? Could they use it?"

"The Torn Cards want to destroy the Great Engine," Isobel said. "They wouldn't do that with a program. If they ever got access to the Engine Room, they'd just drop a few bombs between the gears."

"I see. Well, thank you." Cristof began gathering the cards back up. "If you think of anything that might help us figure out who . . . who killed my brother, would you please let me know? It would probably be fastest to send a message to Taya Icarus."

"Just drop a line through Dispatch, or tell any icarus that you need to talk to me," Taya said, nodding.

"We'll do that." One by one the programmers shook her hand, then ducked quick bows to Cristof.

"What now?" Taya asked, as they walked back down the marble steps to the campus plaza again. The autumn wind whipped dry leaves across the walkway. "Do you think the bomb was meant for Alister?"

"Now we know it's a possibility. But Caster's still the more likely target."

"When can we investigate him?"

"Not tonight." Cristof paused, taking off his glasses and wiping them on his coat front before putting them back on. "Tomorrow I'll visit Viera."

"Can I come?"

He looked at her, clearly not enchanted by the idea.

"I want to," Taya insisted. "It would be rude if I didn't offer my condolences."

"Oh, all right," he said gracelessly.

"Thank you." Taya took the lead this time, heading for the University flight dock. "When are you going to see her?"

"No earlier than noon. You won't have any problem getting off work?"

"Not if I tell them I'm working for an exalted. Everyone will be on search and rescue, anyway, so schedules are going to be flexible." She sighed, thinking again of the wreckage in the mountains. "I'll meet you at noon. Where?"

"In front of her estate."

"All right." She reached the dock, a metal tower that rose over the rooftops of the University buildings.

"Fly safely."

"I will." She swung herself up onto the rung ladder and began to climb, turning her face toward the moon.

Chapter Ten

When she arrived at Estate Octavus the next day, Taya removed her armature in the foyer and left it with the servants. A few minutes later she was glad she had, because Viera turned from embracing Cristof to throw her arms around Taya's shoulders.

"I'm glad you came," the exalted said, fiercely.

"I'm so sorry." Taya hugged her back, surprised but flattered. "How's Ariq?"

"He's quiet. I'm afraid he's just starting to understand what this means." Viera stepped back, smoothing the front of her layered robes. Her strong features looked haggard. "Do you know who did it yet?"

"No, but we're looking into it," Cristof said. "I'll have some answers soon, I promise."

"Do they—" Viera stopped. "Who was the target? Alister or Caster? Do they know?"

"Not yet." Cristof took her arm and led her to a chair. Both he and Taya sat as soon as Viera was settled. "I've found one or two reasons why someone might want to kill Alister, but it's still possible that Caster was the target, or that this was just a random act of terrorism. It's too soon to tell."

Viera nodded, folding her hands in her lap.

"Would you be willing to answer some questions?" Cristof studied her. "I realize it's difficult to talk about, but—"

"Of course I will," Viera replied, cutting him off. "I spent all night trying to figure out why someone would want to kill my husband. The only thing I can think of is that it must have been Council business. Something political and dangerous."

"What was Caster working on? Did he have any important votes coming up? I know votes are confidential. . . ."

"He told me a lot about his work. Maybe more than he should have, but he liked to ask my advice." Viera looked at her cousin. "I know he was going to vote against Alister's experimental program. And he was going to vote for an increase in the import tax on luxury items from Si'sier, and for a series of new safety regulations in the textile factories. None of those votes were worth killing him over."

"Alister told me yesterday that your husband had changed his mind about the program," Taya objected. "He was going to support it."

"Clockwork Heart?"

"Yes."

"I don't think so. Caster thought the whole idea was preposterous. He said that a machine would never have been able to predict a marriage like ours, and that he wasn't going to discourage anyone else from trying to find what we had." Her voice cracked on the last word, and she took a breath to steady herself.

"I'm sure he was right," Cristof said, taking her hand. "But you know Alister. He was convinced technology would solve all our problems."

Viera gave him a weak smile.

"I know. It's so funny that he would write that program after teasing you so much. He trusted machines and spent all his time around people, whereas you trust people and spend all your time around machines."

"I don't trust people that much. They're just as likely to malfunction as a machine."

Taya was only half-listening, still puzzling over Viera's previous answer.

"Could he have changed his mind and not told you? Because Alister was very certain . . . ."

"Maybe he misunderstood something Caster said. That could be why they were out on the wireferry together," Cristof suggested.

"They were probably arguing, then," Viera sighed. "They respected each other's talents, but couldn't agree on how to run Ondinium. Our dinners together were always very loud."

Taya frowned. Alister had seemed adamant that Caster was on his side. But Emelie's accusations nagged at her memory.

"Do you think he might have lied to me?" she asked.

"Are you still thinking about that programmer?" The lines around Cristof's mouth tightened. "Don't. Alister would have no reason to lie to you about a Council vote."

"Unless he thought it would impress me," she ventured. Neither Cristof nor Viera immediately protested, so she hurried on. "He told me he'd shown Exalted Octavus some evidence about what broken marriages did to the economy, and that Octavus had finally seen things his way. That doesn't sound like a misunderstanding, to me. He even said the attack on the wireferry could have been because the Torn Cards were worried that Caster would convince other decaturs to change their votes."

"Caster didn't change his mind," Viera said, with confidence. "He would have told me, if he had. Clockwork Heart had become something of a joke between us."

"Oh." Taya sank back in her chair, discouraged.

It hadn't bothered her to think that Alister was flirting instead of looking for a serious romance. It hadn't even bothered her very much to think that he might have told her secrets to try to impress her. But if he'd lied to her— that was completely different.

A liar writing a true-romance program. It didn't make any sense.

"Did Caster leave any of his papers here?" Cristof asked, as she brooded. "And if so, may I look at them?"

"I would let you, but his papers are confidential," Viera said with regret. "The lictors are getting a warrant to take all his work away with them, and they won't be happy if I let you go through it, first."

Cristof pulled off his glasses, polishing them and gazing blindly out one window. Taya looked at Viera with confusion. Had the exalted already found out that Cristof was suspended?

Oh.

Viera didn't know that Cristof worked for the lictors at all.

Oh, Lady, Taya thought with sudden panic. *What if Cristof was lying to me, too?*

But no sooner had the thought crossed her mind than Cristof pushed his glasses back up his nose and reached into his suit jacket.

"I know you won't be happy about this, Vee," he said, pulling out a folded piece of paper and handing it to his cousin. "I had good reasons for not telling you. But the reasons don't matter anymore."

Viera unfolded the letter and read it, her eyebrows rising when she reached the end.

"Is this why you left Primus, Cris?" she demanded, handing the document back. Cristof took it, paused, then handed it to Taya.

She knew what it was even before she looked. It was his letter of appointment, confirming that he worked for the Ondinium Civic Police Force.

She read it, anyway. At least this wasn't a lie. She'd seen the lictors' official letterhead and seal dozens of times on other documents.

"No. I started working for the lictors a few years after I left. I would have said something, at least to you and Alister, but the military thought I'd be more useful if nobody knew what I was doing."

"In other words, they turned you into a spy." Viera's tone was frosty. "That's not a gentleman's profession, Cris."

"I'm not a gentleman." Cristof, too, must have heard her disapproval, because an acid note had returned to his voice. "I never lied to you, Viera. I just didn't volunteer the information."

"That's called a lie of omission, and it's no better than a lie of commission." Now Viera's annoyance was more apparent. "Apparently all my years of defending your character have been in error."

Color rose in Cristof's cheeks, darkening the wave-shaped castemarks on his cheeks.

"I've done good work for the lictors. I've helped them catch smugglers, spies—I was one of the people who figured out Neuillan was selling our secrets to Alzana—"

"All of which would be very admirable if it had been done in an honorable manner. But I'm not going to condone you pretending to be something you're not."

"Like every other exalted in Ondinium?" Cristof snapped, gripping the arms of his chair and half-rising. "Hiding behind masks in order to pretend that they're flawless?"

"Not that again, Cris."

"It's the same thing!"

"If it were the same thing, then you wouldn't have any right to disdain us, would you? A mask of flesh is no different from a mask of ivory. But I think what you're doing is worse—at least people know when you're wearing a mask of ivory."

Cristof made a disgusted noise, dropping back into his chair.

"You and the icarus. . . ." he snarled. "Neither of you understands anything."

"When I said you were still wearing a mask, I wasn't talking about spying," Taya said, looking from one exalted to the other. Family spats were much more difficult to finesse than merchants' arguments or foreigners' misunderstandings. "Exalted Octavus, your cousin has been honest with you today because he wants to find the person who killed your husband and Alister. I'm helping him because I care, too. We can disagree about other things and still agree that the killer needs to be found, can't we?"

Viera nodded, her eyes still narrow as she regarded her cousin.

"Yes, but you and I are going to discuss this matter at greater length in the future, Cris."

"Agreed." Cristof's tone was curt. "In the meantime, do I have your permission to see Caster's papers?"

"Before you say yes," Taya interrupted, "there's something else you should know. Cristof's superiors have suspended him. He says his suspension only applies to investigating his brother's murder and that he's free to investigate a theft from the Oporphyr Tower. Your husband's papers might help him investigate that theft, but they're more likely to help him work on the case he's not supposed to touch."

Cristof shot her an angry look, his lips tight, but he didn't say anything. Well, he could be as angry as he wanted, she thought, but she didn't intend to lie to Viera Octavus for him—not by commission or omission.

"Were you going to tell me that?" Viera asked, turning to Cristof. He bared his teeth in a humorless smile.

"I don't have to tell anybody anything anymore," he said, in a voice like vinegar and honey. "I'll just leave all my talking to the icarus."

"Perhaps that would be a good idea." Viera stood. "I'll show you the papers, for the family's sake, but you can't take them away, and I intend to tell the lictors you were here."

Cristof nodded once, looking grim. They followed her out.

On the way down the hall, Taya caught Cristof's eye and raised an eyebrow.

"What?" he snapped. She decided to let his snide comment about speaking for him pass and asked another question, instead.

"Did your brother lie a lot?"

"I don't know." He looked away from her. "My brother cared what people thought. That can make a man do stupid things."

"I don't like it when people have hidden agendas and try to use me to meet them."

"My agenda isn't hidden." They followed Viera up a flight of stairs. "I want Alister's killer. I'm letting you work with me because you want to and because if I didn't, you'd just get in my way."

"You're 'letting' me work with you because you're too bad-tempered to get information out of anybody on your own," she retorted. "I don't know why the lictors thought you might be useful to them. What do you do, stab prisoners with the sharp edge of your tongue until they beg for mercy?"

He gave her an amazed look, then turned away again.

"Here." Viera opened the door to Caster's office. "Keep his things in order, Cristof. And leave Taya alone. Right now, I like her more than I like you. Taya, please make sure my cousin doesn't walk off with anything."

"I will," Taya said, putting her palm on her forehead and bowing. "Thank you, exalted."

"I'm not angry at you." Viera touched her cheek a moment, then turned. "Come again without Cris, so that we may enjoy a civil conversation together."

"Thank you," Taya repeated, as Viera walked back down the stairs. Then she turned. Cristof was already sitting at Caster's desk, his thin face intent as he rummaged through his papers. "You're going to apologize to her, right?"

"Of course I will," he said, sounding preoccupied.

Taya rolled her eyes and sat down at the desk. "What am I looking for?"

"Anything useful."

They spent two hours going through Caster Octavus's papers and files, searching for anything that might have led to his death. Taya confirmed from his correspondence that he'd intended to vote against the Clockwork Heart.

"Alister really did lie to me," she sighed, leaning back in Caster's oversized leather chair and pulling her legs up.

Cristof set down the file he was perusing.

"He's dead. Making yourself sick over him won't do you any good."

"I'm supposed to be a good judge of character. I have to be, if I'm going to be a diplomatic envoy." She rested her arms on her knees, staring out the window. The autumn sun was already low, although it was only afternoon. "I hate to think a man could just smile at me, and I'd forget everything I've learned about human nature."

"You care what people think, too."

"Not really." She glanced at him, saw his skeptical look, and gave him a rueful smile. "All right. Maybe a little. I don't want people to think I'm an idiot, anyway. And I'm feeling pretty idiotic right now."

"You're not an idiot." He picked up the file again. "I'll tell you when you're an idiot."

"Thanks."

"Just returning the favor."

Well, how about that, she thought. *He has a sense of humor, after all.*

"You sound better."

"Work's therapeutic." He turned a page in the file. Taya nodded, looking out the window again. It was too high up for her to see the Octavus's gardens. All she could see was sky and clouds. A bird flew by.

"Icarus."

"Hmm?"

"I don't have a hidden agenda. Nor do I intend to use you or mislead you with my charm."

Despite herself, she smiled, glancing at him. His face was studiously neutral.

"The day you act charming, I'll know something is wrong."

"Good."

Taya watched him as he looked back down at his work. He still reminded her of a crow, his unruly black hair sticking on end and his black greatcoat wrapped around him. Just like a crow. Loud and mocking, but not without a sardonic sense of humor.

"It's nice to know that you care what I think about you," she added. "And it hasn't even made you do anything stupid yet."

He looked up and blinked at her once, puzzled. Then he realized what she was saying. He frowned.

"Wanting to avoid yet another unfounded accusation isn't the same thing as worrying—"

"Be careful, exalted. You're about to talk yourself into a corner."

"Have you finished looking through all those papers?" he asked peevishly, sticking his beak back into the file he was holding.

They abandoned the office as the sun began to hang low between the mountains. Back in the Octavus foyer, Taya strapped on her icarus armature.

"Did you find anything useful?" Viera asked, holding a sleepy Ariq as they took their leave. Subdued voices from the parlor indicated that she had more visitors.

"A list of his intended votes on upcoming issues, and a better understanding of what kind of man he was," Cristof said. He took her hand and held it a moment. "Caster thought things through very carefully and did his research. I'm impressed."

"I wish you had known each other better." Viera sighed, then leaned forward and kissed his thin cheek. "Good luck, Cris. I'm still annoyed at you, but be careful. Don't let them take anyone else away from me."

"I won't." He returned the kiss and stepped back as Viera hugged Taya, Ariq squirming between them.

"You be careful, too."

"I will." Taya looked down at Ariq. He stared at her, his cheek against his mother's shoulder. "Bye-bye, Ariq. I'll see you later."

They walked down the estate path to the gate. A cold wind blew past them as they stepped out into the street, and long shadows stretched across the cobblestones.

"I told Dispatch I was working with you, so I don't need to report back," Taya said, glancing up at the red-streaked sky. "What time is it?"

"A little past four," Cristof replied, glancing at his gold watch.

"I think the bomber was after Alister." A gust of wind tugged her wings, carrying the faint smell of smoke from the factories far below on Tertius. "There doesn't seem to be any reason to target Exalted Octavus, but Alister was working on all those important programs. Plus, he knew something was going on, even if he thought you were the one involved. He must have said something to tip off the real spy."

"Unfortunately, any proof of that would be up there." Cristof pointed to the isolated Oporphyr Tower. "Do you know how long it will take to fix the wireferry?"

"A week or two, if they can beat the first snow," Taya said. "If it snows, it'll take longer."

"Damn." Cristof stared up at the mountaintop. "That's the next place we need to go to search for clues."

"I could fly up."

Cristof paused, then looked thoughtful as he contemplated her metal wings.

"Would you know what to look for?"

"Anything useful," she said, deadpan. He made a disgusted sound and looked back up at the mountaintop.

"It's too dangerous. We don't know where the killer's hiding."

"I could take you with me." She glanced at the low sun. "But not until dawn."

Cristof's expression grew guarded.

"What do you mean, take me with you?"

"Flying. You know, Alister kept joking about going flying. He wanted me to bring him some wings and take him aloft. I never did, though." If Cristof hadn't been suspended from the investigation, it would be easy to get him to the Tower. But doing it secretly posed some problems. She thought through the problem out loud. "We could leave tomorrow morning, as soon as it gets light. Paulo's on midnight-to-dawn shift. If we're lucky, he'll be dozing and won't notice that we're using the dock. First shift starts when the sun crests the mountain, so we could be long gone before anyone else gets there. If we use guest wings, someone might notice, but check-in and check-out are a little chaotic right now. And it'd be safer than taking somebody's personal wings."

"I'd have to wear wings?"

"Well, it's the only way up. I can counterweight you and keep a safety line between us. You wouldn't be in any danger." She nodded, satisfied. "I think it would work."

"If we're caught—"

"If we're caught, you're going to use every ounce of influence you can muster make sure I'm not grounded for the rest of my life," Taya stated. "I'm willing to help you, but not at the price of my freedom."

For a moment Cristof seemed to debate with himself, taking off his glasses and pinching the bridge of his nose. Then he sighed, pushing the frames back into place again.

"I'm certain that between Viera and I, we can keep you safe from prosecution. And I can't think of any other way we'll be able to search Alister's offices in a timely fashion." He shoved his hands into his pockets, looking down at the street. "Tomorrow morning?"

"We'll kick off the moment you can see your hand in front of your face," she affirmed.

"All right."

"By the way, what did you do with those punch cards?" Taya asked. "Are we going to take them with us?"

"No. I returned them to Lt. Amcathra this morning. I'd prefer to have kept them, but they're safer under lock and key. I've also put in a recommendation that the Labyrinth Code be rewritten as soon as possible."

"Maybe Kyle's team could do it."

"I suggested them."

"That was nice of you."

"I owed it to Alister."

Taya was pleased. Underneath Cristof's prickly exterior and lack of interpersonal skills, he had a sense of fairness she was starting to appreciate.

They fell silent as they walked.

"How did your work go this morning?" Cristof asked, at last. "Did the search teams find anything new?"

"No. More metal scraps, but that's all." She glanced at him. "Some searchers found a few bones, but they were too old to be . . . anyone's. The coroner said they're probably wild dog bones."

"Did you see them?"

"No. I decided to work with the engineers." Taya swallowed. It took a particular kind of person to work on a body reclamation team. Just the thought of finding something she might recognize made her feel sick. "They think they found part of the bomb."

"I'd like to see it."

"A team of experts was examining it."

"I wonder if I know any of them."

Taya shrugged, looking around. They were turning toward the switchback road that descended to Secundus.

"Did you did you find anything at your brother's house?"

"The mansion?" Cristof stopped. "The lictors searched it. But I was being questioned, and then they pulled me off the case." He made a sharp turn left, instead of taking the road to Secundus. "I'm an idiot. It's about half a mile away."

"Do you want me to go with you?"

He gazed at her, puzzled.

"You're free for the rest of the day, aren't you?"

"Yes. I just thought it might be too personal for you. Going through your brother's things."

"Oh." He looked away and gave an abrupt, dismissive shrug. "I have no intention of bursting into tears, if that's what you're afraid of."

"Your mask is in place."

"I did all my grieving last night." His voice was hard. "Now all I want to do is give Alister a peaceful rebirth by putting his killer behind bars."

Taya walked side-by-side with him, her wings straining against the harness when the winds caught them. She was glad he'd said 'behind bars' and not 'to death.' At least he wasn't going to do anything stupid.

Ondinium would execute the killer, anyway. The city wasn't tolerant of murderers.

That reminded her of her own fight. She glanced down at the cuts on her hand, which were nearly healed.

"Do you know if the Demican I stabbed is still alive?"

"So far."

"Did they find the Alzanans who were with him?"

"Not the last I heard. I expect the investigation has been suspended."

She mulled over that a moment, then attempted a joke. "Maybe after we've borrowed you a set of wings, we can walk around Tertius and try to get mugged. See if we can tempt them out."

"As long as we're walking."

"Oh, I wouldn't take you flying down there. Too many towers and wires. Flying up to the Tower will be a lot safer."

"Good." Cristof took a deep breath. "Alister learned how to fly when he was fourteen or fifteen. He said it was the most exhilarating thing he'd ever done. I didn't pay much attention to him. He was always getting excited over some new adventure or another. His enthusiasm would last a month or two, and then he'd move on to the next thrill. I imagine that being with you made him want to strap on a pair of wings again."

"He could fly?"

"Yes." Cristof looked at her. "He didn't tell you?"

No. But he'd led her to believe that he'd known nothing about flying.

A lie of omission, Viera would have called it.

She would have brought Alister a pair of wings, expecting to teach him what to do, and he would have been able to show off. To impress her.

Taya took a deep breath, shaking her head. *Just forget about it. It doesn't matter anymore.*

"But you never learned how?" she asked, forcing herself to sound natural.

"No."

"You'll do all right. Knowing how armatures work will give you an advantage."

"Knowing how armatures work is different from actually using them."

"It's easy," she assured him. "The icarus docks are above all the towers and cables, except the wireferry to the Council building, and we won't have any problem avoiding the broken lines. The only danger will be the wind, and I'll help you navigate it."

"It's not the wind that worries me. It's the distance to the ground."

"You aren't afraid of heights, are you?" Taya teased, glancing at his sharp profile, which was cast into relief by the late afternoon sun. He was wearing a cross expression again.

"I'm terrified of them."

He said it so tonelessly that she burst into laughter. He shot her a dark look, stopping in the street.

"I'm sorry! I'm not laughing because you're afraid," she apologized. He glared, hunching his shoulders. A gust of wind flapped his coat around him, making him look like a crow with its feathers ruffled. "It's just that it explains so much. That's why you keep track of wireferry repairs, isn't it? I wish you'd told me sooner." A dry leaf whirled up and stuck to his hair. She reached up and plucked it away.

"It's not something I felt comfortable admitting to an icarus."

"Don't be silly." She let the leaf go, watching it tumble away in another gust. Cristof reached up and irritably brushed at the place where it had been. "If you're afraid of heights, you shouldn't go. I can keep you from falling, but if you freeze or panic, you might still get hurt."

"I won't panic."

"You never know how you'll react until you're up there."

"I'll be fine. I don't have a choice, so I'll do it." Impatience was creeping into his voice.

"All right. You don't need to get angry."

"I'm not angry." His voice was taut. "I'm not snapping, shouting, shaking, or lecturing. Nor am I pretending to be anything I am not. In fact, I am being very honest. Is that satisfactory, icarus?"

"Yes, exalted." She sighed. He *would* get moody again, just when they were starting to have a real conversation. "Is your brother's house nearby?"

He stared at her a moment, then tugged up his collar and turned away.

"It's right over there."

Estate Forlore didn't seem any different from the other houses around it; a huge edifice behind an iron gate. Cristof strode toward it as though eager to get away from her.

Taya drew in a deep lungful of the cold autumn air and watched Cristof search through his pockets until he found a ring of keys.

"You have a key to Alister's house?"

"It's my house too. And Alister had the keys to my shop."

When he got the gate open they walked up the path to the door, and he rang. A famulate woman dressed in mourning opened it, then stepped back, bowing. Taya recognized the servant from her dinner with Alister.

"Good afternoon, exalted. We've been awaiting your visit."

"I should have come by yesterday. I was distracted." Cristof stepped inside, dropping his gate keys back into his pocket. "Is Mitta here? I need to talk to her about—arrangements."

"Of course."

"This is Taya Icarus. See that she's made comfortable." He turned to her. "I need a few minutes to talk to Alister's housekeeper." He looked wary, as if expecting her to argue with him. But the servant's black livery and the black cloth draped over the mirrors in the foyer served as stark reminders of why they were there, and Taya just nodded.

"That's fine," she said. She should have guessed that Cristof would be the executor of his brother's will. "I'll wait."

"Would you prefer to doff your wings, icarus?" the servant asked, as Cristof vanished through a side passage. Taya nodded and left her armature behind in the cloak room. The servant led her into a parlor where a small fire burned, and she was soon settled in with a glass of warm spiced wine. It might have been pleasant, if she could forget that she was in a dead man's house.

Alister's taste had run to contemporary artists, she saw, studying the names on the paintings that hung on the walls. One of the works she recognized from last year's exhibition at the Ondinium Museum of Fine Art. She'd gone with Cassi and Pyke, but they'd abandoned Pyke after about half an hour of listening to him rail against the 'anti-aesthetic' of contemporary art. They'd wanted to enjoy the paintings, not think about the politics surrounding them.

Alister's furnishings looked up-to-date, too, which fitted her evolving mental image of him. He'd decorate the way he lived, she thought, looking around. Always looking for something new. The only thing that didn't fit was the parlor's neatness. Alister's office had been a mess. But then, he hadn't had servants in Oporphyr Tower to pick up after him.

She leaned back in the leather chair by the fire and sighed, cradling the glass between her cold fingers. A long-case clock ticked by the door. Had Cristof taken care of it? Her eyes moved to the mantel. It was bare. *Maybe that's where the clock Cristof repaired would have sat*. The clock that had been destroyed along with the wireferry and its two passengers.

Suddenly restless, Taya stood and left the room, walking down the hall. More paintings hung along the walls. She stopped to study one that depicted two icarii in flight and remembered Alister's joke about skydancing. He'd pretended he'd never heard of it, but Cristof's story and this painting proved otherwise. Had he been taught by some icarus girl who'd been flattered by the attentions of a handsome young exalted? Had he flown with a mask over his face, or, surrounded by icarii, had he dared to take it off and hope that nobody on the ground would look up and see the waves on his cheeks?

Her anger at his lies was fading. She stepped back to look at the other paintings. They could have belonged to a complete stranger.

I didn't know him, she thought with resignation. *I'm sorry he's gone, but I wonder if I would have liked him, once I'd figured out who he was?*

Maybe not.

She turned, then started as she realized she was being watched. Cristof stood at the end of the hall, his pale eyes fixed on her. He'd taken off his greatcoat, and his dark suit blended in with the hall's shadows. Only his white cuffs and collar stood out.

"I got tired of sitting in the parlor."

"You look pensive."

"I was just looking at this painting." She gestured to the icarii. "The artist did a good job."

"You can have it, if you want."

"No! No, that's all right." She didn't want anything of Alister's in her little eyrie apartment. "I live with icarii. I don't need paintings of them on my walls."

"I didn't mean to leave you for so long. The staff had a lot of questions."

"What will happen to them now?"

"They can stay here until I decide what to do with the house." He walked forward. "Alister's office is upstairs. Are you done with your drink?"

"Yes." She followed him as several clocks began to toll, all at the same time. Five in the afternoon. "Did you take care of Alister's clocks?"

"Usually." He glanced back at her as he started up a flight of stairs. "Is your landlady going to fix hers?"

"I don't know."

"If she doesn't, you should buy an accurate clock for yourself."

"Clocks are too expensive for an icarus."

"I thought you earned a reasonable salary."

"I do all right, considering the Council takes care of my food and housing and provides me with a uniform and armature. But a clock would just be a luxury. There are plenty of public clocks I can look at, and the church bells, of course."

"Are you saving your money for something important?"

The question surprised her. It seemed intrusive, although she didn't have any reason not to answer. "Retirement, I guess. I don't know. I don't need much to be happy. Just a few friends, my wings, and the sky."

"That sounds like a good way to live."

"It is. Although seeing the way you exalteds live makes me feel a little deprived." She looked around. "My room is going to seem awfully bare when I go back to it."

"I have nothing for you to envy."

She remembered his spartan living quarters. "But you don't have to live like that. Don't you like paintings, or comfortable chairs, or nice furniture?"

"I live on Tertius. I don't want to attract thieves."

"So why not move to Secundus and be more comfortable? You told me you had money."

"Maybe I'm like an icarus. I don't need much to be happy."

"Are you? Happy?"

His shoulder twitched, and he turned as he reached the top of the stairs. Late afternoon light from one of the second-story windows ran in a bright bar across his face.

"I was happier before my brother died."

"I'm sorry." She touched his sleeve as she joined him. "I mean, are you satisfied with the way you live? Don't you ever feel left out, seeing all the things Alister and Viera own?"

"I chose to walk away from all that." Looking ill at ease, he disengaged his arm and pushed up his glasses. "Alister's office is the door behind you. I'm sure it's a mess."

She pushed open the door and gave a sad laugh, looking around. Cristof had guessed correctly. Alister incorporated his floor filing system at home as well as in the Tower. She picked her way inside, setting her wine glass on a bookshelf.

"I can't believe he got anything done like this."

"Somehow he managed." Cristof followed her inside, making his way to the desk. "I assume he learned how to read this mess the same way he learned how to read the holes on a punch card."

"He joked about it, the first time I met him."

"He joked about a lot of things." Cristof looked around, his expression unreadable. "I'll go through his desk. I think that the important part of this disarray will be in the glass-fronted cabinet over there, where he kept his programs. Why don't you start there?"

Taya nodded and squeezed around a pile of books to get to the cabinet. She reached for the door, then paused.

"Is the cabinet supposed to be locked?"

"Oh, of course. He kept his Council programs in there. Do you need me to pry it open?" Cristof started to reach for his pocket, then frowned. "I have a small repair kit in my coat downstairs. It has a screwdriver."

"No, the door's unlocked. That's why I asked." Taya pushed the doors aside, revealing shelves full of long, labeled boxes. Unlike the rest of his filing system, this one was obviously alphabetical. Three boxes were missing from the "C" section. Marks in the dust on the shelves indicated that they had been removed recently.

"There's a program missing. Clockwork Heart, I'll bet."

"What?" Cristof joined her. "Maybe his team took it. This might have been the copy they were running last night."

"How would they have gotten it?"

"I'll check with Mitta." They both stood shoulder-to-shoulder, reading the labels off the other boxes.

"Well, at least he didn't keep the Labyrinth program in here," Taya said.

"He wouldn't be that careless." Cristof closed the cabinet door and glanced at the lock. "It wasn't forced." He shrugged. "Either he took it or his team did. Maybe he was still tinkering with it down at the lab, since it was coming up for vote in Council."

They continued the search, each settling down with a separate stack of papers. Several times Taya looked up to catch Cristof staring at nothing, his thin face tight and miserable. She didn't say anything, and after a few minutes he always started working again, rubbing his eyes.

The sight depressed her. For brief moments at a time she could forget about the deaths, but their memory always returned, casting a pall over everything. Even though his irascibility exasperated her, she had to respect the way Cristof kept pushing forward. It would have been easier for him to just give up and grieve.

Work's therapeutic.

If only he weren't so stubborn about hiding his feelings. She sighed.

"What's wrong?" Cristof turned, his face almost invisible in the shadows that stretched across the room. Taya realized she'd been straining to see the papers in front of her for the last ten minutes or so. The sun had set below the mountains.

"It's dark."

"Oh." He stood, rummaged through the desk for matches and lit a gas lamp on the wall. "Better?"

"Yes." She studied the shadows that hollowed out his cheeks and eyes. "How are you doing?"

"I haven't found anything that seems relevant."

"That's not what I meant."

He hesitated, then shrugged.

"I told you I wasn't going to burst into tears."

"I wouldn't think any less of you if you did."

"It's not going to happen." His voice brooked no disagreement. She sighed and dropped flat on her back, staring up at the ceiling. The leather of her flight suit creaked as she folded her arms under her head.

"Don't you ever relax that iron grip you keep on yourself?"

"I'll relax it when this is over."

She lifted her head to glance at him. He sat rigidly in his chair.

"Sure you will." She sighed again. "I'm sorry. I'm just thinking out loud. If I start getting annoying, just tell me."

"You're long past 'start.'"

She dropped her head again and smiled at the ceiling. If he could be sarcastic, he couldn't be too bad off.

"I'm starving. Can we take a break for dinner?"

"I plan to avoid eating until after our flight tomorrow, but don't let me stop you."

"You should eat something," she urged him. "You don't want to get light-headed out there."

"I don't think that's avoidable, and I'd rather not get sick, as well."

"I told you, I'll take care of you." She propped herself back up on her elbows. "Anyway, come to dinner with me. Even if you're not hungry, it'll be better than sitting up here on your own. Then we can go ask Kyle if he took Alister's copy of Clockwork Heart."

"Now you're my voice *and* my counselor?" He stood, casting dark, narrow shadows against the opposite wall.

"Sure," she said, holding out a hand. "I don't know what it's like for exalteds, but among icarii, after you've eaten, argued, and cried together, you're friends."

He looked at her hand, then drew back.

"Then perhaps we should avoid sharing a meal," he said, turning away.

"What?" Taya gaped. "What in the Lady's name does that mean? An exalted can't be friends with an icarus?"

"That's not it at all."

"Then what?" she demanded.

"I'm not Alister." His voice was cold and dispassionate. "I don't need a friend who only tolerates me because I'm the last link to her lover."

Taya scrambled to her feet.

"Is that what you think I'm doing?"

"It's obvious."

"Well, you're wrong. First of all, Alister and I never even kissed, so we're hardly lovers, and second of all, you're no link to him at all. Alister might have lied to me, but he was never rude." Taya jerked around and stormed out of the room, throwing the door open as she went.

"He told me you were lovers!" Cristof shouted, behind her. She ignored him and clattered down the stairs, heading for the foyer and her floating armature.

Like him? Pity him? What in the Lady's name was I thinking? She grabbed her armature. Forget it. She'd made a heroic effort to be diplomatic, even to be friendly, but she wasn't going to be a masochist about it.

"Icarus?" The servant appeared, hesitating. Taya snapped the keel shut over her chest and began running straps through buckles.

"Tell the exalted I'll meet him at the dock gate at dawn," she snapped. She heard Cristof descending the staircase. She gave her shoulder straps a yank, eager to be gone.

"What about the University?" Cristof asked, standing in the hallway facing her. His voice was tight. "I thought we were going to talk to the programmers."

"Talk to them yourself." She fixed the last of her buckles and gave him a withering look. "You don't need me to be your voice, your counselor, or your friend. So I'll give you exactly what you want, exalted. Nothing."

Cristof gestured to the servant to go. The wide-eyed famulate darted away.

"It's clear I didn't have all the facts. I spoke poorly."

"Yeah, you've got a real knack for that." She turned and pushed the doors open. "Dawn. By the dock gates. And only because I said I would."

"Taya, wait!"

"Forget it, exalted. You're not the only one in the world whose pride can be wounded." She headed down the steps, relieved to feel the crisp, cold autumn air on her face and the familiar brush of wind against her arching wings.

After tomorrow, I'm through with this. Reaching the front gate, she pushed it open. *Pyke was right—exalteds are nothing but trouble. I'll take him to the tower for Viera's sake, but that's the end of it. I've got real work to do.*

The wide Primus street was empty. Lights glowed in the windows of the neighboring estates, and the moon was bright overhead. She slid her arms into the uplifted wings and shrugged to unlock them, spreading them wide.

"Taya! Wait!"

She turned. Cristof was hurrying out the gate, his greatcoat askew.

Taya took a step away from him, turning her face into the wind.

"Stay out of my way," she warned him, fanning her metal feathers wide. He ducked beneath them.

"Would you listen to me, please?"

"I've got nothing to say to you."

"Please!"

She gazed up at the stars, then lowered her wings, berating herself for being a weak-willed fool. She fixed Cristof with a steely eye as he stumbled to a halt in front of her.

"You've got ten seconds."

He grabbed her forearm, which was encased in protective ondium struts. "I'm sorry—Alister told me you were lovers. I thought it was true."

"We already know he was a liar." She tried to shake him off, but his grip tightened.

"I shouldn't have accused you like that. I'm sorry. I'm the one who sees my brother, every time I look at you."

"Why?" Taya regarded him with suspicion. His pale eyes were wide behind his glasses.

"Do you have any idea what you looked like, dancing together?"

"It was just a dance."

"You looked—" his voice cracked. "You looked happy. You looked like a couple. That was the last time I ever talked to him. The night I saw you dancing together."

"Oh, Lady." Taya's shoulders sagged, and metal feathers clanked against the cobblestones.

"After—I wanted to talk to you about what you'd overheard, but you were on the dance floor and Alister was bragging about how you were going to spend the night with him, so I gave up. I shouldn't have believed him, but I knew you'd been seeing him before the party. And when you were together it was so obvious that you were meant for each other—" he stopped, clutching the ondium struts as if to physically hold her in place. "Every time I look at you, I feel guilty because he died and I didn't. And I can't replace him for you."

"Of course you can't." Taya suddenly felt tired. *I should have left without listening to him. Being angry is better than being depressed.* "There's nothing to replace."

"You loved him."

"No, I didn't. I liked him, and I thought it might turn into love, but after everything I've found out about him, I'm glad it didn't. I don't know. Maybe it *is* better to be rude. You piss me off, but you don't lie to me."

"Only by omission." Cristof looked down at his white fingers. "It's been making me sick, envying my dead brother. I'm sorry."

Envying? Taya gave him a searching look. The exalted hunched his shoulders, a picture of sharp angles and shadows, and lifted his hands from her armature.

"Don't worry about tomorrow, icarus. I'll find some other way up to the tower. Maybe Amcathra will let me back in on the investigation if I tell him what I've found so far."

Taya stared up at the sky again and gave a long, pained sigh. *Oh, Lady. I need to learn how to be hard-hearted.*

"You're a real slagging pain in my tailset, you know that, exalted? I don't know how much more of you I can take. I've got lots of other people I could spend my time with."

"I don't." The gas lamps turned Cristof's glasses into white flames against the darkness as he pushed them higher on his nose and turned away. "Fly safely, icarus."

She stared after him a moment, then lifted her arms and shrugged her wings back into their locked position. *Forgefire,* she thought. *What else am I going to do tonight? Sit in my bedroom and brood?*

"We already shared a meal, anyway," she called after him. "Back when you weren't being so rude."

He stopped, the hem of his greatcoat swinging around his legs.

"I said I'm sorry."

"Among icarii," she said, to his back, "when two friends fight, one of them buys the other a drink to make up."

He stared straight ahead, into the darkness.

"What kind of drink?"

"A cold beer to wash down a spicy Cabisi stew would be perfect." She folded her arms over her chest. "I told you I'm starving."

He turned.

"Then I'll buy your dinner, too," he said, his grave tone leavened by the profound relief in his face.

Chapter Eleven

Taya's favorite Cabisi restaurant was close to the University campus, where it served foreign students and the occasional adventurous Ondinium like her. Cristof stuck to his decision to fast, only nibbling on shreds of the flatbread served with the meal. They discussed what they knew so far. It wasn't much, but it was safe territory. Taya didn't know what to think about Cristof envying Alister. She didn't know what to think about Cristof, period.

It was easier not to.

When she'd finished eating, they walked the four blocks to the University, heading back down to the basement of the Science and Technology building. The familiar sound of an argument greeted them, but Taya didn't hear the clatter of the analytical engine or the chugging of the steam engines.

"Hello," she sang out, as they entered the room. The argument stopped as the programmers looked up. Palms hit foreheads and heads bobbed when they saw Cristof.

"This isn't a good time for a visit," Kyle cautioned them. A large schematic was spread on the table in front of him. "A bug cropped up this morning and we've been trying to hunt it down all day."

"Did something go wrong with one of your programs?" Taya looked at the huge analytical engine that stood motionless across half the room. The thick cables that led down to the steam engines in the basement were disconnected.

"No, it's mechanical, we think." Lars was inspecting a gear assembly. Cristof crossed the room to join him. "Some torsion in the spindles, maybe some gear drift . . . ."

"What happened?"

"We came in this morning—"

"Afternoon," Victor corrected. He was sitting next to a box of punch cards, glancing at each and then setting it to one side. "We were hung over this morning."

"This afternoon, early, and we found the engine running on its own."

"Is that bad?" Taya pulled around a chair and sat in it backward, her wings rising behind her.

"It can't be very good for the mechanism," Cristof murmured, squinting as he examined the gears. "This is a precision machine, like a clock. Does it lose accuracy with metal wear?"

"Absolutely." Lars rubbed oil off a spindle.

"Lars thinks the mechanical problems might have affected Heart's results," Emelie said, smirking.

"That, or Alister had a serious glitch in his program," Lars growled. "Anyway, it's not just the fact that the engine ran all night. Its encryption keys were overridden, too, so anyone could have gotten in and used it while we were gone."

"Did they?" Cristof asked, suddenly intent.

"Not that we can tell, but . . . ." Isobel shrugged. "The place was a mess when we left. We couldn't tell if anything had been moved when we got in this morning."

"Afternoon." Victor tapped a card on the table and then put it back into his stack.

"Whenever."

"So, what went wrong with the Clockwork Heart program?" Taya inquired.

"It told us that Lars and Kyle had the best chance of a successful marriage," Emelie replied, grinning.

"The deal was, if any of us scored well together, we'd go on a date and see if the program was right." Kyle glanced up and smiled impishly. "But Lars has cold feet."

"I'd rather be ground through the Great Engine's gears," Lars grumbled.

"We all agreed to it," Kyle pointed out. "Don't worry. I'll take you someplace nice."

Taya laughed. "Isn't there some kind of—I don't know, some kind of program rule about couples being men and women?"

"That's what Victor's looking for." Kyle was still smiling to himself as he glanced down at the schematic again. "Either another function overrode it, or Alister was more of a free thinker than we thought."

"Good for Alister," Isobel said, unscrewing a metal panel.

Taya glanced at Cristof, wondering what he thought, but he was crouching and regarding the analytical engine with a furrowed brow.

"You'd think he'd put sex selection on top of the deck," Victor griped, "but it's not there. And some of these cards are ridiculous. He's got registers in here that don't make any sense at all."

"Did he write the whole program himself?" Cristof asked.

"Pretty much. It was his project." Victor scowled, putting another card into the stack. "I would have written this routine with much more elegance. It's as though he didn't care how much slagging computational power or time his program would take."

"Well, he was going to run it on the Great Engine, wasn't he?" Taya asked. "I mean, that's pretty powerful, right?"

"Aesthetics are essential. Programs should be as clean as possible. Alister was usually very efficient, but this mess is positively baroque."

"That's not the Great Engine's version of the program, is it?" Cristof asked. "The cards are too small."

"This was his test version, the one he ran here. Nobody tests a program on the Great Engine. It costs too much, and you wouldn't want to cause a crash," Kyle said.

"What would happen if the Great Engine crashed?" Taya cocked her head, imagining huge gears tumbling down against each other. "Is it something the Torn Cards might try? You said running a partial program like the one Cristof had last night could shut down an engine."

"It wouldn't be the end of the world," Lars said, handing Cristof a clean gear. The exalted began piecing the cleaned assembly back together again, looking as engrossed as he'd been while dismantling the eyrie clock. "But you'd panic a lot of engineers. An abrupt stop would throw gears and spindles out of alignment, and it might ruin a storage drum if the data were being written. Everything would have to be recalibrated before the Engine was started up again. That would take a few days. The program schedule would fall behind, you might lose some data, and Ondinium could get stuck with a surplus of widgets or something. Nothing serious."

"You keep saying that the Great Engine isn't very important, but I thought it was the main reason Ondinium's so powerful."

"Don't listen to the Organicists *or* the Social Engineers," Kyle advised, glancing up from the schematic. "They both credit the Engine with far too much power. It's just a fancy calculating machine. People decide what to do with the data it provides. If you looked at your watch and it said five o'clock, but you knew it was the middle of the night, would you believe your watch or your senses? Same with the Great Engine. If it gives the Council obviously inaccurate data, the Council will notice and make corrections."

"'Obviously' being the key word, of course," Isobel said as she pieced together more metal parts.

"There's something very skewed here," Victor muttered, flipping back a few cards. "What in the Lady's name was he doing with this? Some kind of look-up. . . ?"

"By the way," Taya said, "did you take that program from Alister's house? His copy is missing."

"This is his copy, but we found it here. He must have been working on it the night before he died," Emelie replied. Taya winced at her matter-of-fact tone.

"He was at a party that night."

"He might have come here afterward. He did things like that. Sometimes the best time to work is after midnight, when nobody else is around." Victor scrutinized a card. "Emelie, can you figure this out?"

She leaned over his shoulder, then picked up the cards that preceded it.

"Looks like it should loop. Where's the end?"

Kyle set down the schematic.

"If a loop set the program buzzing, it could keep the engine's gears spinning all night," he observed. "But an error that obvious should have come up during testing."

"This card is pretty new. Maybe he was experimenting," Victor suggested. He held up two cards. Even Taya could see the smudges of oil and wear around the perforations on the older card.

"Could a loop bypass the security on this engine?" Cristof joined them, studying the cards as if the punches might render up their meaning to him.

"No, but take a look at this." The other programmers huddled around Victor as he pulled out cards and spread them on the table, over Kyle's schematic.

Taya and Cristof backed away, giving each other blank looks.

"How soon can we get up to the tower?" Cristof asked, his voice low.

"Not until there's light. We can leave as soon as we can make out shapes, but you wouldn't want to fly into a tree or a cliff on your first time out."

"Or ever." He jammed his hands into his pockets, frowning at the motionless analytical engine.

"What are you thinking?"

"You don't want to know."

"How'd you like me to drop you while we're flying?"

He glanced at her.

"I'm thinking about what happened to Decatur Neuillan."

"Why?" Taya swallowed. "You don't think Alister had anything to do with that, do you?"

"What if Emelie was right?" His voice had dropped to an uncertain murmur. "What if Alister *had* given Neuillan too much information? Enough for Neuillan to circumvent the loyalty test?"

"If he did, it was just an accident."

"Let's say it wasn't." Cristof sounded defeated. "Neuillan was a family friend, and Alister's judgment wasn't always the best when it came to keeping secrets. What if Neuillan convinced Alister to tell him how to get around Refinery? And what if somebody found out what Alister had done, blackmailed him into writing a program that would harm the Great Engine, and then killed him to keep him quiet?"

"The Clockwork Heart program?"

"It's just coincidence that the team ran it last night. Otherwise, if it had gotten Council approval, it would have been run on the Engine."

"That's pretty far-fetched," Taya objected. "And Alister really believed in this program, I could tell."

"He fooled you before. He could be very convincing, when he wanted to be."

"Clockwork Heart wasn't about impressing me. It was personal."

Cristof looked troubled. "Maybe. But he also cared what people thought about him. If someone threatened to tell the world that Alister had a hand in Neuillan's treason. . . ."

"But if Clockwork Heart didn't work right, that would make him look bad too, wouldn't it?"

"Making a programming error is one thing. Aiding and abetting a traitor is another." Cristof rubbed his eyes, knocking his glasses askew. "I don't want to believe that Alister would sabotage the Engine, but think about it. If he'd written a program that would break into the Engine's security, someone would have a very good reason to kill him and Caster. Killing Alister would keep the program's secret safe, and killing Caster would make sure Clockwork Heart got accepted in the Council's vote."

"But that doesn't explain the stolen Labyrinth program cards. Alister thought you did that."

"Hey, exalted." Lars looked over, his round face troubled.

"What?"

"No offense, but I think your brother was writing more just than a matchmaking program."

Cristof gave Taya a heavy look, then stepped up to the table.

"What is it?"

"Well, we haven't gone through the whole thing, but he's got routines here that look more like decryption functions than compatibility match-ups."

"This is the last program we ran last night," Kyle added. "It has to be the one that affected the engine, unless Lars finds a mechanical problem."

"I haven't found anything yet, and I've been over about two-thirds of the metal. It's still a possibility, but after seeing these cards. . . ." Lars shook his head.

"It's all Alister's work?" Taya asked, casting about for a better explanation. "Could someone else have inserted those cards into his program?"

"No, it's his," Victor assured her. "I've seen him use some of these functions before."

"Was the program sitting here when you came in yesterday?" Cristof asked.

"It was in his storage area."

"Locked?"

"Yes, but we all have each other's keys. When we heard he was dead, we decided to pull it out and run it."

"It doesn't make sense," Cristof muttered. "Why would he leave it here, where anyone could see what he was doing?"

"You wouldn't want to carry a program all day," Victor said, nudging the boxes at his feet. "A box of punch cards is heavy."

"Besides, this room's secure," Lars said. "And nobody would have any reason to think Clockwork Heart was anything other than a matchmaking program."

"Hey, wait a minute," Isobel protested. "You don't think Heart was specifically written to get access to an engine, do you? Alister wouldn't do that."

"I don't know," Cristof said, pulling his coat around him. "But if it was, somebody might be coming after this copy."

Taya and Kyle both spoke at once.

"Not necessarily." "If he is—"

They looked at each other. Kyle gestured for her to go first.

"If we're assuming this was written to run on the Great Engine, these are the wrong kind of cards. He would have had a second copy to run on the Engine, and that copy's probably still up in Oporphyr Tower," Taya said. "So if someone wants to get access to the Engine, they'll have to go up there to get it."

"And only icarii can get there right now," Cristof mused.

"The only other engine worth accessing would be the one in the Bank of Ondinium," Kyle added.

Taya felt a surge of excitement.

"A bank robbery! Maybe that's what this is all about!"

"But the Labyrinth Code . . ." Cristof objected.

"Does the bank use it?"

"Not that I know of," Lars said, looking thoughtful. "But you could be right, Kyle. Messing with the Bank of Ondinium would cause a lot more trouble than tampering with the Great Engine, and the bank uses paper cards."

Cristof stood deep in thought, his usual frown in place.

"As much as I'd prefer to stay in the bank than go up to the tower," he said at last, "there's too much evidence pointing to the Great Engine."

"But how would someone get up there?" Emelie asked.

"You can hike up to the Tower," Isobel pointed out. "It's dangerous, but it's possible. The wireferry service path runs all the way to the top."

"So somebody could already be up there." Cristof looked at Taya. "Is there any way—"

"No. I'm not taking you up in the dark."

"But if someone's trying to sabotage the Great Engine—"

"They're not climbing up in the dark, either. It's too dangerous."

"How long would the hike take?" Cristof asked Isobel.

"Depends. From Primus, at this time of year, two or three days, depending on how athletic and well-equipped you are. The cliffs are the hardest part. You'd need to know what you were doing, and you wouldn't want to get caught on the cliffs at night."

"Is the only access to the Great Engine through the Council tower?" Taya asked.

"As far as I know, yes," Kyle replied. "All the construction tunnels were blocked and sealed after the Engine was put into place."

"There's got to be some kind of maintenance tunnel. What if one of the steam engines needs replacing? Or a megagear?" Cristof insisted.

"Well, if there's another way in, it's a state secret. You'd know it better than we would."

Cristof looked frustrated as he pulled out his watch and checked it.

"It's not even nine yet," he muttered.

"How long would it take you to examine this program and find out exactly what it does?" Taya asked, turning to the programming team.

"A few hours, maybe."

"Would you do that? So far, all we have are suspicions. We could be completely wrong, and there's no point in speculating until we know what this does for sure."

"We might as well," Victor said, eying the boxes. "We can't do anything else until Lars reassembles the engine."

"Good." Taya grabbed a graphite pencil and scribbled her address on the corner of Kyle's schematic. "When you find out what it does, send a message to me here. No matter what time it is, okay?"

"What if we find out it *is* some kind of security workaround?" Lars asked. "Do you want us to tell the lictors?"

She looked at Cristof. He nodded.

"It could make Alister look bad," Kyle warned.

"I know. I trust that you won't raise any alarms unless you're certain there's a security risk. But if you feel there's a genuine threat to the city, warn the lictors and tell them your suspicions about a bank robbery."

"Don't mention that we're going to the tower, though," Taya added. "Please."

"All right. And don't worry, we'll be careful. Our reputations are linked to Alister's." Isobel shook her long hair back over her shoulders. "I can't believe he'd do anything shady, though. This has to be some kind of mistake."

"I hope it is," Cristof agreed.

"We'll leave you to work," Taya said, putting down the pencil. "Come on, Cristof."

The exalted equivocated a moment, then followed after her.

"Where are we going?"

"All we can do now is spin our gears, so we might as well go home and try to get some sleep."

"Just stop? When we finally have some idea of what's going on?"

"All we have are suspicions until they analyze that program. And all you can do with suspicions is give yourself a stomachache."

"There's such a thing as being too pragmatic, icarus."

"Do you have a better idea?"

"I'm going back to Alister's office to look for more information. We barely made a dent in that mess."

"You're just going to frustrate yourself," she predicted.

"I'm used to that. And I don't expect I'll get much sleep tonight, anyway."

"All right. I'll walk you back."

"No. Don't bother." His eyes slid away from her. "Get some rest. You're going to have your hands full tomorrow morning."

"Are you sure?"

"Yes."

Taya sensed Cristof's reserve kicking in again. She didn't have the energy to fight it again. "All right. I'll see you at dawn, then. Meet me at the gate next to the flight docks."

"Shortly after five." He hesitated, then reached into his vest. Gold glinted in his hand as he held it out. "Don't be late."

"I don't need that."

"Just in case. Since your eyrie clock is inaccurate."

She met his eyes a moment, then took it. The pocket watch's gold case was warm. She curled her fingers around it.

"I'll see you at dawn."

He nodded, and she turned and headed for the University dock, tucking the watch into her flight suit.

As she circled up into the night sky, she spotted him standing under a streetlight, peering upward. She tipped her wings to him, and he waved.

THE LANDLADY KNOCKED on her door. Taya rolled over in bed, pulling her covers under her chin.

"What?" she groaned.

"That clockwright is here to see you," Gwen said, her voice quivering with disapproval. "He says it's important."

Taya stared at the ceiling.

"What time is it?"

"Almost eleven. I told him we don't open the doors for groundlings after ten, but he insists, and he *is* an exalted, even if he's a freak."

"All right. I'm coming." She rolled out of bed, grabbing her slippers.

Gwen sat downstairs in the cloakroom, matching Cristof scowl for scowl. She outweighed him by a considerable amount and wasn't cowed by his castemark.

He broke their mutual glare when Taya walked in.

"It isn't dawn." Taya rubbed her face. "Maybe you need your watch back, so you can tell the time?"

"I need to talk to you."

"I was asleep!"

He turned to the landlady.

"May we have a moment in private, please?"

"Not in here," Gwen declared. "I don't care what my icarii do elsewhere, but this boarding house stays quiet after ten. If you want to talk, you can take your conversation outside."

"Taya—" he turned to her. "It's important."

"It's also freezing." She was already cold, wearing nothing but her red flannel nightgown and threadbare slippers. "And late."

"Here." He pulled off his greatcoat and held it out for her. "Just for a minute."

Taya took it, giving Gwen a resigned look.

"I already told you what I thought about him," Gwen said, darkly. "You can do better."

Cristof cast the woman a resentful look before opening the door.

"So, what is it?" Taya asked, shivering as they stepped out onto the porch. Cristof's coat was still warm from his body, but her feet felt like they'd been plunged into ice water.

"The lictors have issued a warrant for my arrest. The engineers confirmed that the bomb was in the clock."

"I thought you'd already gone through all that."

"It was just a suspicion, then. Now they have enough evidence to detain me for questioning. I spotted lictors staking out Alister's house when I returned, so I avoided them and tracked down Amcathra. He told me what happened and said if I was still around by the time he pulled on his boots, he'd have to arrest me." He rubbed his eyes, frowning. "Under any other circumstances I'd go to headquarters and answer their questions, but what if Alister really was writing a security bypass program?"

"It won't make any difference if the lictors get the proof or you do. Unless you're planning to cover up for him."

"No." He shook his head. "I wouldn't do that. But—maybe it's arrogance, but I won't believe Alister's guilty until I see the proof with my own two eyes. Accusing him without evidence would be a poor way to avenge his death. And . . . you said he was going to do the same thing for me."

"All right." Taya yawned. "Then nothing's changed, unless Amcathra's going to turn you in."

"He seemed to be having some trouble finding his boots. But something *has* changed. If you help me now, you'll be aiding a fugitive. I promised that you wouldn't lose your wings if you took me up to the Tower. I can't promise that anymore."

Taya frowned.

"If I refuse to take you up, will you turn yourself in?"

He met her eyes.

"No. I'll figure out some other way to get there."

"Why don't you just talk to the lictors and let them sort it out?"

"We're talking about a potential plot to take over Ondinium's Great Engine and a criminal who will apparently stop at nothing to keep his secret. I need to know how deeply my brother was involved, and who was involved with him. If there were other decaturs . . . ."

Taya studied the determined set to his mouth. She'd seen that expression before, in mirrors. There was no arguing with it.

Lady. She leaned on the porch railing. *Do I really want to risk my wings for this? Alister was a liar, Cristof's a pain, and Viera—*

Viera's nice enough, but I don't owe her anything. In fact, she owes me.

But I like her, and I like her son, and they deserve to know the truth.

And I want to know the truth, too.

She closed her eyes, weighing her options.

"I'll find another way up," Cristof said, sounding downcast.

"Just shut up and let me think this through."

One short flight. Up and back. She could claim that she hadn't known Cristof was suspended. That she hadn't known there was a warrant out for his arrest.

He needed her. He'd helped her escape her attackers, he'd shared his lunch with her, and he'd let her borrow his handkerchief and watch and coat.

He was snappish and sharp-tongued, and he had envied his brother's flirtation with her.

She opened her eyes and glared at him. He looked irresolute, his thin face pinched by the cold.

"You're still a pain in my tailset, Cristof," she grumbled. "But I'll take you up and trust that Viera will bail me out of prison."

"She wouldn't let you down."

"Where are you going to go tonight?"

"I don't know. Does your landlady have any rooms to let?"

"You'd get a warmer reception from the lictors."

"I'll find a squat in Tertius, then," he said with resignation.

She eyed him. "Stay there. I'll be back in a minute." She ran back into the eyrie, waving to Gwen, and burst into Cassilta's room.

"Wha—?" Cassi rolled over in bed, waking up.

"It's me. Go back to sleep." Taya grabbed Cassi's purse and headed downstairs again.

Cristof was huddled in a corner of the porch when she got back, shivering in his thin cloth famulate's coat.

"Oh. Sorry." She pulled off his greatcoat and handed it to him. Then she rummaged through the purse. "Perfect. Sit down."

He wrapped the coat around himself and sat on the porch rail, watching her with wary curiosity. When she pulled out Cassi's small jars of cosmetics, his eyes lit up with understanding.

"I think this will do it," Taya said with satisfaction, choosing a color.

"This isn't your foundation, is it?" he asked as she dabbed a coppery base color over the blue waves on his cheeks.

"No. My friend Cassi's. Why?"

"It isn't your shade."

"So you're an expert on cosmetics, as well as a clockwright and a secret lictor? Are you living *another* secret life I should know about?"

He shook his head, and she tsked, dabbing at a splotch with her fingertip.

"I've had to cover my castemark before."

"Too bad. I know a dressmaker who'd love to have an exalted as a patron." She corked the bottle and opened a small pot of eye darkener. "Do you want to be cardinal or plebeian?"

"Plebeian. I'm going back to Tertius."

She leaned over him and drew a famulate castemark on his forehead.

"It's not perfect, but it'll do," she said, drawing back and assessing her work. "Don't reach up and smudge it."

"I won't." He grabbed her fingers, warming them a moment between his hands. "Thank you."

Taken off-guard by the gesture, Taya stared at him. Even half-sitting on the porch rail, Cristof's head was an inch or two higher than hers.

Gawky. Skinny. Crowlike.

Not such an awful guy, after all.

"That's what friends are for," she said, at last.

He didn't say anything, scrutinizing her with his hands curled around her fingers. Taya felt like some kind of machine he was trying to figure out and forced a laugh to dispel the tension.

"Although," she added, "this friendship ends if you keep waking me up in the middle of the night."

He released her, standing.

"I'll keep that in mind. Good-night, Taya Icarus."

"Good night."

THREE HOURS LATER Gwen knocked on her door again. This time the vexed woman held out a message from the University.

Taya opened it, groaned, and shoved it under her pillow.

She'd deal with it tomorrow.

Chapter Twelve

Taya could barely see her hands in front of her as she hurried down the path to the flight dock. The dawn *diispira* hadn't kicked up yet, and it was cold enough for her breath to form visible clouds as she ran.

Cristof was a dark, narrow figure huddled by the gate.

"It's locked," he said, as she approached.

"Of course it is." She pulled out her key and let them in. "Ondium's expensive. Did you find a place to sleep last night?"

"More or less."

"What does that mean?"

"The floor was cleaner than the mattress. I didn't sleep well."

"Stiff muscles?"

"Not too bad."

"Good." She led them across the open practice field to the flight prep building. "I got a message from Kyle last night."

"What did he say?"

"The Clockwork Heart program affected the University engine. I guess that once it runs, it keeps other security programs from locking off access to the engine, or its storage drums, or something like that. He seemed to think it was pretty important. He said he's sending a formal report to the college president and the lictors this morning."

"Oh, Lady." Cristof leaned against the building wall, staring into space. "What was Alister doing?"

"That's what we're going to find out." She unlocked the door to the flight prep building and struck a lucifer match as soon as they were inside. Candles and lamps were stored by the door. She handed him a lamp and took one herself. In the light, she saw that he'd wiped off last night's handiwork, leaving his castemark visible once more. "You decided to be an exalted again?"

"It might give us an advantage if we're caught."

"Good idea. We'll need all the advantages we can get." She led him to the men's changing room.

That morning, she'd done what she could to set up her own advantages. She'd left a note in Cassi's purse containing Kyle's letter and describing where she was going and why. She didn't know what Cassi would do when she found it, but no icarus flew without filing a flight plan.

Besides, if they got caught by the lictors, she wanted her friends to know she wasn't a criminal.

"Don't worry." Cristof tapped his bulging coat pocket. "You can always say that I forced you at gunpoint."

"It wouldn't work. They'll just ask why I didn't drop you once we were aloft." She opened up the flight suit closet. "How tall are you?"

"Six three."

"Hmm." She looked dubiously at the selection. "Well, do your best to find a suit and boots that fit. The suit needs to be snug, but not so tight that it binds. Don't wear anything but your drawers beneath it. Fold your clothing and bring it out with you, and we'll store it in my locker. Then we'll find you a harness."

He nodded, and she left him, going to the women's locker room to change into her own suit and harness. Fifteen minutes later she was showing him how to step into a complicated arrangement of straps and buckles.

Cristof had done the best he could, but his flight suit was several inches too short in the arms and legs and a little too wide around the chest and shoulders. Transferring the contents of his coat pockets into the pouches built into the suit gave him a bulky look. *Crow with his feathers plumped,* she thought, irreverently.

"The needlegun I can understand, and even your identification papers, but do you really need this?" She held up the slim leather tool kit.

"You never know when you might need a screwdriver." He tucked the leather case away and she shook her head. Cassi and her lip paints, Cristof and his tools.

"You really are a gearhead, aren't you?"

"We gearheads consider that term a compliment, icarus."

Amused, Taya buttoned up his collar until it rested under his chin. He tugged at it, frowning.

"Leave it alone," she instructed. "It may feel tight now, but you don't want a breeze down your suit while you're flying."

"It's no more uncomfortable than robes and a mask," he said, dropping his hand and cinching his belt tighter. "But the suit's heavier than I expected. Especially the boots. You don't look big enough to carry around so much weight every day."

"I'm stronger than I look," Taya said, with a trace of pride. "And the ondium makes make it feel lighter. The boots are heavy because of the metal toes and thick soles. Even so, we have to replace them pretty often. Which reminds me. . . ." She grabbed a pair of jointed metal-and-leather knee pads. Kneeling in front of him, she attached them to the harness straps that circled his legs, bracing a hand against his shin as she pulled the buckles tight. "We're not going to try an upright landing today. You're going to land on your knees and skid to a halt."

He shifted uneasily while she worked and finally cleared his throat.

"I've seen little icarii doing that. I thought they were playing."

"It's the first landing we learn. It isn't elegant, but sometimes it's the best you can do, especially when the winds are high or the approach is awkward." She slapped his calves and straightened. "This job is tough on the joints."

"I feel like I'm wearing armor." He took a few steps. "Excuse me." He turned and readjusted the straps around his thighs.

"Make sure they don't chafe," she said, smirking at his back. "Remember, the straps will pull up once the armature is strapped on."

"Wonderful," he muttered, his back still turned.

"I'll go get you some wings and weights while you fix that," she said, chuckling. "How much do you weigh?"

"About one hundred and seventy."

"Heavy."

He glanced over his shoulder.

"People have called me scrawny all my life."

"Heavy for an icarus," she amended. "But you're tall for an icarus, too. I'll be back in about ten minutes."

She found a pair of visitor wings and grabbed a wire cage of ondium counterweights. By the time she returned, Cristof was pacing the room, testing the straps. She led him outside, locking the door behind them.

"Paolo's on watch, but he usually dozes off at dawn," she said. "Still, let's move quickly." The sky was lighter now, although the sun hadn't risen above the mountains. The air was crisp and cold. She took Cristof to the docks, which jutted out over the city. The peaks of the surrounding mountains were starting to glow with the imminent dawn. The city of Ondinium stretched out below them, still in shadow, crammed with buildings, tenements, and factories.

Cristof glanced down and shuddered.

"Oh, Lady," he breathed, fixing his eyes on his hands as he pulled on his leather gloves.

"Don't worry. You'll be fine." Taya clipped the floating wire cage to a ring in the ground and helped him buckle the icarus armature onto his harness. "Snap the keel around your chest and run the straps through the rings."

"Exactly how is this going to work?" he asked, his voice strained.

"I'm going to put so much ondium on you that even if you lose control and stall, you'll just drift to the ground," she said, adjusting the padding around his shoulders and over his chest. His heart was pounding so hard she could feel it through her gloves. "Breathe, exalted."

He nodded and drew in a deep breath. She gave him a reassuring smile and tousled his hair. Then she paused and plucked at several strands of it.

"Who cuts this, anyway?"

"I do." He brushed her hand away.

"I guess that explains it." She stepped away and opened the hatch at the bottom of the ondium cage. "You do a lousy job."

"Didn't I just see you wearing red flannel pajamas and slippers with holes? I don't think you have any right to lecture me about what looks fashionable," he retorted. His voice seemed steadier.

Taya pulled out a five-pound counterweight, pleased with herself. Her diversion had worked.

"I like those slippers. They're broken in." She slid the buoyant ondium bar into a pocket on his belt and buttoned it. "Anyway, nobody sees them except me."

"Nobody?"

She pulled out another five-pound counterweight.

"Well, my best friends."

"So seeing them should be construed as a privilege, not a punishment?"

"Watch it, clockwright." She slid another counterweight into his belt. "How do you feel?"

"Light." He stepped away from her a moment. "Strange."

"We don't usually counterweight ourselves this much. It makes wind hard to handle. But I'm going to be doing most of the flying, so I want you to be as maneuverable as possible." She slipped out two more five-pound counterweights and added them to the others. "Are you floating away yet?"

"Almost." He eyed the edge of the cliff and took a step back toward her again. "What would happen if I got too light?"

"Well, in theory, you'd float up until you hit the moon. But in practice, you'd slide one of the counterweights out of your belt and release it into the air." She eyed him. "And then you'd reimburse me, because each of these weights is worth about a year of my salary."

"As long as you keep me alive, I'll handle the expenses," he promised.

"Deal. It's time to practice." She stood in front of him, her own wings locked high, and showed him how to slide his arms into the straps and bars. He had no trouble mastering the release and engage mechanisms, locking his wings into high, glide, and close positions.

"The mistake most beginners make is to flap too much," she said as he spread his wings and practiced an up and downstroke, feathers closing and opening. The downstroke lifted him and she reached up to grab the metal keel over his chest, pulling him back down to earth. "But birds glide as often as they can because it's less effort than flapping. What I'll want you to do most of the time is lock your wings into glide position and let me guide us."

"How are you going to do that?" he asked. His heart was pounding again, thumping against her fingers and the harness.

"We're going to be connected by a safety line. Are you remembering to breathe?"

He took another deep breath, his grey eyes fixed on her face. They were wide behind his glasses.

"There are only two dangers up there," she lectured. "The biggest one is that you panic and tangle your wings with mine. If that happens, we're going to stall and fall. We don't want to do that."

"I never panic." His coppery skin was going pale again.

"Good. The second danger is that we get caught off-balance in a wind and I have to unhook from you until I can regain control. You're so light right now that you don't have to worry about falling. Even if you folded your wings into a dive position, you'd just float down. So let the wind blow you and do your best to keep your wings spread wide. I'll come get you. All you have to do is stay calm and make yourself visible. I'll find you even if you end up floating over another mountain. Okay? Just don't panic."

He swallowed and nodded.

"Hey!"

Taya turned and saw the dispatch office door open. Paulo had seen them.

She turned back to Cristof, shoving a flight cap into his hands.

"Lesson over. Time to go."

"Wait! I don't have any idea what I'm doing yet!" Cristof protested, pulling on his cap.

"No time. Buckle the chin strap. That's Paulo." She pushed him by the harness to the edge of the dock as he fumbled his goggles into place over his glasses. "Stand still."

"Oh, Lady," he groaned, looking down. His fingers yanked on the cap strap.

"Eyes straight ahead. Take three deep breaths." Taya stood behind him, pulling out her safety line. It was twenty feet of tightly wound silk cable with a braided wire core, safety hooks on each end—the same kind of line Pyke had dropped to her in the wireferry accident. She hooked their harnesses together and pulled her goggles down.

"Hey, icarus, you haven't cleared this flight!"

She glanced over her shoulder. Paulo had been grounded years ago with a bad leg, and now he hobbled toward them on a cane. Plenty of time. She yanked the line, snuggling up against Cristof's back. Lady, he was tall. Her face was even with his shoulder blades.

"Is this—"

"Lock your wings into close position," she ordered, spreading her wings wide. His wings folded back, their metal primaries brushing against her legs. "Walk with me to the edge."

"Exactly how do we take off?" he asked, agitated.

"We jump."

"Can't you be in front?"

"Walk!" She took a step forward, her knee nudging the back of his leg. He took one step, a second.

"We're at the edge!"

"Wait."

They teetered on the edge. Paulo shouted behind them.

Taya leaned against Cristof's back.

"Crouch and jump forward as far as you can. Keep your wings folded. We'll fall for a few seconds, and then I'll stop us. Don't flap your wings. Keep them tight. If you panic and spread them, we'll get tangled up and it'll be a really short flight."

"I understand."

"Jump on the count of three. One. Two. Three!"

Cristof leaped.

Taya leaned against his back, her wings downstroking as hard as possible. They sagged, then thrust upward and forward. Unable to see clearly, Taya scooted herself higher on his back, wrapping her legs around Cristof's waist and tucking her feet next to his hips to seal them together.

His extra mass dragged against her as she beat her wings, but he was well counterweighted, and she pulled them up over the city and into the pale sky. As soon as they were clear of the launch dock and Secundus wireferry towers, she straightened one leg to awkwardly kick down the tailset on his armature.

"Legs up and in," she shouted, straddling his back again.

For a moment they bobbled as Cristof tried to find the rung under the tailset, and then she felt their balance steady as he got his ankles hooked over it. The ondium tailfeathers counteracted the drag of his legs. Until she could separate from him, his tail was going to be her tail.

For a moment she was silent, concentrating on finding the air currents. Cristof's short hair blew into her face and she nudged up higher on his back, putting her mouth close to his ear.

"Good job!"

"Are we safe yet?"

"We're fine. It's a beautiful morning for flying."

"Okay."

He sounded frightened.

"You're not looking down, are you?"

"I'm not looking anywhere."

"Are your eyes open?"

"No."

"What? Scrap, open your eyes! You can't fly blind!"

A moment later he groaned. She felt his muscles tighten beneath her thighs.

"What?" she asked.

"The ground."

"Cristof! Keep your eyes up and open and don't panic! You have to see where you're going!"

"No, I don't." His voice was faint. "I trust you."

"Open your eyes!" she commanded, digging her boot heels into his ribs for emphasis.

"Oh, Lady. . . ." His voice dropped into the steady murmur of a prayer and she felt him tensing beneath her again.

"Breathe. Long, deep, slow breaths. You're safe. Keep your eyes forward so you can see where we're going."

She was beginning to get tired, maneuvering for them both, but she kept them rising until she felt his sides and back begin to relax. She felt an updraft and leaned them into it. For a second she felt him resist her, and then he caught himself, letting her take the lead. She touched her head to his for a moment to speak.

"Are you okay now?"

"No."

Her eyebrows rose. At least he'd stopped hiding his feelings.

"Unlock your wings, stretch them out, and lock them into glide."

He straightened his arms and she shifted her weight, pressing her collarbone against his shoulders so that their wings matched up. The metal bars of their armatures clicked as their forearms tapped each other. Ondium feathers rattled in the wind.

They began to soar, arm to arm, cheek to cheek. Taya drew in a deep breath, her heart leaping at the sight of the city wheeling below them, the brightening morning sky, and the craggy mountain cliffs glowing gold in the dawn.

"Beautiful!" she cried out, delighted. "Isn't it beautiful?"

He didn't answer. After a moment, Taya sighed. Some people had no appreciation for nature. Maybe he'd enjoy it better after a few more lessons.

She squeezed her legs to get his attention.

"Do you feel me against you?" she asked.

"I—er, yes."

"I'm going to give you a quick flying lesson. Relax and let me guide you through it."

She felt, rather than heard, him clear his throat.

"Do I still have to keep my eyes open?"

"Yes." She maneuvered awkwardly a moment, then managed to kick down her own tailfeathers. She tucked her legs into the tailset and stretched out flat against him. He was tall enough that the match wasn't perfect, but it would do. She rested on top of him, leg to leg, arm to arm, stomach to back, cheek to cheek.

"Okay, we're going into a right turn. The right wing's going down, and the left wing's going up. Left wing downstrokes harder. Feel me move, and move with me."

His breath caught as she pushed his right arm down with hers, letting herself tilt in the wind. They were moving more slowly than she liked, but the city's thermal updraft and the extra ondium counterweights in his suit kept them from stalling.

"Good! I want you to keep your legs straight for now. If you were alone, you'd bend your left knee when you turned. Wing, tail, and tilt. That's how we steer. But just concentrate on using your wings."

They soared into a long circle, cold air whistling against their faces, the industrial mass of the city sprawling out beneath them. Cristof's body was warm and stable beneath hers, and pale light gleamed against his metal wings. Taya lifted her arms, feeling his shoulders move beneath her as she guided him.

"Good," she said, as they rose on the thermal. "That's it. Fast downstroke, even and hard."

Metal feathers beat against the air, lifting them higher. She arched her back, lifting their tails higher to give them more upturn. Then she evened them out again in another long circle and showed him how to make a left turn. They wheeled next to a dark cliff, then out into the pale sky again. Taya smiled, feeling Cristof's body moving comfortably against hers at last. It felt good not to be fighting him anymore.

"Do you think you've got it?" she asked.

"I think so," he said. He sounded a little out of breath.

"Are you remembering to breathe?"

"Sometimes."

"Work on it. I'm going to lengthen the line between us. I'll be right above you, but you'll have to keep yourself up without my help."

"Wait! Don't!"

"I have to. We can't land together. Our wings will tangle."

"Not yet. I'm not ready yet."

"Sure you are. Keep your eyes open. Breathe."

"No—Taya—don't. Stay there!" She heard genuine fear in his voice. His wings tilted and she pulled hers back to keep them from tangling.

"Don't flap! I'm still here. Come on, let's get some height together."

For a minute they flew in silence, rising higher up the cliff face. The peaks of Oporphyr Tower gleamed in the first rays of sunlight, silhouetted against the clear sky. Taya sensed the morning winds increasing. When the sun rose over the mountain, the *diispira* would kick up and their landing would become much more difficult.

"Look ahead," she called out. "We're almost there."

"How—how do I land?" he asked with trepidation.

"We're going to land on the ground, not on a balcony. Put your face into the wind, lock up your tailset, and spread your wings. The ondium gives us lift, so we don't need to maneuver much. Backbeat your wings to slow down. Bend your knees like you're kneeling. If you don't keep them bent, you could break a leg. Head for a wide open space. Lean backward and let your knees hit the ground first and skid. Keep your wings high—you don't want them to touch the ground—and keep backbeating until you slide to a stop."

He was silent a moment.

"How do I backbeat?"

"I'll show you." She lifted them higher, then arched her back against his chest, throwing her wings out. Cristof faltered a moment, then followed her lead, leaning against her breast, keeping his arms in contact with hers. She quickly backbeat a few strokes, feeling them start to fall.

"Taya!"

"Trust your metal!" She twisted, wings out, forcing him to move with her. With a powerful downbeat they caught the wind again, pushing back up.

"Oh, Lady." He had tensed up again, his sides heaving as he breathed heavily. "I don't think I can do this."

"It's all right. You're doing fine. Just relax and don't think too hard."

"I always think too hard," he grated.

"This would be a good time to learn to trust your instincts."

"Do you have to let go?"

"Yes. I'll still be tied to you, and I'll reel myself back down if I have to. But if I try to land with you, we're both going to crash. There's no way we can synchronize our backbeating well enough to land together, not on your first flight."

He was silent, but at last she felt him nod.

"Okay. Keep your arms locked into a glide for a minute."

As soon as they'd steadied into a glide, she locked her wings and pulled one arm free, uncoiling the line that bound them together.

"Remember, I'm right here. I'm not going to let you fall. Do you trust me?" She worked her arm back into the wing.

He nodded again, jerkily.

"Okay. Stay in a glide until I tell you otherwise." She lifted her wingtips up and let them separate, moving ahead and over him. The safety line slithered down in a long arc between them.

"One stroke up. Lift your wings. That's it. Now downstroke." Taya kept herself behind him as he gingerly pushed forward. The line cleared his wings. "Good. Again. Up—down."

She let the distance between them increase. They drew closer to the mountaintop as the sun rose higher, its bright rim peeking over the cliffs.

"Good! Now, tilt your wings down just a little. A little! Don't flap so hard. We're heading to that bare spot of dirt on the left of the courtyard. See it?"

"Yes."

"We're on the descent. Remember, if you flip or stall, you're still going to stay aloft, so don't panic. Now. Keep tilting your wings down as you fly, and gently tilt your tail down, too. Easy!"

Together they flew lower, heading for the council grounds. Cristof still moved too abruptly but, engineer that he was, he'd grasped the mechanics of flying. She seldom had to repeat an instruction.

Still, landing was the most dangerous part of a flight. Taya prayed he wouldn't panic or mistime his movements. If he broke an arm or leg, their investigation would be over before it began, and he'd never trust her again.

Her own heart started to beat faster as they drew closer to the ground, and she sucked in a deep breath, forcibly calming herself. He'd be fine. He was doing fine.

"Okay, now kick your tailset up out of your way and bend your knees," she shouted. "Cup your wings and backbeat. Remember, you want to slow down as much as possible! You *will* float!"

She fell in behind him, as far back as the safety line would let her go, and started to slow down, herself.

"Open your wing slots!" she shouted, watching him. "Knees forward! Like you're jumping on a bed!"

Had Cristof ever jumped on a bed in his life? It was hard to imagine.

She kicked her own tailset up. The winds weren't too bad. She could probably make a running landing, but she was afraid that if she tried, she'd stumble over Cristof. The only thing worse than him breaking an arm would be her breaking one. She could fly for help if he got injured, but she didn't think he'd be able to do the same for her.

"Slow down and lean backward! Lift your arms up!"

His knees hit the ground, their heavy protective pads digging furrows into the dirt as he threw his weight as far back as he could, nearly flat on his back. She breathed a sigh of relief as he skidded to a halt, buoyed by the extra ondium on his harness.

Her own landing was only a little more graceful as she let herself slide in behind him.

"Are you all right?" She locked her wings high and staggered to her feet, wincing as her knees protested. She stripped off her cap, goggles, and gloves.

Cristof's wings had fallen to the ground, and his head was slumped forward as he panted. She walked over and knelt in front of him.

"Hey." She cupped his cold face in her hands. He was shaking and pale. "You did it. We're here."

He swallowed and nodded.

"Come on, exalted. Concentrate on what you're doing. Dragging your wings is bad form. Lift your arms up. Lock your wings upright."

Moving slowly, he followed her instructions, then slipped his arms free of the armature and yanked off his cap and goggles. They fell to the ground between his legs. His eyes were wide, his pupils dilated and his glasses askew.

"Easy, now." Taya smoothed his sweat-dampened hair and adjusted his glasses. "That was good. That was really good." She leaned forward and hugged him. "Silly crow. I told you that you could fly."

He stiffened a moment, then he grabbed her, pulling her close and clutching her as though his life depended on it.

Taya's heart lurched. She closed her eyes, pulse pounding.

In a minute he's going to let go and make some self-deprecating quip, and everything will be normal again.

Seconds passed. His breathing slowed and his trembling subsided. Taya waited for him to pull away, but instead he rested his forehead against her shoulder, still holding her.

She swallowed. Her fingers curled protectively in the thick, ragged thatch of his black hair, then ran down the sharp angles of his shoulders.

"I still feel like I'm falling," he said at last, looking up. A gleam of morning sunlight played around the wire rim of his glasses. "I'm afraid to let go."

For a moment she stared into his pale eyes.

"It's all right. You're safe." Her pulse pounded in her throat. Had anyone ever looked at her so desperately before? She'd wanted a glimpse behind his mask, and now she knew what was back there—a deep, aching loneliness. "There's nothing to be afraid of anymore."

"If I let go, you might fly away without me," he said, his voice cracking.

"I won't—"

He leaned forward and kissed her, one gloved hand sliding up into her hair.

For a moment Taya stiffened. Then she closed her eyes, letting herself relax into the moment. His tentative kiss slowly grew more confident as he realized she wasn't going to pull back.

Some critical part of her pointed out that it was ridiculous to kneel in the dirt and kiss this ungracious, ill-tempered outcaste, but the rest of her felt a surge of affection for him. The uncertain, eager way his fingers touched her cheeks and the back of her neck made her heart ache.

Poor, awkward crow. So much more determined and honest than his handsome brother had ever been.

Taya laid a hand against his jaw, tasting salt on his lips, and hooked the fingers of her other hand into the harness straps across his back as he pulled her as close as their metal keels would allow. He was so tall it felt like he was

folding himself around her. He slid his hand from her hair
to the small of her back as their tongues touched and their
breath mingled. His kiss and his body seemed to provide
the only warmth to be found in the cold mountain air.

For a long minute they held each other, lost in each
other's lips, breath, and touch. Then, at last, Cristof pulled
back and tugged off his glasses with one hand.

"I can't see," he said, breathlessly.

She glanced at his steamed lenses and laughed. *There's
the self-deprecating quip I was waiting for*, she thought,
relieved to be on familiar ground again. Her cheeks were
flushed and her nerves were tingling. *And in a moment
he'll push me away.*

But she felt comfortable kneeling in front of him, his
knees flanking hers, their bodies held inches apart by their
ondium armatures. More comfortable than she'd ever felt
with Alister.

"Keep them off," she suggested. "You don't need them
right now."

"Lady." He rubbed the lenses on his flight suit sleeve
and put his spectacles back on again. His lips tilted in a
wry, sad smile as he gazed at her. "Don't tempt me. If we
keep doing that, we'll never find Alister's program."

Taya studied him. There it was, the gentle push away. She
couldn't blame him, really. He had to be as surprised by the
moment as she was. But she still felt disappointed as she stood
up, stretched her legs, and unsnapped the line between them.

"We'd better get to work then," she said, forcing a light
tone.

Cristof clambered to his feet, picking up his cap and
goggles. She saw him tug irritably at the harness straps
that ran around his thighs, when he thought she wasn't
looking, and she felt a little better.

They walked to the tower silently, both lost in their own
thoughts.

Taya had never entered Oporphyr Tower from the
ground. The front door was locked, and nobody responded
to their pounding. She flew up until she found an open

icarus dock door on the tower's second floor. She leaned over the balcony and managed to talk Cristof through an ungraceful hop up to it. He was light enough, with all his extra ondium, for her to grab his harness and haul him in as he staggered through an upright landing.

"You're doing fine," she assured him. "Better than our fledglings."

He shot her a sour look.

The building was dark, empty, and cold. They lit a lantern in the icarus dock office and carried it with them, their heavy boots loud on the tile floor.

"Wait." Taya laid a hand on Cristof's arm as they reached the stairs to Alister's office. "Look at that."

Dirt was scattered over one of the steps. Cristof picked it up and crumbled it between his gloved fingers. Then he looked at the thick soles of his boots and behind them.

"We've left a track, too. Do you think it's from one of the icarii who helped evacuate the place?"

"I don't think so. An icarus would have flown straight to the dock, where there's no dirt. Maybe it was tracked in by a lictor."

"Tower employees arrive by wireferry, which docks directly inside the tower," he pointed out. "But people might have been walking around outside the Tower during the rescues. I don't know why, though." He pulled off his gloves and jammed them into his belt, then unbuttoned the bulkiest pouch around his hip and pulled out his needler.

Taya made a face. "I'm really glad that didn't shoot me in the leg while we were flying." *Or kissing*.

"It has a safety." He tilted the barrel down and flipped a stiff switch by the trigger.

"Well, don't shoot some innocent lictor who stayed here to guard the place."

"I'll be careful." He stepped in front of her and headed up the stairs, muttering to himself whenever his metal feathers scraped the walls. He wasn't used to thinking in terms of wings yet. Taya followed, maneuvering more deftly through the halls.

The door to Alister's office was unlocked. Cristof pushed it open, looked inside, then let them both enter.

"It looks pretty much—" Taya stopped as her eyes fell on an empty patch on the floor. "Something's missing."

"A box?" Cristof leaned over the small rectangular area and brushed the papers next to it aside. "Not much dust. Whatever was here was taken recently. Can you tell what it was?"

Taya walked over and looked at the books and papers surrounding the empty spot. To her chagrin, she couldn't conjure up a clear mental image of what had been there when she'd last visited the office. She hadn't spent much time looking around. Most of her attention had been on Alister. "Let's see. There's a collection of Council minutes, two books on Si'sier economic theory, a book on, uh, reptiles of the Donweyr Waste? Wait, they're all written by people with C-names. So the box was probably a C, too. Clockwork Heart."

Cristof turned, looking around. "If this pile is C, where's L?"

"P is over there." She pointed to the place where she'd set down the plaster bust of Abatha Cardium.

Cristof knocked over a pile of books with his wings as he passed, swore, and looked around. "Plenty of ledgers here, but I don't see anything that looks like the Labyrinth Code."

"P is for program." Taya moved to the bust and stopped in front of a cabinet that matched the one in Alister's office. The lock on this one hung loose, too. She swung open the doors.

Row upon row of boxes, neatly labeled. None were missing.

"Maybe it's in here."

They quickly removed the lid of each box, checking the numbers stamped into the tin punch cards.

"The official code wouldn't be LC. What was it?" Taya muttered, setting a box aside.

"SA? Security Access?"

"If he wasn't using the programs' nicknames, then Clockwork Heart might not be the missing C." Taya looked up, feeling a trace of panic. "We might not recognize it, even if it's here."

"He filed it under C in his office." Cristof rocked back on his heels. "And I don't see it in here, so it probably *was* in the box on the floor. So someone's taken it. And this version would be the one formatted for the Great Engine."

"If someone's got it, and it really can disable the Engine's security, then we're in trouble." Taya bit her lip, trying to remember everything the programmers had told them. "But whoever it is will need the Labyrinth Code to run Clockwork Heart the first time, right?"

"You should have left me behind and brought Kyle." Cristof scowled. "He'd understand this better than I do."

"No, I've got it," Taya said, earnestly. "Before the killer can run Clockwork Heart, he's got to run Labyrinth. But after Clockwork Heart has been run once, it doesn't matter what other security programs are set, because Clockwork Heart will let him bypass any security code that's added later. Right?"

"I don't know. Is that possible?"

"I'm pretty sure that's what got Kyle so upset."

Cristof looked grim. "I thought the twenty-five cards Pins had gotten her hands on were the first ones to be stolen. But remember what Emelie said about the technicians not noticing if the whole backup program were stolen? What if those cards were the last twenty-five? What if the thief already had seventy-five percent of the program?"

"But . . . once he found out from Pins that the last twenty-five cards were gone, he'd realize that his plan had been uncovered." Taya's eyes widened. "Maybe that's why he killed her. And that meant the only copy of Labyrinth Code he could use was the one still stored up here in Oporphyr Tower. And there was no way he could get access to it unless he moved everyone out of the Tower."

"So the explosion might not have been about Alister or Caster at all," Cristof said, looking pained. "It might have simply been a convenient way to isolate the Tower."

Taya rose with the lantern. "How do we get to the Great Engine?"

Cristof reached down to pick up the needler.

"The access doors are through the Council chamber," he said, standing. "Let's go."

Chapter Thirteen

The Council chamber was a wide, circular room dominated by a huge oak table in its center. The walls were paneled, each panel bearing a neatly executed oil painting depicting one of the great moments in Ondinium's history.

Two of the panels had been pushed aside, revealing a broad metal sliding door. It, too, had been opened, just wide enough to allow a person to pass through.

"I guess that's it." Taya circled the table and set down the lantern. "Although whoever went through here wasn't wearing wings." She leaned against the edge of the door, then yelped as it moved easily, nearly sending her sprawling. She straightened up, studying it. "Must have ondium counterweights."

"Be careful." Cristof joined her. "If there are any Torn Cards in there—"

"They'll be planting bombs, not running programs," she reminded him.

"Let's hope there are no more bombs involved." He picked up the lantern and looked down the dark tunnel. "I don't want to lose you, too."

Taya glanced at him. He was still frowning into the darkness. Feeling daring, she wrapped a hand around his shoulder harness and tugged him down, kissing his cheek.

His copper skin flushed as he glanced at her.

"What . . ." he pushed up his glasses. "What was that for?"

"For saying something sweet for a change."

"I—oh." He looked disconcerted. "I hadn't intended to be sweet."

Taya rolled her eyes. "That doesn't surprise me."

"Last night I was a slagging pain in your tailset."

"That's why you need to work harder on sweet." She took the lantern from him. "Come on, let's go find your Torn Cards."

THE TUNNEL to the Great Engine was wide enough for two people without wings to walk abreast and almost as tall as a normal room, which meant they had to walk in single file and lock their wings into tight position—only head-high, but with the joint sharply angled forward over their shoulders and their primaries jutting backward an arm's length behind them. After twenty feet they came to another door, also metal and also ajar.

Cristof eased it wider, needlegun pointing inside. After a moment he stepped through, waving Taya after him.

The momentary playfulness that had affected her in the Council chamber had passed, and now Taya found herself growing tense. A deep, rhythmic rumbling vibrated through the air, tickling the thick soles of her flight boots and trembling through her wing feathers. The sound of the Great Engine, she guessed, her palms sweating.

They came to a third open door. A sign on it declared, *Oporphyr Council Analytical Engine: Authorized Personnel Only Beyond This Point*.

Cristof stepped through, pistol out.

Beyond it, stairs spiraled downward into the center of the mountain. The air was still and warm, and when Taya put a hand on the walls, she felt the stone shivering beneath her fingertips.

Cristof locked his wings into high position for the stairs, scowling at the inconvenience as he juggled his needlegun from hand to hand. Taya, better accustomed to the inconveniences of an armature, followed suit.

The rumbling grew stronger as they descended, finally becoming audible as a constant mechanical thumping. The sound came from the steam engines that powered the Great Engine, Taya guessed, although they were much louder than those that powered the analytical engine in the University basement.

The stairs ended in a short hallway and another door.

*Oporphyr Council Analytical Engine. All visitors must
be accompanied by Security.*

Cristof gave it a push. Pale light spilled into the stairwell
and the rumbling, thumping sound increased. The exalted
peered through.

Taya turned down the lantern and set it on the stair step.

Satisfied with whatever he saw, Cristof opened the door
the rest of the way and twisted, slipping his wings through.
Taya slid in after him, then straightened.

The door opened onto a long, wide catwalk that ran in
either direction around the hollow core of the mountain.
Metal lines coiled around the walkway and stretched across
the wall like thick spider webs, feeding banks of lights that
gave off a brighter glare than any gas lamp Taya had ever
seen. The lights all faced inward, highlighting the huge
hollow chamber at the heart of Ondinium Mountain and
the gargantuan, floating, constantly moving mechanism
that was the Great Engine.

Stunned by its size, Taya stepped up to the iron railing
and looked down.

The Engine plunged down as far as she could see,
level upon level of moving clockwork. Pistons as tall as
trees shifted back and forth. Gears and wheels the size
of wagons and mansions spun in midair, locked to each
other by the intricacy of their design and the light, narrow
wires that held the lighter-than-air components together.
Levers as tall as wireferry towers shifted up and down
with jarring clicks, and thick cables carried power from
the steam engines that chugged on every catwalk. Giant
drums the size of Taya's eyrie apartment spun in the center
of a weaving, bobbing network of metal arms.

They stood at the very top of the hollow mountain. But
even here, at its narrowest point, Taya couldn't see the other
side of the catwalk. The chamber was too breathtakingly
vast, the Great Engine too colossal.

She didn't know how long she stood there, staring. At
last she released the rail and looked around for Cristof.

He was as enraptured by the sight as she, his needlegun dangling from one hand and his eyes wandering over the cables and moving parts. She reached for the gun and he started, his hand tightening on it again.

"That's carbon-filament incandescent lighting," he said, raising his voice to be heard over the clatter. He pointed at the banks of lights. "I've never seen it used outside a technology exhibit. Look—it's powered by the steam engines. No smoke!"

"Come closer and take a better look," she said, waving him over. He shook his head.

"I'm fine."

"After flying all the way to the top of Ondinium, you're still not over your fear of heights?"

"Not in this lifetime." He craned his neck to look through the open railing. "Do you see anyone?"

"No, but it's a long way down." She held out a hand. "Come on and look. I'll hold you steady."

He gritted his teeth, then edged forward, ignoring her hand and standing sideways to the railing.

"Stubborn." She hooked her fingers through a strap on his harness. "See, I've got you."

He grabbed the railing with his free hand and glanced down, his muscles tense. Then his head snapped back and he pushed up his glasses as though afraid of losing them.

"It's impossible to see anything down there," he complained. "It's all hazy."

"Probably smoke from the steam engines, or grease spray from the gears. They must keep the machine oiled somehow." Taya leaned over the rail, heedless of Cristof's flinch. "This space is so big, I'll bet it has own weather patterns. I can feel an updraft." She released Cristof's harness to lean out as far as she could and held her hand palm-down, flat over the chasm. Warm air pushed against it.

"Be careful!"

"Relax. There's plenty of room to fly here. Lots of clearance around the sides of the Engine, and even some around the gears and pistons. I'll bet flying through the

Engine isn't much more dangerous than flying through the lines on Tertius." She frowned, studying the mechanism. "Although I wouldn't want to get a feather caught between those gears."

"I'm sure there are stairs." The exalted stepped backward again. "Let's go find them. We need to figure out where the punch cards are fed into the Engine."

"It'll be faster to go straight down." Taya gauged the distance and began unhooking her safety line. "It'll be just like the hop you took to get up to the balcony, but easier. The next catwalk is only twenty, thirty feet below us."

Cristof closed his eyes and sighed.

"I don't like sounding like a coward, Taya. And there really aren't many things in the world that scare me. But I don't like heights, and I would prefer to avoid them as much as possible." He sounded pained.

"It's all right." Taya gave him a sympathetic look. "I don't think you're a coward, not after forcing yourself into a first flight. I've got a phobia, too—I don't like crowds. If I'm stuck in a real shoulder-to-shoulder press, I get faint. Cassi has to drag me down to the Markets each winter to do my Ladysday shopping."

He opened his eyes, looking down at her.

"I don't like crowds, either," he said.

"This won't be so bad. I'll hook our two safety lines together. We'll drape the lines over this railing and use them to guide our descent. Remember, with all the ondium you're wearing, you're going to float even if you lose your grip on the ropes. We'll climb to the next catwalk, I'll shake the lines loose while you hunt for the punch card whatchamacallit, and if it's not there, we'll do it again."

"Tray. The punch cards are fed into a tray."

"Does it look like the one on the University engine?"

"I don't know." He sighed, his apprehension obvious. Taya tentatively reached out to pat his shoulder, trying to reassure him.

It was strange. Alister had made her feel warm and admired, but he'd never made her feel needed. He'd paid her plenty of compliments, but she'd never felt like she offered him anything he couldn't get from someone else.

Cristof, on the other hand, had never tried to impress her and had never hesitated to acknowledge that she could do things he couldn't. He just stepped aside and let her work.

Taya liked the fact that he didn't try to make himself seem perfect. He was defensive and sarcastic and not very handsome, but he trusted her, and that made a big difference.

Still, I'd better fly carefully, she thought, studying his sharp face. *We're both negotiating a lot of obstruction currents right now.*

"The tray must be connected directly to the Engine," he said after a minute, looking down through the grillwork under their feet. "I'll bet there's at least one level where a catwalk extends out to the machine itself. That'll be where the technicians feed in the program."

"Then we'll keep descending, level by level, until we see it," Taya said, lifting her hand. "Let's hope it's not on the other side of the mountain, though."

Cristof turned and contemplated the machinery-filled abyss.

"Obviously," he said, after a moment, "flying is the most efficient solution." He paused, and she saw him brace himself. "How long do you think it would take to make a circuit of the entire Engine?"

"I can't even begin to guess." She leaned over the railing again, scanning the horizon. "I'd have to spiral. Fifteen minutes? Twenty? It depends on how close the catwalk is, and what the air currents are like."

"Can you guide me down again?"

"Here?" She straightened, surprised that he'd suggest it. "No. Rappelling is one thing, but flying in a completely new airspace, next to so many parts and cables—I'd need to pay attention to what I was doing. Guiding you would distract me too much. I'll tell you what. I'll take the first flight down by myself, and when I find the tray, I'll come back to tell you. Then we can decide how to get there."

"I have no intention of letting you go down there alone. There could be a killer in here."

"If I see anyone, I'll head back up."

"Investigation is my job, not yours."

"And while we stand here arguing about it, someone could be running Clockwork Heart through the Great Engine."

Cristof's jaw tightened. Then he jerked one shoulder, turning away.

"All right." He pinched the bridge of his nose, under his glasses. "Be careful."

Taya nodded and climbed on top of the wrought-iron catwalk railing. The metal trembled from side to side beneath her boots and she swayed. Cristof stepped forward, steadying her, his eyes averted from the chasm as he grabbed her harness and held her in place. Taya slipped her arms into her wings and unlocked them. The exalted ducked as a wing swept over his head.

"Sorry."

His fingers tightened for a moment on her harness straps.

"Let go," she ordered. He released her and jumped backward as she kicked off from the railing.

Taya let herself drop until she was well under the first catwalk, then spread her wings and flapped hard, tilting to keep her body parallel to the inner curve of the mountainside.

The air was warm and filled with unpredictable thermals and currents caused by the steam engines and incandescent lights, spinning drums and coiling springs, thumping pistons and clicking levers. The Engine's constant movement at the edge of her vision kept drawing her attention away from the air currents until she bobbled and her awareness snapped back to maintaining her balance.

Taya concentrated. She was used to flying through cables and towers—that was a given, in the closely developed cityscape of Ondinium—but usually the only movement around her was the slow coast of a wireferry, the quick dart

of a bird, or the lazy glide of another icarus. Flying next to
the Engine required a very different set of skills.

She was glad she hadn't brought Cristof with her.

Thinking of him, she swept in a circle in the empty space
between the catwalked mountain wall and the moving
immensity of the Engine and looked up.

He was leaning over the catwalk, his wings glinting over
his back as he watched her.

He looked down, she thought, pleased, and tilted her
wings in salute before starting a slow, spiraling descent
around the Engine. He didn't wave back. He probably had
a death grip on the iron railing.

She flew around the Great Engine of Ondinium,
marveling again at its complexity. She'd learned in school
that it had taken fifty years to build, and engineers had
been tinkering with it ever since, expanding, adapting,
and experimenting. As the Engine had grown, so had
the chamber in which it was housed. Whenever one of
the mountain's ondium mines had been tapped out, the
tunnels had been destroyed, their leavings cast into new
gears and their stone hauled away to build the houses,
mansions, bridges and statues that had turned the surface
of Ondinium Mountain into the most densely populated
city in the world.

The air shuddered with the Engine's heat and vibrations,
and air currents danced and broke against each other as
gears turned and pistons pumped. Cables suspended by
ondium counterweights criss-crossed the empty space
around the vast Engine, carrying power and oil and she
couldn't guess what else. Every few levels she saw steam
engines built on top of massive platforms, chugging away
to power the bright lights and giant machine. Some of
the catwalks were lined with the same kind of huge iron
cylinders she saw spinning in the machine, wrapped in
blankets and strapped to the walls with thick cables.

No wonder they call it the heart of Ondinium, she thought,
soaring across the miles of space that surrounded it. Her
own heart seemed to pump in time to pounding beat, and

her wingtips trembled whenever she flew too close to one of its oversized mechanisms.

Every catwalk she passed was empty, but as she circled the inner circumference of Ondinium Mountain, she saw offices built into the walls and opening out onto the metal walkways. She wondered if the chamber's emptiness were normal or if the Engine had been abandoned only because of the wireferry explosion.

Cristof was right, though. There had to be another way into the chamber. Those giant gears and mainsprings would never fit through the hall and stairwell they'd taken.

It probably *was* a state secret.

At last she spotted a crosswalk running perpendicular to the catwalk, stretching out across the empty space to end in a small platform beside the Great Engine. Taya caught a thermal current and let herself rise higher again, squinting down at it.

Was that someone on the platform next to the Engine? Despite the glaring, unnatural light, she found it difficult to discern whether it was a human figure or a trick of the chamber's constantly moving shadows. She tilted her wings and tailset and swept back down again.

The figure turned, and Taya caught a glimpse of a startled, uplifted face.

She gasped and tilted too far. The air broke around her and she tumbled, one wing catching beneath her and twisting.

For a moment the walls and Engine spun and gravity fought ondium for possession of her body. Heart pounding, Taya contorted herself, throwing her arms wide and arching her back. The fall didn't frighten her nearly as much as the intruder—she knew how to deal with gravity and open air. She gave one last half-spin until she was falling face-down again. Then she swept her arms down, hard, feeling metal feathers snap shut against each other to catch air.

Something burned across the back of her left leg and she flinched. Her downsweep checked her fall and propelled her back up. Taya aimed herself at the metal-mesh crosswalk overhead, her eyes fixed on the ondium rods that crisscrossed its bottom and held it suspended. She spread her wings again and felt a welcome push of hot air as excess pressure was released from one of the steam engines far below.

Her calf was starting to hurt. She looked down, but she couldn't see anything beneath the hinged bars that extended from the armature back to her tailset.

She looked back up.

The intruder was crouched on the catwalk, staring down through the meshwork. Amazement and admiration gleamed in his green eyes as he gazed at her.

She hadn't been mistaken.

The intruder was Alister Forlore, complete with embroidered robes, jeweled ornaments, and an ivory mask hanging from his belt.

Their eyes met, and for a moment all Taya could think of was how relieved Cristof would be that his brother was alive. Then she realized what that meant, and a surge of righteous anger swept away her relief.

The decatur looked up, then leaped to his feet, holding out a hand as if to stop something.

Taya craned her neck over her shoulder and saw a lictor standing on the side catwalk, aiming an air rifle at her.

Lady! She swerved, soaring up and to the right to put the crosswalk between her and the gunner.

A series of sharp, metallic pings warned her that the lictor was firing again. Taya had no idea where the bullets had gone—buried, perhaps, in the enormous grinding cliff of gears behind her—but they hadn't hit her.

A crosscable nearly caught her and sweat broke out on her forehead as she swept beneath it. The lictor who'd fired at her lowered the barrel of his rifle to the catwalk floor, unscrewing its used air reservoir.

Out of the corner of her eye, Taya glimpsed a second lictor running along the catwalk, trying to keep abreast of her. He was carrying a rifle, too, but he was moving too fast to aim.

"Stop shooting!" she shouted, furious. "I'm not your enemy!"

Or was she? Were the lictors secret Torn Cards, working for Alister? Or—her heart leaped—could Alister be innocent, somehow snatched from death to protect the Engine?

Another burst of warm air swept up around her. She spread her wings to catch it, letting the thermal pull her up and over the crosswalk, away from the level the shooters were on.

Alister's head was tilted upward, and he held a hand over his eyes to shade them from the bright glare of the incandescent lights as he stared past her.

Taya tilted to see what he was looking at.

"Oh, no!"

Cristof must have heard her shout, because he was plummeting down, a dark winged shape hurtling through the empty space between the mountain and the Engine. He was falling fast, his wing-clad arms spread wide but their ondium feathers slotted open to let the air whistle past their metal edges.

Taya swiftly calculated the angle of attack she'd need to intercept his fall. He was wearing enough ondium that it wouldn't take more than a glancing blow to drive him back toward the catwalks, but she had to hit him without getting their wings tangled together. A conscious icarus who was out of control could help a rescue attempt by locking his wings up, but frightened fliers all too often caught a rescuer's wings in their own.

Then Cristof swept his wings down, awkwardly emulating the strokes she'd taught him. His flightfeathers snapped shut and his descent slowed. Taya held her breath, watching him fumble through the morning's lessons to angle himself toward the crosswalk.

Lady, he was freeflying! Badly, to be sure, but the ondium counterweights she'd packed into his suit were giving him the margin of error he needed to keep himself aloft.

She tilted, trying to catch the last wisp of her dissipating thermal.

Then she saw the second lictor swing his rifle around.

"Cristof!" Taya shouted at the top of her lungs and plunged down, angling herself sideways so that the stretch of her metal wings would be between the gunman and the outcaste. Her leg protested the twist needed to steer with her tailset, but the maneuver worked. The lictor started as she swept past him, and his shots went wild, lead pellets ricocheting off the walls and machinery around them.

She pulled out of the dive and saw Cristof backbeating hard, his feet aimed at the crosswalk where his brother stood. Alister stood motionless, watching his brother with an expression of sheer incredulity.

One of Cristof's heavy boots hit the railing and he hovered there a moment, suspended, teetering.

Taya swooped over him.

Alister reached out and grabbed his brother's keel, yanking him down to safety.

Cristof's soles hit the iron crosswalk. He slipped an arm from the wingstruts and swept it upward, his fist slamming against Alister's chin and snapping the decatur's head back.

Taya turned and saw both lictors running toward the crosswalk to assist Alister. She circled wide, her wings teetering as she lost the current she'd been riding. Then she turned and aimed herself for the top of the crosswalk.

Her timing was almost perfect. She swept over the crosswalk just as the riflemen stepped onto it. They ducked, instinctively throwing their arms over their heads, and one of the air rifle barrels clipped the front edge of her left wing.

The impact tore the weapon from the man's hands and sent it falling into the chasm, but it also threw her off-balance. She spun, struggling to right herself. The Great Engine loomed before her with sickening speed.

Backbeating as wildly as Cristof had a moment before, Taya jerked her ankles from the tailset and lifted her feet in front of her. Her thick boot soles hit one of the Great Engine's giant spinning gears, hard. Her left foot slipped against a slick coating of machine oil, but the other got enough of a grip to push her back, away from the mechanism, as the gears' teeth ground against each other. She snatched her feet away before they could get trapped. Sweat dripped down her face, running along the edges of her flight goggles.

She fought her way back up again.

Cristof had his needlegun out and pointed at Alister, but in his haste to subdue his brother, he'd forgotten to lock his wings up and out of the way. One of the floating wings had become tangled in the iron railing, trapping him in place.

The lictor who'd lost his rifle drew a knife. With one hand, he grabbed Cristof's trapped wing and yanked on it, trying to distract the exalted while he waited for a chance to use the blade. The other rifleman pressed against the far railing, leaning backward as he tried to aim his weapon at Cristof without risking Alister. Taya swore. She'd missed the lictor who'd replaced his air cylinder.

Then she heard the hissing that signaled a new release of hot air from the steam engines below. Thanking the Lady, she caught the updraft and aimed herself at the crosswalk, starting high and angling down at a forty-five-degree angle. As soon as she was close, she swung herself around into landing position.

The rifleman looked up in time to see her boots slam into his chest. Already off-balance, absorbing her impact was enough to flip the lictor backward over the rail, still clutching his rifle. He screamed as he plummeted.

Taya used the jar of hitting him to backbeat and caught the rail with both feet. A jolt of pain went through her injured leg. She craned her neck, trying to see whether she had any chance of saving the falling man. She hadn't meant—

"Look out!"

She heard Cristof's shout at the same time she felt hands on her wing, yanking it down. She tumbled, her back slamming against the crosswalk. The impact wasn't hard enough to knock the breath out of her—the ondium kept her light—but she was momentarily helpless as the knife-wielding lictor kicked her in the side, right beneath her keel.

Gasping for breath, Taya struggled to free her arms. The lictor leaned over and grabbed her harness straps, his blade flashing. She futilely tried to kick him back.

Over the lictor's shoulder, she saw Cristof swinging his needler around.

The weapon spat, and the sharp tips of long steel pins abruptly protruded from her attacker's throat. Blood spurted as the man clutched his neck. The knife fell from his fingers and slipped through the grillwork into the emptiness below.

Taya freed her arms and wiped the dead lictor's blood off her face, her hands shaking.

"Nice work, Cris," Alister said agreeably, then grabbed his brother with both hands. With a heave, he lifted Cristof by his harness and hauled him over the catwalk rail.

"Wait!" Cristof shouted, his loose wings floating around him. He made a grab at Alister's forearms and missed.

Taya rolled to her feet, her own unlocked wings clattering against the metal railing as they floated upward. She stood just in time to see Alister drop his brother into the depths.

If Cristof shouted, his cry was lost in the roar of the Great Engine and the ugly grating and squealing sound of his metal wings rattling over the guard rail as he fell.

Taya threw herself forward, leaning over the edge of the railing. She had one boot wedged in the grille, ready to jump, when Alister grabbed her around the waist. She twisted, yanking at his wrists.

"Easy, little swan! He'll be all right." Alister picked her up and pivoted, planting her on the small platform next to the Engine. "The worst he'll suffer is a broken arm or leg."

"You bastard!" Taya kicked and ducked. Alister cursed as a floating wingfeather cut his cheek. He shoved her against the Engine.

Taya hit the Engine's ondium panel and turned, putting her back against it. Pain burned up the back of her leg, and her tailset scraped and flexed against the catwalk. She kicked it up behind her. Her wings floated at her sides.

Alister frowned, dabbing a drop of blood from his face.

The hem of his robe was covered in dirt, and a few leaves jutted out from the golden hoops and clasps that were slipping out of his once-ornate hairstyle. Gold glittered on his hands, but his fine manicure had been destroyed.

Taya looked down, through the open mesh floor, and saw the receding mass of metal that she was sure was Cristof and his floating, broken wings. Suddenly her anger was replaced by convulsive shivering, and bile rose in her throat.

"How could you do that?"

"I wouldn't have thrown him over if I didn't think he'd survive," Alister chided her. "You did a fine job of counterweighting him."

"He thought you were dead!"

"Oh." Alister blinked. "That." For a moment he looked ashamed of himself. "Was he upset?"

"Of course he was!" Taya felt the Engine thrumming behind her, rattling her wings. She glanced to one side, looking for an escape route—some way to help Cristof. Alister shifted his weight to stand in front of her.

"I'd really prefer you didn't retrieve him. He's safer down there, where he won't feel obliged to stop me."

Still trembling with reaction, Taya wiped her palms on her pants legs.

"What if he's swept toward a gear? The air currents in here are all over the place."

Alister glanced down, uncertainly. Then he shook his head.

"He'll be fine. And if you rescue him, you'll just keep bothering me and I might have to hurt you."

"He's afraid of heights!"

"I know that." The exalted gazed at her, his green eyes wide. "I was astounded when he leaped down to save you. Or was he simply leaping down to hit me? Hard to say. My brother plays his cards close to the chest."

"He's not the only one," Taya said, bitterly. How far down was it to the floor, anyway? The fall would be slow, because of all the ondium Cristof wore. Was a gradual descent a blessing or a curse for someone who was afraid of heights? "What are you doing here, anyway?"

"Nothing that will harm Ondinium, I assure you." The exalted held out a hand. "My swan queen. I'm sorry. I truly regret any pain I may have caused you or my family."

Taya ignored his hand and slid her arms into her loose wings. Alister tensed. Realizing there was no escaping him for the moment, she simply locked the wings high and pulled her arms free again. She'd have to wait for an opening.

Her calf felt like someone had laid a hot iron across it. She hoped it wouldn't stiffen up before she needed to vault past him.

"What about the pain you caused Pins' family?" she asked, to distract him. "Her daughter found her body. You're the one who killed her, aren't you?"

Alister made a face.

"She was a criminal. I didn't do anything the lictors wouldn't have done, eventually."

"That's a horrible thing to say." Taya recoiled. "I liked you. I was even thinking about sleeping with you!"

"Really? How flattering." He smiled, stepping closer. "I still like you, Taya Swan. You never fail to impress me. When you came swooping down out of nowhere like a silver bird, you took my breath away. You're an example of everything that's right about Ondinium."

"Is that so?" Taya pulled herself as tall as she could. "Then why are you trying to destroy it?"

"I'm not destroying it. I'm fixing it." He reached out and caressed her cheek. "I'd like to convince you and Cristof not to tell anyone I was here. With your cooperation, nobody will hear about this, and the city will be better off. I'm not going to cause any harm. I'm just going to update a few programs to make everyone's life a little safer and a little more predictable."

She turned her face away. "Clockwork Heart was meant to circumvent security, wasn't it? It was never a marriage program at all."

"Actually, it can do both. All I need to do is switch out a few sets of cards."

"Some marriage program. It matched up Lars and Kyle."

Alister laughed, sounding delighted.

"They ran it on themselves? That's wonderful. I would have loved to have seen Lars' face when he saw the results. I'd guessed about Kyle, but . . . ."

Taya shoved him in the chest, forcing him to take a step backward.

"They ran it in your memory!" she snapped, her eyes flashing. "They held a wake for you!"

"That was thoughtful of them." He seemed unperturbed by her violence. "Listen, my swan. We can all be friends again. I'll be found, thrown clear of the wreckage, tonight. You and Cristof will find me. I'll be shaken up, feverish . . . ." he touched his face ruefully. "Scratched and bruised. You'll be heroes, and everyone will be happy to have me back. Is Cristof in trouble over the bomb?"

"Yes! How did you—"

"I'll clear his name. One of the lictors you've just killed must have tampered with the clock while it was sitting in my office overnight. They were saboteurs, stopped just in time."

"Cristof will never lie for you."

Alister started to speak, then paused.

"Well. Maybe not. I hadn't realized he was working for the lictors until you told me about Pins. That was a real surprise, although it explained a lot. Still, we're family." He looked wistful. "Cris and I have gone through a lot together."

"You just threw him over the railing!"

"Oh, for the Lady's sake, I wouldn't have done it if I'd thought he'd get hurt. I'm sure he'll understand. He loves Ondinium as much as I do, although he shows it differently." He caught her eyes again. "It's convincing you that worries me, my swan. What do I have to do to prove I'm not your enemy?"

Despite the heat, Taya felt ice crawl down her spine. Her calf was starting to throb in time to the Engine's pounding.

Behind Alister, a lone bead of blood dripped down from the rifleman's needle-punctured neck, falling through the crosswalk's grille floor and into the depths. She shuddered.

"I'm not going to lie for you, either."

"I could guarantee you a position in the diplomatic corps."

"I don't want it badly enough to protect a murderer."

"You don't even know what I'm doing. I—did you hear something?"

Taya listened, but all she could hear was the Engine's roar, its vibrations making her wingfeathers jingle.

"No."

"This place. A man can't hear himself think." Alister reached down and picked up a tin punch card that had fallen to the crosswalk floor. Taya tensed to kick him while he was looking down, then flinched as a jolt of pain ran through her calf. The exalted straightened, oblivious to her aborted action. "All I'm doing is setting up a few new permanent subroutines. I'm not stealing any data, and I'm not sabotaging the Engine."

"What kind of subroutines?"

"Iterative simulations. They'll need regular checking and adjustment, which is why I need Heart in place. I can't afford to waste my time guessing the Labyrinth Code every time I need to run some cards."

"You stole the Code."

"I was just borrowing it," Alister corrected her. "I was planning to return it. Unfortunately, losing the last few cards to Cris rendered months of effort completely worthless. That's why I had to do it this way, instead." He sounded proud of himself. "But I replaced all the cards I bought from Pins. Nobody will ever know they'd been stolen. Well, of course they'll know about the twenty-five Cristof got, but we can say the lictor who set the bomb was the same one who was smuggling out the cards. This could be flawless, if you'd just cooperate with me."

Taya looked down at the wire-mesh platform beneath her feet, wondering if she should lie and agree to work with him so she could fly down to find Cristof. She couldn't see any sign of him.

He'll be all right. I counterweighted him well. He might be terrified, but he's safe.

She looked up and took a deep breath.

"What kind of simulations do you want the Engine to run for you?"

"Immigration, crime, breeding . . . I want to make sure Ondinium stays healthy over the long term. That means making careful choices about whom we allow to become citizens and how the composition of future generations should fall out. The ideal population ratio is ten to five to two to one, plebeian to cardinal to icarus to exalted. But Ondinium's always been open to immigration, and my research indicates that we're starting to accumulate too many plebeians. That's what's causing our higher rates of poverty, violence, and crime."

Taya nodded, reserving judgment. So far he hadn't said anything she hadn't heard before from self-styled social critics.

Alister smiled as if her nod had been an endorsement.

"I plan to run the simulations on a regular schedule to calculate the city's ideal immigration and childbirth rates each year."

"And you couldn't have done that legally?"

"The Council has a strong conservative element when it comes to relying on simulations to inform public policy. Look at the fuss they kicked up over Clockwork Heart, and all it does is ensure stable marriages and healthy, caste-appropriate children. Who could argue with that?"

"I can. A program can't tell you how well a marriage will work or whether a child will be 'caste-appropriate.' What does that mean, anyway? I'm completely different from my sister, and you're completely different from Cristof."

"You're being distracted by surface differences. I'm looking at deep, behavioral similarities. Now, I grant you, nothing's guaranteed, but if I can control enough of the variables, Clockwork Heart should be able to reach satisfactory statistical likelihoods." His eyes gleamed with enthusiasm. "Logically matched marriages and rationally directed childbearing programs can help Ondinium raise a stronger and smarter generation of citizens."

"Childbearing programs?" A fresh wave of dizziness overtook her and she leaned on the Engine, trying to collect her thoughts.

"Certainly. Mareaux has been breeding superior horses, cattle, and dogs for centuries, and if a group of uneducated farmers can set up a successful breeding program without an analytical engine . . . ."

"Wait." Taya frowned. "You want to breed people like farm animals? That's insane."

"You're grossly simplifying the matter."

"We're reborn according to the Lady's judgment. You can't breed for caste."

"Yes, yes." He waved a hand. "And there will always be a certain amount of movement between the castes due to the social and environmental variables of individual upbringing. Those issues are too difficult to control, which is why we established the Great Examination to reassign children who are poor fits with their birth caste. But I believe that as a society we can take logical, progressive steps to improve the quality of the bodies into which our spirits are reborn. It's not a matter of breeding better people; it's a matter of breeding stronger castes."

"What if Clockwork Heart recommends a cross-caste marriage? Everyone says they never work out."

"It won't. I built in caste as a selection parameter. After all, the idea is to *strengthen* desirable caste traits, not dilute them. Consider it social engineering. A rational, civilized world is a blessing to everyone. The Lady gave us intelligence so that we can improve ourselves and work toward the perfect final rebirth."

"And the Lady also gave us the free will to choose who we love." The pain in her leg was growing worse. "What about Viera and Caster? Would Clockwork Heart have let them marry? Would your childbearing program have come up with Ariq?"

"I'm sure it would have."

"Cristof said both of you objected to the marriage." Taya leaned over and felt the back of her leg. Her flight suit had a ragged rip in it, and she felt something damp. She pulled her hand back.

A thin smear of blood. Just what she'd been afraid of.

"We—" Alister's eyes fell to her hand. "You're hurt."

"One of your men shot me."

"I thought they'd missed." Alister stepped forward and knelt, examining her left calf. Taya flinched and braced herself on his shoulder with her left hand. "It looks like a bullet went in and out. You're bleeding into your suit padding. Give me your knife. I want a better look."

She reached up with her right hand and pulled the utility knife off her harness. Alister's back was protected by layers of silk, but his bare neck was vulnerable, draped with loops of long, gold-wrapped black hair.

She steeled herself and pressed the knife blade against Alister's carotid artery.

"Let go of me, Alister."

The decatur's left hand shot out and grabbed her wrist before she could move. He stood, his grip tightening as he forced her arm up and aside, over her left shoulder.

"Taya—"

She jerked herself around, spinning all the way to her left. Her wings screeched over the metal face of the Great Engine, and then the metal feathers sprang free, slapping Alister across the face and chest. He swore and released her, more startled than injured.

She dropped to her left knee, gasping as her wound sent a fresh pulse of pain shooting through her leg, and slashed behind her with the knife.

The blade slammed harmlessly into Alister's leather boots, but the impact was enough to make him hop backward.

"Stop that! You're being foolish!"

She looked down. A square basket of tin Engine cards sat on the platform—Clockwork Heart, she presumed. She shoved it sideways and it hit the metal guardrail.

"No!" Alister dropped to his knees and grabbed the basket.

For a moment they knelt shoulder-to-shoulder, yanking the basket back and forth as the tin cards inside jingled against each other. Then Taya jammed her knife into the side of the basket and sawed the blade down through the woven reeds, ripping out one of the corners.

Slick metal cards poured out of the ragged hole, tumbling down into the chasm.

"Scrap!" Alister grabbed the basket and tore it from her grasp before all of its contents could vanish into the depths. She slashed at his wrist. He slid the basket behind him and sprang to his feet.

Taya tried to do the same. Pain skewered her and she dropped back to her knees, tears stinging her eyes.

"Now look what you've done," Alister growled, reaching down. He snatched the knife from her suddenly weak hand and put it into his jacket pocket. "You're bleeding to death and you're still trying to fight me."

"Nobody bleeds to death from a calf wound," she gasped. She was almost certain she was right, but Lady, she'd never been shot before, and her calf hurt like Forgefire. She looked down through the grillwork.

The incandescent lights flashed off a small mass of moving metal that was crawling up the side of the Great Engine.

She blinked.

"Take off your armature."

She looked up.

"No."

"Take it off or I cut it off." Alister reached down and grabbed her arm. "I need to see that wound, and I can't get a good look with your tailset in the way. If the bullet left any leather or padding under the skin, your leg could get infected."

She looked up at him. His expression was a picture of concern, as if she hadn't just foiled his plan to penetrate the Great Engine.

"Why do you care?"

"You still don't understand, do you? I'm trying to take care of you—you and Cristof both. But you aren't making it easy."

"What about Caster Octavus?" she asked. "Were you taking care of Viera when you killed him?"

"I—" He looked away, distressed. "I'm sorry about that. Caster was in the wrong place at the wrong time."

"You murdered him!"

The exalted sank into a crouch, facing her. She pulled her arm back and he let it slip out of his grasp.

"I'd intended to get on the wireferry alone. But at the last minute, Caster hopped on with me, wanting to talk about the Clockwork Heart vote."

"You could have waited."

"No, I couldn't have. The alarm was set, and I couldn't pull the clock open and disarm the bomb while Caster was standing there arguing with me, could I? Besides, it was obvious from what you'd said that Cristof was close to discovering me. I had to do something drastic to knock his investigation off its cables."

"So you framed him for your murder?"

"I left the possibility open. I wired the bomb into the clock in the hope that it would implicate him. I knew if the lictors arrested Cris, it would keep him off my trail. I've always intended to show up again to clear his name."

She swallowed. "But why did you kill Octavus? Couldn't you have taken him prisoner?"

"It was hard enough to climb out of the car on my own. I couldn't have done it carrying another man. I knocked him out, though. He didn't feel any pain."

Taya shuddered, thinking of the body parts in the wreckage. The body parts . . . .

She looked at Alister again, filled with cold fury. "No. You *needed* Caster. If you'd been on the ferry alone, there wouldn't have been any blood found in the wreckage. Everyone would have known you weren't dead."

His green eyes shifted, and in that moment she knew.

He was still lying. Even now he was trying to charm her, trying to convince her that all the deaths in his mad scheme had been accidents.

But he'd known exactly what he'd been doing when he'd gotten on that ferry car with Caster. Not only would Viera's husband provide the gore for the search team, his dissenting vote would be removed from the Council chambers. The decatur's murder had been deliberate.

"You're a monster," she spat. She grabbed the railing with one hand and pulled herself up, ignoring the pain in her leg.

The flash on the side of the Engine caught her eye again. It was closer now. She squinted, then spun, turning her back to it.

She had no idea how he'd managed it, but somehow Cristof was climbing up the shifting, floating, cliff-like face of the Great Engine, his ondium wings strapped in a bundle on his back.

"How did you get out of the car in time?" she demanded.

Alister's expression seemed colder now. He wasn't trying to charm her anymore.

"It's easy to reprogram a wireferry driver. I had it pause at a maintenance tower for a minute, just long enough to swing out and climb down."

"And you hid on the mountain for two days?"

"Hiding from the rescue teams by day and traveling at dusk and dawn." Alister shrugged. "I've done some hiking before, although I hadn't anticipated how cold it would get at night."

"You hiked in your public robes."

"Of course not." He smiled. "I had climbing gear and supplies hidden by the maintenance tower. After Neuillan was arrested, I realized a wise decatur needs to be able to drop out of sight at a moment's notice."

"Emelie said you helped Neuillan avoid the loyalty program." She dredged its name out of her memory. "Refinery. Is that true?"

"She must have been mistaken."

"She seemed pretty certain." Taya gave him a steady look. "You were working with Neuillan, weren't you? Did you know Cristof helped catch him?"

"In his role as a lictor's spy?" Amazingly, Alister seemed as disapproving as Viera had been. "Cris shouldn't have gotten involved. Neuillan took good care of us when we were orphaned. Arresting him was poor thanks."

"Was he really a traitor?"

Cristof sighed. "Yes, I'm afraid he was. But I didn't know. I thought he was an idealist, like me; someone willing to bend the rules for the greater good. I was as shocked as anyone else when his ties to Alzana came to light. But if I'd been the one to find out, I would have tried to reason with him, not arrest him."

"How did you cheat Refinery?"

"I've never cheated it," he said, surprised. "I'm not a traitor. Don't you understand? Everything I've done, I've done for Ondinium."

She felt sick. "Refinery can't identify murderers?"

"It can only calculate someone's likelihood to kill. Certain types of bloodshed are desirable, you know. Lictors need to be able to kill as part of their job. And look at you! You threw a man to his death to protect my brother." Alister's voice softened as Taya twitched with guilt. "But I respect that, just as I respect Cris killing to protect you. It's perfectly rational to defend yourself and your friends. Believe me, if I could have done this without causing any deaths, I would have. If Pins hadn't been giving evidence to the lictors, if Caster had only seen reason, if Cristof hadn't been so close to identifying me . . . ."

Taya ignored his excuses, still brooding over the man she'd thrown over the side of the crosswalk. "Who was he? The man I killed?"

"I'm not sure. William, I think. He thought you were a terrorist, breaking in to stop me from doing my job."

"You mean, he was innocent?" Fresh horror swept over her. "I thought he was your accomplice!"

"He was one of the lictors who stayed behind to guard the Tower. He didn't have any reason to doubt me when I informed him I'd hiked up from Primus to check on the Engine. He and his partner escorted me down here and stood guard while I worked."

Taya felt like she were about to vomit. The man had just been doing his job. *Lady.* She began to shake. *Oh, Lady, grant him a swift rebirth and forgive me my sins.*

She grasped at a straw. "Why didn't he recognize you? The lictors would have known Exalted Forlore was supposed to have died in the explosion."

"I didn't give them my real name, and they could hardly recognize me from my robes and mask." Alister shrugged. "I was carrying convincing security papers and I wrote down the correct passwords. Lictors are taught to be obedient, bless them."

"They would have figured out the truth eventually." Taya drew in a deep breath. "What were you going to do with them when you were finished? Sooner or later they would have told someone about you, and inquiries would have been made."

"Ah . . . ." Alister frowned at his chipped nails, then looked up. His face was hard. "Take off your armature, Taya."

"So you can throw me over the side, too?"

"Are you going to make me? So far all of this can be explained away, if you'll agree to cooperate. But if it boils down to my word against yours, I don't need to tell you which one of us will be believed, do I?"

"Cristof will support me."

"It won't be that hard to prove that you're both Torn Cards who came here to destroy the Great Engine after trying to kill me and Caster. You were close to the last wireferry accident. Maybe you were there to make sure it killed the right man and only rescued Viera when it became

clear Caster wasn't on the car. And Cris, well, he's already
a suspect in the attack. Those two lictors were heroes who
rescued me in the middle of the night and then died in an
effort to keep me safe from your attack. I can make you a
hero or a villain, Taya Swan. Which will it be?"

Taya shifted, rising on her toes and planting her back
more firmly against the railing. Pain made her head swim.

"You wouldn't do that to Cristof," she argued. "You
might ruin me, but you wouldn't hurt your brother."

"I would rather not hurt either of you." His voice dropped.
"Work with me, Taya. We'll retrieve Cris and explain to him
that the lictors were forcing me to reprogram the Engine at
gunpoint and that all of this has been a misunderstanding.
I'll make you both heroes, and then, if you'll let me, I'll
prove to you that I'm not such a bad man."

He stepped closer. Taya pushed herself up until she was
sitting on the railing, her back to the open chasm. "Don't,"
she warned.

"Please." Bright light glittered off his golden jewelry
and highlighted the tattoos on his face and the smear of
blood along his cut cheek. "You know how much I admire
you. You said you felt the same way about me. Do you
remember our dance? You looked so beautiful in that
dress. I wish you'd gone home with me that night. Pins
might have stayed alive, if you'd kept me occupied."

For a moment Taya was caught by his emerald gaze,
remembering his strong arms holding her as they danced.
Then she thought of Caster Octavus and of Pins, and she
jerked her gaze away with disgust.

His expression darkened, and he lunged. Taya let herself
fall backward, tumbling heels-over-head off the rail.

"Taya!"

She saw Cristof stare at her, wide-eyed, as he held on to
the side of the Great Engine, just beneath the crosswalk.
Then he looked up at his brother, lifted his arm, and fired
his needlegun through the grillwork.

Taya closed her eyes, feeling the air rushing against her
face. She reached up and slid her arms into the wings by

touch. Without the spinning depths to disorient her, she stretched and unlocked them.

She opened her eyes, waited until her tumbling put her head-up again, and spread her arms.

Air pressure pushed against the feathers. She glanced down. The floor was nowhere in sight and no immediate danger threatened. Warm air whistled past her ears as she kicked the tailset down, hissing as her calf protested. The armature jolted as the tailset created more air resistance.

Groaning, Taya worked her ankles beneath the bar. A kick-tilt and she maneuvered herself belly-down in free fall and took another look beneath her.

So far, so good. None of the chasm-crossing cables or catwalks had caught her. That had been her only concern. Falling backward off a ledge was an icarus game she'd played often as a teenager, dangling from wireferry towers and sitting on cliff tops. The only danger was the unknown.

Now she held her wings at full spread, testing the air and steering herself.

There—the gentle push of a thermal. She swept her arms down and transformed her drop into an ascent.

The thrill of free fall had, at least momentarily, cleared her mind and pushed the pain away. She took advantage of the respite, forcing herself to gain altitude as fast as she could.

Above her, she saw Cristof clinging to the outside of the platform railing. Alister had grabbed the air pistol's barrel and they were struggling for possession of it. Taya swept her arms down again, flying up in the hope of breaking the stalemate.

Alister glanced down, over Cristof's shoulder, and saw her. He redoubled his efforts.

Cristof released the gun and rolled himself over the railing, awkwardly falling to the crosswalk floor. As Taya shot up to the platform, Alister thrust the barrel of the gun into Cristof's face and pulled the trigger.

Taya made a strangled protest, but nothing happened. With an oath, Alister fumbled for the safety.

"Alister!" Taya swooped around to give herself enough height, then twisted and began to backbeat. Alister glanced up at her, then back down at the gun.

Cristof was fumbling in his belt pockets as Alister's thumb snapped the safety back. Alister aimed the weapon just as his brother's hand reemerged.

The outcaste opened his fingers and a five-pound ondium counterweight shot into the air, clipping his brother under the chin. Alister's head rocked backward and a spray of needles stitched the air, one sending a shudder through Taya's wing as it hit an ondium feather.

Taya's heavy boots slammed into Alister's chest and drove him backward, into the Great Engine. The metal punch card tray on the Engine's face snapped off beneath him, and her wounded leg felt like it was on fire.

For a moment she frantically backbeat to keep her balance, and then Cristof ducked between her wings, grabbing the harness straps between her shoulders and steadying her until she got her feet beneath her again.

Limping, Taya grabbed the front of Alister's robes and slammed him against the Engine again.

"I hate you!" she shouted. Tears of anger and pain streaked her face. "You make me sick!"

"My gun," Cristof protested. Careless of her own safety, Taya yanked the weapon from Alister's hand and held it over her shoulder. Cristof took it from her.

"Taya." Alister looked at her, stunned. "I'm sorry."

She spat in his face, then stepped back to let Cristof have him. Alister wiped off his cheek, looking hurt.

"What was that for?"

"Trying to kill your brother."

Cristof stepped to one side on the platform, the needlegun held steady.

"You punched *me* when you'd thought I'd killed my brother," he observed. "Why does Alister get off so lightly?"

"I thought you'd succeeded." Taya was shaking with released tension. "Alister only tried."

"Twice." Cristof turned a hard gaze on their prisoner. He looked as forbidding as he had the first time she'd seen him.

"Don't exaggerate, Cris." Alister's emerald eyes darted back and forth as he took a measure of the situation. "I knew the fall wouldn't hurt you, and I wasn't trying to kill you with the pistol."

"You didn't think shooting me in the face would be fatal?" Cristof was squinting, and Taya realized he wasn't wearing his glasses. He must have lost them in the fall. "You must not have been paying attention earlier. Maybe you were too excited about throwing me into the abyss to see what I did to your lictor?"

"You'd better let me take the gun," Taya said, worried about Cristof's nearsighted aim.

"I'm sorry, Taya, but I don't think you have a cold enough heart to shoot." The tall exalted's voice was flat. "I, on the other hand, am very tempted to run a few needles through your legs right now, Alister."

"And then what would you do?" Alister straightened up and smoothed the front of his embroidered robe. "Are you going to turn me in, Cris? You know what they'll do to me, don't you? Are you really going to let them blind me and flog me out the city gates? After all we've been through together?"

Cristof's needler trembled a moment. Then he shifted his grip and the trembling stopped.

"Blinding is for traitors, Al. You aren't going to be that lucky. Murder carries the death penalty."

"So you'll let me die? That would make you the last Forlore. Will you go back to Primus and take up the mask again? Or you will you let our family line vanish from the ranks of the exalted?"

"I don't see any compelling reason to keep it going. The last two generations have been full of murderers."

"You're as guilty as I am," Alister said, pointing to the lictor's body sprawled on the crosswalk behind them.

"Exactly," Cristof said, evenly. "As I said, no compelling reason."

"Cris, let me tie him up," Taya said, reaching for her safety line and remembering that she'd left it on the catwalk high above. "I need your line."

Cristof pulled the coil off his harness and held it out. She limped forward and took it.

"Our swan's been shot," Alister said, watching them. "Did you notice the blood on her leg? I don't think you should make her walk around on it."

"Shot?" Cristof turned, giving her an alarmed look. "I thought—"

Alister lunged, tackling him. Taken off guard, Cristof staggered and fell to one knee, his needlegun skittering across the grillwork from his hand.

Taya grabbed for the weapon. Its barrel brushed her fingertips as it slipped over the catwalk edge.

The two brothers grappled. Cristof was taller, but Alister was stronger and heavier. The younger brother laughed as Cristof realized his ondium-buoyed harness put him at a distinct disadvantage. For a moment Taya was afraid Alister was going to hoist Cristof up and throw him over the side again, but then Cristof grabbed Alister's neck with both hands, squeezing.

Alister's hand plunged into his jacket pocket and reappeared with Taya's knife.

Taya grabbed the first thing that came to hand, the torn basket of tin punch cards, and leaned over the struggling men. She slammed it down on Alister's head.

The basket split, sending the remaining cards tumbling everywhere. Alister winced and Taya grabbed the back of Cristof's harness, yanking him up and away from his brother. Then her leg gave out and she sagged, darkness swimming before her eyes.

Through the haze, Taya could barely make out Alister recovering and flicking her knife toward his brother. A line of red appeared on Cristof's jaw, jarringly vivid against the spots that floated in front of her eyes. She groped across the catwalk and grabbed a handful of wide tin cards. When Cristof shifted to one side, she hurled them at Alister's face.

The decatur flinched. Cristof shoved him and they hit the
metal railing, which shook and bent at the rivets.

Alister's eyes widened as the metal sagged beneath him.
He grabbed Cristof at the same time that Cristof's hand
closed on his arm. For a moment Cristof held him safe—

—and then the railing snapped and they both fell over
the edge.

Without stopping to think, Taya grabbed the abandoned
safety line and rolled off the catwalk after them.

This time she didn't try to put on her wings. Instead, she
extended her arms and legs into a dive, the line snapping
against her arm as she fell.

The two men were tumbling, gaining speed on the descent.
Taya reached for her nearest counterweight pocket and
pulled out the ondium bar, releasing it and letting it dart up
to the ceiling. Her speed increased as her weight increased.

She had time. They hadn't reached terminal velocity.
She yanked another counterweight out and let it go. Then
another.

She began to draw closer. She hooked one end of the
safety line to her harness and reached out.

Alister and Cristof were clutching each other, their anger
forgotten in the horror of the unexpected plunge. Taya's
first attempt to clip the rope to Cristof failed. Her second
attempt succeeded. The hook snapped onto his belt.

He looked up, his eyes widening.

"It's okay!" she tried to shout, but the words were ripped
from her mouth. She began the struggle to re-wing herself.
It wasn't easy, with the safety line dangling between
them.

At last her arms slid between the struts. She threw her
wings out. All three of them jerked, then began to fall
again.

She wouldn't be able to carry them, she knew that.
She was in the same position Pyke had been during the
wireferry rescue. The best she could do was slow and
guide their fall. She let the line run taut, then began to
angle all three of them toward the Great Engine.

It grew larger and larger as they drew closer, and she searched for an opening. At last she found a landing spot, a makeshift platform created by two huge, flat, ponderously grinding ondium gears. She steered them toward it as they dropped, hoping Cristof and Alister knew enough to brace for impact.

The gears grew larger, each one as wide as Viera's ballroom floor, slowly rotating.

Cristof dropped Alister, who tumbled on the gear and lay motionless. Taya yelped as the two of them bobbed upward with the released weight. Then Cristof snapped the hook off his belt and fell, landing about ten feet away from his brother. One foot slid perilously close to the gear teeth before he yanked it back, scrambling to safety.

Knowing that a graceful landing would be impossible, Taya braced herself, backbeat, and dropped onto the second gear on her knees.

This time the pain was too much to bear.

Chapter Fourteen

"Taya? Taya?"

She groaned and opened her eyes. She was surrounded by noise and motion.

"Don't move." She felt the hard leather of a harness shift under her cheek and realized she was propped against Cristof's shoulder. Her arms were still encased in wings and spread out in front of her. "Are you all right?"

"We should get her out of that armature." Alister's voice, a little farther away.

"Does anything hurt?" Cristof sounded worried. Fingers stroked her cheek. "Don't move. You may have broken something."

"I'm all right." Taya tried to push herself up, swinging an arm around. Metal feathers scraped against metal, and she realized they were still on the megagear. The Engine loomed above and below them, its clattering and chugging forcing them all to raise their voices to be heard. She glanced at Cristof and saw the pallor in his cheeks as he studied her. The cut on his jaw was still bleeding. The fall had made the blood streak up the side of his cheek.

She couldn't have been unconscious for more than a few seconds, then.

She tried to pull her leg under her and a fresh streak of pain ran through her calf. Involuntary tears sprang to her eyes.

"What?" Cristof's hand tightened on her shoulder. "What hurts?"

"My leg."

"Where you were shot? Or someplace new?"

She pushed herself up again. "Shot."

"Give her room, Cris," Alister said, sounding annoyed. "She doesn't need you hovering over her."

"Move slowly," Cristof directed her, ignoring his brother. Still, he backed away.

Her primaries were bent. She looked at them with dismay, flexing her arm and rolling her shoulders, testing to see how much damage her body had sustained.

"Be careful. You rolled when you fell." Cristof frowned. "Nothing's sprained? Broken?"

"No." But her arms and shoulders ached, and she gasped as she stretched them over her head to lock the wings upright. Both Cristof and Alister grabbed a wing to help. Taya grimaced as she twisted her arms out of the struts. "I think I pulled some muscles."

"You're lucky it wasn't any worse." Alister flexed the crooked feathers. "I don't think these are going to work anymore, Cris."

"Don't touch my wings!" Taya glowered up at him. Alister dropped his hands.

"We're going to have to cooperate to get off this gear," he pointed out, mildly.

Taya gave him a hard look.

"You should tie him up," she said, to Cristof.

"I should, but he won't sit still for it."

"And chasing me across the gears would be dangerous," Alister pointed out. "This time we wouldn't have our brave icarus to save us."

"Then I'll—" Taya started to stand, but both brothers protested. Cristof dropped back to his knees and pressed his hands against her shoulders.

"Wait," he insisted. "You can't fly anywhere with bent feathers, and you need to rest and let us bandage that bullet wound before it gets any worse."

"You two are obsessed about wounds, aren't you?" she griped, but she settled back down again. Part of her was glad that she didn't have to prove herself yet. She felt weak and nauseous, although she didn't want to let Alister see her vulnerability.

"We still have a few things in common," Alister said. "Cris, hand me your knife."

"No." Cristof pulled the utility knife off his harness and shifted his weight. "I'm sorry, Taya, but either you need to take off the suit, or I'll have to cut the leg open."

Taya made a face. "Cut it open. But one of you owes me a new flight suit."

"I'll see you get it, my swan," Alister promised. Taya didn't miss the annoyance that crossed Cristof's face.

"Stop calling me yours," she snapped, as Cristof lifted the leather by the bloodstained bullet hole and slit it open.

Alister looked offended, but she saw Cristof's lips quirk in a small smile as he worked. Blood seeped through the cut on his face.

"You're still bleeding," she said. He dabbed his face with his flight suit sleeve, wincing.

"It won't kill me. There." He stood. "Let Alister look at it. I want to see if I can repair your armature. I don't think he'll hurt you."

"Of course I won't!" Alister took his brother's place. Taya gave him a dark look as Cristof pulled out his small repair kit and stood behind her. She could feel the vibrations through her armature as he shifted her wing feathers.

Alister shrugged off his two outer robes. "This may hurt," he cautioned, taking her leg in one hand and wiping away the blood with one of his robes. Taya tensed.

"When Cris and I were boys," he said as he worked, "one of the estates in Primus was being remodeled, and the family had moved out while the work was being done. The two of us decided to explore it. Of course it was dangerous, and of course I got hurt. I was climbing over a pile of scrap wood and fell. I gashed my arm. We bandaged it up and left and didn't tell anyone, because we were afraid we'd get into trouble for trespassing."

Taya flinched as Alister probed the wound, his fingers around her calf.

"Unfortunately, the cut began to fester and I grew feverish, and it wasn't long before our servants noticed the blood on my sheets and found the torn robe hidden under my bed. Our parents called in the family physician, who did everything but scour the wound out with a bristle brush. He lectured us about dirt and infection and amputation and basically put the fear of the Forge into us. And after he left, our parents lectured us all over again. We were both in tears by the end of the day. We honestly thought my arm was going to be cut off."

Cristof laughed once, startling her. Taya glanced up. Had she ever heard him laugh with real amusement before? This seemed like a strange time for it.

"The wound healed, of course, but it left a scar, and neither of us ever forgot the lesson." Alister lifted his arm and pulled up his sleeve. The scar was old and pale against his dark copper skin, but long and uneven.

Taya discarded the few uncharitable comments that leaped to mind and just nodded.

"I'm afraid this is going to leave a scar, too," he said.

"How bad is it?" Cristof asked. Taya looked up at him again. He was removing one of the intact primaries from his own broken wings.

"Not as bad as it could have been," Alister replied. "It looks like the bullet went straight through the muscle. You were lucky, my swan."

"I told you to stop that. I wouldn't have been shot, if it weren't for you."

Alister's jaw twitched.

"You'll need a physician's attention. Cris, if you'll give me your knife, I can cut up one of my robes for bandages."

"I don't trust you with a knife, so stop asking."

"You don't think I'd attack you, do you?"

"Yes," Cristof said. "Right now, I think you're capable of anything."

Alister rocked back on his heels, stone-faced. "You're going to have to trust me eventually. Taya shouldn't fly with a hurt leg, and you'll only get yourself killed if you try it in her armature. I'm the only one here who can get help now."

"More likely you'll get one of the lictors' rifles and come back to finish us off," Taya retorted. "I can fly well enough to get out of here. Flying's mostly arms and hips, anyway."

"Landing isn't. And what will you do when you get to the top of the Engine Room? Do you plan to limp all the way up the stairs to the Tower, and then even farther up to the signal flags?" Alister's voice was gentle. "Neither of us wants you to suffer like that. It has to be Cristof or me, and you know how hopeless my brother is in the air."

"Cris, can't you hit him or something?" Taya asked, irritated.

"I *am* hopeless in the air," Cristof pointed out. He looked down at her, holding a metal feather. "But I'll hit him, if that's what you want. I'm reasonably talented at fisti-cuffs."

"You can barely see me," Alister scoffed. "And that's another thing. Without your glasses, you'd never be able to maneuver past all the cables running to the Engine."

"Stop it, Alister." Taya felt one of the feathers slide out of her wing, and then Cristof handed it to her as he replaced it. "Neither one of us trusts you, and neither of us is going to let you go free."

"So you'll go get help and leave us down here, alone together?" Alister raised an eyebrow. "Blind as a bat, light as a feather—I could throw Cris between those gears and watch him get crushed to death."

"Don't believe him." Cristof was tightening the screws against her back.

"I don't," she said. A flash of annoyance crossed Alister's face and he stood, walking to the edge of the gear and looking out at the chasm as they rotated.

"Here." Cristof took the feather from her, sliding it into his bundle of broken feathers, and then picked up one of the robes Alister had left behind. With effort, he hacked out a chunk of the heavy silk with his utility knife and packed it between her suit and her wound. "Do you really think you can fly?" he asked, in a low voice.

"I'll do what I have to do. We can't let him go up there on his own."

Cris combed his dark hair with his fingers, leaving it standing on end. "We *could*. I don't trust him not to escape, but he'd probably send out a distress flag before abandoning us. He has that much honor."

"Do you want him to get away?" Taya searched Cristof's angular face. His eyes narrowed, but she knew his irritation wasn't directed at her. He was irritated with himself.

"Part of me does. If he hadn't killed anyone . . . if he hadn't killed Caster . . ." His jaw tightened. "I can put on your armature and fly up. It doesn't matter if it's not a good fit or if I can't see well. All I have to do is get up to the nearest catwalk, and then I can find stairs, or a lift. You don't need to go."

Taya's leg hurt too much for her to muster a smile, but she gripped his hand briefly, reassuringly.

"I know. But I'll be all right, and it'll be faster." She glanced over his shoulder at Alister. "You know, before all this, he kept pestering me to bring him a pair of wings. I bet if I had, he would have kept them and gotten up here a lot faster after the accident."

Cristof nodded and straightened, walking around her to begin working on the wings again. Each bent feather he removed was bundled with his broken armature, the whole thing kept from floating away by the safety line tied to his harness.

"What happened when you fell?" she asked, after a moment. "I was afraid you were going to float to the bottom of the mountain."

"I hit a crosswire and hung on for dear life."

Her lips curved at his sour, self-deprecating tone. It seemed like something reassuringly familiar in this whole bizarre situation.

"Then what happened?"

"I sat there and panicked for a while. It seems I *do* panic, under the right circumstances. Then I screwed up enough courage to start moving. I was closer to the Engine than to the walls, so that's the way I went. I was hoping to find a platform, but there wasn't anything there. I could see one above me, though, and the Engine didn't look too hard to climb, so that's what I did. All that ondium you put into my suit helped. When I got to the next catwalk, I bundled up my wings and began unscrewing every counterweight attached to the catwalk floor that I could find. At first I thought I could make myself light enough to float back up to you and Alister, but then I realized that if I did that, I wouldn't be able to control my ascent, so I just counterweighted myself enough for an easy climb."

"That was smart," Taya said, looking over her shoulder. Her strained muscles twinged, and she winced and rolled her shoulders, looking forward once more.

"I have moments of lucidity," he said, dryly. "When I'm not falling to my death."

"I wanted to go after you, but Alister wouldn't let me."

"I know."

"I feel bad about it. You came after me when you heard shooting."

"That was *not* one of my moments of lucidity."

She laughed, remembering his awkward plummet.

"It was brave, Cristof. It was really brave."

He made an impatient sound and stepped back. "All right, I think we're done. Unless the mechanism itself took damage, you should be able to fly in that."

Taya lifted a hand, and Cristof helped her to her feet. She stood, favoring her injured leg, and brushed his blood-smeared face. She wanted to kiss him again, but not here, not with Alister so close. Instead she looked into his eyes, hoping he could read her impulse. "Thank you."

He shrugged, looking down at his suit and pulling open a pocket. "We'd better give you more counterweight. It'll make walking up the stairs easier, and I need to be heavier so Alister can't throw me around."

"You don't really think he'll fight you when I'm gone, do you?" Taya took the metal bars from him and began sliding them into her suit pockets and harness slots.

"He might, but—"

"Ready to fly?" Alister interrupted, striding back. He picked up his discarded robes, looking unperturbed by the missing fabric, and slid them over his shoulders. "I still think this is unwise, Cris."

Cristof waited until Taya signaled that she was light enough, then turned to his brother. "You have less faith in Taya than I do."

"Maybe I just care more."

"Are you going to be all right with him?" Taya asked, looking from one to the other.

"If you leave, there will be nobody to stop me from killing him and calling you a traitor," Alister warned her.

"He's not going to kill me, Taya. Go."

Taya delayed another moment, but she knew she had no choice. She had to trust that Cristof knew what he was doing, just as he trusted her. Pushing back her misgivings, she limped to the edge of the gear. Alister started to move toward her, but Cristof stepped between them, his utility knife in his hand.

Giving them one last look, Taya slid her arms into her wings and tested them. Everything opened and closed correctly. She crouched, flinching with pain, and kicked off.

Strained muscles and her wounded leg made her flight awkward and slow. She caught thermals and glided as often as she could. She was worried about what Alister and Cristof were doing, but she didn't dare push herself into a faster flight.

She had almost reached the top of the Engine Room when she saw two other icarii sweeping back and forth across the face of the Engine.

She tilted her wings to acknowledge them and made an effort to fly up to the topmost catwalk. There she let herself collide with the rail, sliding one arm loose to grab it and clamber over. She fell to the floor, whimpering. Tears of pain streaked her face and she shrugged out of her wings to wipe them away.

The two icarii landed next to her, locking their wings and pulling off their flight goggles.

"What the hell are you doing?" Pyke demanded.

"The lictors are looking for you," Cassi added, looking worried.

TAYA SAT on the catwalk, her back to the wall, and watched as lictors and icarii worked around her. After she'd told them what had happened, Pyke had flown down to stand guard over the two exalteds and Cassi had gone back upstairs to get help. Now Taya was under arrest, although other than confiscating her wings and making sure she wasn't going to die of blood loss, the lictors were ignoring her.

Being ignored gave her time to think, and her thoughts were haunted by the lictor she'd kicked over the railing. William.

She'd killed an innocent man. No matter how often she reminded herself that it was an accident and that he would have shot Cristof if she hadn't, she couldn't make it feel right. She'd killed a man, and Cristof had killed another, and the thought made her stomach churn.

Within an hour both exalteds were brought back up in rescue harnesses and the lictors' bodies were retrieved. Alister had drawn his ivory mask back over his face and was exercising his exalted's right to remain mute in public. Cristof had shown the lictors his identification papers and insisted a physician be called to tend to Taya's wound. He'd paused long enough to grab her hand and squeeze it before the lictors had hustled him off. As always, his hands had been cold.

The lictors took them all back to the Tower and put them in separate rooms. Taya gave her statement while a physician cleaned her wound and called for a pair of crutches. The questioning took a long time, and then Lt. Janos Amcathra walked in and she had to tell the whole story over again, searching his impassive Demican face for some sign that he believed her.

Several more hours passed. At last she was allowed to leave, given her wings and escorted by military icarii back to the lictor station on Primus. This time she didn't have to wait in a cell; she sat in a room and read a copy of her statement, then signed it. After a warning that she was grounded until further notice, she was released, wingless.

Cassi and Pyke were waiting for her outside the station.

"We found your note pretty much just as the warning was going out that there'd been an unauthorized flight," Cassi explained, as they walked down the street. "By the time we got to the launch docks, it was complete chaos. The lictors had heard about the flight and were telling us there was a suspected terrorist loose, and someone pointed out that your armature was missing, and there was a huge argument over whether or not you were a terrorist or if you'd just been kidnapped by one."

"We volunteered for one of the search parties and broke away as soon as we could," Pyke chimed in, as they stopped at the hack station. "We knew from your note that you'd gone to the Tower, so we searched it and found the tunnel to the Engine."

"We knew you weren't a terrorist," Cassi said. "Pyke, will you get us a coach?"

"Sure."

"Ask for Gregor," Taya said, sitting on a bench and setting her crutches next to her. She felt exhausted, emotionally and physically. Pyke nodded and turned to talk to the hackmaster.

"I wish we'd gotten there faster," Cassi said, looking at Taya's torn and bloodstained flight suit. "Did that decatur shoot you?"

"No. It was one of the lictors. It was a mistake. He didn't know who I was." Taya shivered, her guilt over the senseless deaths returning. "He's dead now. Cristof and I killed them both. They were innocent. They didn't know Alister was a criminal."

Cassi put an arm over her shoulders. "It's okay."

"It's not okay."

"You didn't have any choice."

Taya shrugged despondently. Wasn't there always a choice? Maybe she could have put herself between the lictor and Cristof, or—

"Taya, don't eat yourself up over it. You were in danger and you did what you had to do. Nobody's going to blame you for it."

"Their families will."

Cassi hugged her, not answering. After a moment, Taya sighed.

"Do you know if Alister and Cristof are under arrest?"

"Nobody is telling us anything. We want the whole story from you as soon as we get home."

"Deal," Taya agreed, closing her eyes.

When they got back to the Eyrie, Taya assured the rest of the tenants that she wasn't a terrorist and then headed straight to her room. Cassi and Pyke spent the afternoon with her, bringing up food and talking about what had happened. Pyke left a few times to pick up the broadsheets that were starting to hit the streets, their ink wet and their type poorly set. Large headlines marched across the page, comprised of equal amounts of rumor and guesswork. Taya's father, her sister Katerin, and her new brother-in-law Tomas all came to visit toward nightfall, looking concerned and bringing her the best wishes of her childhood friends on Tertius. She hugged them, grateful for her family's support.

Cristof never showed up.

At last Gwen chased all the visitors away and locked the eyrie up for the night.

Taya fell into a restless sleep, awakening throughout the night to the sound of Cristof's watch steadily ticking on her bed stand.

SHE FELT CALMER the next morning, sitting at a breakfast table with her second cup of black tea and a stack of newspapers. The rest of the eyrie had gone to work, and only the famulate staff was left, washing dishes and chattering in the kitchen. Taya had been reading for hours.

The printers must have been up all night. The stories were closer to the truth this morning, and Taya read them all. Nobody had fabricated quotes for her this time. In fact, only the *Courier Regnant* bothered to mention her name. The rest of the papers referred to her as only as "an icarus."

Alister and Cristof received the bulk of the coverage. Alister's educational and political background was covered at length, and any hope Cristof might have had of continuing to work undercover was dashed by the papers' scandalized accounts of the exalted who'd scorned his caste to serve the military.

She also read the names and descriptions of the two lictors who'd died. The papers were fair, at least, describing them as dupes who'd become unwitting casualties during the fight. After a moment, Taya tore out the article and put it into her pants pocket. She wasn't sure how she could atone for killing a man, but she was determined to do something. She'd apologize to his family in person, at the very least, and she'd do more if she could.

Making that decision made her feel better, and she was finally able to set her guilt aside for a while as she read.

A small item in the back of one of the less reputable papers made her stop dead. Taya folded the page over and leaned back in her chair to focus on the story.

One of the journalists had managed to dig up the details of the Forlore murder/suicide, and for the first time Taya had access to a full account. She read it with horrified fascination. The article described the elder Forlore's violent madness and his brutal attacks on his wife and children; attacks that had culminated in the argument that had left his wife dead. He'd killed himself immediately afterward.

The two boys, Alister and Cristof, had been found hiding in the cellar, bruised but alive. They'd been put in a hospital for a while to recover and had then been taken in by their aunt and her husband. The names weren't published, but Taya knew who they were. Viera's family.

She lowered the paper and stared into space, thinking about the different ways the two boys had dealt with their father's abuse.

A familiar voice startled her from her absorption.

"Taya?"

She looked up, her heart leaping. Cristof stood in the dining room doorway, holding a black leather bag.

"Cris!" Taya set the paper face-down and reached for her crutches.

"Wait. Don't get up." He started across the room.

"Now, don't you plan to sit there and talk all day," Gwen said tartly, appearing behind him in the doorway. "I'm paying you to fix my clock, not bother my tenants."

"You won't have to pay me anything, if you'll just leave me alone for a while," Cristof shot back over his shoulder.

"Hmph." Gwen gave Taya a long look, her eyebrows rising. Taya nodded. "All right, clockwright, but you two stay downstairs. I don't allow tenants to bring outsiders to their rooms. This is a boardinghouse, not a brothel."

"Don't be ridiculous." Cristof said over his shoulder, then stopped by the table and looked down at Taya. She was smiling. "What's so amusing?"

"Did you really come here to fix the clock?"

"I found your landlady's service request in my mail last night." He set the bag down. "How are you?"

"Bandaged and grounded. The physicians gave me these awful crutches and some medicine to dull the pain and told me no more crash landings for a month or two."

"But you're going to be well?"

"They said they wouldn't need to amputate."

"That's good. May I join you?"

"Of course. I was hoping you'd come by yesterday. I was worried about you."

He pulled out a chair and sat, giving her a searching look. Taya met it, assessing him in turn.

He'd replaced his lost glasses with an older pair, judging from their battered wire arms. The cut across his jaw had become a narrow, scabbing red line. Other than that, he looked the same as ever, his angular body enclosed once more in a crow-black suit, his ragged hair in disarray from the long walk up to the eyrie.

"They kept me for questioning until midnight," he said, at last. "Alister's in jail. He didn't say anything for hours, and then he began to confess everything."

"I read a little about it."

"He admitted to killing Pins and Caster. He also took the blame for the two lictors. He said they wouldn't have attacked us if he hadn't misled them." Cristof's expression tightened. "There's going to be an inquiry into their deaths."

Taya met his eyes and saw her guilt reflected there. It wasn't reassuring, but she felt better knowing that she wasn't alone.

"What about Viera's wireferry? Did he do that?"

"No. He said it was a coincidence. I have to believe him. It doesn't make any sense for him to work with the Cards."

"Are you sure it was sabotaged by the Cards?"

"They left their usual torn copper punch card close to the vandalized girders."

"What about the bombing that night? The refinery fire?"

"Alister says he didn't have anything to do with that, either." Frustration passed over Cristof's sharp features. "I hate coincidences. Still, it could have been the Torn Cards again. We didn't find a card in the initial search, but it might show up during repairs."

"I'm glad Alister didn't try to kill Viera. That's something, at least."

"Hmm." Cristof's lips tightened.

Taya reached out and took one of his hands. "Are you holding up all right?"

He closed his eyes a moment.

"They'll execute him. The Council won't forgive him for killing a decatur."

"Can he bargain?" Taya thought of Neuillan's blinding and exile and wondered if Alister would consider that any better. But Cristof shook his head, looking troubled.

"I don't see how. The laws are clear."

"I'm sorry."

"So am I." He paused. "Viera isn't. She wants him dead."

Taya nodded. It wasn't hard to imagine how furious Viera must be, finding out her husband had been killed by her cousin, instead of both of them dying in the same tragedy. She searched for something reassuring to say.

"You know, she's still angry and grieving. But she's not heartless. She'll change her mind, in time."

"Maybe. But it won't matter." He drew his hand back. "We talked last night. I thought I owed it to her to tell her what we'd discovered. But she got so angry that I had to leave. I couldn't stand hearing her shouting that she wanted him dead. Even after everything, I don't want him to die. Again."

"Of course you don't," Taya said, quietly. "If you did, you wouldn't be human."

"He tried to kill me."

"I don't think he was thinking straight."

Cristof leaned back in the chair and massaged his forehead. Lines of tension ran vertically down his brow and bracketed his mouth. "I wonder if he's ever thought straight. Sometimes I think there's some kind of poison in our blood. Alister's just like our father. Charming, charismatic, and violent."

Taya bit her lip.

"And the worst part is, it doesn't make any sense," he continued. "He didn't have to kill anyone. Pins didn't know who was buying the Engine cards, and Caster's vote might not have swayed the entire Council. Alister was powerful. He was building up a following among the decaturs. Why couldn't he wait? Even if the vote had gone against him, he would have had years to get his program accepted."

"I don't think his ideas would ever have been accepted," Taya protested. "He thought people could be controlled, like little analytical engines he could program to do whatever he wanted."

"He was always good at getting his way. But up until now, he'd never done anything to hurt anybody. I thought his ambition meant he was a natural leader. I let him take over the estate because I thought he'd do a better job than I would."

"Don't start blaming yourself," Taya chided him. "You're not responsible for your brother's decisions."

"What if my decisions affected his?"

"You can't start thinking that way. It'll make you go crazy."

"Crazy's already in my blood."

Taya frowned. Cristof needed shaking out of his black mood before it overwhelmed him.

"That's stupid," she snapped. "You're not crazy. You're nothing like Alister. For one thing, you aren't charming, charismatic, or violent."

Cristof's distant gaze snapped back to her. She lifted her chin.

"You're a slagging pain in the tailset and sometimes, very rarely, you show signs of being a little sweet. But you're not crazy."

He stared at her, several expressions warring on his face. At last he settled for a crooked, humorless smile.

"Only very rarely?"

"At best."

"I see." He closed his eyes and pinched the bridge of his nose. "Forgive me. I'm talking too much about myself. I didn't mean to come here and complain."

Taya leaned forward, propping her elbows on her knees.

"I want to help. You know that, right?"

"Yes."

"So I'm not going to let you waste your time being bitter and self-pitying."

"Is that what I'm doing?"

"Pretty close." She dropped a hand on his leg. "Look, you did the right thing. And Alister did, too, by confessing. Now he's going to need you. He's all alone in that cell, facing execution, and he's going to need his older brother to support him. That's all you can do for him now, so if you love him, do it."

Cristof drew in a deep breath and nodded once, his eyes still screwed shut.

"Viera's going to need you, too," Taya continued. "You don't have to agree with her. Just let her be angry and let her know that you're not going to abandon her."

He opened his eyes, giving her a bleak look.

"It would be easier if you were with me. They both like you better than they like me."

"That's not true. But I can be there if you want me." She shrugged. "I'm grounded for two weeks. I'd rather be an exalted's personal assistant than sort mail up at Dispatch."

He put his hand over hers, holding it.

"Do you have to consider it a duty? Wouldn't you do it as a friend?" His voice was strained.

"Of course I would. But let's make it official, anyway. 'Friend' won't get me out of stuffing mail bags." She tilted her head, looking at his tense expression. "Thanks for asking, though. You have your moments, exalted."

The lines in his face smoothed, almost imperceptibly. "Am I up to 'rarely' yet?"

"No, but I don't expect miracles."

He laughed, once, a gasp that contained less humor than it did relief, but Taya was still glad to hear it.

"Taya Icarus, I don't know why you humor me, but I'm glad you do."

"You'll pay me back." Taya tugged his hand, struggling to her feet. "To start off, you can carry my chair into the foyer. I want to watch the master clockwright at work."

He rose, clinging to her hand, and gave her a wry, grateful smile.

The late morning sun streamed through the foyer's front windows, and Cristof set Taya's chair in a pool of light. She laid her crutches on the floor next to it and sat to watch.

The exalted's deadpan humor returned as he began to work. He explained each step and brought over the dirty clock parts for her to clean and oil. "It's only fair," he pointed out. "I learned your job, so now you can learn mine." Taya made a point of complaining about the messy work just to please him.

Watching Cristof fix the clock gave Taya time to examine him. She enjoyed watching the satisfaction on his face as he replaced a worn spring or polished a gear back up to a dull shine. With his coat off and his sleeves rolled up, only the castemark on his copper cheeks revealed that he was anything other than a regular craftsman. The sharp angles and furrows of his face had become familiar to her now, and the smudge of grease on his nose, where he'd shoved his glasses back up as he worked, amused her.

Taya chewed on her bottom lip, watching his grease-blackened fingers as he deftly reconstructed a gear fitting, and thought about their one kiss next to Oporphyr Tower.

Any other man, she mused, *would have come in and greeted me with a kiss this morning. Alister would have*— but she thrust that thought away. Alister would have, but it wouldn't have meant anything.

Why hadn't Cristof? Was it just his social ineptitude, or was he starting to separate himself from her in anticipation of returning to Primus?

She bit too hard on her lip and winced, straightening up. *He'd better not withdraw. Not when I've just started to like him.*

At last he cleaned his hands on the rags in his toolkit, closed the clock case, and wound it up again. Both of them fell silent, listening to its loud ticking as it filled the room. Shortly after noon. The repair had taken two hours. Taya thought it would have taken less time if she hadn't been there distracting him with questions and jokes.

"Oh! I still have your pocket watch," she said, remembering. "It's upstairs."

Cristof glanced at her, then away.

"You can keep it," he said, gruffly. "For now, I mean. Until I find you something better."

"You don't need to do that," she protested. "I mean, now that you've got this clock working again . . . ."

"It's all right. I own plenty of watches."

"I—" she closed her mouth. What was she doing, arguing with him when he was trying to do something nice? Lady, if anything, she should be encouraging him. "Thank you, Cris. I appreciate it."

He knelt on the floor and began packing his toolkit.

"I expect to be up to 'rarely' in no time."

"Huh? Oh, you have a hidden agenda, do you?" She laughed. His straight-faced humor always surprised her. "You promised me you didn't."

"There's nothing hidden about it," he replied. "My objective is obvious. I've decided that I'd rather have you describe me as 'sweet' than a 'slagging pain in the tailset.'"

"Really?"

"Well . . ." he looked up from the bag. "Maybe not in public."

"I might be able to confine myself to saying it in private, if you gave me a reason." Taya met his eyes, and he blushed. He averted his gaze and grabbed a handful of greasy rags, stuffing them into his bag.

Taya stood, grabbed one of the crutches, and limped over to him. She braced a hand on his shoulder and leaned over to kiss him on the cheek. "I'm sorry," she said, unrepentantly. "I shouldn't tease you."

He glanced up at her, his expression serious.

"No, you shouldn't. I don't have much experience with teasing. I could end up taking you seriously."

Taya felt a jolt as he met and held her gaze. Her fingers curled on his shoulder. She leaned over, braced against him again, and he slid a hand up over her cheek.

For a moment they gazed at each other, the promise of another kiss trembling between them.

Then, behind them, Gwen cleared her throat.

Taya jumped, nearly stumbling. Cristof half-rose, grabbing her arms to steady her. They both looked over their shoulders, giving the landlady guilty looks.

She eyed them, her beefy arms folded firmly over her chest.

"If you're finished here, Master Clockwright, I'll go get my pocketbook," she said, unmistakably satisfied with herself. "And I'll expect a receipt."

"I really *ought* to charge you, now," Cristof muttered, making sure Taya was stable before he stood and brushed at the dust on his trousers. He raised his voice, sounding annoyed. "I thought you were going to leave us alone if I repaired your clock for free."

Taya clapped a hand over her mouth, not sure whether to be embarrassed or amused. Amusement won out, and she had to struggle not to laugh as the thick-waisted landlady and skinny exalted glared daggers at each other.

"You said 'for a while,'" Gwen snapped. "I did leave you alone for a while. But if you think I'm going to let you ravish one of my little girls—"

"Ravish!" His eyes widened with disbelief.

Gwen snorted, irreverently snapping her fingers at him. "The bill?"

Cristof ground his teeth. "I, at least, will keep my end of the bargain. I'm not charging you for this repair."

"Then if you don't have any more business here—"

"He's going to take me to lunch," Taya said, hastily. Then she gave Cristof an uncertain look. Would he mind? Did he have more important things to do? "Weren't you? Or are you busy?"

"Of course we're going to lunch," he said, still glowering.

"Good." She smiled. "Just give me a minute to get my cloak."

"Wait. You can't walk down Cliff Road on crutches."

Gwen snorted. "Send one of the neighborhood boys to hire a hack, you maskless ninny. They'll run messages for a penny or two."

Cristof scowled, then turned and headed outside.

"Have him ask for Gregor and Bolt, if they're available!" Taya shouted. Cristof nodded once, shoving through the door.

As soon it shut behind him, Taya turned on Gwen.

"You enjoyed that," she said, accusingly. Gwen gave her an innocent look, then burst into raucous laughter.

"Oh, I did. You both looked so disappointed! If only you could have seen yourselves! Absolutely priceless!"

Taya tried to resist, but then she started giggling, too, until both of them were reduced to helpless laughter and snorts, glancing at the door to make sure Cristof wasn't going to come back in and find them like that.

"That's not fair," Taya said at last, wiping her eyes. "I like him."

"Clear proof that love is blind," Gwen retorted. "What in the world would a nice girl like you see in that squawking crow?"

"He's brave, and honest, and intelligent—"

"—bony, bad-tempered, poorly dressed, outcaste—"

"Oh, Gwen! He's not perfect, but . . . the perfect one turned out to be a murderer."

"Hmph." Her landlady sighed. "You know I'm only giving him a hard time because I can. But I worry about you, Taya. You're flying in such dangerous skies, with all these criminals and spies and bombs . . . ."

"It's all over now."

"Is it?" Gwen looked dubious. "And what will you do when that awful decatur is executed and your crow puts on his mask again? It would be one thing if I thought you were just having a fling, but I know you better than that. I don't want you to get your heart broken when reality catches up with you."

"Reality." Taya straightened her shoulders. "I can outfly reality any day."

"Not even the fastest icarus can do that, dear." Gwen sighed. "Well, enjoy yourself while you can, even if it *is* with an outcaste. And don't forget to take your pain medicine, if you're going to be gone for any amount of time."

Taya nodded, grabbing her other crutch and limping up the stairs.

Cristof's mood had improved by the time they were settled into the hack. The message boy had found Gregor, and the cheerful coachman greeted Taya with enthusiasm and Cristof with respect. They jolted into motion. Cristof steadied his toolbag with one hand, stretching his legs across the narrow gap between their two facing seats.

"Where are we going?" Taya asked. "If you have work to do, I don't mind getting lunch on my own. I didn't mean to invite myself like that."

"No? I thought we'd go to that foreign restaurant you like. The Cabisi place. I didn't eat there the other night, so I thought I should try it today."

She smiled. "You have time?"

"My suspension is still in effect. In fact, this time they took away my lictor's papers to ensure it."

"I'm sorry."

"It's all right. I don't know what I'm going to do after this, anyway." He looked out the window, then flinched and looked back. Taya glanced out and saw that the hack was making its way down Cliff Road, revealing a sweeping vista and long drop. "I'll never be able to work as a spy again."

"You don't sound too upset about it."

He absently tapped his fingers on his toolbag. "I'll find something else to do."

She hesitated, but the opening was there, and she had to take it.

"Will you go up to live like an exalted again?"

"No." His answer was fast and firm. "I can't go back to a mask and robes anymore. Could you go back to working in a factory, after living like an icarus?"

"But that's different. I'd be giving up my freedom if I did that," she protested.

"And I'd be giving up my freedom if I covered myself again. You have no idea. It's not just the public restrictions, although those are bad enough. It's all the other rules and traditions and expectations. No . . . the Lady made a mistake when she incarnated me as an exalted. I'm not ready for it yet."

"Maybe the Lady wanted you in the caste for a reason," Taya suggested. "To make it more honest, or to shake up

the traditions, or something like that. Maybe it's your duty
to live like an exalted."

"Do you want me to go back?"

"No!" She looked at him and saw that he was serious, so
she became serious, too. "But I want you to do what's right. If
you have to go back to help your family, then you should."

"My family doesn't need my help. Not the kind of
help that requires me to put on a mask, anyway," he said,
forestalling her protest. "Besides, it's too early to think
about returning to Primus. We don't even know what's
going to happen yet."

Taya glanced at him. It was clear what was going to
happen, and they both knew it. But she didn't argue.

"All right." She made an attempt to lighten the mood.
"I was wondering what you might look like with long hair
and jewels, though."

"Ridiculous."

"I *was*."

"I mean, I look ridiculous."

"Well, somebody needs to do something about your hair.
You have to stop cutting it yourself. Even that little sweep
girl of yours could do a better job."

"Jessica? She'd cut off my ears."

"She was cute. 'Clockite.' I like that."

"She's a pest. I can't get rid of her." He sounded put out.
"For some reason my shop fascinates children."

"Well, it's filled with all kinds of fascinating things. Did
you show them the flying birds?"

He muttered something. She laughed.

"I don't know why you can't just be nice to them, for a
change."

"If I'm nice, they'll come around even more often than
they do now, and I'd never get any work done."

"I see. So by that logic, if I decide I don't want you
hanging around—"

He gave her an alarmed look, and Taya realized he wasn't
confident enough for that kind of teasing. She adjusted her
response.

"—then I'll have to suggest something unpleasant, like taking another flight together."

"Yes, that might scare me away."

"Too bad. I liked flying with you." She put on a thoughtful expression. "I liked landing with you even better."

He closed his eyes and sighed. "I don't suppose there's any chance you really mean that."

"You'll never find out if you keep sitting so far away from me."

He swallowed and opened his eyes again.

"I am aware the correct response would be to swing across to sit next to you," he said, sounding pained, "but if I tried, I'd hit my head on the ceiling, or fall on top of you, or do something equally graceless that would embarrass us both."

She laughed. "You're thinking too much again."

"Thinking isn't a habit I'm likely to break."

Taya shook her head, exasperated. A minute later the hack rattled to a halt and Gregor sang out the name of the restaurant.

"Allow me." Cristof unfolded himself first, exiting and setting his toolbag and her crutches onto the cobbles. He helped Taya slide out. The manuever was a little inelegant as she tried to avoid putting too much weight on her wounded leg.

"Are you all right?" he asked, steadying her.

"Just cold." She started to lift her hand to fasten the cloak-clasp around her neck, only to find that he wasn't letting go. "What—"

He cupped her cheek with one hand and kissed her.

Startled, Taya stood frozen a moment. Then she collected herself, wrapped her arms around his neck, and lifted herself up to return the kiss.

She felt him shiver as he lowered his head again, his lips soft as they brushed against hers. Taya closed her eyes, surprised by how content she felt to be held by him as her cloak slipped off her shoulders and passers-by whistled.

When they separated a second time, Taya lifted his glasses from his face. The lenses were steamed opaque.

"That was nice," she murmured, smiling up at him. The autumn wind stirred his hair, and he wore an expression she didn't think she'd ever seen before. She touched his lips with her free hand. "Why, Cris, you're positively handsome when you smile."

Gregor cleared his throat from his driver's bench.

"Maybe you'd like a tour of Secundus, you two?" he asked, fighting to keep a poker face. "Take me a couple hours to make a complete circuit of the sector, most like."

Cristof looked up, blinking as he tried to focus without his glasses.

"Um—not today." His hands slid from Taya's waist. "Here—" He reached into his greatcoat for his pocketbook.

"Oh, you needn't worry yourself about that, exalted." Gregor's eyes crinkled with humor. "I weren't going to charge you anyway, not the city's heroes. You two have a nice lunch, then." He saluted them with his coachman's whip and shook the reins.

"Thank you, Gregor!" Taya shouted, as the hack rattled away. He waved.

When she looked back, Cristof's smile had shifted back to his more familiar mocking expression.

"What?" She faced him and carefully slid his glasses back on.

"You make friends with everyone, don't you?"

"It's better than making enemies."

He nudged the frames back down to the right angle. "Interesting concept."

"By the way, I think you've reached 'rarely' now."

"What comes after that?"

"'Sometimes.'"

"A new goal."

He held her closely until he'd settled her into a seat by one of the restaurant windows. Taya set her crutches against the wall, enjoying the attention. Since Cristof didn't know anything about Cabisi food, she suggested a few dishes, which led them into a discussion of her curiosity about foreign lands and the diplomatic corps exams. He listened to her with a grave air, asking probing questions.

They were halfway through their lunch when Taya heard her name called. She twisted in her seat.

Lars stood in the restaurant doorway, looking uneasy. She gestured, and he lumbered past the other diners, shaking his shaggy hair back over his shoulders.

"Taya, I'm glad to see you. I'm looking for Kyle. You haven't seen him, have you?"

"No." Taya set down her spoon, hearing the concern in his voice. "Why?"

"What's wrong?" Cristof asked, his face settling into its usual frown. Lars gave the exalted a startled look, noticing him for the first time, then bowed, palm against forehead.

"You haven't seen him, have you?" the big man asked, plaintively. "He talked to the lictors yesterday about Alister and Clockwork Heart."

Cristof shook his head. "He didn't talk to me. Has something happened?"

"He—the prototype—" Lars grimaced. "We've got a problem, exalted. You're a lictor, right? Or something like that?"

Cristof looked across the table at Taya. "Do you want to wait here?"

"No." She pushed her bowl away and reached for her crutches. "Let's go."

Lars looked relieved, hurrying back out. Taya followed, pulling her fur cloak around her neck and limping after him. Cristof grabbed his toolkit and spoke to one of the servers as they left.

Outside, Lars pulled them into an alley.

"I didn't want to notify the lictors, not until I was sure what happened," he said nervously. "I tried Kyle's flat, but nobody answered, so I thought maybe he'd gone out for lunch, but—"

"Lars!" Cristof's voice was cold. "Stop babbling."

The programmer's mouth closed and he nodded.

"Now. Why are you looking for Kyle?"

Lars licked his lips. "The prototype engine. It's missing."

Taya gave Cristof a swift look, and he returned her gaze, his expression grim. Her first thought was of Alister, and she knew that he was thinking the same thing.

"That's the new analytical engine?" she asked, turning her attention back to the programmer. "The one Alister was inspecting?"

"Yes. It's, um—" he gestured, at a loss for words. "It's something brand new. Ground breaking. I mean, it's only duplicating the functionality of the Great Engine, but to do it on a human scale—"

"When did you find out it was gone?" Cristof cut him off.

"Maybe . . . two, three hours ago?" Lars sounded uncertain. "I couldn't sleep, not with the news about Alister, so I decided to go do some work while I was up. Nobody else was down there, but things had been moved, so I thought maybe one of us had curled up to take a nap in one of the other rooms. That happens, sometimes. I went looking and saw scratches and scuff marks, so I knew something wasn't right—"

"Scratches?"

"On the wall. You know how you mark up the walls when you move something big? I saw these long black scrapes and knew something was wrong."

"How did you know it was the engine?" Cristof was pulling on his coat now, his grey eyes fixed on Lars' face.

"I looked. There are four rooms down there, and we've got keys to them all. I just started opening doors." Lars looked ill. "And it's gone. The whole engine. It must have taken all night to dismantle."

"The team wasn't at the University last night?"

"No." He shifted from foot to foot. "The news, you know. That Alister was alive but under arrest, that he'd been caught trying to sabotage the Great Engine—we couldn't believe it. We were at PT's, reading every paper as soon as it came out, trying to parse out what had happened. I mean, none of us could concentrate on writing code while all of those rumors were flying around."

"PT's?" Taya asked, puzzled.

"The Pickled Thalassonaut. It's a programmer bar," Lars explained. "Every programmer in the city was there. We were stunned. And then the lictors came in and started asking questions, and they took our team down to the station . . . it was just too much. I don't think a single card got punched in the city yesterday."

Cristof was scowling.

"You're on suspension," Taya reminded him. "And you know who they're going to suspect."

"It couldn't have been Alister. He was in jail last night."

"Did he really. . . ." Lars looked at Taya.

"Yes. I'm sorry. He confessed."

"Lady." He shook his head, looking like a heartbroken bear. "I just can't believe it."

She patted his arm, watching Cristof. She could sense the gears turning as he tried to think of some way to take the case, but the frustration on his face showed that he wasn't having any luck.

"Everyone on the team had the key to the room?" she asked.

"Yes. Including Alister, of course, and the engineering team in the College of Science and Technology who built the engine. Probably an administrator or two, as well, but you'd need to ask the dean about that."

"How many of them visited the engine on a regular basis?"

"Just Alister and the chief engineer. They were still testing it. I don't think it had run anything more complex than some simple mathematics programs, just to test the — um, the parts."

She sensed that he was avoiding something. "Is it a secret?"

He looked uncomfortable. "Nothing that would mean much to you, but we signed confidentiality agreements . . .

"All right." Taya nodded, curious but not inclined to pursue the matter. She was used to carrying secret messages and mysterious packages, and if she ever became a diplomatic envoy, the secrets would only multiply. "How hard is it to dismantle an analytical engine?"

He grimaced.

"If you want to use it again, you have to know exactly what you're doing, and you need an expert to put it back together. You can't just take a piece of complex machinery like that apart with a hammer and a wrench."

"Who on your team could do it?" Cristof asked, looking up.

Lars took a deep breath.

"Me. Kyle. Emelie. Vic and Izzy aren't mechanics."

"Have you tried looking for anyone on the team besides Kyle?"

"No . . . he's the boss. I wanted to tell him, first. If this . . . it's bad enough that Alister's in jail. For the team to be implicated in a theft, too . . . ."

Cristof nodded and looked at Taya.

"I'll take Lars to the lictors," he said, sounding resigned. "You—"

"If I'd wanted to go to the lictors, I would have!" Lars growled. "I need to find Kyle."

"I don't care what you want," Cristof shot back. "The city's in the middle of a security crisis. The Great Engine's out of operation, the Tower's all but abandoned, one of our decaturs is in jail, and now our newest analytical engine has been stolen. This is bigger than your team's reputation, Lars."

The programmer caviled a moment, then muttered and agreed.

"I'll go talk to Alister," Taya volunteered. "I'll ask if he knows anything about this."

"What makes you—no, never mind." Cristof looked sour. "All right. I'm going to try to talk my way onto this case. How can I reach you, if our paths don't cross?"

"If it's late, send a message to the eyrie, but I'll try to find you before then."

Cristof ducked back into the restaurant to pay for their aborted meal. Taya angled herself next to Lars so that his bulky frame blocked off most of the wind.

"Did Alister really kill Decatur Octavus?" Lars asked.

"Yes."

"And that woman?"

"Uh-huh."

"It's hard to believe. He always seemed so normal."

"I know."

"You think he's involved in this? The theft?"

Taya thought about it a moment.

"He could be if he thought stealing the prototype would benefit the city."

"But he was in jail last night, so he couldn't have been one of the thieves."

"That's true."

"There are lots of troublemakers in Ondinium."

Taya glanced at him. "He told me he was glad you ran the program in his honor. And he laughed when he heard what it said."

The big man's cheeks colored over his brushy stubble. "Probably some kind of prank he and Kyle hatched up together."

"Oh, I don't think so."

Cristof returned. "All right, let's go. Taya, stay off that leg. Take a hack around town. Do you have money for the fare?"

"Enough. Don't worry about me. I'm used to getting around."

"On wings." He frowned. "I should have hired that coachman of yours for the day."

"I'll be all right."

"If you're certain." He hesitated, then quickly stepped forward, laying a hand on her shoulder and giving her a fleeting kiss on the cheek. "I'll see you later."

Taya rested her cheek against his cold fingers a moment. "I hope you get the case." She turned to Lars, who was giving them a bemused look. "You know, you'll be treated better by Cris than by anyone else. He knows you and your team. Maybe you shouldn't talk freely to any lictor but him."

The programmer closed his mouth, then scratched his chin with a thoughtful look.

"Yeah, that makes sense. The rest of the team would probably feel the same way."

"You're devious," Cristof said to her, with appreciation. Taya leaned on her crutch and winked at him.

Chapter Fifteen

When Decatur Neuillan had been arrested for treason, he'd been held in a special cell on Primus. Taya guessed that was where Alister would be held, too, so she took a hack to the station. Two lictors stood at the station door, each carrying air rifles. The sight of armed guards was unusual enough to suggest that her guess about the decatur's location was correct.

"Hi." She caught her breath. "I'm Taya Icarus. Can you tell me who's in charge of Decatur Forlore?"

The lictors' attentiveness transformed into wariness and something else. Dislike?

"Captain Scarios," one said, coldly. "Ask for him at the desk."

"Thank you." She limped to the front desk. Within a few minutes, she was sitting in the captain's office.

Scarios was an older man. Streaks of grey ran through his dark hair, and his black lictor's stripe had grown soft-edged with age. He looked tired, and Taya suspected that it was the kind of bone-deep weariness that set in after too many years at a thankless job, rather than the result of temporary sleeplessness.

"Some of the caste resent the fact you killed a lictor," he said, after they'd exchanged the necessary pleasantries. "Those two men had friends at this station."

Taya lowered her eyes. "I'm sorry, captain. I feel terrible about it."

"I expect the investigation will clear you. It'd be hard to argue you weren't defending yourself when you've got a bullet hole in your leg. But there's going to be hard feelings, anyway. You should try not to do anything that would cause trouble."

"Like coming to the station today?"

"Right."

She looked up, searching for anger or resentment in the captain's features, but he just looked worn out.

"I wouldn't be here if it weren't important. I need to talk to Alister—to Decatur Forlore. It's, um, a private matter."

"A private matter."

"I need to ask him a few questions. I think he, well, his brother and I . . . ." her voice trailed off as she wondered what to say. If she brought up the theft, the captain would demand to know why it hadn't been reported yet. She could tell him Cristof was doing that now, on Secundus, but he'd probably make her wait until he could check it out, and then he'd take over the questioning.

Taya wanted to talk to Alister herself. They had more to discuss than the missing prototype engine.

"His brother. Cristof Forlore?"

"Yes."

"He defended you last night."

"Really?"

"He said you took him to the tower under orders—that you didn't know he was suspended." Scarios gazed at her from beneath hooded eyes. "Interesting thing is, when Alister Forlore started confessing, he defended you, too. He told us how you saved Exalted Octavus and her son, and that you only killed William to save his brother Cristof. He said if it wasn't for you, he and his brother would be dead at the bottom of the Engine Room. Made you sound like a real hero."

"That was . . . generous of him."

"I thought so. But he said lots of nice things about his brother, too, so maybe he's just a generous guy."

"For a killer."

"Exactly." The captain kept watching her. "I don't have any reason to keep you from talking to him. But there's gonna be a lictor nearby to listen in on the conversation. I don't like it when captives and captors get too chatty. Makes me wonder what I'm missing."

"The only thing you're missing is that Alister's a master manipulator." Taya met the captain's eyes. "He's being charming and generous because he knows he can't save his life by being rude. But he tried to shoot Cristof in the face, and he would have framed both of us with murder if he could have gotten away with it."

"I got the impression he liked you."

"He pretends to. He fooled me before I found out what kind of person he is. But he doesn't mean it. It's just the way he acts, throwing compliments around and trying to make everyone feel special."

Scarios grunted and pushed himself to his feet. "You'll have to be searched before you go in to talk to him. You want to see him in his cell or an interview room?"

"What's the difference?"

"If you talk to him in his cell, he won't mask up, but there won't be any lictors around to protect you if he decides to take you hostage. If you talk to him in an interview room, we'll put guards in with you, but he'll stay covered and mute."

"His cell, please. I don't want to try to communicate with him when he's behind a mask." She gazed at him curiously. "How do you do it?"

"Eventually we'll get him legally outcaste. In the meantime, we ask lots of yes or no questions. Last night he agreed to talk to his brother and let me listen in." Scarios gave her a tight smile. "I didn't get to see his face, but I got to hear his voice. Maybe he was trying to make me feel special. You think?"

"It wouldn't surprise me."

"I'm flattered. C'mon."

The "cell" where Alister was being held had an antechamber arrangement much like Rhodanthe's, leading into a parlor from which two more doors indicated other rooms. The room's furnishings included a desk, a table, several chairs, some bookshelves, and a small fireplace. Only the lack of windows suggested that it wasn't the best suite of a travelers' inn.

Scarios waited until a female lictor searched Taya and pronounced her safe, then took his leave. The lictor, a silent woman with hard eyes, stopped at the antechamber and sat down. Taya walked through the curtained but doorless frame.

Alister was already on his feet, waiting for her.

"Taya. I was surprised when they told me you were coming." His smile was as warm as ever, although his green eyes flickered to her crutches. "I was afraid you were angry with me."

"I am, exalted." Taya wondered for a fleeting moment whether she should bow or not. *Good manners are always appropriate.* Unable to bend on the crutches, she settled for pressing her palm to her forehead and inclining her head. "I'm here on business."

"Please, sit down. Those crutches can't be comfortable." He walked around the low tea table and pulled out a chair. Taya's neck prickled at his proximity, but he did no more than take her crutches as she sat and prop them up close to her.

He was wearing fresh robes, and his public robe and mask sat on a nearby chair, ready to be pulled on. His jewelry had been confiscated, though, leaving his hands and ears naked. His hair ornaments were gone, too, and with nobody to dress his long hair for him, he'd settled for tying it back with a scarlet ribbon.

She remembered wondering what he'd look like in a more casual setting, that night at Rhodanthe's. She'd imagined him looking like this on some lazy morning, perhaps over a leisurely breakfast.

Not in a cell.

"How's your leg?" he asked.

"Good enough. The doctor said it'll heal cleanly."

"I could have wrung that man's neck when I realized he'd shot you."

"Really." She wasn't impressed. "I need to talk to you about the prototype engine."

"Why?"

"It's part of a new case that's come up."

"One of Cristof's cases?"

"Maybe."

"I see." He inclined his head. "I'll tell you as much as I can, although some information about the engine is confidential."

"Is the prototype valuable?"

"Of course. All our engines are valuable, but especially the analyticals. They cost a great deal in parts and workmanship, and of course their reverse engineering value to another country would be inestimable."

"But this prototype is special?"

"It's a significant improvement over the other small engines we've built. The Great Engine is still superior, but that's hardly a fair comparison—we can build much more complicated mechanisms when we're working on that scale. It's bringing that level of functionality down to a human scale that's always been the challenge. Frankly, I don't think anybody will be able to replicate the Great Engine's complexity with smaller components, but this prototype brings us one step closer." Alister smiled at her. "Why are you asking me questions, instead of Cris? You aren't going to give up your wings to take a lictor's stripe, are you? Or perhaps you plan to give them up for a life of gears and springs?"

Taya shot him a sharp look.

"I'm not going to give up my wings at all. I'd be wearing them now, if it weren't for you."

"Good. I'll die happy, knowing that you're still my silver-winged hawk."

"Despite your best efforts."

"That's not fair. I never wanted to hurt you. If Cris hadn't dragged you into his investigation, you would never have been harmed at all." Alister raised an eyebrow. "And speaking of Cris, I couldn't help but notice a certain . . . tenderness . . . in the way he was treating you yesterday."

"That's none of your business."

"When one is facing imminent death, matters of family seem extremely important. It's all right. I approve. In fact, I'm jealous. I never thought my gearhead of an older brother would have enough spirit to steal a woman away from me. I used to say he had a clockwork heart."

"Cristof didn't steal me from you. I'm not anybody's to steal, and you were dead. Or you were supposed to be, anyway."

"If I'd known my death would throw you into each other's arms, I might have changed my plan."

"To something that didn't involve murder?"

Alister sighed. "Maybe."

"The prototype. Who else knows it exists?"

"Its existence isn't a secret. The details of its construction are, but anybody with an interest in AEs will have heard about the Council's experiments with a new model. Why? Are you going to tell me what happened?"

"Somebody stole it last night."

She was watching him closely, but all she saw on his face was honest astonishment.

"Stole it? How? When did you find out?"

"We ran into Lars about an hour ago, and he told us it was missing. He went into the office early this morning and saw that it was gone."

"The whole thing?" Alister looked stunned. "How could somebody steal an entire engine without anyone noticing?"

"That's what we're wondering. Was it as big as the other engines, the ones your programming team was working on?"

"Yes. It filled the entire room, with power cords running down to the steam engines. They must have dismantled it. Lady, I hope they had someone who knew what he was doing. You said Cris is on the case?"

"Not yet," Taya admitted. "He was suspended, but he's down on Secundus right now trying to argue his way back onto active duty."

"That's why you're here."

"Yes."

"Do you think I'm the thief?"

"No. You had access to the engine while you were free, so you could have taken it then, if you'd wanted to. And having it stolen now won't gain you anything, even if you could have arranged the theft in one day."

"Thank you, my hawk. You're right. I didn't have anything to do with it."

"So, who did?"

Alister clasped his hands in front of his face, gazing over his knuckles into the air.

"I don't know anything about the theft," he said at last. "But I have some very good guesses." He rested his green eyes on her. "And I'll pass them along to Cristof, if the Council agrees to change my sentence from execution to exile."

Taya shivered. For the first time she heard a raw edge to his voice, a hint of the dread he must be feeling as he contemplated his death.

"You know. . . ." She stared at him. "Even if they agree to exile you, you'll be blinded and outcaste."

"I know. I was a witness at Neuillan's exile. But I'm not ready to face the Forge yet. As long as I'm alive, I can try to work off Caster's death. If I'm executed now, I'll face rebirth with his blood on my hands."

"So are you feeling regret, or just fear?"

"A little of both."

"They might not agree to make a deal. Murdering a decatur is a lot more serious than selling secrets to the Alzanans."

"I think I know who arranged the theft. And I have Neuillan's contact information; a list of all the Alzanan spies he talked to and a list of the passwords he used. It might not be accurate after a year, but it would give the lictors a head start on their investigation. The Alzanans must be behind this, even if they used an Ondinium citizen to carry it out."

"How did you get the list?"

"I found it in Neuillan's house. Cris and I were his executors. I didn't see any reason to give the information to the military."

"Does Cristof know about it?"

"He chose to handle the legal issues, rather than go through Neuillan's personal belongings. He's always been more comfortable with the intellectual than the emotional. Take that as a warning, if you like."

"Why didn't you destroy the list?"

"A wise man never destroys information."

"Neither does a crook, apparently."

"Please, Taya. Make this deal for me. I don't want the engine to fall into enemy hands. I'm sure we've already lost months of effort troubleshooting and calibrating it."

"Would it really make a difference if other countries got analytical engines of their own?"

"Not every country is governed as well as Ondinium, Taya. I know there are many people who think our trade restrictions are selfish, but the Council hasn't forgotten the lessons of the Last War."

Taya slowly nodded. Centuries ago the Last War had been brought to Ondinium's doorstep using the ondium boats and liquid fire the kingdom had been selling to other countries. Ondinium had won the war, but only after losing half its population and being burned to the ground. The social chaos that had followed had led to the fall of the monarchy, the metamorphosis of the ancient caste system, and years of political upheavals before the current republic was established.

Ever since then, Ondinium had refused to sell its metal and weaponry to other countries, and it strictly prohibited the manufacture of ondium craft. Every generation some young idealist pointed out how antiquated the icarus system was, and how much better it would be if armatures left a person's arms free and how much more efficient it would be to carry packages in an ondium-plated skiff. And in response, every generation an older and wiser politician reminded the idealist that it's impossible to wield a weapon when one's arms are encased in metal wings.

"You aren't convinced," Alister said, watching her.

"I guess I just don't understand why Lars was so upset that the engine was gone."

"I imagine he's afraid the team will be suspected of its theft."

"They were taken in for questioning after you were arrested."

"They didn't know anything about my plans."

"You're being very careful to clear everyone's reputation."

"I don't see any reason to drag anyone else to the headsman. Or to the blinding irons, as the case may be. I'm not a vengeful man. I only want what's best for Ondinium."

Taya let out a long breath. She didn't know how Alister could talk about his fate with such calm. She hoped that if she were ever in the same position, she'd be as brave.

"I'll see what I can do." She took her crutches and stood. "It might take a while."

"I'll be here," Alister said, with rueful humor. Taya nodded and limped out the curtained doorway, deep in thought.

After a quick stop at a mail station to send a note to Cassi, she headed back to the lictor's headquarters on Secundus.

Lars was sitting in the front room, huddled in a corner and looking as bear-like as ever. His glum expression brightened when she walked in, and he hurried to pull out a chair for her.

"He's in there. There was some shouting at first, but it's been quiet since then," the big man said, jerking his head toward the back.

"Are they doing anything about the missing engine?"

"The lieutenant sent out some lictors to secure the building and ask questions. I guess they'll be grilling the rest of the team and the engineering crew that worked on the engine. Did you talk to Alister?"

"He wants to make a deal."

"Then he knows something."

"He suspects something."

"Is he all right?"

Taya gave him a sympathetic look. Lars had a kind heart, and she could tell he still wasn't entirely convinced of his friend's guilt.

"He's worried about his sentence. But he's in good health and he has a comfortable cell."

"Benefits of being an exalted, I guess."

"Until he's thrown out of caste."

Lars fingered the dedicate's spiral over his left cheekbone, looking nervous at the thought. Taya swung her crutches around.

"I'm going to go interrupt," she said. "Wish me luck."

She explained her news to the desk sergeant, who went back to check with the lieutenant and then waved her through. Both Cristof and Lt. Amcathra fell silent when she entered.

"You spoke to Exalted Forlore and did not wait for us?" Amcathra demanded, his usually impassive face showing perceptible annoyance.

Taya made a show of tucking her crutch under one arm and pulling out Cristof's pocket watch. She opened it and examined its mother-of-pearl face.

"We talked to Lars almost an hour and a half ago, lieutenant, but you're still in here wrangling with *this* Exalted Forlore. When did you plan to send somebody to question the other?"

Amcathra's pale blue eyes narrowed, but instead of answering, he waited. Knowing that Demicans could sit in silence for hours, Taya tucked the watch back into her pocket.

"Decatur Forlore says he had nothing to do with the theft," she reported, "but he may know who set it up. He also said that it could be an Alzanan plot. He has a list of Alzanan spy names and code words that he found in Decatur Neuillan's personal possessions last year that he's willing to hand over in exchange for a deal."

Cristof muttered under his breath.

"He'll tell the lictors everything he knows if the Council agrees to change his sentence from execution to exile," she finished.

"The decatur believes he can blackmail the Council?" Amcathra sounded offended at the thought of such effrontery.

"I guess he does."

"It's not an unreasonable demand." Cristof turned to the lieutenant. "Not if he can help us get the engine back in one piece."

"You are not without bias in this matter, exalted."

"That's true, but I also want to find the engine before they get it out of the city and damage it on the mountain trails. Put me on the case. Alister will work with me."

"I will send a message to the Council, asking for its decision."

"They could argue for days."

"I will impress upon the decaturs the need for haste."

"Janos!" Cristof leaned on the desk. "We don't have time for that!"

"I can neither speed nor slow the march of the sun across the sky, exalted," Amcathra observed. "Nor will putting you on this case convince your brother to reveal his secrets. He will keep them until he is promised his life. Your presence on the case cannot affect that outcome."

"But—"

"Come. You may accompany me while I search the engine room."

Cristof growled.

"What about Taya? She's working as my assistant while she's grounded."

"Is she?" The lieutenant gave them both a dispassionate look. "Wait outside for me. And tell Mr. Wycomb that he will come with us."

"Mr. Wycomb?" Taya looked puzzled.

"Lars," Cristof explained, holding the door open for her.

LICTORS GUARDED the door of the Science and Technology Building, ignoring the abuse Isobel and Emelie were heaping upon them. Dark-bearded Victor, on the other hand, was standing to one side, gazing down the building's steps and across campus. He saw the small group approach and raised a hand.

"What's going on?" Lars asked, bounding up the stairs.

"It would be a straight walk from here to the university gates if they carried the engine out in crates," Victor observed. "But that would take dozens of men. On the other hand, a wagon couldn't be brought to the bottom of the stairs without going around Froshcourse."

Lars turned from him to Isobel. "Iz? What's going on?"

"They won't let us in."

Taya worked her way up the broad, shallow steps. Cristof paced himself, walking next to her. She appreciated his thoughtfulness; she knew he was impatient to reach the top.

Amcathra jogged up the steps past them.

"Is this the entire team?" he inquired of Lars. He looked at Victor. "Ah, Mr. Kiernan. I thought I recognized your name."

"Lieutenant," Victor greeted the lictor, looking uneasy.

"This is Isobel Vidoc and Emelie Wilkes," Lars said, introducing the two women. "They're on the team, too." He turned to Isobel. "Where's Kyle?"

She shrugged.

"I stopped at his flat and he wasn't there."

"Em?"

"I haven't seen him." The smaller woman frowned, giving the lictors a nervous glance. "What's going to happen now? Are we under arrest?"

"Vic? Any sign of Kyle?"

"The stripes already asked me about him." Victor scratched his beard. "I haven't seen him, either. That makes him suspect number one, doesn't it?"

"Kyle?" Lars recoiled. "Kyle's no thief!"

"I know that. But the stripes don't. And until he shows up . . . ."

The programmers looked at each other, crestfallen.

"You're *all* suspects," Cristof informed them, as he and Taya reached the top of the stairs. "Lieutenant, why not have them accompany us, too? They know the area and the engine. They might spot something we'd miss."

"You will all walk behind me," the Demican directed, then turned and passed through the doors.

Black-robed students gathered to watch as the group walked through the hall. Lictors had been stationed at the top of the stairs down to the AE labs, and a warning chain had been strung across the head of the stairs with a lictor's seal dangling from it. More students leaned over the banister of the stairs above, watching as the chain was unhooked and the small procession headed down to the basement. Taya could hear them gossiping about Alister and speculating that the lictors were collecting evidence from the labs.

"It seems strange that the University is still in session," she murmured to take her mind off the increasing annoyance of negotiating stairs on crutches. "I feel like the whole city should be in an uproar."

"The Council may be shaken, but Ondinium remains untouched," Amcathra said, overhearing her. "It is the strength of the city. And the weakness."

"Why do you think it's a weakness?"

"I feel sometimes there is nobody in Ondinium who cannot be replaced. We are like the gears in one of Exalted Forlore's clocks. That is a strength, because the clock will keep running even after every gear inside it has been replaced. But it is a weakness because it is impossible to respect a man when one thinks of him as nothing more than a replaceable part. 'We must have a dedicate here. Go, send a lictor there.' A man's name and spirit become unimportant."

"Maybe that's why terrorists throw bombs," Taya suggested. "So people will remember their names."

"Yes, that is why terrorists throw bombs," Amcathra agreed. "They have not been taught to respect life. How can a man learn to respect life in a city of clockwork castes?"

"You're a philosopher, lieutenant." Taya reached the bottom of the stairs and leaned against a wall, rubbing her shoulders. "But a grim one."

"I do not understand how a philosopher in this city could be anything but grim." Amcathra paused in the hallway until the rest of the group joined them.

"'The hawk sees the meadows and streams that lie beyond this dark forest,'" Taya quoted, in Demican.

"'Let the sun shine upon the mountains; their peaks remain encased in ice, and my heart, also,'" Amcathra countered in the same language.

"Good one," Taya said with appreciation, reverting to Ondinium. "You win. I haven't read enough Demican poetry to compete. I just liked that line about the hawk."

"Perhaps an icarus, whose eyes are fixed upon the horizon, cannot be other than optimistic. Those of us who do not fly so high are not as fortunate." Lt. Amcathra saw that the rest of the group had gathered. He turned and began pacing down the hall, his blue eyes moving over the walls and floor like one of his hunter kin.

The programmers murmured as Lars pointed out the marks on the walls outside the prototype engine room. Isobel handed over her key when Amcathra stopped to inspect the door, and after a moment scrutinizing the door and frame, the lieutenant unlocked it.

Taya's first impression was of a large, empty room. But then she noticed the marks on the walls and snips of wire and small screws on the floor. Thick cables ran into the room through a hole in the wall and ended in a cascade of bare wires.

"We need light," Amcathra said.

"Just a minute." Lars hurried down the hall, then returned with an oil lamp from the other room. In a moment it was lit and handed over.

"Stay here," Amcathra ordered. He took his time circling the room, crouching often to inspect the floor before taking another step. Cristof squatted in the doorway, and Taya leaned on her crutches behind him. The rest of the programmers crammed close, trying to look over their shoulders.

"How much of the room did you search?" Cristof asked Lars.

"I didn't search it. All I had to do was glance inside to see that the engine was gone. Why?"

"If you left anything in the room or took anything with you, the lieutenant will want to know."

"Nah. I don't think I even stepped inside. Maybe one or two steps, because I was surprised. But that's it."

"They packed the engine in straw-filled crates," Amcathra said. "I see nails, splinters of wood, and wisps of straw. Is that safe for an engine, straw?"

Lars nodded. "Safe enough. Are there any signs of oil?"

"A few drops, yes."

"They probably wrapped the parts in oiled rags before packing them. That's what I would have done."

"The crates will be a fire risk," Amcathra observed.

The programmers all looked at each other.

"Could a good hound track the scent of the oil?" Cristof asked.

"They would have put the crates into a wagon outside," Victor said. "A dog would lose the scent, eventually."

"We will still try," Amcathra said. Suddenly he stopped and crouched, holding his lantern close to the floor.

Taya watched, fascinated, as he set the lantern a foot or two away and lay on his stomach, studying the ground. She'd never seen a grown man so careless of his dignity. On the other hand, she thought, if you took Janos Amcathra out of his lictor's uniform, wiped away his black stripe, and dressed him in a Demican hunter's furs and leathers, his behavior would seem absolutely in character. She wondered what kind of family he'd came from. He'd preserved much of his Demican heritage.

"What color is the hair of Mr. Deuse?"

"Brown," Lars said, after a moment. "Brown hair, blue eyes. About average height and weight."

Taya realized they were talking about Kyle.

"He had a key to this room?"

"Yeah."

"Lots of people have brown hair," Isobel protested, even though she, like Amcathra, was Demican blond. "Just because you find some brown hair doesn't mean Kyle stole the engine."

"Where was Mr. Deuse last night?"

"He left the station with the rest of us."

"Did any of you go home with him?"

A chorus of 'no's.

Amcathra stood and began to search the room again, skirting the area he'd just inspected so intently.

"What did you find?" Taya asked, her curiosity getting the better of her. He shook his head and kept looking.

At last he walked back, waving everyone away from the door. He closed it and locked it.

"I will take your keys to this room, please," he said, holding out his hand. One by one, the programmers slid their keys from rings and cords and laid them on his palm. He dropped them all into his pocket with a metallic jingle.

"Exalted, icarus, please stay. The rest of you may leave. You will of course remain in Ondinium where we can find you if we must."

"What did you see in there?" Lars asked, repeating Taya's question.

"Clues." The lictor would say nothing more.

"Look, Taya, we'll be at the PT," the big man said, turning to her. "You'll tell us if you learn anything, won't you?"

"If I can." Taya leaned on her crutch and patted his arm, feeling like a doll next to him. "I'll try, I really will."

After the team members had left, throwing worried looks over their shoulders as they headed up the stairs, Cristof turned to Amcathra.

"Kyle helped us figure out what Alister's program was doing. He seemed like an honest man."

"I think Mr. Deuse may have been coerced into assisting the thieves," Amcathra said. "I saw blood and brown hair on the floor, as might come from a head wound."

Taya drew in a worried breath. "Do you think he's alive?"

"If they had killed him, I think they would have left his corpse locked in the room."

"Well, if he's been kidnapped, that would explain why nobody can find him." She wanted to run out and tell the rest of the team, but she knew Amcathra must have refrained from mentioning it in front of them for a reason.

"Lars said Kyle was one of the team members who'd know how to reconstruct the engine," Cristof added, his eyes narrowed behind their lenses. "Plus, he's the head of the programming team, now that Alister's in jail. He'd be a nice catch for the Alzanans."

"It does not need to be Alzanans."

"Who else who do something like this?" Cristof pulled off his glasses and began polishing them fiercely. "I'm going to call the thieves Alzanan until we learn otherwise. They waylaid Kyle and forced him to unlock the door; maybe even made him dismantle the engine."

"The amount of blood was significant. It is possible he protested at some point and was knocked unconscious."

Taya felt sick, imagining the pleasant young programmer sprawled in a pool of his own blood.

"Then they packed up the crates and carried them up the stairs and out. What was Victor saying about wagons?" Cristof looked at Taya.

"He said either the thieves would have to hand-carry the crates across campus to the gate or pull a wagon around on some kind of road . . . something-course . . . ."

"Froshcourse. Right. It runs along the perimeter of campus for deliveries." Cristof turned to the lieutenant. "It's a long route, and it passes in front of the dormitories. One of the students may have heard a wagon go by late at night."

"I will have lictors speak to the students." Amcathra stood. "Let us examine the foot path to the gates."

Outside, Taya sat on an iron bench and watched the two men work. Her leg was starting to throb again, warning her that the painkillers were wearing off, and her shoulders ached from working the crutches. Sitting down was a relief.

This time Amcathra permitted Cristof to search with him. Both men bent over the path, Cristof constantly pushing his glasses back up as they slipped down his sharp nose. Taya grinned, trying to imagine him in a Demican hunter's furs. He wouldn't be very convincing. He still looked like a crow, bobbing along the path looking for something to eat.

Her grin faded as she considered Amcathra's speculations. Kyle had seemed like a nice man, intelligent and responsible. He'd been the one Clockwork Heart had chosen as Lars's best match. Well, Lars might have been irritated by the program's decision, but he seemed concerned enough now. He wouldn't be very happy when he found out that Kyle might have been kidnapped. But how could the thieves have taken Kyle out with them? Had they folded him into a crate or hidden him under a tarp? Pretended he was a drunken friend and let him sprawl against the driver?

"They must be storing the crates someplace until they can get them out of the city," she said, out loud. "And if they aren't hiding them on Secundus, they would have had to take them through one of the sector gates last night. The crates and Kyle, both."

"The sector gates are locked after midnight," Amcathra replied at once. "The theft could have occurred before then, but I think it would have been carried out much later, when nobody would be walking around the campus."

"So if they transported the crates to another sector, they either lied to a lictor to let them through late at night or waited and passed through this morning," Taya finished.

"It's unlikely they'd call attention to themselves by going through after lockdown. If I were a thief, I'd leave the sector the next day, probably a few hours after the gates had opened again," Cristof said. "Actually, breaking the load into several wagons, or a wagon and some handcarts, would be even smarter."

"It's still worth questioning the gate guards. They might have noticed Kyle, since he was hurt." Taya wanted to run off to interview the gate guards herself. She cursed the crutches that slowed her down.

"Where's the nearest cart gate?" Cristof asked.

"A few miles east." Amcathra turned to Cristof. "Go to the station. I want a tracking hound brought to the engine room and lictors questioning the students in the dormitories. I will inquire at the cart gates, starting at the nearest and proceeding west. You may rejoin me when your messages have been delivered."

Cristof gave the lictor a sour smile. "So, I'm trustworthy enough to run your errands but not investigate your crimes?"

Amcathra pulled a narrow black wallet out of his coat pocket and handed it over. Cristof flipped it open, then looked up.

"I thought you were going to wait for the captain's approval."

"This is a field decision. I will clear it with him later." Amcathra was as stone-faced as ever. "I recommend you do not speak to your brother without another lictor present, and if you do speak to him, do not promise him anything you cannot deliver."

"I understand." Cristof slid the wallet away. "Thank you, Janos."

"Why are you still here?"

Taya grinned at Cristof as they headed out the University gate. "Are those papers what I think they are?"

"My credentials. I'm back on the job." He sounded pleased, although he was clearly trying to hide it.

"He was going to give them back to you all along, wasn't he? Because you're friends."

"He's my supervisor, Taya. Not my friend."

"Men." Taya laughed. "So, what are we going to do now?"

He stopped, outside the University gates, and looked askance at her crutches.

"I need to deliver the lieutenant's messages and start investigating these leads. I'm going to be running all over the city. How do you feel?"

"Tired," she admitted. "And my leg's starting to hurt, but I'm not supposed to take any medicine for another half an hour."

"I'm sorry." He frowned. "Maybe you should rest for a few hours. It's not that I don't want your company, but you might hurt yourself trying to keep up with me."

"I'm not going to go stuff mail bags."

"They'll give you the day off, won't they?"

"I don't want to sit around the eyrie all day, either." Taya let her gaze climb up the side of the mountain, over stacks of houses and shops to the mansions of Primus. The stubborn part of her wanted to stay with Cristof, but the practical part of her knew that she'd only slow him down. "Do you think Viera's ready for visitors yet?"

"I'm sure she'd like to see you. But she's not very happy right now."

"Well, she wouldn't be. But I want to see her again."

"Should I look for you there?"

"I don't think I'll be staying long. I might go down to that bar Lars mentioned. Is there any reason I can't tell them about Kyle?"

"You'd better not. We don't have any proof that he's involved. That hair and blood could have come from a janitor or one of the engineering team. It's too early to tell."

"But—"

"Please, Taya. There's no sense frightening his friends if he's just off visiting his mother or spending the day with his girlfriend, is there?"

"Hmph." Taya wasn't so sure Kyle had a girlfriend, but she let it pass. "Okay, but if you haven't found anything by this evening. . . ."

"I'll find you, and we'll talk about it."

"Promise?"

"I promise."

"Good." Taya leaned on her crutch and touched his face. "No matter how late."

He nodded, looking preoccupied. "Take a hack and charge it to me if you have to."

Taya sighed and dropped her hand. Whatever romantic stirrings Cristof had felt earlier that day had vanished in the excitement of the new case.

"What's wrong?" He blinked, focusing on her again.

"Nothing," she said, ruefully. "I'll see you later."

SHE SPENT two hours with Viera, which was longer than she'd expected to stay. Viera had welcomed her with relief and pressed her for all of the details of the previous day's adventures. As Cristof had warned, she was still furious with Alister.

"My family took him in when his parents died," Viera raged. "I looked up to him as though he were my own brother. And when I got married, I welcomed him into my house, fed him at my table—and he betrayed me!"

Taya nodded, watching the exalted pace back and forth across the parlor. She'd seen Viera take a dose of something medicinal, but it hadn't done much to calm her down.

"I don't blame you for being angry," she said. "He betrayed a lot of people."

At last Viera dropped back onto her sofa, wiping her eyes with a handkerchief.

"I wish he'd died with Caster," she said at last. "It would have been easier if they'd both been victims. Finding out he killed my husband . . . it's like losing him all over again."

Taya didn't ask which 'him' she meant. Instead, she pushed out of her chair and limped over to sit next to Viera.

"I wish I could help. I'm sorry I've brought so much pain to you."

Viera shook her head, sighing.

"It's not your fault. I'm glad Alister was caught. I hate it, but I'm glad for it."

Taya nodded, understanding.

"You can't stay away," Viera added. "I've already lost too many people."

"As long as you want me to keep visiting, I will," Taya promised.

She left some time later, sobered and depressed. What would have happened if she'd agreed to Alister's ruse and pretended he'd survived the explosion? Viera and Cristof both would be happier, and Alister wouldn't be under a sentence of death. But no. She thrust the thought away. One way or the other, the lie would have come out and destroyed them. It wouldn't have been possible to keep the secret forever, and it would have made her an accomplice to his crimes.

"Taya!"

She looked up and saw Cassi sitting on top of a hack, her ondium wings bright in the afternoon sun. Taya limped across the street and saw her friend had found Gregor and Bolt.

Cassi hopped down and gave her a quick hug, careful not to jab her with the armature's ondium keel.

"I got your note," she said. "Took me a while to find you, though. I ran into your exalted and he told me you were either up here or at some punch-jockey bar. He told me to make sure you were staying off your leg, so I rounded up your favorite coach."

"Thanks." Taya turned to Gregor. "Can I put you on retainer for a day or two?"

"Of course." The coachman smiled.

"I appreciate it. If I don't have enough money with me—"

"We'll settle up later, then." Gregor slid from his seat and opened up the hack's doors, letting the folding steps clatter down to the cobblestones.

"I asked Pyke to get your armature," Cassi said. "His uncle works in the repair shop, so he's got a better chance of nicking it than I do. He said he'd leave it in the eyrie for you."

"Thanks. I hate these crutches."

"No flying, though," Cassi warned her. "If you rip out your stitches, you're going to have an awful scar."

"I'm going to have an awful scar, anyway." Taya sat on the hack's steps, making the coach rock, and set her crutches on the street. "But I don't plan to fly. I just need to get lighter before these things put permanent bruises under my arms."

"Good idea. But listen. I found Exalted Forlore down at one of the gates, and he bought me a cup of tea. I thought he was just going to thank me for yesterday, but as soon as we sat down, he started asking questions." Cassi grinned, squatting in the road next to the steps. "He looked like he was in a hurry, but I think he couldn't resist the chance to investigate you."

"Me?"

"Uh-huh. He grilled me for ten minutes, fidgeting constantly, and then he shot out the door without even saying goodbye. Do you like him?"

"What do you mean, he grilled you? What did he want to know?"

"Oh, the usual. What kind of flowers do you like, how many boyfriends have you had, what's your favorite color, how many boyfriends have you had, what kind of jewelry do you like, how many boyfriends have you had . . . ."

Taya groaned, covering her face with her hands.

"I think he's prude," Cassi concluded, sounding cheerful. "He looks like a prude."

"He's not a prude! Well, maybe he is. What did you tell him?"

"That you like irises, you look good in blue, and you hardly wear any jewelry at all."

Taya dropped her hands and swatted her friend across the head.

"The boyfriends! What did you tell him about the boyfriends?"

Cassi laughed.

"I told him every man in the eyrie adores you and it wasn't any of his business how many boyfriends you've had, because if he doesn't respect you for who you are now, he doesn't deserve to have you."

Taya stared down at her friend, then let out a long breath.

"I love you."

"I know." Cassi sounded smug. "And you better remember that answer if anyone ever asks you about me."

"I will," Taya promised, fervently.

"So, do you like him?"

"He used to be kind of a pain, but . . . ."

"That's a 'yes.'"

"That's a 'there's hope.' We haven't had much quiet time together, and I'm worried about how he's going to handle his brother being sentenced. He's the kind of man who'd rather pull away than open up."

"Aren't they all." Cassi reached up and patted her arm. "Hey, no worries. Third time's the charm, right?"

Taya made a face.

"I hope so. You hated the last two guys I was serious about. What do you think about Cris?"

Cassi shrugged, her silver wings rippling.

"He's smart. Intense. Stressed."

Taya nodded.

"Not ugly," her friend continued, "but not as cute as the other two. That's probably a good thing. He won't count on his looks to get him what he wants."

"I don't think he expects to get anything the easy way."

"Probably comes from living out of caste. I have to admit, seeing his marks out in the open like that is pretty creepy."

"He said he's not going to put a mask back on again."

"That'd be better for you. And, you know, it's a good sign that he was asking about your boyfriends. If all he wanted was a mistress, he wouldn't care, right?"

"You think so?" Taya looked hopefully at her friend.

"Your friend's right, she is," Gregor said. Both women jumped, looking up at him with startled indignation. The coachman looked apologetic. "I'd no intention of eavesdropping but, you know, there ain't a man in the world cares about a woman's past until he's thinking of her in his future. That's when a man starts to muse over reputation and reliability, now, ain't it?"

"So you've got nothing to worry about," Cassi assured Taya. "If I were him, I'd be more worried about my own reputation. The guy's an outcaste clockmaker with two murderers in the family. He's going to have to be one awfully sweet boyfriend to be worth your time."

"He's working on it," Taya said, with a half-smile.

"He'd better be."

"Anyway, it's too early to be sure of anything." Taya picked up her crutches. Gregor offered his hand, steadying her as she stood.

"As long as you're not settling for second best."

"That would have been Alister."

"Are you ready to go, then, icarus?" Gregor asked. Taya collected her thoughts.

"Yes. Do you know the lictor hospital on Secundus? A few blocks from headquarters?"

"I know of a hospital there — whether it belongs to the lictors, I've no idea, do I?"

"Let's go. Take off your armature, Cassi. I want to talk to you on the way over."

"I'm supposed to be working." Cassi glanced up toward the docking cliffs, then shrugged. "I guess they won't miss me for a few more minutes."

"I think you and Pyke might be able to help the lictors."

"Really?" Cassi began unbuckling straps. "Do they know you're asking?"

"Well, not yet. But I'll tell Cristof tonight."

"Great. We'll all have reprimands in our files by the time this is over."

They maneuvered Cassi's wings into the hack with some effort and contorted themselves around the unwieldy armature as the coach rattled down to Secundus. Taya filled Cassi in about the stolen analytical engine and the missing programmer.

"Are you sure this doesn't have anything to do with Alister Forlore? I mean, it's a pretty big coincidence, if you ask me. Secret programs, analytical engines . . . ."

"What I think is that this theft has been planned for a long time, and the thieves took advantage of the confusion around Alister's arrest to make their move."

"I guess that's possible." Cassi frowned. "So, what can Pyke and I do?"

"Keep your eyes open for any wagon with lots of crates in it that might be moving around at an odd time of the day, or any activity around buildings that might usually be empty. The lictors can only see everything sector by sector, but icarii see the whole city. If we keep an eye out—"

"You mean, if Pyke and I keep an eye out. You're supposed to keep your feet on the ground."

"You know what I mean."

"Won't they already have military icarii looking around?"

"Sure, but the military don't know the city the way we do."

"So if we see something suspicious, alert the authorities."

"Right. And Pyke's got all his spooky conspiracy contacts, right? Maybe he can get something from them."

"Maybe." Cassi drew the word out. "Okay, I'll ask around."

"Except nobody can be told that an engine's missing. Not until the lictors release the information."

"No problem."

The coach slowed and pulled over. Taya looked out and saw that they were in front of the same hospital she'd visited with Lt. Amcathra, a few days before.

"You'll tell Pyke?"

"Sure." They pulled Cassi's armature out, and Cassi buckled back in. "I'll look for you at that punch-jockey bar later on?"

"Could you bring my armature with you? Just in case I don't make it back to the eyrie?"

"If Pyke can get it out of the shop." Cassi pulled on her flight gloves. "You be careful, okay? Don't let anyone else shoot at you."

Taya waved as Cassi left, then asked Gregor to wait for her as she limped into the hospital.

A nurse directed her to the same hospital room, but this time the Demican was sitting up in a chair and playing cards with his lictor guard.

"Excuse me," Taya said, standing in the doorway. "May I come in?"

The lictor frowned, setting down her cards, as the Demican regarded her crutches with open curiosity.

"The little warrior has met her match?" he asked, not unkindly, in Demican.

"The man who shot me is dead," Taya replied in Demican. She wasn't happy about it, but it was the response that would most impress him. As she expected, he laughed with appreciation.

"Good. That is the best fate for a man who would use a gun on his prey."

"I am glad to see you are healing," she continued, studying him.

"It seems my spirit will not be visiting you on Darkday."

"Excuse me," the lictor said with annoyance, "but who are you?"

"I'm Taya Icarus," Taya replied, dropping into Ondinium again. "I was responsible for putting this man into the hospital, and I wanted to see how he was doing."

"Taya Icarus." The lictor's voice was cool. "So I guess this man was the lucky one, huh?"

"Yeah." Taya winced, then turned to the Demican and began to speak in his language again. "The two Alzanans you were working with—did they ever mention anything about stealing one of the city's metal brains?" It was the closest Demican came to 'analytical engine.'

"They talked about stealing many things. Your wings, 'punch cards'"—he used the Ondinium words, so heavily accented they were almost meaningless—"people, metal brains, weapons. I should have known better than to work with carrion birds."

"Did they talk to anyone else about their plans?"

"Other Alzanans." The Demican shrugged. "Have you looked for the tavern with the red door yet?"

Taya chewed on her lip. Had Amcathra followed up that lead? Maybe, but the wireferry bombing happened right afterward, and it would make sense if less important cases had been shoved aside for the investigation.

"Icarus, unless you have clearance to talk to this prisoner, you should leave," the lictor said, giving her an acrimonious look.

"Can you tell me anything else about them?" Taya asked quickly, in Demican.

"I think they found somebody to sell them the weapons they wanted. Bombs. They were very pleased." The Demican shrugged. "Bombs are no better than guns. They are both cowardly ways to kill."

The lictor was standing, one hand dropping to the pistol at her belt. Taya hopped backward on her crutches.

"I agree," she said, in Demican, then added in Ondinium, "I'm leaving, I'm leaving."

"What was that about?" the woman asked, her expression full of suspicion.

"Spirits, scavengers, and guns." Taya glanced at the woman's weapon. "Demicans think firearms are a coward's weapon."

"I don't give a damn what Demicans think."

"No reason why you should." Taya nodded to the prisoner, then limped out, feeling the back of her neck crawl under the lictor's glare.

Gregor helped her back into the coach.

"Do you know of a bar with a red door in Slagside?" Taya asked, setting her crutches by her. Gregor leaned in the coach door, frowning.

"Slagside, is it? There ain't much call for hacks down there, even where the roads would be wide enough for one. You've no desire to go there, now, do you?"

"Actually, I do." Taya sighed. "Do you know anyone else who's familiar with Slagside?"

"No, not a one." Gregor shrugged. "People who pass their time in Slagside ain't people I'd care to count as friends. Smugglers, thieves, and cutthroats all."

"Surely not all of them."

"Enough of 'em for it to be a bad place for an outsider to visit. A pretty girl on crutches, especially, don't you think?"

"How about the Pickled Thalassonaut?"

"The only danger you'll be facing there is being bored to death," Gregor said, chuckling. "Be that our next stop, then?"

"If you don't mind. And I'll pay for your meal there, too, because I'll probably be there a while."

"Fine with me. Bolt and I could use a rest, the two of us could." Gregor closed the door and climbed back to the driver's seat.

Chapter Sixteen

Taya found Alister's programming team, with the notable and worrisome exception of Kyle, desultorily arguing about a new program and keeping a close eye on the door. She left Gregor to tend Bolt and joined their table. It didn't escape her that the other programmers in the bar were watching Alister's team with open suspicion. Alister might have cleared the team's reputation with the lictors, but not in the court of public opinion.

Minding Cristof's request to avoid telling them about Kyle's possible kidnapping, Taya filled them in on everything else she'd learned.

"Slagside, huh?" Victor asked, his eyes narrowing. "Dangerous place."

"It's not much of a lead," she admitted, "but it might be worth looking into."

"Give me half an hour." The programmer stood, then stopped. Taya followed his gaze and saw Pyke and Cassi walking in, holding her armature and flight suit.

"You got it!" Taya leaped to her feet, then dropped back into her chair again with a wince. "Ouch."

"Yeah." Pyke was staring at Victor. For a moment the two men held each other's gaze, and then the icarus looked away, maneuvering the floating armature through the tavern to her table. "I signed out for it, too, so if you break it again, I'm the one who has to answer to my uncle."

"I won't break it," Taya promised, grabbing his hand and squeezing it.

"Better not." He grinned at her.

"Watch it," a programmer at another table growled, ducking Cassi's wings as she maneuvered around to join them. "This isn't a bird bar."

"Mouth off to me and you'll never get a letter again, punch jockey," Cassi warned him, leaning on the back of Taya's chair. She addressed her friend. "We're off work now."

"Good. Sit down." Taya made the introductions, then stood to inspect her armature. The programmer at the table behind them snarled and moved. Cassi put a leather-booted foot on his table and shoved it several feet away from them to give their wings more clearance.

"We've met," Pyke said, nodding to Victor.

"Taya was asking about a bar in Slagside." Victor paused. "If we're heading down there, I thought Scuro might be useful."

"You're friends with him?"

"We've had a few drinks together."

"I'd like to get to know him better. He's got interesting things to say about technological colonization."

"Did you hear him last week?"

"You mean his talk about the Cabisi?"

"Oh, Lady save us, they're conspirators," Cassi groaned. "If you two are going to talk spook stuff, do it outside."

"I'm so glad somebody else thinks that stuff is way outside normal operating parameters," Isobel said, reaching across the table and offering her hand. "If you get Victor started on politics, he'll rant for hours."

"Pyke's the same way," Cassi said, shaking hands with her.

"Pyke!" Taya said. "There's a hack outside, driven by a man named Gregor. He can take you and Victor on my tab, if you've got a long way to go."

Pyke nodded, deep in conversation with the dour programmer.

"I wonder where they're off to," Emelie said as they walked off together. "We don't need any more political trouble."

"Politics is always trouble," Lars muttered, with his chin on his fist.

Cassi waved to the bartender for another pitcher. Meanwhile, Taya tethered her floating armature to a table leg and inspected her flight suit. The physicians had exacerbated the damage Cristof had started, slicing the suit's leg open to help her out of it the day before.

"Do you think this can be fixed?" she asked, fingering the tear.

"Probably not." Cassi poured her a beer. "But as long as you aren't going airborne, a torn leg won't matter."

"I guess not." Taya sighed, running a hand over the oiled leather. "I liked this suit, though."

"Get the top cut into a jacket." Cassi grinned and stroked the fur draped over the back of Taya's chair. "Then I can borrow this."

"So, why are you here, anyway?" Emelie asked, in a challenging tone.

"Taya said we might be able to help you find the you-know-what," Cassi replied. "And I've never been in here before. It never hurts to try out a new bar."

"They carry an interesting liquor from Tizier," Isobel volunteered. "None of these other wretches will drink it. It's a kind of a spicy, anise-flavored rum."

"Wow." Cassi made a face. "Is it as bad as it sounds?"

"Worse."

"How much does it cost?"

"I don't understand why Kyle hasn't shown up yet," Lars sighed. Taya turned to him as Cassi and Isobel continued talking. "Do you think Vic was right? Could he have been working with the thieves?"

"All Victor said was that Kyle was a suspect," Taya corrected him. She wanted to tell him about Amcathra's suggestion, but she forced herself to stay silent. "Kyle struck me as an honest, responsible man. I don't think he is a spy."

"No, but I would have said that about Alister, too. I was thinking . . . ."

"What?"

"What if Kyle got there before me and ran into them? Maybe they did something to him."

Taya tightened her hands around her metal tankard until her knuckles were white.

"If they did," she said, choosing her words with care, "he'd be too valuable to hurt. Anyone who wants an engine will want a programmer."

"Yeah, that's true." The big man looked thoughtful. "And Kyle's smart enough to let them know that, too. So if the lictors find the engine—"

"They might find Kyle, too. If the thieves have him. But he could be someplace else, couldn't he? Visiting family, or a girlfriend or something?" Taya echoed Cristof's words.

"Nah, Izzy asked at his brother's house. They haven't seen him."

"And the only person Kyle likes is you, Lars," Emelie said, standing. Isobel glared at her, but Lars just stared at his drink. "This is too depressing. I'm leaving."

"Are you sure?" Taya asked. "Cris—Exalted Forlore said he'd stop by tonight, if he can, to tell us how the investigation is going."

Emelie vacillated for a few seconds, then shrugged.

"Maybe I'll stop by later. But I can't stand sitting around here doing nothing."

"We'll send a message to your flat if anything changes," Isobel said. Emelie nodded and walked off, buttoning her coat. The tall blonde turned and patted Lars on the shoulder. "Cheer up. It'll be all right. A lot of people are looking for him."

"Let's order that anise drink," Cassi suggested. "Sounds like we could all use something stronger than beer, and if it tastes bad, it'll take our minds off our worries."

They sat around drinking and talking for another hour. Taya excused herself for a few minutes and went into a back room to change into her flight suit. She felt better wearing it, even if one leg flapped. By the time the city clocks struck six, Victor and Pyke had returned, looking satisfied and paying for Gregor's delayed meal. The coachman sat at a table by the door, keeping an eye on his hack, while the two men rejoined them.

"Where's Em?" Victor asked, dropping into a chair. Isobel slid the squat bottle of greenish-black liquor over to him. He helped himself to Lars' small glass and poured.

"She went home," Isobel said. "She said she might be back later."

"Sure." The bearded man made a face and drank, then shuddered and refilled the glass, handing it to Pyke.

"Did you find out anything about the red door?" Taya asked.

"Nothing useful," the programmer said. Next to him, Pyke took a shot of the Tizier liquor and made a strangling noise, slamming the glass on the table.

"Lady and spirits above, that's the most disgusting thing I've ever tasted," he gasped.

"Isobel collects bad drinks," Cassi said, laughing. "She says this isn't even close to the worst."

"Well, so far nothing's been worse than the fermented goat's milk," Victor agreed, catching his team-mate's eye. Isobel smiled at him, sharing a private joke.

Disappointed that they hadn't learned anything about the red door, Taya slumped in her chair. "Your friend wasn't any help, then?"

"Scuro gave us some advice about entering Slagside." Victor waved a hand. "We can go down and find it ourselves."

"You aren't worried about getting into trouble?"

"Three icarii, three programmers, and a hack driver walk into Slagside—it sounds like the beginning to a bad joke, doesn't it?" The bearded man chuckled and Pyke laughed out loud. Taya wondered if they'd been drinking at Scuro's. They seemed flushed with excitement. She shook her head, then glanced up as the conversation around them died.

"We are not here to arrest anybody," Lt. Amcathra announced, walking in. The bar's patrons muttered, looking askance as Cristof followed the lictor. A few of the programmers made awkward bows. Others just stared with shock at the castemarks on his bare face.

The two men brushed past the tables and joined them. The team and Cassi bowed. Pyke waved a hand vaguely in front of his face. Cristof ignored them all.

"You have your wings again." He sounded disapproving as he dropped his hands on the back of Taya's chair. "I thought the doctor said you were grounded."

"Oooh, the exalted's bossy, as well as a prude," Cassi said, her voice carrying as she stared Cristof in the eye.

Cristof's lips tightened, and Taya realized that everyone around the table was staring at him with various degrees of interest. A number of programmers at the other tables were gaping, too.

For a moment the outcaste and the icarus locked gazes. At last Cristof gave the same low, irritable noise that Taya recognized from their arguments past.

"I'm also a slagging pain in the tailset and very rarely sweet. Do you have a problem with that, icarus?"

"'Rarely' sweet," Taya corrected. "You've worked your way up to 'rarely,' remember?"

The tension broke, and Cassi rolled her eyes while the others chuckled.

"'Sweet' is a side of you I have not seen, exalted," Lt. Amcathra remarked, deadpan. "I have, however, noticed the other three traits."

"Then he *is* a prude," Cassi said, triumphantly.

Cristof leaned over the chair and gave Taya a faint, crooked smile.

"How are you feeling?" he asked in a low voice as Isobel offered the lieutenant some of the Tizier liquor. The Demican shook his head.

"All right. We've got some news and maybe even a lead or two."

"So do we. Why does your friend think I'm a prude?"

"Because you were asking about my former boyfriends."

"Oh." He glanced across the table at Cassi. "I should have known she'd talk."

"Not all the stereotypes about icarii are true, you know."

"I just wanted to know how many jealous exes I'll have to deal with."

Taya flushed, not sure whether to be annoyed or flattered. "The only person you need to worry about is Cassi. She'll make your life hell if she decides she doesn't like you."

"Lady help me." He brushed a finger down her cheek, then straightened as Lars hoisted two chairs over the table for the newcomers. The rest of the patrons in the bar were being incrementally shoved back to the walls.

"We cannot stay long," Amcathra objected, looking around. His eyes settled on Taya. "We have come here to pick you up."

"The Council approved Alister's reduced sentence," Cristof said, his voice tense with excitement. "I think it's the fastest I've ever seen them move."

"Cris." Taya felt her heart leap, and she gave him a smile of pure relief. Viera would be furious, and Alister probably didn't deserve to live, but Taya couldn't help but be happy for Cristof's sake. "That's great."

"Reduced to what?" Isobel asked.

"Blinding and exile," Lt. Amcathra replied. "Some people would call the sentence worse than death."

"Not Alister." Taya touched Cristof's arm, and he nodded.

"So." Lars sighed. "I guess that's good, then."

"It's good," Victor agreed. "But a lot of citizens are going to call it favoritism."

"Damn right it's favoritism," Pyke growled. "Doesn't sound to me like they even paused to discuss it. I hope the Council's ready for the backlash."

"Did you get the information you needed from him?" Taya asked, to forestall Cristof's irritation.

"We're on our way to see him now," he said, giving Pyke a hard look before glancing back at her. "I thought you'd want to be there."

"Us, too," Lars said, standing. "We're his friends."

"We are visiting the exalted to discuss a criminal investigation, not to celebrate his successful blackmail of the city Council," Amcathra said, chillingly.

"Sure, but it's a criminal investigation in which we're the primary suspects," the big man objected.

"Do you have any good reason to exclude us?" Victor challenged the lictor.

"You, of all people, should not annoy me, Mister Kiernan."

Victor and Pyke traded quick looks, and Taya felt a moment's alarm. What were they involved in, anyway?

"I might be more help than you think," Victor countered.

"We all know what's going on," Cassi pointed out. "And we all want to get the you-know-what back. You might as well make us useful, or we'll just hang around outside the station and follow you everywhere you go."

"I cannot stop you from doing that," Amcathra admitted. "But perhaps when it grows late and cold you will lose your enthusiasm."

"Keep hoping," Isobel said, smiling. Amcathra glanced at her, then inclined his head in acknowledgement of their shared northern heritage. Still, his next words were directed to Taya.

"Come, if you wish to accompany us."

"Absolutely." She untethered her armature and snapped the keel over her chest, leaving the harness straps secured. "Gregor's waiting for us, lieutenant."

"I'm afraid we've hired him away from you," Victor cut in. He gave her a significant look. "I'll pay for a different coach, if you need one."

"I'll take care of it," Cristof interrupted with a frown. Taya wanted to ask more questions, but the closed expressions on Victor's and Pyke's faces were enough to make her stay silent. They were up to something, and they'd gotten Gregor involved. She didn't want to know anything else. She grabbed her crutches and fur cloak.

Walking was much easier with the ondium armature carrying part of her weight, although she chose to sit next to the driver on their hired hack rather than try to jam her wings into a carriage with two grown men. They reached the Secundus headquarters in twenty minutes. Pyke and Cassi were already at the station, perched on the back of one of the iron benches by the street. Gaslight from the street lamps glimmered off their silver wings.

"Show-offs," Taya muttered, sticking her tongue out at them. Cassi winked.

"How's Viera?" Cristof asked, holding the door open as Taya ducked through. Amcathra strode up to Captain Scarios, handing him a formal-looking document.

"She's still angry." Taya set one of her crutches by the door. With her wings, she could maneuver with one. "Did you find anything about the crates and wagon?"

"We confirmed that something heavy went by on Frosh-course a little before midnight, and we're pretty certain the wagon passed through the sector gate to Tertius around ten in the morning. The hounds lost the scent after the wagon left the university gates. We've got military icarii sweeping the roads in case the wagon already left the city, but security's been high ever since the bomb went off on the Tower ferry, so we think it's more likely that the thieves are lying low."

"Risky," Taya said. "Someone could find them."

"They'd be taking a risk either way; they'd have to know we'd monitor the roads as soon as the theft was discovered. One good thing is that the weather's in our favor. The thieves will have to leave Ondinium within the next two months, before the passes close. We can step up security until then."

"But what about Kyle?"

Cristof pushed up his glasses, looking at the two lictors. "He's one of the reasons the Council agreed to Alister's deal. Kyle's one of the city's top programmers, now that Alister's been arrested."

"What were the other reasons?"

"The prototype's important, and they want Alister's information about the Alzanan spy network."

Taya sensed from the way he was avoiding her gaze that he wasn't telling her everything. *Lies of omission*, she reminded herself.

"What else?"

He lifted a shoulder.

"I agreed to give them all of the work Alister was keeping at home, instead of handing it over to the newspapers with an exclusive interview."

"You would have done that? I don't believe it."

"I also promised to donate the remainder of Alister's inheritance to the Council coffers. I didn't want it anyway."

Taya narrowed her eyes. He still wasn't looking at her.

"And what else, Cris?"

He sighed and pulled off his glasses, pinching the arch of his nose.

"They need me to dress like an exalted again. But it won't be as bad as before."

Taya stared, shaken.

"You said you wouldn't."

"Don't get angry until I can explain."

"You promised you wouldn't go back." Gwen's warnings came back to haunt her. "You told me you were never going to wear a mask again."

He looked at her, his spectacles dangling from one hand. He seemed strangely vulnerable without glass and silver between his eyes and her gaze.

"I had a choice between keeping my promise to you and saving my brother's life," he said, quietly. "I did my best to respect both. Will you trust me a little longer? I don't know if you'll approve of the deal I made, but it's not—"

"Exalted? Icarus?" Captain Scarios interrupted them. Cristof gave her a long look, then slid his glasses back on.

"Not all the stereotypes about exalteds are true, either," he said, stiffly.

Taya hesitated, then nodded, once. Fair enough.

"You're going to tell me everything," she warned him. He adjusted his frames and picked up her other crutch as she limped past.

She was startled, at first, to see that Alister was waiting for them in a chair. His public robes were draped around him and his blank ivory exalted's mask hid his face. The robes were heavy with jewels and embroidery, their hems folded on the floor and draped over his lap to hide his hands and feet. His mask looked like every other exalted mask she'd ever seen, a smooth ivory disk with slits for the eyes and a wave mark shining on one cheek in inlaid gold.

She'd never seen Alister in his public robes before; but then, she'd never seen him in front of strangers, either. Neither Amcathra nor Scarios were permitted to see an exalted unmasked.

"Alister." Cristof stepped forward, then dropped his eyes. "I talked to the Council. They've agreed to reduce your sentence to Neuillan's, in exchange for your assistance." He dragged his gaze up and held out both hands, palms up. "The paperwork's already in the captain's hands. But if you agree, you'll forgo your right to trial. You'll be automatically admitting your guilt and accepting exile from caste and city. Starting now."

For a very long minute the figure in the chair didn't move, and Taya wondered if it were even real. Maybe Alister had managed to set up a mannequin and escape. But then, at last, the exalted's arms rose, his hands still covered by draped material. Embroidered hems touched the sides of the mask and lifted it away.

To Taya, the gesture only seemed full of melancholy, but both Scarios and Amcathra leaned forward. She glanced at them and was taken aback by the awed, almost guilty fascination on their faces as they stared at the exalted's naked face.

Alister set the mask into Cristof's waiting hands. His cheeks were flushed, and Taya realized that he felt humiliated at being unmasked in front of a lower caste. For the first time in her life, she understood how privileged she was to be an icarus. For her, this forbidden sight was a matter of course.

"It's better than dying," Cristof breathed, holding the mask. The two brothers were staring at each other, Cristof with a peculiar expression of pity and Alister with a tense expression of shame.

"It looked easier, when you did it."

"It wasn't. But you'll survive, just like I did."

"What did they make you give up, to save my life?"

"Nothing that was mine to begin with."

Taya wanted to object, but she ground her teeth together and stayed silent. *Will you trust me a little longer?* he'd asked. All right. She'd give him a chance to explain before she got angry about it.

Before she let anyone else know how angry she was about it, she amended.

Scarios cleared his throat, an oddly polite interruption for the brusque man. Alister tensed, not looking at the lictor.

"Your part of the deal is to spill everything you know about who stole the engine," the captain reminded him.

"Has anyone been arrested yet?" Alister asked, his voice and bearing taut. He'd dropped his hands back in his lap, the folds of his robe still covering them.

"Kyle's missing," Taya said, limping forward. For the first time his green eyes flickered up and registered her wings, and when he looked at her, she thought some of the tension in his face eased. "Was he working with the thieves, or was he kidnapped by them?"

"If anyone's working with thieves, it would be Emelie," Alister replied.

"Not Victor Kiernan?" Amcathra sounded surprised.

"Victor's a nonconformist, but he isn't a thief," the exalted answered, still looking at Taya. She nodded, encouraging him to continue. "But Emelie's always been dissatisfied. She got through the University by cutting corners and cheating on tests. She's a good programmer. You can't fake that. But she wants to be rich, and she doesn't want to work for it."

"You two were lovers." Taya couldn't help the note of accusation in her voice.

"She thought she could get special favors that way." Alister raised an eyebrow, his green eyes still fixed on her. "It worked until I got tired of her and broke it off."

"Nice."

"Do you have any proof she's involved?" Scarios asked, cutting in.

"I never said I had any proof. Just suspicions." He never looked at the captain.

"What about the Alzanans?" Cristof pressed.

"All the data on them is in my office." Alister shifted his gaze to his brother. "There's a cabinet with my punch cards inside. At the bottom of Resources and Allotments is an envelope with Neuillan's cards. Anyone on my team should be able to read them without sending them through an engine. They aren't encrypted."

"Cassi and Pyke can get them," Taya suggested, looking at Cristof. "And Victor said the team was going to be waiting outside—"

Cristof nodded, already reaching into his pocket. He handed his keys to Amcathra.

"You can walk out there faster than Taya," he said. Amcathra gave him a cool look, then turned and left the room.

"I'd like to see my team," Alister said, looking at his brother. "May I?"

Cristof turned to Scarios.

"Another day," the captain said, tersely.

"Did the information say anything about a bar down in Slagside?" Taya asked. "One with a red door?"

Alister shot Cristof a look.

"A red door means it was a brothel, not a bar," Cristof said, looking uncomfortable.

Taya frowned. "Wouldn't a sign be better advertising?"

"Only for the literate," Alister pointed out. Cristof seemed discomfited by the entire subject. Maybe he *was* a little bit of a prude.

"You know, I deliver messages for some of the most prestigious brothels on Secundus," she told him. "But they have signs."

"I didn't know prostitutes conducted their business by mail," Cristof muttered, his cheeks flushing.

"There was a brothel listed among Neuillan's contact points," Alister said. "I remember it because I'd wondered if Neuillan had ever delivered messages there. It would have made quite a sight, a covered exalted entering a brothel in Tertius."

"The Alzanans who tried to steal my wings meet there, too." Taya felt a leap of excitement. "If we go, we might catch them."

"*We?*" Captain Scarios frowned at her. "Don't get carried away with yourself, icarus. A raid is lictor business."

"And you're injured—" "Your leg—"

Alister and Cristof glanced at each other and fell silent.

"All right," Taya surrendered. "But I think it's a good place to start."

"Emelie wouldn't hide in a brothel," Alister said.

"We don't know for sure she's involved." Captain Scarios straightened. "You got anything else, Forlore? I was expecting something more useful."

Alister looked at Taya. "Emelie has family in Cantery, but I doubt she'd try to hide there. It's a two-day walk from the city, and I don't think her family is wealthy enough to be much help to a fugitive."

"We can still send an icarus out to ask questions," Amcathra said, from the doorway. Scarios nodded.

"She's attracted to power," Alister added, "so if you find the ringleader in this theft, you'll probably find her, too. She'd stay close to him to make sure she gets her share of whatever reward has been promised."

"That it?"

"I said from the beginning that all I had was speculation."

"Huh. Hardly seems worth your neck. I hope something in those records of yours pans out." The captain's gaze was cool. "Since you accepted the plea bargain, I've got the authority to move you to a regular cell. Enjoy your soft bed tonight; it'll be the last time you sleep on it."

Alister's copper cheeks grayed.

"Do you know when the . . . the sentence will be carried out?"

"Not yet. You'll get a few days' warning. More than your victims got."

Taya shifted, biting her lip. She understood Scarios' anger, but she couldn't help but feel sorry for Alister.

"I'll try to visit tomorrow," Cristof said, awkwardly.

"Good luck." Alister held his gaze. "Don't let anything happen to our little hawk."

"I'll do what I can."

Taya gave them both a disdainful look and limped out the door.

Cristof caught up with her as she stood on the station steps, looking up in the sky for some sign of Pyke or Cassi. It was dark already. Lars, Victor, and Isobel were inside, talking to Amcathra and Scarios. About Emelie, she presumed. She set her crutch against the wall and leaned against the iron railing.

Cristof stood beside her, close enough for the hem of his greatcoat to brush her legs.

"So, tell me about this deal of yours," Taya said, after they'd both stood looking at the stars for a long minute.

"There are some benches about half a block down the street. Do you want to walk with me?"

"There's a bench right there." She nodded to the bench at the bottom of the steps, where Pyke and Cassi had been waiting for them.

"I'd rather discuss this in private."

"I wouldn't."

Cristof looked down, and Taya saw that he was still holding his brother's ivory mask. He turned it over once, then slid it into one of his coat's capacious pockets.

"All right." He looked back up at the sky again. "The Council wanted more than vague promises of information in exchange for Alister's life. I offered them the Forlore estate and told them I'd be happy to retire with my shop down on Tertius, but they turned me down. They said I'd be more useful to the city if I took up my role as an exalted again."

Taya turned to watch him. His face was easy to read in the light from the station windows and the gas lamps that lined the streets. She'd expected that he'd look guilty or upset, but he only looked determined.

"I told them I wasn't willing to live under the restrictions of caste. I told them everything I told you. And they said that was exactly why I could be useful to them. They need an exalted who's willing to take off his mask in front of foreigners."

Despite herself, Taya's interest was caught. She grasped the diplomatic implications at once. "You're going to be the exalteds' public face."

He nodded, finally risking a glance at her.

"I wouldn't be replacing the icarii. But Ondinium has had a lot of trouble with other countries because exalteds won't speak to foreigners. Negotiations have to go on between foreign ambassadors and icarii envoys, which is slow and awkward and apparently offensive. The Council thinks that if they call me a 'special liaison' instead of a caste pariah, they can smooth over some of the problems they've had in the past. I'd dress up to put on a good show for the ambassadors and foreign dignitaries, but then I'd take off my mask and talk to them face-to-face, instead of doing all my business through icarii."

"That's smart." Taya frowned. "Really smart. They didn't just think it up, did they?"

"I doubt it." He turned to her. His grey eyes were steady. "I imagine the Council's been waiting for an excuse to force my hand for a while. If it weren't in exchange for Alister's life, it would have been for something else."

Taya gave him a wry smile.

"You'll make a terrible ambassador, Cris."

"I know. I was hoping you'd help me."

"I don't think I could stand having you as my boss."

He shook his head.

"We'd be partners. Envoys are usually sent abroad for a year or two to immerse themselves in a foreign culture. While you were telling me about the diplomatic corps at lunch, I kept thinking that if you joined it, I'd lose you. So when the Council made this offer . . . if you pass your exams and get sent to Si'sier, I could travel with you. The Council likes the idea of its new ambassador making a tour of the embassies." He cleared his throat. "Of course, it all depends on whether you could stand traveling with me. I know I'm not an easy person to get along with. But you . . . you seem to manage better than most."

Taya looked up at him and slowly smiled. "I asked to be assigned to Cabiel, not Si'sier."

"I'm sure the food will disagree with me no matter where we go." He hesitantly reached out and tucked a lock of hair behind her ear. "So. Will you forgive for going back on my word?"

"I suppose," she sighed, glad that she hadn't let him know how angry she'd been. "As long as you don't make a habit out of it."

He leaned down and pressed his forehead against hers, then kissed her.

She slid her hands into his greatcoat and under his suit jacket, letting the flaps of his coat fall around her like great black wings. Cristof's angles felt warm and comfortable. He bent over her, one hand sliding around her waist beneath the metal bars of her armature keel, and the other running up through her curls. Their lips touched again, lingering this time. He pulled her closer.

A shrill whistle interrupted them. Taya looked up and saw Cassi and Pyke both landing in the street. Pyke glowered at the exalted, but Cassi just locked her wings up and slid her goggles into her hair.

"Making out is easier without the armature," she advised, climbing the stairs.

"Mind your manners," Pyke warned, jamming a finger at Cristof and giving him a hard look as he followed Cassi inside.

Cristof looked at Taya and adjusted his glasses.

"If we'd walked down the street. . . ." he said meaningfully.

"I'd still be wearing my wings." Taya pulled him down for another quick kiss. "Someday you have to take me on a real date, instead of dragging me around to lictor stations and crime scenes."

"I tried a real date," he pointed out, straightening. "Lunch, remember? And Lars showed up. Trouble follows me."

Inside, the station's waiting room had become crowded. Victor, Lars, and Isobel were inspecting the cards and scribbling notes. Pyke and Cassi sat backward in their chairs, watching from the sides with the lictors. Scarios, leaning over Victor's shoulder as the programmers worked, ignored Taya and Cristof as they re-entered the station. Amcathra glanced up at them.

"A successful hunt?" he asked Taya, in Demican.

"Very funny." Taya dropped into a chair next to Cassi.

"The Forlores have a nice house," Cassi said, her eyebrows rising. "He doesn't look rich."

"He doesn't live there anymore. But I think he'll be moving back soon."

"Uh-oh. Is that bad?"

"No." Taya smiled. "I think it's going to be all right."

"You know, if she's a suspect now, shouldn't somebody search Emelie's rooms?" Lars asked, looking up from his notes.

"Do any of you have keys?" Cristof patted his hair, smoothing down the locks that Taya had disarrayed outside. The three shook their heads.

"It seems you will have to go back to work now, exalted," Amcathra said. "I believe your kit contains the appropriate tools for this job."

"Do you have a writ of entry?"

In a few minutes Amcathra called Scarios away to put a seal on the paperwork. As soon as the wax seal cooled, Cristof tucked it into his coat.

"I'll go with him," Cassi volunteered, pushing the chair away and hopping to her feet. "I can courier messages back and forth faster than he can walk."

Cristof looked skeptical. Cassi gave him a charming smile.

"Besides," she added, "I'm looking forward to getting to know you better. Our conversation this afternoon was so one-sided."

He looked to Taya for help, but she just winked. Cassi would be relentless.

The exalted scowled and walked out, jamming his hands into his pockets.

"Lieutenant, I want an icarus team sent to Cantery, and send a message to the captain of Tertius that we're going to be mustering a team down there," Scarios said, glancing over the programmers' shoulders. "Tell him we'll want ten lictors, armed."

"We are running short on nightflyers," Amcathra warned. "We have four at Oporphyr and four searching the mountain roads. If I send two to Cantery, we will only have one team left in the city."

"That's enough."

Amcathra began pulling out fresh sheets of paper.

"That's it," Isobel announced, collecting the notes from everybody and handing them to Scarios. "We put a star by the brothel you were asking about."

"Good. Lieutenant, as soon as you're through." Scarios turned and walked back to his office. When Amcathra finished sending lictors off with orders, he turned and vanished into the office after his superior officer.

"So, do you think Em really did it?" Isobel asked, at last. Both Victor and Lars shrugged.

"She has a selfish streak," Victor said at last. "But to accuse her of theft on this scale. . . ."

"If she hurt Kyle, I'll wring her skinny neck," Lars growled.

"They always got along," Isobel said. "I don't think she'd do anything to him."

But her accomplices might, Taya thought, worried. She hoped the thieves understood how valuable Kyle was to them.

"So, does anyone else have any dark secrets they want to reveal?" Lars demanded, glowering at Isobel and Victor.

"Most of my secrets aren't mine to share," Victor said, fingering his beard. "I've been arrested a few times for protesting. You know that."

"Have you?" Taya asked, turning to Pyke and glaring. He raised his hands.

"I can't afford to get arrested. Programmers are given more leeway than icarii."

"Don't you drag Pyke into anything illegal." Taya shot Victor a stern look. "He can't afford to lose his wings."

Victor shrugged. "Social criticism isn't illegal."

"I don't see what either of you two have to criticize. You're both lucky to be living in Ondinium," Taya said.

"True." Victor raised his eyebrows. "But you can love something and still want to clean up its routines, can't you? Make it safer, fairer, more generous—"

"Alister thought the same thing."

"I don't think lasting change can come from an analytical engine."

Taya looked at Pyke, who was avoiding her gaze. Sighing, she promised herself they'd talk about it later. She didn't want him falling in with a dangerous crowd.

"And you know everything about me," Isobel said, looking at Lars. "The worst thing I've ever done was climb through the provost's window, and that was your fault."

Victor chuckled, and even Lars smiled.

"Why'd you do that?" Taya asked.

"Oh, it was silly." Isobel's blue eyes twinkled. "The university provost had this old difference engine everybody used to joke about—it was hardly better than an abacus. So one night I entered his office and opened up the door for these guys. We pulled out his engine's front panel, removed the mechanism, and replaced it with a cage full of white mice."

"The next day none of his programs ran." Lars picked up the story, grinning. The cards just dropped through the feeder slot and landed in the empty box we'd rigged up inside. So he sent over a complaint that his DE was broken and making strange squeaking noises. The dean of the school of engineering came to his office to find out what was wrong."

"We were in class, but apparently the dean opened up the front panel, took one look at the cage, and demanded to know how long it had been since the provost had fed his mice." Isobel giggled. "The provost began stammering that nobody had told him anything about feeding mice and that he was sure it was his secretary's job."

"Were you ever caught?" Taya asked, after they'd finished laughing.

"No, never. The dean kept the mice as pets."

"We couldn't have done it without Izzy," Lars said, nodding in her direction. "She scaled the brick wall to the provost's office as easily as I'd climb a ladder."

"And now that leaves you." Victor leaned back in his chair and gazed at Lars. "What are your dark secrets?"

"I don't have any secrets," the big man said. Victor and Isobel traded looks. He became defensive. "Clockwork Heart was broken, and you know it!"

Victor shrugged. "Hey, I don't care who you sleep with."

"Well, I do!"

"My mother told me that Demican warriors had hunt-partners," Isobel said, not quite looking at Lars. "Usually men with men and women with women. They had to like each other's company enough to spend weeks in the wild together under dangerous conditions. Most of the time they only shared furs when they were on the trail, but some hunt-partners lived with each other all their lives."

"How nice for the Demicans."

They fell silent, Lars with his arms folded over his chest, sulking. Taya wondered why he was so upset. Belonging to a caste with a reputation for moving as freely from bed to bed as it did from sector to sector had its disadvantages, but at least nobody ever made a fuss over who an icarus slept with.

Voices heralded the officers' return.

"We appreciate your help," Scarios said, looking around at the programmers. "You can go home now. We'll contact you if we find Miss Wilkes or Mr. Deuse."

"We'd just as soon wait." Isobel looked up. "At least until Exalted Forlore comes back."

"We'll keep out of your way," Victor added. The captain was already shaking his head.

"We can tell you about the engine," Lars said, grasping at straws. "Your men wouldn't know AE components from a box of broken clocks. You'll need one of us along to tell you if you've found the right crates."

"I think we can—" Scarios broke off as Cassi burst through the door. The pockets of her flight suit were bulging, and she walked straight to the table and began pulling out slender boxes of cards.

"Pyke, he's walking up Trisent and he has a bag full of boxes," she said, over her shoulder. Pyke nodded and left without a word. She looked up at the lictors. "Emelie wasn't there, so we took all her notes and cards, in case any of them were important."

Lars gave the captain a triumphant look and picked up one of the boxes. In moments the three programmers were thumbing through cards and dropping boxes on the floor.

"I think she left," Cassi said, turning to the captain. "A lot of her clothes were missing, unless she's got a smaller wardrobe than Taya."

"Hey!"

"Give me a few minutes and I'll bring back whatever Pyke can't carry," Cassi continued, grinning at her friend.

"Do you want me—" Taya started to stand, but her friend pushed her back into the chair.

"Stay off your leg."

"You know, someday *you're* going to be the one who's grounded."

"And I'll be smart enough to spend my time in bed reading lurid love stories and having handsome guys wait on me hand and foot," Cassi shot back, heading out the door.

"Forgefire, Em must have saved every program she ever wrote," Lars groaned, closing another box and dropping it on the floor.

"Not all of these are hers." Victor tossed a box to the ground. "Some of these are class demos, and this looks like Alister's work."

"I doubt any of them are important." Isobel frowned. "Emelie was sneaky. She wouldn't leave anything significant behind."

"Look anyway," Scarios ordered. The programmers shrugged and turned back to their work.

Pyke returned with more cards and a bundle of letters that he handed to the captain.

A few minutes later, Cassi came back and unloaded more letters and papers. Amcathra handed bundles to each icarus and the few lictors who remained.

When Cristof finally walked in, the station was quiet, everyone busy reading.

"This is strange," Isobel remarked, turning a box upside-down. Small flecks of bright metal rained down onto the table top. Everyone pressed close to look at it.

"Copper," Victor said, picking one of the tiny pieces up on a fingertip.

"Punches," Lars burst out. "That's punch chad!"

"Great Engine cards are made out of tin—"

"But Torn Cards aren't," Cristof said, grimly. "The Torn Cards mark each of their attacks with half a copper punch card."

The three programmers looked at each other, dumbfounded.

"Well, so much for your theory that a Torn Card would rather throw a bomb than learn to program," Victor said at last, turning to Isobel.

"But a Torn Card would have put a bomb in the university lab, not stolen an engine," she insisted. "It doesn't make any sense for Em to be a Torn Card."

"Well, she had access to the right tools to punch a card," Lars said, looking up at the captain. "And I suppose she couldn't leave copper keypunch droppings around in our chad box where we would see it. She probably brushed it into whatever program she was working on at the time."

"Do you think she vandalized the wireferry?" Pyke asked, speaking up at last.

"She couldn't have. She was with us the night before the accident," Isobel said. "We were all working late, even Alister."

"What about the refinery bombing?" Taya asked, remembering her hurried night flight to the site of the disaster. "That was the Torn Cards, too, wasn't it?"

"No card was ever found, but the rubble hasn't been cleared away yet."

"She wasn't with us that night," Victor mused. "None of us were working. Alister told us he needed to spend time with his cousin, since she was still recovering from the scare, and we all decided to take the night off."

"But women don't plant bombs," Isobel reminded her friend. Victor sighed.

"Well, that bomb didn't kill anyone, did it? Maybe a woman would plant a bomb if she knew it was only going to cause property damage."

"You're so narrow-minded. Women can make as much of a mess as men."

"The refinery never made sense," Scarios said, looking at Cristof and ignoring the two programmers. "Octavus is a legitimate target for terrorists, but refineries are low-technology. The Cards prefer high-profile vandalism."

"Was the explosion ever investigated?" Cristof asked.

"The case wasn't closed, but with everything that happened afterward, it wasn't given a high priority."

"Maybe someone should take another look down there, just to make sure we didn't miss anything. The refinery wasn't owned by a decatur, was it?"

"No. We checked the obvious leads. It belongs to one of the Big Three mining companies. Nothing screwy in its records."

"It could have been a disgruntled worker," Victor suggested. "Labor isn't very happy with the Big Three."

Scarios waved off the suggestion. "Right now, I don't care about the refinery. The only thing that matters is that your friend was either a Torn Card or working with Torn Cards, and that makes this investigation a lot more urgent. We have to move down to Slagside."

"Can we—" Victor had barely started before Scarios was shaking his head.

"You've done your part. Now it's time to step aside," he said, his tone brooking no disagreement. "The Torn Cards are violent. I'm not going to involve civilians."

"What about us?" Cassi volunteered. "Could you use some overhead reconnaissance?"

"Sorry, icarus, but you haven't been trained to fly in a firefight. Under other circumstances, I might be tempted, but this time I can't take the risk."

The argument continued another minute, but Scarios was adamant, and he and Amcathra were already issuing orders to the lictors left in the station.

"Exalted." Scarios turned at last to Cristof. "I want you to stay here, too. You're too important to get killed by crossfire."

"I'm not—"

"You're an exalted, you're a key witness in your brother's case, and this is lictor work. The Council would bust me back to Tertius gate guard if you got hurt."

Cristof seemed to consider the captain's words. Taya held her breath.

"All right," he said at last. "But I think I'll run by the refinery on my way home, just to double-check."

"There something you're not telling me?"

"No. I'm just bothered by the fact that the refinery was vandalized so soon after the Torn Cards attacked the wireferry."

Scarios gave the exalted an evaluating look, and Taya could tell he was thinking the same thing she was—that Cristof was desperate to find something to do that would take his mind off his brother. Then the captain shrugged.

"Do you want a lictor?"

"No. You'll need all the firepower you can get."

"All right," Scarios said, turning away. "Lieutenant, let's go."

Amcathra lingered, his pale blue eyes resting a moment longer on Cristof.

"What are you thinking?" the Demican asked, as the captain headed out the door.

"The refinery isn't that far from some of the contact points on Neuillan's information."

"It's not that far from where I was nearly mugged, either," Taya said.

Amcathra glanced at her, then back to Cristof.

"Do not risk yourself or the icarii."

"Don't worry, lieutenant, we'll protect him," Cassi said, with a small smile. Pyke grunted, less pleased by the prospect.

"Send one of the uninjured icarii to inform me if you discover anything."

"I will."

Amcathra gave a brusque nod and followed his captain.

The only people left in the Primus office were the night clerk and themselves.

"We want to go search the refinery with you," Isobel said, gesturing to Lars and Victor next to her. "We can be your backup if something goes wrong."

"That won't be necessary," Cristof demurred.

"We're not as helpless as you might think," Victor added. He shot a glance at Pyke, who nodded. "I can explain better when we get back to Gregor's coach."

"It's a long walk to Tertius," Cristof pointed out. "I live there, so it isn't inconvenient for me, and Cassilta and Pyke can fly back. But for the rest of you, it's a meaningless journey that could keep you out past lockdown."

"If I go with Gregor, I can get them through the gates," Taya said.

"Look, we want to help," Lars added. "I understand not taking us on a raid, but what's wrong with poking around an old factory? If we find one of those torn punch cards, we'll be helping the investigation, right?"

"Kyle is our friend," Isobel added. "Anything we can do to help find him, even if it's just closing off loose ends, will make us feel better."

DRU PAGLIASOTTI

Cristof let out a long, exasperated breath and pushed up his glasses.

"If any of you get hurt, I'll be held responsible."

Pyke's eyes narrowed. "Don't patronize us."

"But you're not lictor caste—" Cristof stopped abruptly, but not before Cassi snapped back, "—and neither are you."

"Taya?" Cristof gave her a pleading look. She shrugged.

"I don't want to go home and spend the night tossing and turning, either."

"All right." He rubbed the bridge of his nose, under his spectacles. "But please do what I say. I'm licensed to work for the lictors, and if you investigate with me, I'll expect prompt obedience."

Pyke muttered something about expectations and Cassi rolled her eyes, giving Taya a meaningful look.

"That's fine with me, exalted," Lars said. Isobel nodded. Victor hesitated, then inclined his head.

"Bossy," Taya teased. Cristof frowned and she raised her eyebrows. "Whatever you say, exalted."

"You should stay here, Taya. You've already put too much strain on your leg today."

"I grew up in Tertius, right around that area, and I fly over it all the time to visit my family. I know it better than anyone else here, and I can tell Cassi and Pyke what to expect in the air. Do you have a sector map?"

"But your leg—"

"It's going to hurt whether I'm flying or in bed, and you're not leaving me behind." Taya pushed herself out of her chair to stand. "When all of this is over, I'll do whatever you say. But right now, you aren't the only person here who needs to stay busy."

Cristof glowered. The rest of the group fell silent, watching with interest.

"Whatever I say," he repeated, dangerously. "Is that a promise?"

Taya wavered a second. Then she considered the possibilities and smiled.

"When this is over—yes."

Shaking his head, he strode back to the offices.

"Better watch out," Cassi said with a grin. "A repressed guy like that. . . ."

"You're the one who said he's a prude."

"Prudes are the worst, once they loosen up," Isobel pointed out. "Or maybe I should say 'the best'?"

Taya laughed, torn between embarrassment and amusement.

"I can't believe you like that guy," Pyke complained. "What's so attractive about a skinny, glasses-wearing outcaste?"

"Oooh, listen to the pretty boy." Cassi patted Pyke's head. "Jealous again."

"Hey, remember, Taya asked my advice about that guy's brother. I said 'leave him alone,' and he turned out to be a murderer." Pyke folded his arms over his chest. "I'm one for one right now."

"The exalted is all right," Victor said. "He has integrity."

"He'd better," Pyke muttered.

A moment later Cristof returned and spread a map out on the station table over the discarded punch cards and letters. They leaned over it and began to work out their route.

Chapter Seventeen

Gregor's hack clattered to a halt, and Taya pushed off from the rooftop where she'd been waiting. She'd taken another dose of painkilling medicine before leaving the station. Despite the medicine, it still ached; a dull sensation at the edge of her awareness, warning her not to overdo anything.

Now she kicked her feet up into the tailset and swept her wings down, seeing Cassi and Pyke spreading out to either side of her.

This part of Tertius was quiet at night, with no tenements, bars, or theaters to attract people and noise. The factories were all closed down and the streets were empty and dark.

The three icarii flew in near silence, concentrating on the airspace around them. The lights from the upper sectors gave the sky a dim glow, and lamps had been lit every hundred feet on the wireferry towers, but it would still be easy to mistake a factory chimney for a patch of shadow or forget about a crosscable stretching diagonally between two towers.

From above, the bombed refinery didn't look very different. In the darkness, the soot and broken windows from the fire weren't visible. A makeshift barrier had been set up around it, but parts had gone missing, pilfered away by neighbors.

Taya tilted her wings and let herself sink lower in a long circle. Pyke stayed high, watching for approaching traffic, but Cassi kept a few body lengths behind her.

The openings where the refinery's windows had been were dark and empty. Taya landed on a factory roof across the way, gasping as she took most of the impact on her good leg. She touched her calf, then made a face and pulled her hand away.

Nothing I can do about it. Tomorrow I can take Cassi's advice and spend the day in bed. Maybe she'll lend me one of her lurid novels.

Cassi cut across to the other side of the street and landed. In a moment she'd unhooded her small lamp and signaled to Pyke, three swift flashes of light reflected from her silvery wings.

Pyke rocked back and forth in acknowledgment and flew back to inform the others that the coast was clear.

Taya perched on the edge of the roof, searching the burnt building. Still no sign of life. She didn't expect any, but anything that kept them all busy seemed like a good idea.

She glanced to her left. The hack had stopped, and the three programmers and Cristof were piling out.

Rifles jutted over their shoulders.

Cristof hadn't been very happy when they'd arrived at Gregor's coach and Victor had pulled the percussion weapons off the floor, where they'd been shrouded in canvas.

"Firearms are restricted inside the city," he'd protested, as Victor had handed one of the guns to him. "Where did you get these?"

"Friends of friends. I thought we'd be going into Slagside ourselves, and I didn't want to go unarmed." Victor had shrugged, handing a rifle to Isobel. "They're just a precaution."

"Vic's playing soldier again," Isobel sighed, examining her weapon. "He and his friends like to think of themselves as Ondinium's second line of defense. You should get some of those lictors' air rifles, Vic."

"These are cheaper and sturdier."

Cristof gave the bearded man a hard look. "So who are your friends, Victor? Liberationists?"

Victor shook his head. "I don't sign up for causes. I just think that sometimes you have to take the law into your own hands if you want to ensure justice."

"Loose gears don't help a clock run better."

"Life isn't as simple as clockwork, exalted. We both know that."

"What makes you think I'm not going to report you?"

"The fact that you've been bending some rules yourself, lately."

Cristof made a familiar, impatient sound, checking to make sure the gun was loaded, but he hadn't said anything else. Victor had handed the fourth weapon to Lars.

"Thanks, but I can't imagine shooting anybody," Lars had said with a shudder, handing it to Gregor. "You can watch our backs."

The coachman had taken the weapon with a bemused expression.

"What're you going do if somebody draws on you?" Victor insisted. "You may be good in a bar fight, but those ham-sized fists of yours won't be any protection against a bullet."

"I don't see how a skinny little gun's going to protect me." Lars snorted. "I'm too big to miss if somebody starts shooting."

"The idea is that they'll be too afraid of your weapon to shoot."

"How about I just look harmless and keep my hands up?"

Victor hadn't offered the icarii a weapon, and they hadn't asked for one. To carry a firearm would violate one of the most fundamental rules of icarus protocol. They could lose their wings over it. Not even Pyke had suggested it, although he'd gazed at the rifles with palpable longing.

Now Taya watched as Gregor climbed up to the top of his coach and sat down, his rifle by his side. He'd taken the hack around the refinery and parked on Drover's Way, the wide road that led to the biggest gate in Ondinium's walls. He'd seemed just as excited by the late-night mission as the programmers, even though Cristof had assured him that it would likely turn up nothing more interesting than a few piles of rubble and, if they were lucky, a torn copper punch card.

Cristof had chosen to team up with Lars, Taya saw, and Isobel with Victor. The two teams split up, one going left and the other right, to circle the broken shell of the refinery.

She waited until they were close and then kicked off again, taking a long, silent sweep over the building. Pyke did the same, while Cassi, their designated signaler, stayed on her high perch and watched.

Both Cristof and Victor seemed to have had similar training. They stayed in the shadows with their partners, popping up to look through the broken-out windows with their rifles aimed, then crouching and moving to the next. They continued until they met at the far wall and hunkered down to consult.

Isobel stepped out of the darkness and waved. Taya tilted her wings in acknowledgement and turned to see if Pyke had seen. He was heading down, too.

They both landed, Pyke on his feet and jogging to a halt, Taya on her knees. The landing hurt, and she began to wonder why she'd argued so hard to be a patroller instead of a signaler.

It was a stupid question, of course. She'd go crazy sitting away from all the action and wondering what Cristof was doing. Thank the Lady, Cassi had understood.

Pyke walked up as she locked her wings. Sliding a hand under one arm, he helped her to her feet.

"How are you feeling?"

"Fine," she whispered, trying to keep the weight off her wounded leg. He supported her as they joined the small group.

"I didn't see anything from above," she murmured as she joined them.

"No, but the exalted and I smelled something strange," Victor replied. "Ammonia, he says. Smelled like methanol, to me."

"What does that mean?"

"I don't know, but it's a funny smell to come from a refinery that's been shut down for nearly a week."

Taya gave the shattered walls a second, worried look.

"Victor and I will go inside to look around," Cristof said to the group. "I want the rest of you to spread out and give an alarm if anyone runs outside. Don't shoot. Just shout. Pyke, can you stay up in the air to follow anyone who leaves?"

"Sure."

"You think there's still someone inside?" Isobel asked.

"Chemical fumes disperse quickly, so the fact that we both smell something worries me." Cristof checked his rifle. "I should probably send one of you back to alert the nearest Tertius station, but I don't want to risk raising a false alarm while the captain has another operation going."

"Send Cassi," Pyke said. "Taya needs to stay grounded."

Taya started to object, and Pyke laid a hand on her shoulder.

"Hey, I just saw you land. Your leg can't take many more jolts like that. You want to hurt yourself so bad you'll be grounded the rest of your life, like Paulo?"

Taya thought of the crippled night watchman and shook her head. Her leg was still throbbing. She had a bad feeling she might have pulled a few stitches.

"I'll stay grounded unless I have to go aloft," she acquiesced. Pyke squeezed her shoulder.

"Why does she listen to *you*?" Cristof demanded.

"She likes me better," Pyke said, with a smug smile.

Taya shot them both a disgusted look.

Frowning, the exalted took off his glasses and cleaned them with a handkerchief. "All right. There are three doors: the big bay door in front and the two smaller doors in back. Gregor can watch the front, and Isobel, you watch the back. You should be able to cover both doors at once. Cassilta's already got a clear view of the west side, so Lars, I want you on the east. Taya, stay with Lars. Neither of you is armed, so if you see someone, stay hidden and shout an alarm."

"Got it." The big man nodded. Taya nodded, too. She would have preferred to be with Cristof and Victor, but she knew she wouldn't be much use with a bad leg.

The group broke up.

Lars and Taya found a doorway where they could sit on the sooty stone steps and see most of the east wall of the refinery. Lars sat on the bottom step, and Taya sat higher, her wings brushing the brick sides of the entryway.

"You okay?" Lars asked, as she bent over and looked at her injured leg.

"I think I'm bleeding again." She tugged at the laces that were tying down the shredded leather of her pants leg and winced. "I hate being hurt."

"You should take it easier."

"I can't."

"Yeah. I understand."

They waited, their eyes fixed on the shadowy building. The gaping windows looked like wounds in its walls, and the rubble in the street glittered with shards of broken glass.

Minutes crawled past, and then Taya saw a glimmer of light inside the building. She straightened, straining to see it again.

A shot echoed through the building, and she was on her feet, stumbling into Lars. He steadied her and they both rushed into the street as a woman shrieked.

Now lamplight was clearly visible from the windows, as if some barrier had fallen.

"Don't move," Cristof shouted, inside the building.

"Come on!" Taya ran across the street and scrambled over broken rocks, hardly noticing the pain shooting through her calf.

"Wait, wait!" Lars wrapped a hand around one of the metal bars of her tailset as she braced her leather-gloved hands on a windowsill. "What are you doing?"

"Somebody might be hurt!"

"Emelie!" Victor's voice, from inside the refinery. "Emelie, wait!"

Lars shoved in front of her, heaving his bulk through the window. Taya waited until he was clear and then started to climb through, only to have the big man grab her by the metal keel and lift her through. She yelped as a wing hit the side of the windowsill and sent vibrations rattling through her armature.

"You're lighter than you look," he grunted, setting her on her feet.

"Ondium." She looked around, getting her bearings. There—the light was to the northwest. "Look!"

They stood in a huge open space filled with equipment that blocked the light, but it was clear that some kind of makeshift encampment had been set up to one side, where several lamps were burning. Lars began to run toward it, and Taya limped after him, cursing the machinery that kept looming up out of the dark and forcing her to swerve or stumble.

Another gunshot rang out, and then a third. Voices began to shout in Alzanan:

"Put your weapons down!"

"I only see one! Where'd the second one go?"

"Toss me that box of bullets!"

Taya flinched, swerving toward the wall again, and ran into a metal staircase. Surprised, she looked up and saw that it led to a catwalk that circled the open workspace.

A door slammed. "Vic?" Isobel's voice.

Taya considered her options. If the catwalk encircled the area, she could get over the firefight, which would give her a chance to shout directions to her friends. On the other hand, it would also make her more vulnerable to stray bullets. Her aching leg reminded her of what a bad idea that would be.

Then she heard a clatter and felt the metal vibrate under her hand as somebody ran above her. She grabbed the staircase railing and half-climbed, half-hauled herself upward.

"Lars, get down!" Cristof cried out as another shot cracked through the building. Taya yanked herself up to the catwalk and saw a figure leaning over the railing, aiming a rifle.

"Wait!" she shouted, panicked. Then, switching to Alzanan: "Stop! You must surrender! The building is surrounded!"

The man turned, his rifle barrel dropping. Taya threw herself forward.

The Alzanan yanked the rifle back up, but ondium and desperation gave her the momentum she needed to close the distance before he could squeeze off a shot. Taya's gloved hands grabbed the weapon's barrel, shoving it aside, and she rammed a metal-protected shoulder into him. The man staggered and the rifle went off, bucking in both of their hands.

Then she tore it from his grasp and he tried to ram an elbow into her ribs, only to hit the metal of her armature keel. He winced and used an Alzanan word she hadn't learned yet.

Taya slammed the rifle's butt against the side of his head. The Alzanan staggered and his legs buckled underneath him.

"Sorry," she said as she kicked him in groin with her metal-toed flight boot. With a strangled groan he collapsed, holding himself.

She put the rifle down with a sense of distaste, then turned and looked over the railing.

From her vantage point over the encampment, she could see everything. The Alzanans had cleared away the fallen rubble to set up a small lair with scrounged blankets and boards serving as makeshift walls. The center was dominated by a work table covered with wire and metal pipes and buckets and cord. The lamps next to it gave off the light she and Lars had seen a few minutes before. Sleeping mats were scattered along one side of the room, and a wagon filled with crates stood at the northernmost end, close to the bay doors in front.

One man was lying on the soot-covered floor next to the table, holding his arm. Blood trickled through his fingers, and his face was pale as his dark eyes darted back and forth.

Three gunmen were crouched by the wagon, two aiming, the other reloading. They were intent on Cristof, who had taken cover behind a low stack of wooden crates. He was digging in his coat pockets for something, but from the looks of things, he wasn't finding it. His rifle was on his lap, its breech open. The crates had several splintered bullet holes in them.

A few feet away, Lars had ducked beneath some kind of heavy equipment that had been twisted and bent by the explosion. The Alzanans had a clear shot at him, but he was low and in shadow and the Alzanan with the gun seemed more worried about Cristof.

She didn't see Isobel, Victor or Emelie, but from where she was standing, she could just make out someone huddled against one of the makeshift walls in an awkward position.

Cristof stopped searching his pockets and pinched the arch of his nose. Then he set the rifle aside and rolled onto his stomach, peering around the boxes.

One of the armed Alzanans tensed, but Cristof ducked back and the man's finger loosened on the trigger.

"Out of cartridges?" the Alzanan mocked, his voice loud.

Cartridges! Taya crouched and began searching the groaning Alzanan at her feet. Her hands closed on the paper-wrapped cylinders. Hoping that all rifles took the same kind of ammunition, she leaned out as far as she could.

"Here!" She threw them down at Cristof, then scampered forward.

The second Alzanan spun toward her, squeezing off a shot that slammed into one of the catwalk supports. The whole walkway shuddered.

"Dammit, be careful!" the fallen Alzanan shouted, hoarsely, in his own language. "I'm up here!"

Taya edged back to him, grabbed his weapon, and kicked him again to make sure he'd stay down.

"Cris!" She hurled the Alzanan's rifle toward the exalted as hard as she could. It clattered several feet beyond him. She'd done better with the cartridges, which were now scattered around his crate.

"I thought I told you to stay outside!" Cristof shouted, snatching up one of the cartridges and loading his rifle.

"There are three men by the wagon. One's reloading. It looks they've got four pistols between them," she reported, gambling that the Alzanans wouldn't take another shot at her voice and risk hitting their friend.

She gambled wrong. She shrieked as the bullet tore into the catwalk and made it shudder and creak again.

"Taya!"

"I'm okay!" She backed up as far as she could, finding a shadowed area out of the circles of light cast by the lamps below. "There's another man by the far wall. He's not moving. It might be Kyle."

"Kyle!" Lars stood, his hands wrapped around a twisted metal bar that he held like a club. "Kyle, is that you?"

Both Alzanans turned to aim. Cristof swore and leaped to his feet, rifle pointed at the armed men.

Lars charged.

"No! Don't!" Taya lunged against the rail, jamming her arms into her wings.

Cristof's shot winged one of the gunmen, who shouted and staggered backward. The other Alzanan fired at Lars and ducked.

Lars stumbled, then grabbed the worktable with his free hand and flung it toward the wagon as he ran. Glass and chemicals flew, and the Alzanan flinched, throwing his arms over his face.

Taya swung her legs over the railing, holding her arms wide.

Cristof stood upright, holding a second cartridge between his teeth as he broke open the rifle's breech.

The third gunner grabbed one of the loaded pistols as Lars swung his metal club at the man who'd just fired. The club smashed into the side of the wagon, sending splinters of wood flying everywhere. His would-be victim whacked him across the shins with his empty pistol. Lars snarled and swung again. This time the Alzanan howled.

The third Alzanan rolled under the wagon and aimed his gun at Cristof.

"Look out!" Taya shouted, kicking away from the catwalk.

DRU PAGLIASOTTI

It was a short drop, and she took it hard, the ondium
barely managing to slow her fall. Cristof was still jamming
his cartridge into place when she landed in front of him,
her metal wings spread as wide as possible. The Alzanan's
shot rang out through the building.

The bullet hit one of her ondium feathers and sent a jolt
running through her arm, but that was nothing compared
to the agony that tore through her calf as her foot hit the
ground. She staggered, her wings sweeping down and
clattering on the floor as she tried to catch herself.

Then Cristof was beside her, one arm sliding under hers.
Gasping, she threw her arm over his shoulder, her ondium
feathers fanned out around his back.

He spun her out of his way and fired his rifle one-handed.

The weapon jerked out of his hand and the bullet buried
itself in one of the crates on the wagon.

Lars stomped on the fingers that were reaching for the
last loaded pistol, then kicked the weapon away into the
shadows.

Taya gasped with pain as Cristof hauled her back behind
the boxes.

"Taya?" His face was white. "Were you hit?"

"No." She leaned against him, tears stinging her eyes.
She was sure she'd torn out her stitches, this time. "Help
me sit."

"What happened?" He lowered her to the floor. His
hands were shaking.

Taya shrugged out of her wings, letting them float
uselessly around her as she looked at her leg. Blood was
seeping around the edges of the torn leather. She rested her
forehead against her knee, feeling faint.

Then Isobel rose up from the shadows, a rifle in her hands.
She gave them a cursory glance, turned to the wagon, and
swung her firearm up to her shoulder in a practiced move.

"Lars, I have you covered," she said, her voice calm.

"It's about time you got here," he growled. Taya heard a
thud. Someone grunted with pain. "Keep these assholes in
line while I look for Kyle."

"You got it."

Taya felt Cristof's cool hand on her forehead and looked up.

"I'm all right," she said, knowing her voice was thin with pain but unable to make it steadier for him. "Go help them."

"Just a few more minutes," he promised, still looking ashen. He grabbed the rifle she'd thrown from the catwalk and stood, taking aim next to Isobel.

"Got him," Lars roared, in triumph. "It's Kyle! He's all right!"

Despite her pain, Taya smiled.

FIFTEEN MINUTES LATER, Cristof and Isobel finished tying up their captives. Taya sat next to Lars, who had only admitted to having been grazed by a bullet after Cristof had noticed the blood staining his shirt. Now he was bare-chested, his shirt pressed against his side, inspecting the boxes in the wagon.

"This is our engine, all right," he said, fingering a splintered hole. "I hope your bullet didn't go all the way through, exalted."

"If it did, we'll blame it on the Alzanans," Kyle said. As Lt. Amcathra had guessed, he'd suffered a head wound, but his captors had bandaged it. Other than some bruises and scraping, he seemed none the worse for wear.

"Fine with me." Lars stood, then winced and peeled his balled-up shirt away to look at his wound. "I can't believe I got shot for you, Kyle. I expect a raise when we get our next contract."

"Oh, stop complaining," Isobel said, checking a knot. "You're looking good compared to this guy." She gestured to the Alzanan that Lars had caught across the ribs with his metal club. The man was fighting to breathe, wincing each time he inhaled. "He's going to need a doctor."

"He shot me." Lars scowled. "I got scared. I don't like being shot."

"Me, either," Taya said, leaning sideways against a crate. After leaving Isobel to take care of the prisoners, Cristof had helped her lock her wings back and had wrapped her wounded leg in fresh bandages.

"If that's how you react when you're scared, Lars, I'd hate to see you angry," Kyle joked.

"Hello?" Pyke edged in, then relaxed when he saw that everything was under control. "Everyone all right?"

"We're alive," Cristof reported. "Have you seen Victor?"

"He caught Emelie about two blocks from here." Pyke looked serious. "She started babbling about bombs, so he's taking her to the Tertius station in Gregor's hack, and Cassi's flying ahead to warn the lictors. If everyone's okay here, I'm going to head up to Primus to spread the alarm."

Cristof's jaw tightened. "What bombs? How many?"

"She called them triton bombs and said the Alzanans had made about ten of 'em. They're set to go off at four in the morning. They were supposed to be a distraction while these guys drove the stolen engine out the city gates."

Cristof yanked out a pocket watch and checked it. Diamonds glittered in the lamplight, and Taya realized he was wearing his brother's watch.

"Three more hours." He sounded relieved, then turned a cold look on his five prisoners. "What do you know about the bombs and their locations?"

The Alzanans looked at each other.

"Talk, and your cooperation will be taken under consideration when they sentence you," Taya said, in Alzanan. "Believe me, you'd rather be sentenced as thieves than as terrorists. The Council's not very happy with the Torn Cards right now."

"We're not Torn Cards!" one of the men protested. "Those cards were fakes, to fool the police. Everyone knows the Torn Cards are blamed for everything in Ondinium."

Taya translated.

"He's got a point," Pyke agreed.

"They'll have to prove it in court." Cristof picked up one of the Alzanans' loaded pistols and set it against a prisoner's kneecap. "Where are the bombs?"

"You'd better tell him," Taya said, in Alzanan. "He's in a really bad mood." She gave Cristof a warning look, but his face was blank. She hoped he was just bluffing.

After a hasty conference, the Alzanans began to talk, and Taya translated. Pyke lingered long enough to get a list of locations, then ran outside to carry the information to lictor stations across the city.

About half an hour later, a group of lictors arrived with a wagon to pick everyone up. They stopped at the hospital to drop off the programmers, Taya, and Cristof, and then continued onward to take the prisoners to the nearest jail.

"You don't have to report in?" Taya asked, as Cristof slid an arm under her armature and helped her up the hospital steps.

"I'll do it tomorrow."

"Do you think the bombs will be found?"

Cristof's arm tightened around her waist.

"I hope so," he said at last. "The Alzanans don't have anything to gain anymore, and everything to lose."

The group split up, Cristof and Taya going one way and the programmers going the other. A physician pulled out and replaced Taya's stitches, a painful procedure that she bore with clenched teeth and tears in her eyes as she clung to Cristof's hand. The physician recommended another dose of painkiller, but she refused. It would put her to sleep, and she wanted to make sure Lars and Kyle were all right.

To her dismay, the physician then proceeded to give her the lecture Cristof had been biting back all evening, delivering stern warnings about infection and permanent muscle damage. He handed her a second set of crutches and ordered her to use them, this time.

Taya meekly agreed to everything he said. Her leg throbbed and her head hurt, and she would have said anything to get out of there. By the time she limped into the main room, the programmers were already waiting for her.

"How are you?" she asked.

"Three stitches and some new bandages," Kyle said, touching the back of his head. "I'll have a bald spot for a while."

"I'm glad you're okay." Taya gave him a quick, awkward hug, careful not to jab him with her armature. "We were worried about you."

"The Alzanans treated me all right. I guess they needed me in one piece to help them with the engine."

"Did Emelie arrange your kidnapping?" Isobel asked, her voice cool. Kyle shook his head, then winced.

"No. In fact, she was pretty mad when she came in and saw me. I think she was supposed to be the only programmer they took. It would have ensured her a comfortable place in the Alzanan court, that's for certain. Having me along reduced her value."

"I'm still going to wring her neck," Lars rumbled. He was wearing his bloodstained shirt again, over the bandages around his side.

"How did they catch you?" Taya asked.

"It was my fault. I surprised them. I couldn't get over Alister's arrest, so I went down to the engine room to do some work, and suddenly there I was, staring a bunch of Alzanans in the face." Kyle shook his head, then winced. "I'd like to say I put up a fight, but I'm not like Lars here, charging a bunch of armed men with nothing but a stick. They knocked me down before I could do anything."

"Lars was worried about you," Taya said, looking over at the big man. "He's the one who raised the alarm when he found the engine missing."

"The lictors thought you might be involved in the theft," Isobel added, "but Lars never doubted you."

Lars was turning red, and the two women shot each other satisfied glances.

"Thank you," Kyle said, looking up at his friend with affection.

"I'm going to go see if I can find us a hack," Isobel said, rising. "You two want one?" She looked at Taya and Cristof.

"Yes." Cristof stood and handed Taya her crutches. "I'm going to drop you off at your eyrie and pay your landlady to keep you locked in your room until I return."

"You won't have to," Taya said, standing. An icarus on crutches. She sighed and began to limp down the hall. "I told you I'd behave myself, now that we've got the engine back."

Cristof kept pace next to her. "If you're behaving yourself, why did you set up poor Lars back there?"

Taya paused and glanced over her shoulder. The large programmer was slumped down in his chair, shaking his head as he said something to Kyle.

"I didn't set him up. I just wanted Kyle to know what happened. Lars might not want to admit that he cares, but as soon as he heard that Kyle was in that corner, he charged right in without a second thought."

Cristof was silent a moment.

"You did the same thing."

"Me?"

"You put yourself in front of a bullet for me. You could have been killed." He took a deep breath. "In fact, for one very bad moment, I thought you had been."

Taya blushed, looking down at her boots.

"Well . . . you were so busy trying to defend Lars, you weren't paying any attention to defending yourself."

"It was a very brave thing to do." He tilted her head up. "I'm not going to forget it, and I'm not going to forget the way my heart stopped when you stumbled."

Taya didn't know what to say, and then she didn't have to think of anything, as he pulled her into his arms.

"You know," she said, after a moment, "someday you should do this when I'm not wearing my armature."

"Maybe tomorrow. Although," he added, "I'm not going to let you leave the eyrie, and the way your landlady keeps hovering around us, we may have to spend the entire day sitting in the foyer admiring how nicely the eyrie's clock keeps time."

Taya grinned. Rules or not, she'd think of some way to get Cristof alone. If Gwen still harbored any hopes of breaking them up, she was going to be disappointed.

"How about you bring me lunch and tell me and Cassi and Pyke everything we'll be missing tonight, instead," she countered. "The Slagside raid, the bombs, what's going to happen to Emelie and the Alzanans—we'll want to hear it all. I know you're not going to sleep tonight until you find out, anyway."

"Don't forget which one if us is in charge now," Cristof countered. "You promised you'd do whatever I say."

"For a while," she amended. "As long as you don't get too annoying about it."

He sighed. "I will do my best to avoid being bossy, rude, prudish, a pain in the tail, or too rarely sweet. Will that do, icarus?"

"Yes." She gave him a thoughtful look. "It should be quite a change of pace."

He gave her a dark look and she laughed, hugging him.

Chapter Eighteen

His public robes were covered with dusty jewels and tarnished silver embroidery. The fabric weighed ten pounds and was cut in a boxy shape meant to hide the wearer's stature and gender. The robes' hems trailed on the ground to make it impossible for him to walk any faster than with a slow, measured pace, and their sleeves were cut two feet longer than his arms to prevent him from engaging in any form of manual labor.

His long black hair was held up in ornate loops secured by a complicated arrangement of golden ornaments and pins. Like the robes, the hairstyle kept him from moving too quickly.

And, finally, the ivory mask in front of his face erased his individuality with its narrow, glassed-in eye slits and its shallow bump of a nose that provided minimal air holes for breathing. The mask's pale expanse was mouthless and impersonal, only a golden wave on one cheek indicating the wearer's caste, as if anybody could mistake such a figure for anything other than an exalted.

Taya shivered, disquieted. Next to her, Jessica hid behind her mother's skirts, and even the girl's two older brothers seemed subdued.

"Is that really Master Clockite, then?" Jessica whispered, tugging on her mother's hand. "He looks *scary*."

Her mother, Ann, stroked the girl's hair.

"It works, don't it, exalted?" she asked, anxiously. "You'll be finding it satisfactory, then?"

Cristof lifted his arms, his sleeves hanging over his hands and obscuring them.

"Here, I'll get it," Taya said, standing and steadying the mask with one hand as she tugged on its silk cords with the other. The ivory surface felt slick and unnatural, and it was with some relief she pulled the mask away from his face and set it on the work table.

Cristof rubbed his forehead where the mask's padding had left a red mark, and then nodded to his neighbor.

"The wig's very convincing," he said. "It should do fine."

"Oh, that pleases me right well." Beaming, Ann stepped forward and began unpinning it. "I'll box it and have it sent up to your estate, shall I? Your servants will know how to take care of it?"

"You'd better come up to show them. Your family can have dinner with us."

"Oh!" Jessica's mother faltered. "Why, that wouldn't be proper, would it, exalted? I mean, what would people think?"

"Don't be ridiculous," Cristof said, with asperity. "Since when I have cared what other exalteds think?"

"She's talking about her own caste," Taya said, sliding his spectacles back on his face for him. "Ann's family is perfectly respectable, and dining with someone like you . . ."

"No, Taya, you mustn't say that!" Ann protested, blushing. Her two sons were giggling. "But we've no fine clothes to wear, or—"

"I don't care what you wear." Cristof tried to shove up his sleeves so he could begin untying his robes, but the hems kept tumbling down over his hands. "I don't want some incompetent servant jamming a pin through my skull because you weren't there to show him how it's done. I'll send a hack for you tomorrow evening. Just wear what you have on now; it'll be fine. You, your husband, the three loathsome brats—"

"Will you be wearing those stupid robes, then?" the youngest boy asked.

"—maybe only two of them—and Taya. It won't be formal."

"Well. . . ." Ann gave Taya a hesitant look. Taya nodded encouragement as she began untying the knots that held

Cristof's robes closed. "That'd be a great honor indeed, exalted, if you really don't mind."

"I don't."

Taya was pleased. Cristof would never come out and say it, but she knew he was uncomfortable in Primus. Most of the other exalteds treated him with distant mistrust, muttering about a taint in the Forlore bloodline. Cristof needed the company of his few friends.

Two months had passed since they'd rescued Kyle and retrieved the prototype engine. The raids on Slagside and the refinery had led to the arrest of fifteen spies, crippling the Alzanan spy network in Ondinium. Several bombings that had been attributed to the Torn Cards were found to have been the spies' work, and the Council had confirmed what Cristof had long maintained—that the Alzanan king was providing money and encouragement to fringe political groups in an attempt to destabilize Ondinium's government. The Alzanans who could be definitively pinned to murder had been executed. The rest had been sent away to labor in Ondinium's mines, Emelie among them.

Pyke and Victor, and hundreds of others who shared their political viewpoints, had been dragged in by the lictors for questioning and forced to take a special second administration of the loyalty test. Both men had passed, as had most of their friends, leading to critical articles in the activist newspapers that lambasted the Council with accusations of persecution and abuse of power.

As Victor had predicted, Alister's reduced sentence had drawn a storm of protest. Mobs had ringed the plaza when he'd been blinded and, two weeks later, most of the city had turned out to jeer at him as he'd taken his exile march across the city and out the gates.

Cristof, Taya, and Viera had attended both events. None of them had enjoyed the punishment, not even Viera, whose desire for vengeance had evaporated during the public blinding. In fact, she'd been instrumental in helping Taya draw Cristof out of the black mood that had engulfed him after Alister's mutilation and exile. Those weeks had been difficult, but somehow they'd persevered, and after Alister had been led down the mountain under an armed escort, they'd started to put their lives back together again.

Taya knew that Cristof had set up a secret—and illegal— account for his brother with a bank in Mareaux. She'd seen the paperwork when they'd established a fund for the families of the two lictors they'd killed. It was all they could do; neither family had wanted to see or talk to them. It hurt, but Taya understood. And she didn't blame Cristof for trying to make exile a little easier for his brother, either.

"Well, now, we've packed every last thing you own but your robes, haven't we, exalted?" her father said, walking into the shop and stamping snow off his boots. Katerin and her husband Tomas followed, pausing to watch Cristof as he tugged at the knots on his public robe.

"Thank you," Cristof said, glancing up.

The shop was empty. All of the exalted's clockwork and tools had been packed up to be taken to Primus. Taya had wanted Cristof to keep his business, but he'd protested that he wouldn't have time to make the trip back and forth between Tertius and Primus anymore. Instead, he planned to set up a small workshop in one of the spare rooms in Estate Forlore.

"May I? If you'll permit me, exalted?" Katerin moved forward and helped her sister untie the robe. Cristof stopped trying to do it himself and sighed, letting his arms fall.

"Pyke calls this 'ostentatious incapacitation,'" Taya commented, as they worked.

"That's exactly what it is." Cristof squirmed as Ann lifted the wig from his head, leaving his short hair standing up in unkempt spikes. "I can't even scratch an itch while I'm wearing it."

"You'll have to suffer for another second or two," Taya said, unsympathetically. "We're almost done."

"Look, I'm an exalted, I am!" one of the boys shouted, holding Cristof's mask against his face.

"Put that down right now!" Ann cried out, horrified. The child flinched and dropped the mask on the table. She rushed over to examine it, her hands shaking. "Exalted, forgive him. There's no harm done it; no damage at all."

"Don't worry. The brat doesn't know how lucky he is that he doesn't *have* to wear that thing."

Taya and Katerin lifted the heavy robes off his shoulders, and Cristof sighed with relief, scratching his head. He was wearing his usual plain black suit beneath the robes. He'd only put on the outfit at Ann's insistence that he try out the new wig before packing it.

Taya folded the garments, placing the ivory mask in their center, and handed the bundle to Tomas. He carried it out to the last crate. A moment later she heard him nailing the lid into place.

"That's it, then." Cristof looked around, a little wistfully. "I'll see you tomorrow, Ann?"

The woman nodded. "I'll bring up the wig, then, and instructions for your servants."

"Good."

For a moment everyone stood in awkward silence, trying to figure out how to say goodbye across caste. Finally Taya stepped forward and shook the wigmaker's hand.

"Thank you for your help. I'm looking forward to seeing you tomorrow."

"Me, too, Taya. Good luck." Ann smiled at her, relieved, and herded her children out the door.

"Off we go, as well," Taya's father said. Taya hugged him.

"Thanks for helping, Dad."

"A pleasure, sweetness. Exalted, we're honored to see you again. Best of luck to you." Her father bowed, his palm on his forehead. "You'll be at our table for Ladysday the week next, now?"

"As promised," Cristof agreed, although he looked a little daunted by the prospect. Taya had warned him about their annual Ladysday dinner, where two-thirds of the neighborhood was invited, half the gifts that were exchanged were alcoholic, and the singing and dancing continued until midnight. It wasn't the kind of thing the reticent exalted would normally attend, but she thought the noise and merriment would be better for him than spending a quiet Ladysday on Primus.

"See you later, then," Katerin said, hugging her sister. She tapped the gold envoy feather that Taya wore pinned to her fur cloak. "Don't be flying off to any strange countries without telling us."

"They won't let me leave until spring," she replied, cheerfully. "Until then, it's back-to-back lessons." Katerin grinned as Taya turned to embrace her brother-in-law. With good-humored bows to Cristof, her family headed outside, pulling up their collars against the ash-colored snow.

At last Cristof locked up the shop. The wagon full of wooden crates was already on its way up to Primus, but Gregor's hack waited for them by the curb.

"Where to, exalted?" Gregor asked. He was bundled against the cold, but his voice was as cheerful as ever.

"Estate Octavus," Cristof said, as they climbed inside. Gregor saluted and the coach jerked forward.

"Have you already told Viera that we're going to Cabiel, or am I going to have to listen to you two argue about it all afternoon?" Taya asked, nestling comfortably against Cristof's side.

"I haven't told her yet." He shifted, searching inside a pocket of his greatcoat for something. The coach rattled and lurched around them.

"Oh, Lady." Taya groaned. "You know she thinks you ought to stay in Primus instead of playing traveling ambassador. I think that's the only part of the Council's plan she doesn't like."

"Well, she'll have all winter to complain about it," he said, sounding unconcerned. "But not this afternoon. Ah, here we go." He pulled out a small box and offered it to her. "I didn't let your family pack this away."

"What is it?" Taya took it from him. The box was heavy. She held it to her ear and smiled, hearing ticking. "Is it for me?"

"The ambassador's envoy deserves her own watch, don't you think?"

"But I like using yours," she protested, even though she eagerly lifted the lid.

Her smile widened as she lifted the watch out of the box. Cristof hadn't tried to make it small and delicate. Instead, like the timepieces he'd made for himself and his brother, it had a comfortable heft, a sense of solidity and presence. It was the kind of watch she wouldn't be afraid to slip into a leather flight suit pocket. As if to emphasize that it was meant to be carried while flying, its red gold case was engraved with an outswept bird's wing.

"It's beautiful," she said, delighted.

"I would have made the case out of ondium, but I couldn't get my hands on enough," Cristof apologized. "Red gold isn't as valuable, but. . . ."

"It's much prettier."

"I thought . . . the color reminded me of your hair." He sounded nervous. Taya shot him an amused glance and opened the case.

"Oh."

A narrow ring of red gold ran around the outside of the watch's face, marking the hours. But set inside that ring was a disk of transparent glass that revealed all of the watch's inner mechanisms: the coiled mainspring, the tiny gears, the pin holding the watch hands in place, the tiny screws and plates that kept all of the workings together. And set into one of those plates, directly underneath the hands, was a small, heart-shaped ruby.

"Oh—Cris." She felt a lump in her throat.

"The program's name . . . it was an old joke. Alister used to say that's all I had. A clockwork heart. Nothing but logic and predictability." The nervousness in his voice was even clearer now. "So I thought I'd give it to you. The heart. You know. But if you hate it—I made another watch face, a normal one. Just give it back and I'll replace it tonight."

Taya swallowed, leaning against his chest again and watching the gears turn beneath the glass, slowly nudging the golden minute hand forward. Then she closed the cover and pressed the watch against her lips, feeling it vibrate. *Well, what did you expect,* she asked herself, half amused and half exasperated. *Trust Cris to make something so painfully and awkwardly sincere.*

"I think it's perfect," she said, at last, meaning it.

"Good." He sounded relieved. "You—you haven't looked at the watch fob yet."

Taya slid the chain back up through her fingers. A gold ring swung back and forth from its tiny jeweler's clip.

Astonished, Taya twisted and looked up at him. Cristof cleared his throat as the coach clattered over the cobblestone street.

"I know what you're thinking. Cross-caste marriages never work out. But logically, since you're an icarus and I'm hardly any caste at all, I thought—"

Taya threw her arms around his neck and silenced him with a kiss, nearly knocking off his glasses. And for one long moment, the watch in her hand seemed to keep perfect time with the beating of their hearts.